City Girl,
Country Vet

City Girl, Country Vet

CATHY WOODMAN

**Doubleday Large Print
Home Library Edition**

voice

HYPERION / NEW YORK

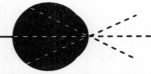

**This Large Print Book carries the
Seal of Approval of N.A.V.H.**

To my family and friends—

both human and animal

City Girl,
Country Vet

First Blood

IT'S A FAR CRY FROM STARBUCKS. IN FACT, THE blue and yellow gingham curtains with matching tablecloths and the paper doilies give the Copper Kettle a rather retro feel. There are no lattes or cappuccinos here. The coffee comes either with milk, or without. The local clientele look decidedly downbeat too with their blue rinses, and floral polyester dresses and macs, and the only buzz about the place emanates from a wasp, which crawls feebly about on our table, having woken from its winter slumber a couple of months too early.

"So what do you think, Maz?" My best

friend, Emma, sits opposite me with a cream tea and a piece of fruitcake in front of her because she can't decide between the two. The sun's rays slant through the window, emphasizing the dark shadows under her eyes.

"I think you've been overdoing it," I say.

"It did cross my mind to book myself in for a quick eyelid tuck when I looked in the mirror this morning," Emma goes on. "I look like some old spaniel."

"Emma, you're exaggerating," I say, smiling. She has the most amazing cheekbones, naturally long lashes, and lips that need little enhancement. "The last thing you need is surgery."

"You're right. A good night's sleep would do." I watch her pour two cups of tea from the pot, which sports a tea cozy knitted from oddments of wool. "Now, where was I?"

"You need a relief veterinarian to run the practice while you're away." I'm glad she's decided to take a break at last—no one can say she hasn't earned it. I pick up a knife, slice my scone in half, and scoop on a generous blob of strawberry jam, real jam with the pips left in.

"When you're in Devon you're supposed

to put the cream on before the jam," Emma whispers. "You'll be drummed out of town if anyone notices."

"As if," I say. "You are joking?"

"We're very set in our ways here in Talyton St. George," she says, her cheeks dimpling and her dark eyes sparkling with merriment as a tractor rumbles past, rattling the teacups. Yes, a real tractor—not one of the Chelsea variety, which I'm more used to.

I wipe my knife and scoop up a small portion of clotted cream instead, then take a second, more generous dollop.

"Have you been in touch with any of the agencies yet?"

"Of course not. I want you to do it." Emma gazes at me through the fringe of her brunette bob, which has grown overlong, like an Old English sheepdog's. "I want you to look after Otter House for me," she goes on as I choke on my scone.

Don't get me wrong—I'm not averse to the idea of helping Emma out, but here in this quiet market town, where nothing ever happens? Let's just say I wish she'd set up her practice even a tiny bit closer to London.

"All right, I know we disagree on a few things like"—she struggles to think of an example—"like how to pronounce the word *scone,* but we have a pretty similar approach when it comes to work, which'll suit my staff and clients."

"I've never taken sole charge of a practice," I say doubtfully. The idea of being responsible for absolutely everything, from dealing with disputes to handling finances, is daunting. I like being a vet, just a vet.

"If I can do it, you can, Maz."

"I haven't had much experience of the business side of things either."

"I've already thought of that. Nigel, who looks after the practice computers, he's agreed to handle the admin and accounts, so you won't have to worry about those."

"I'm really not sure."

"Well, I can't trust anyone else to look after it." I notice Emma stealing a glance at the small child who's squirming about in a high chair at the table beyond ours and squeezing vanilla sponge between his fingers. "It's like . . . well, it's my baby."

At the word *baby,* there's a sudden hush. Scones hover between plate and mouth, teaspoons between sugar bowl and cup.

Cheryl, proprietor of the Copper Kettle, who I could swear was behind the counter slicing freshly baked chocolate cake a moment ago, appears at our table, wiping her hands on her frilly apron.

"Baby? Did I hear someone say they're having a baby?" she says. "Congratulations, Emma—I guessed you were eating for two."

"I'm sorry to disappoint you, Cheryl," Emma says, her eyes overly bright and her smile forced. There's something wrong, something she isn't telling me. She's only thirty, like me, so there's no great hurry, but she used to joke about having a family the size of a football team, until setting up and running the practice took over her life. I realize that she hasn't mentioned babies for a long time.

"So you aren't?" Cheryl says, sounding surprised.

"No," Emma says sharply, and a spoon chinks against a dish, a cup against a saucer, "absolutely not." Her voice softens as she goes on. "Please, don't go spreading that rumor around town."

I suspect from Cheryl's crestfallen expression that the rumor has already been spread, and I'm upset for Emma. It must be pretty hard living in a small town where everyone's talking about you. I know I'd find it difficult to put up with.

"I'm trying to persuade my friend Maz here that Talyton is a much nicer place to be a vet than London," Emma tells Cheryl.

"Our babies are registered with the Talyton Manor Vets," Cheryl says, referring to the other practice in Talyton, a father-and-son outfit, a traditional mixed practice treating farm animals and horses as well as cats and dogs. "The Fox-Giffords have generations of experience behind them. We'd never trust anyone else."

Emma winks at me. I can tell she's more than happy with that arrangement. Anyone who calls their pets "babies" is going to be very demanding of their vet, and Cheryl, with her sharp features and short dark hair set in tiny, precise curls, doesn't strike me as the easiest person to please.

"Cheryl and her sister, Miriam, breed Persian cats," Emma explains when Cheryl drifts away to greet more customers, two young families of tourists, or grockles as they're known in this part of the world. "Cheryl and the Fox-Giffords are welcome to each other." I know there's no love lost between Emma and Talyton Manor Vets, but I'm still surprised at the venom in her voice when she talks about them. The Fox-Giffords were openly hostile when Emma's practice first opened, but I had the impression things had calmed down since then. Obviously not. "I hope they don't start throwing their weight around again," Emma goes on. "If they start accusing you of pinching their clients and undercutting their fees, just ignore them. Don't get involved."

"I haven't said I'll do it yet," I point out gently. Part of me wants to do it for Emma's sake. Part of me wants to stay well out of it. I have no desire to get involved in some silly feud between competing practices. The job can be stressful enough without that kind of complication.

"Excuse me." Emma pulls a mobile out of her bag—from the ring tone, I'm almost expecting one of those old-fashioned Bakelite telephones, but it's a blue slimline model—and answers it with "Otter House Veterinary Clinic. Emma speaking. How can I help?" She listens, chewing one of her fingernails down to the quick, and I think how typical it is of her to be so busy looking after everyone else that she forgets to look after herself.

"I'll meet you at the surgery," she says, ending the conversation and tucking her mobile back into her bag, along with a packet of aspirin that fell out with it when she took the call. "It's an RTA. I've got to go."

"I'll come with you."

"You don't have to . . ."

From the back of the chair, I grab my blazer, a cropped number in citrine that I fling over my tunic and skinny jeans, an outfit that might be considered by the residents of Talyton St. George as outlandish rather than the latest trend. Emma never has had much fashion sense—what's left seems to have become mired in an over-attachment to soft lamb's-wool sweaters and timeless navy skirts. She looks like a county cricketer's wife on her way to make afternoon tea at the pavilion, not a young and savvy professional. I'm not being mean—she needs help and, if I'm going to be the one to do it, I guess I'd better see what I'd be letting myself in for.

I take out my purse, but Emma gets there first.

"It's my treat," she says, leaving some cash on the table before we hurry back along Fore Street and turn up the drive alongside a smart three-story Georgian house that is rendered the same color as the clotted cream I had with scones.

"The client—the one whose dog's been run over—he's the chap who bought the Talymill Inn a year or so back, an ex-policeman. He was in the Met," Emma says, unlocking one of the double glass doors to the modern conservatory-like extension at the side of the building. "The patient's an ex–police dog."

There's a sign to the right: OTTER HOUSE SMALL ANIMAL VETERINARY CLINIC, dark blue lettering on white, with a logo of an otter, surgery hours, and a telephone number. Beneath that is a brass plaque engraved EMMA KENDALL, M.A., VET.M.B., M.R.C.V.S.

I follow her into the reception room. It's a while since I was last here, and the whole area has been redecorated. It's very blue: royal blue chairs; pale blue walls; a blue-gray nonslip, easy-clean floor. And as if there isn't already enough blue (Emma's favorite color, as I now remember), the notice board and posters—three seascapes—have navy frames. I barely have time to take in any more because a man in his fifties has come staggering through to join us. He's well-built with a fair-size paunch and has gone for the shaved rather than the comb-over look to disguise the fact that he's bald on top. He carries a big, old dog in his arms.

"This way." Emma shows him straight through to the consulting room. "Stick him on the table." I follow and close the door behind us. Emma grabs a stethoscope and gives the dog—a German shepherd with a belly to rival any fat fighter's and the distinctive smell of hot dog, earwax, aftershave, and stale beer—a quick once-over. "I'm very sorry—Mr. Taylor, isn't it?"

The dog struggles to sit up, panting for air and whimpering in pain.

"It's Clive. And this is Robbie. It's my stupid fault. I wasn't watching out for him." He shudders. "One minute he was at my feet, the next he was in the middle of the road underneath a bloody great tractor." He has an East London accent. His shirt and jeans are smeared with blood and, like the dog, he appears to be in shock.

"I'm sorry," Emma says, "but I don't think he's going to make it. Robbie's bleeding internally—his gums are very pale." She raises the dog's lip to prove her point.

"You must be able to do something." Clive's voice quavers. "You have to."

"He'll die if I don't operate." The ticking of the clock above the door seems to grow louder, more insistent, as Emma continues, "And very likely, he'll die if I do."

While Emma's waiting for Clive to absorb this information, I reach out and stroke Robbie's head, discovering a crinkled ear and a scar to match a longer one on his chest. He turns his eyes toward me and, somewhere behind his glazed gray pupils, I catch sight of the dog he once was and perhaps still is. A fighter.

"I want you to give it a go." Clive twists a worn leather lead tight around his fist. "Can I wait?"

"It could take some time," Emma says. "A couple of hours, maybe more."

"Now I feel really guilty, because I've got to get back to the pub," Clive says.

"I'll call you as soon as I have any news," Emma promises.

"Thanks, Emma. Please, do what you can. I don't care how much it costs. He means everything to me . . ."

"No pressure then," I say once Clive has left, having signed the consent form and given Robbie one final hug in the sorry knowledge that it could be the very last time he sees his beloved dog.

Emma smiles ruefully.

"I think Clive's right, though," I say. "I'd want to give him a chance if he was my dog."

Within minutes, we're in the operating theater. Emma stands opposite me, scrubbed, gowned, and gloved. On the operating table between us lies Robbie, belly up and almost completely hidden under blue cotton drapes. His tongue lolls out of his mouth alongside the ET tube, which delivers oxygen and anesthetic to his lungs. Fluid pours at speed from a bag hanging from the drip stand, down a tube and into a vein in his front leg.

"How's he doing, Maz?" Emma's surgical cap is riding up her forehead, exposing the roots of her hair, and her eyes peer out anxiously above her face mask.

"Not great." I check and recheck the tension in Robbie's jaw to assess the depth of his anesthetic-induced slumber. "I don't think he's going to leap off the table anytime soon."

I watch as Emma picks up a scalpel and uses it to cut a line in the skin over the dog's belly, then snips right through with forceps and scissors, releasing a gush of blood, a coil of gut, and even more blood.

"I'll need more swabs," she says calmly.

"How many?"

"As many as we've got."

I rip open a couple of packets of gauze swabs and tip them out onto the instrument tray on the stand. Emma uses a fistful to dab at the blood. Sweat begins to form in beads across her forehead. I watch her bite her lower lip as she concentrates on finding the source of the bleeding. If anyone can save Robbie, she can.

"What do you think?" Emma sticks the end of a suction tube into the dog's belly. I flick the switch.

"That it doesn't look like a good place to

lose a contact lens," I say lightly, although deep down my confidence is waning the more the scene resembles something from *The Texas Chainsaw Massacre*.

"Ah, I've found it," Emma mutters. Her voice cuts through the sound of blood spattering around the inside of the suction bottle. "It's the spleen—it's ruptured."

A greasy, metallic scent fills my nostrils, and my hands grow hot with panic. I watch the blood from Robbie's belly trickling down Emma's plastic apron and into her Crocs, while his pulse fades to a barely perceptible flicker beneath my fingers.

"Emma, I can't get a pulse." Using a stethoscope, I try for a heartbeat instead. It's very faint, as if I'm listening to it with cotton wool stuffed in my ears. "I think we're losing him."

"No, we aren't," Emma says fiercely, and she's right, we can't let him die on us now.

Recalling the look in Robbie's half-blind eyes, and the sob that rose in Clive's throat as he held him, I summon all my resources.

"Come on, old boy, you'll have to do better than this," I mutter as I cut the anesthetic, leaving Robbie on oxygen alone to support his vital organs, and fix up a second drip to run in more fluid. I guess in an ideal world we'd have plumped for a blood transfusion, but there isn't time for that. Gradually—it seems like hours, but it's only minutes—Robbie's pulse begins to strengthen. It isn't great, but it's probably as good as we're going to get, considering the circumstances.

Emma continues to operate, and a while later the dog's spleen—a dark and swollen mass, like offal on a butcher's slab—lies on an instrument tray, bristling with every pair of artery forceps I could lay my hands on.

To our relief, Robbie has come through, and is now snoring in one of the kennels.

"I'll make a start on the clearing up," I offer as Emma finishes writing the notes and clips the board to the front of the kennel.

"Oh no you won't." Emma pulls off her gown. "You've done more than enough already. When I asked you down for the weekend, I didn't intend you to end up working."

"It's been a bit of a busman's holiday," I admit, "but I don't mind at all." I'm used to it. You never know when you're going to be called upon—it's a hazard of the job. I thought Emma was used to it too, but I'm not sure she's coping with the demands of running her own solo practice and being on call 24/7.

"I don't know about you, but I could do with a gin and tonic after that," Emma says cheerfully as she grabs the phone. "We'll have one with dinner later."

I catch sight of my reflection in the silvery steel lining of the cage above Robbie's kennel and run my fingers through my short blond crop, half listening as Emma talks through the list of potential post-op complications with Clive.

"It's still touch and go, though," she adds at the end of the conversation. "I'll call you again in an hour or so."

"Now, where were we?" she says as we settle on the sofa in the staff room with a welcome cup of tea, leaving the door propped open so we can keep an eye on Robbie. "When do you have to leave Crossways?"

"In a couple of weeks, when I've worked out my notice." Two weeks? The realization that I'll be leaving Crossways, the place I've called home for the past five years, so soon hits me in the chest. It's my own fault, though. I went and lost my job—okay, I jumped before I was pushed. I broke one of the cardinal rules of the workplace—never fall for a colleague, especially one who's recently divorced. When it all went wrong, I decided I wasn't staying to have my nose rubbed in it.

"I'm really sorry it didn't work out, Maz." Emma takes off her surgical cap and ruffles her hair. "Mike seemed like such a nice guy."

"They always do at first," I say. Mike owns Crossways Vets in southwest London. Charismatic, successful, and good-looking, with the most amazing brown eyes. I really thought he was the one. He was clever and dedicated too, managing to mix working in a practice with some research work at the Royal Vet College, which might partially explain why his marriage fell apart.

He'd been divorced for just a few months when I started work there, and I admired him for admitting the almost instant attraction between us, while wanting to hold back for his ex-wife's sake. Perhaps that's what made it so exciting, the frisson of Mike's arm brushing against mine as he showed me the latest techniques for ligament repair in the operating theater, then the snatched kisses in the consulting room before he announced to the rest of the staff that we were a couple. Funnily enough, they didn't seem surprised.

We moved in together and started making plans for me to buy into the partnership with him. We had four and a half blissful years together. Until he realized he was still in love with his ex-wife.

"I'm going to find the next couple of weeks pretty humiliating, what with the nurses gossiping in the staff room and Mike going around the practice singing like he's James Blunt. He always sings when he's happy . . ." Robbie lets out a deep and noisy sigh from his kennel, matching my own sigh of regret. I try to shrug it off as I watch Emma top up Robbie's pain relief with an injection, but I can't—there's nothing that can deal with the pain of rejection. "I'll get over it," I say, the words rasping out of my throat. "My heart isn't broken this time, just bruised."

"I don't believe you," says Emma.

"Mike wasn't anything special," I reaffirm, but I know I'm lying to myself, and Emma can tell too. "He had a hairy back—spooning with him was like nuzzling a shaggy dog." I wrinkle my nose at the thought. "And he was a bit of a geek. And he liked playing golf. And he was a faithless piece of sh—" I stop abruptly. No point in getting wound up all over again. He isn't worth it. "Men, they're all the same," I say.

"Ben excepted," Emma replies, glancing toward her wedding ring, a simple but weighty gold band, which she wears on a chain around her neck.

"Ben excepted," I say contritely.

"He's my rock." Emma smiles, and I feel a twinge of envy that she's been so lucky in love and I haven't. "In fact, it's partly for Ben's sake that I'm asking this enormous favor of you. We're planning to take six months out to travel—you know he's got all those relations in Australia."

"Six months?" That's a lot longer than I expected, and I try not to let my dismay show. I was beginning to come round to the idea that, if I decided to work here in Emma's place, I could treat it as a bit of a holiday, a couple of weeks in the country.

"It's doctor's orders—Ben's actually." Emma's husband is a GP, which I guess comes in useful sometimes. "He says I'm stressed out, that I'll have some kind of breakdown if I keep going as I am . . ."

Her voice trails off, and I realize that she's been putting on a brave face since I arrived late last night. She does look completely shattered. I've been so wrapped up in my problems, so busy whinging on about my breakup with Mike during our recent phone conversations that it didn't occur to me Emma was having a tough time too.

"I haven't been coping terribly well recently . . ."

"When did you last have a day off?" I ask.

"Not since I opened the practice."

"But that's two—no, three and a half years ago. Emma! Why didn't you ask for help sooner? I could have covered the odd weekend for you."

"I didn't like to bother you—you were busy enough already."

"Not too busy to help a friend." I've known Emma for twelve years now, and she's always been there for me, always ready to help me out of a fix. "Do you remember when we first met? There can't be many people who can say they met their best friend at vet school over a dead greyhound."

"I wonder if Professor Vincent is still stalking the Dissection Room, scaring the life out of first-year vet students." Emma smiles. "What did he used to call you? Gwyneth, wasn't it? As in Gwyneth Paltrow. And I was Catherine Zeta-Jones, which was rather flattering, I thought."

"I didn't make a terribly good first impression, did I?" I say, recalling how I'd been fiddling with the knot on the canvas roll holding my dissection kit when suddenly it came undone and my shiny new scalpels, forceps, and scissors skittered across the floor to land at Professor Vincent's feet.

"There was one person you impressed," Emma says, getting up from the sofa.

"Oh, don't." I know exactly who she's talking about. Ian Michelson. Sandy blond with hazel eyes and a few freckles across the bridge of his nose, good-looking and clean-cut with a brilliant smile and glasses, he shared our greyhound. When our gloved fingers touched, very briefly, across the dog's brindle chest, my heart skipped a beat and I fell for him. We went out together for almost six years. He was my first boyfriend, my first love, my first heartbreak.

I watch Emma walk across to look at Robbie. She checks on his wound and covers him with a blanket to keep him warm.

Emma has stuck by me and helped me through the difficult times—when I thought I was too clumsy to be a vet, and when I ran out of money and nearly had to abandon my studies halfway through the course—which is why I'm going to do this for her. Even if I do have to spend six months stuck in the middle of nowhere, miles from the nearest Starbucks. I owe her.

CHAPTER 2

Country Ways

MIKE DOESN'T HAVE THE COURAGE TO SAY good-bye, but that's the kind of man he is. I glance back in the rearview mirror when I stop at the traffic lights a few yards down the road from Crossways. The figures of the people in the waiting room are silhouetted against the windows, and as far as I know, Mike is hiding behind the blinds in his consulting room.

From the group who came out to wave good-bye—some of the staff and the chap from the corner shop who's also one of my favorite clients—only Janine, the ex-wife who hounded me out, is left. Having turned up at the practice today on the excuse that her dog needed its booster, she stands on the pavement with her arms hugged around her chest—with glee, I imagine, that she's seen me safely off the premises and out of temptation's way. But she needn't worry: to be honest, the way I feel at the moment, I can't imagine being tempted by any man again. Ever.

If you put me in a room with Jude Law, Daniel Craig, *and* Brad Pitt right now, would my heart beat a little faster? I doubt it.

When the lights change, I put my foot down and I'm off, joining the queue of traffic leaving the capital.

There isn't much room for luggage—I've sent most of my belongings ahead by courier—but I've stuffed a couple of clinical waste bags of clothes and books in the passenger footwell. At least one of my contemporaries from vet school is driving about in an Aston Martin with a personalized number plate, something like K9 VET, and others have monster gas guzzlers. But I love my sporty red coupe, even though it's rather impractical for a vet.

On the seat next to me is the box containing my farewell present from Crossways: a brand-new stethoscope, with the card all my colleagues had signed, reminding me not to leave it lying around in men's bedrooms, which is what happened to the last one. (I was helping a client—a C-list celeb, it turned out, who'd once been on *Big Brother*—to catch his cat, which had taken one look at me and scampered under the bed. Really.)

I drive on, with mixed feelings of regret and inadequacy for not realizing what Mike was up to when he was "helping" Janine out by walking their dog, a dippy Irish setter with a penchant for swallowing pebbles. I thought it was fair enough that he did his bit since they shared joint custody. Naive or what?

Eventually I enter the county of Devon, where the radio retunes itself, latching on to a local station that is playing some middle-of-the-road pop harking back to the eighties, and the weather changes from sunshine and showers to a steady drizzle. At the turning for Talyton St. George, the road narrows into a country lane with dense hedges on either side, and I run into the back of a traffic jam of all things, a queue of three or four cars behind a herd of black-and-white cows and a tractor with a sticker in the window reading BRITISH BEEF.

I glance at my watch, and my blood pressure starts to rise, like the steam from the cows' backsides as they wander along, stopping on and off to take a mouthful of grass or release a spattering of muck onto the road. I swap from the radio to the CD player. Beyoncé starts singing "End of Time" and I realize I'm going to have to get used to the slower pace of life down here.

Finally, I reach Talyton itself, passing through Market Square, where red, white, and blue bunting flutters between the elaborately styled Victorian lampposts to tempt tourists to stop at the Copper Kettle or Lupins the gift shop before they continue on their way to the coast. I turn in to Fore Street, and there it is, my destination and home for six months, Otter House Veterinary Clinic.

I leave my luggage in the car and dash through the rain to take shelter inside, where I find a woman behind the desk in Reception, dressed not in blue to match the decor, as you might expect, but in an orange, flower-power smock. When she looks up from a pile of post, I can see that she's in her mid to late fifties, and that locks of thick, honey blond hair seem to have come adrift from the bun pinned up on the top of her head, contrasting oddly with her wispy gray fringe.

She turns her attention back to the envelope on the top of the pile, picks it up and holds it to the light, then takes a small knife from a pot beside the computer and runs the blade along the top fold to open it. She extracts the letter and spends a few moments reading it before slipping it back into the envelope.

Is it possible she doesn't know I'm here? I give her the benefit of the doubt and clear my throat loudly.

"Name?" she barks.

"Er, Maz." I feel my brow tighten into a frown. "I'm Maz Harwood." I step forward, holding out my hand. "You must be Frances. It's lovely to meet you."

"Your pet's name?" the woman says impatiently.

"I haven't got a pet."

"You're in the wrong place then. This is a vet's surgery. Don't waste our time."

The fluorescent tube above me grows dim, then flickers and brightens again.

"I'm not a client," I say, slightly cowed by her manner. She isn't exactly welcoming. "I'm the relief. The vet. Emma's expecting me." I make to go on through to the corridor beyond Reception.

"Stop right there!" Frances says sharply. "You can't go any further—the rest of the practice is out of bounds to anyone who isn't a member of staff."

"But I am."

"Not until tomorrow, I believe. Take a seat. I'll buzz Emma, but I'm warning you— this may not be a convenient time . . ."

Deciding not to cross Frances right from the start, I sit down, eyeing her from a safe distance as she stabs at the buttons on the phone on her desk.

A few minutes later Emma appears in the doorway, in scrubs and surgical gloves. "Hi, Maz." She bounds over to greet me, giving me a hug. "I'm so glad to see you." She releases me and turns to Frances. "I hope you've made our new vet welcome."

"Of course," Frances says, cracking a smile in Emma's direction.

"Has the second post come yet?"

Frances picks up the opened letter. "Is this what you've been waiting for?"

"Thanks." Emma grabs it and turns away to read it.

"Good news, I believe," Frances offers, feigning surprise when Emma turns back, all smiles.

"Phew, what a relief," she says. "I'm in the clear. No case to answer." She tucks the letter into her pocket. "I saw a sick cat and booked it in for some tests—I was busy so it had to wait for a few days. In the meantime the owner took it to guess where, and Old Fox-Gifford diagnosed renal failure. The owner followed up on his suggestion that I'd been negligent, and I've had to go through the rigmarole of contacting the Vet Defence Society, and answering questions from the Royal College." I bet Emma spent hours worrying about it, I think, as she goes on, "I could have done without the extra stress."

"I'm sure it was all a misunderstanding," Frances says, and Emma raises one eyebrow at me.

"Come through. The coffee's on, and I've managed to restrain myself and save you a doughnut." She takes my arm, and I accompany her along the corridor to the ward area, or Kennels as she calls it.

"Did you realize Frances had already opened your post?" I ask on the way.

"Yes, she opens everything to save me time."

"She reads it too. I saw her," I add, which seems to be news to Emma. "Isn't Frances a bit fierce for a receptionist?"

"Maybe, but she knows her job." Emma grins. "I know it's a bit unethical, but I managed to poach her from Talyton Manor Vets a couple of months ago. She'd worked there for years."

"You don't think the Fox-Giffords deliberately set you up with her?"

"No." Emma thinks for a moment. "Definitely not. They've been a pain in other ways, but no, I was the winner this time. She might read my mail, and refuse to wear the uniform—she says blue doesn't suit her—and she still believes that the sun shines out of the Fox-Giffords' behinds, but she has loads of local knowledge, which comes in useful."

I get the impression that Frances treats Emma with more respect than I can ever expect. I'm the outsider, the newbie, whereas Emma's lived in Talyton almost all her life, apart from a few years in Cambridge and then in Southampton when Ben did his GP training.

"Let me introduce you to the rest of the team—not Nigel, though, because he only comes in once or twice a week." Emma touches her hand to her mouth and giggles. "I'm twittering on, aren't I?"

"Like a baby bird" comes a voice from the far side of the room. A woman dressed in navy scrubs like Emma brings a white wire basket over to the bench. Her skin is pale and freckled, and her short auburn hair is run through with silver threads. She looks like she's in her late twenties, but Emma's already told me she's forty-two.

"You've met Izzy before, haven't you?" says Emma.

It was at the party Emma held when she first opened the practice, over three years ago. I recall Izzy getting quietly sozzled on Pimm's and lemonade, claiming afterward that she hadn't realized it was alcoholic, which is probably why she seems a little shy now, greeting me with a nervous hello.

"What do you want to get on with next?" she asks Emma.

"I was going to take Maz to the staff room for a coffee before I finish off here."

"Don't let me interrupt what you're doing," I say hurriedly. I glance around at the surgical instruments piled up beside the sink and the soiled drapes heaped in a bucket on the draining board. I expect Izzy's impatient to make a start on the clearing up.

"There's only the castration left," she says, pointing toward a basket that I notice on closer inspection contains a black feline, more kitten than cat, sitting on a blanket surrounded by toys. "Meet Fang."

"It'll only take a few minutes," Emma says, looking at me apologetically.

"Why don't I help you, then Izzy can get on?" I lift Fang out of the basket and onto the table. He makes to spring off, but I keep him there, hugged to my chest. I catch a whiff of perfume, something floral, in his coat. Emma injects him with a pre-med before he has a chance to notice.

"Where do you want him?" I ask, looking at the rows of gleaming stainless-steel cages against the far wall, designed to house anything from a guinea pig to a Great Dane. "High-rise, or ground floor?"

Izzy picks up a newspaper and lines an empty cage, adding a piece of vet bedding on top for warmth, saying, "Emma, being vertically challenged, prefers me to stick them in the middle."

I shut Fang inside it. He arches his back and yowls at his reflection, then backs off, his tail in the air.

"You wuss." I coax him to turn around so that I can scratch him behind the ear through the bars to reassure him. It must be pretty scary for a young cat to be locked in a cage, surrounded by the smells of dogs and disinfectant, especially when he starts losing control of his faculties as the pre-med takes effect.

"Fang's owner says he's been straying away from home," Izzy says. "She's hoping this'll reduce his urge to roam the countryside."

"I can think of other cases where castration would come in useful," I say, unable to disguise my bitterness as I recall how Mike wandered back to his ex-wife's bed. "Preferably without an anesthetic," I add, fetching a dozy Fang from his cage.

"You scrub, I'll buzz," Emma says, once Fang's lying asleep on the operating table, and I watch her shaving the hair from his balls, wishing there was such a thing as voodoo. She cleans the op site, gives it a squirt of surgical spirit, and opens a foil packet, holding it out to me so I can tweak the blade free, keeping it sterile.

"Are we ready now, Hacker Harwood?" Emma adds, using my nickname from vet school.

The procedure's almost bloodless this time, unlike Emma's epic battle to save Robbie's life, which reminds me to ask her how he's doing.

"I took his stitches out a couple of days ago. He's looking great, considering his age and what he's been through. Clive's over the moon. Although he did have a little dig about the bill—how did he put it, Izzy?" Emma shouts in Izzy's direction.

"Something about it costing him an arm and a leg for a spleen, but he was joking," Izzy calls out, smiling as she dips her head through the hatch between the operating theater and the prep area, where she's washing up. Once we're finished, Izzy offers to keep an eye on Fang so Emma can give me the rundown on the computer and the phones.

Fortunately the systems at Otter House are pretty similar to the ones at Crossways, so it doesn't take long, and Emma provides me with a printout of useful notes and numbers.

"I'm going to put some Post-it notes up before I go home tonight to remind you where everything is," she says, "and I'll leave you Ben's mobile number and his parents' number in case of emergency. Now, you will remember to feed and walk Miff?"

"Of course."

Miff is Emma's Border terrier, a scruffy-looking little brown dog with a broad, otter-shaped head and a lively expression. Emma's family has always had terriers, and Miff is the latest in a long line.

"Have you got wellies?"

I shake my head. I haven't had a pair since vet school.

"You'll need wellies." Emma frowns. "I know, I'll run you up to the garden center," and, in spite of my protestations that I wouldn't be seen dead in wellies, I find myself schlepping up and down the aisles of the local garden center in a pair of bright yellow ones, trying them for size.

"You can't be serious," I say, looking at Emma.

"They aren't supposed to be a fashion accessory, Maz. They're entirely practical."

Unconvinced, I pay for them at the checkout, where a middle-aged woman wearing a tunic over the top of a chintzy blouse chats with Emma and takes an age to serve me.

"I hear congratulations are in order," the woman says, gazing at the slight curve of Emma's belly. "When's the baby due?"

"There is no baby, Margaret. You heard wrong," Emma says, her voice sounding small and sad. "Who told you anyway? I bet it was Cheryl."

"Oh no, it was Fifi." The woman pauses, a flush spreading across her cheeks. "I'm sorry. My mistake. It's just that she was so sure . . ." She changes the subject. "Dollar—she's my dog, a little Westie— she won't see any vet except Alex Fox-Gifford. She's very sensitive, you see."

"That and Margaret fancies Alex," Emma whispers to me as Margaret rustles about looking for a bag for my purchase.

. . .

"YOU KNOW, YOU can't fool me, Em," I say later, while she shows me round the flat above the practice, Miff hot on my heels. Realizing I'm not carrying any biscuits, Miff trots away and settles herself on the sofa.

"Well?" I add, when Emma deliberately doesn't respond.

"Off, Miff," Emma says, "get off." Miff ignores her. "A typical vet's dog." Emma chuckles. "I've never had the time or the energy to train her properly." She pours two small glasses of wine from the bottle beside the bowl of fruit—Emma's thought of everything, as usual. She hands one to me and takes the other for herself. "Here's to you, Maz," she says. "I can't thank you enough for agreeing to look after Otter House. I hope it'll be an enjoyable experience."

"Thank you," I say, "and here's to your holiday. I hope you and Ben have a fantastic time." I take a sip of the wine and return to the subject that I've been trying to broach and Emma has neatly managed to avoid. "That stuff with Margaret today? I got the impression you were upset."

"Wouldn't you be?" Emma says defensively.

I think for a moment. "A little perhaps, but it's only gossip, and it wasn't exactly malicious. Water off a duck's back, no?"

Emma shakes her head, her eyes downcast, staring at her fingers clasped round the stem of her wineglass.

"I should have told you before." She takes a gulping breath, then turns her gaze to me, her dark eyes shimmering. "Ben and I—we don't seem to be able to have children. I can't get pregnant. I wanted to tell you, but Ben didn't want me to say anything."

I can understand that. "It's a man thing, I imagine, not wanting to have aspersions cast on your virility."

"It isn't that." Emma frowns, perhaps a little hurt on Ben's behalf, and I feel bad for thinking meanly of him. What do I know about it? I've never wanted children myself. How can I have any idea how it feels?

"It's just so stressful," Emma goes on. "Ever since we got married we've had everyone going on and on about when we'd hear the patter of tiny feet. And now everyone in Talyton's congratulating me on something that never was and probably never will be." A tear rolls down her cheek. "I'm glad I'm going away. I can't wait to escape from it all."

I'm trying to think of a way to tell her how sorry I am when she continues, "We're going to see someone when we get back to talk about investigations and options for treatment, IVF, that sort of thing."

"That's good, isn't it?"

"Yes, but there are no guarantees, are there?" she counters. "You know, the hardest thing to accept is that you have no control over it. You take the Pill for years, and then you stop and discover you aren't in charge of your fertility at all."

She doesn't have to say any more. I can see that her failure to fall pregnant is completely devastating. I watch her walk to the window and look out on the street below. She takes a swig of wine, then turns back toward me with her vet-in-charge-of-her-destiny face on once more, and she doesn't let her guard down again until she's about to leave at the end of the day to rush through her last-minute packing, before driving to the airport with Ben.

"This is it then," she says, hesitating in

Reception. She grabs a tissue from the box Frances keeps handy on the desk and blows her nose, and I'm afraid she's going to cry again, but she regains her composure and attempts a smile. "I know I said I couldn't wait to get away . . ." She gazes around the waiting area. "It's more difficult than I thought. In fact, I almost wish I was staying."

I know what she means. I wish she was staying too. It would have been fun to work together.

"Don't let the Fox-Giffords give you any hassle, Maz," Emma says.

"Are they really that bad?" I ask anxiously.

"You'll be fine," she says, "as long as you keep your head down."

Reassured, I watch her go, then lock the door behind her. I give her a wave through the window as she reverses her car out of the car park and drives off along the road. Miff whines at my feet, wanting to follow.

"I'm sorry, Miff," I say, squatting down beside her and stroking her head, moving my fingertips from front to back, feeling for the contours of her skull, checking for lumps and bumps. Force of habit. "I'm afraid you're going to have to put up with me for the next six months." She doesn't wag her tail. In fact, she looks like I feel, all hangdog and upset because Emma has gone. I'm wondering what I'm going to have to put up with too, what challenges Emma's patients and the residents of Talyton St. George are going to throw at me.

And then I have to laugh at myself for being so silly. Emma wouldn't have asked me to look after Otter House if she didn't think I could cope.

CHAPTER 3

Perishable Goods

IT'S MY FIRST DAY IN CHARGE. I SHOULD BE LOG-ging on to the computer in the consulting room at Otter House, but instead I find myself down by the river looking for Miff. It's such a beautiful morning, I thought she'd like a quick walk, but she's slipped her collar and done a runner. I followed her into some bushes that I discovered too late were obscuring a ditch, into which I half slid, half fell, ending up thigh-deep in the stinking gloop at the bottom, in the shadow of a regiment of nettles and explosions of hawthorn blossom. Fat lot of good my new wellies are now.

"Miff!" I yell. "Miff!" I try the softly-softly approach. "Biscuit." Unsnagging a curl of barbed wire from my jeans, I listen out for her above the whisper of traffic on the bridge over the river on the far side of the meadow. Nothing.

I don't think she likes me.

I press on through the mud, the like of which you never see in those photos in *Country Living*. (Perhaps they airbrush it all out.) Hanging on to a tree root, I scramble out of the trench and crawl through the prickly undergrowth on the other side to emerge on all fours on a track, where I'm confronted by an enormous horse bearing down on me at speed. I don't know what it is—a pigeon flapping out of the bushes or my sudden appearance out of nowhere—but without warning, the horse puts the brakes on and spins away, throwing its rider up its neck.

"Whoa there! Steady . . ." The rider slips back into the saddle, pulls the horse up, and turns it round to face me. The horse, a bright chestnut mare, tries to rear away again, fighting at the bit. The rider—he, for he is most definitely male—stares at me, his mouth taut and eyes stormy beneath the peak of his hat. "Get up!" he growls.

"Me?" My cheeks grow hot with embarrassment.

"I can't see anyone else about, can you?"

Reluctantly, because not only did he almost kill me but he hasn't said please, I stand up. "Is that better?"

"Now she can see you're vaguely human, not some creature out of *Shrek*."

The mare takes a couple of paces toward me. I notice how the rider flexes and relaxes his fingers on the reins, playing with the bit in her mouth. I also notice that the sleeves of his polo shirt are rolled up, revealing a pair of lightly tanned forearms, and his jodhpurs are so tight across his muscular thighs that it's positively indecent. He's gorgeous, and doesn't he know it.

His gaze settles briefly on my mud-caked legs, and his lips curve into a fleeting smile. "What happened to you?"

"I'm looking for a dog." I feebly gesture at Miff's collar and lead, which hang redundant round my neck.

"What kind?"

"A Border terrier." In fact, I can hear the frantic yelping of a dog after rabbits, moving in our direction. "That's her, I think."

"Border terrorist might be a more accurate description from the sound of it."

Suddenly, the yelping stops and a small brown dog comes trotting out from the brambles beside us. The mare flares her nostrils and champs her jaws, spattering her sleek chest with foam.

"Make sure you keep it under control in future."

"She isn't mine," I say as Miff creeps up to me, her tail between her legs.

"Whatever." The mare paws the ground with her foot, scraping out a deep gouge in the track. "And I'd advise you to check a map next time you decide to go pond dipping, or bog snorkeling, or whatever it is you're up to. This isn't a public right-of-way."

"Oh? I'm s-s-sorry," I stammer. His air of confidence—no, superiority—makes me feel awkward and at a disadvantage.

"You're trespassing," he goes on. "The footpath runs alongside the river, across the other side of the field from here. This is the old railway line."

"I didn't realize . . ."

"Ignorance is no excuse," the rider goes on.

Emboldened and infuriated by his rudeness, I argue back. I wouldn't normally in this kind of situation, but Miff's hackles are up, and so are mine.

"Look, I've got the dog back on the lead and I've apologized. There's no need to be so unpleasant—you don't own this place."

"Actually, I believe that I do." The rider turns the mare side on and delivers his parting sally. "I hope I never see you here again. If my father had caught you, he'd have had you shot—you and the dog." He digs his heels into the mare's sides and gallops away, sending up showers of slag and dust, and flashes of steel.

I scold Miff gently as I clip her collar—a psychedelic canvas affair that I grabbed off the rack in Reception on my way out—securely back around her neck.

"There was no need for you to get me into trouble. I'm more than capable of doing that all by myself," I tell her.

Miff waves her tail just once, her brown eyes downcast.

"Oh, cheer up. I'm not cross with you." I'm annoyed with myself for letting that arrogant, testosterone-fueled—I swear under my breath—get to me. Who is he? The local squire? I try to dismiss him, but he isn't the kind of man who's easily dismissed. I was already on edge, wondering what exactly I've let myself in for, but now . . . I feel as if I could be back in London, having been subjected to a road rage attack on my way to work.

Country life. Country people. Emma made it all sound so romantic, I think, as Miff and I scurry back along the riverbank and across the footbridge that arches over the rust-colored waters of the river Taly.

Crossing the green on the way to the town, we pass two men removing the ribbons from the maypole that stands in the middle.

"Mornin', my lover," one calls out.

I wave back, smiling at his odd, uniquely West Country turn of phrase, then turn right into town, past the end wall of the Duck and Dragon, where someone's sprayed GROCKLES, PER-LEASE GO HOME politely in red paint. (The pub is one of three left in Talyton—apparently, the town used to support eleven.) When I arrive back outside Otter House, I hesitate for a moment.

Taking a deep breath, I finally burst into Reception, only to have my enthusiasm halted by the commanding sight of Frances's raised palm as she uses the other hand to lift the phone.

"Talyton Manor Vets—I mean the other ones. How can I help you?" She listens for a few moments then, "Oh, Gloria . . . yes, indeed. Old Mr. Fox-Gifford would prescribe exactly that—a few days on a light diet, boiled chicken and rice, and he'll be as right as ninepins."

I wait, itching for her to finish. How does it look to a client if your receptionist keeps dropping the name of the competition into the conversation?

Frances puts the phone down and greets me with a brief smile.

"Frances, I know you mean well," I begin tactfully, "but I'd prefer you not to give out advice."

"The Fox-Giffords expected me to use my discretion," Frances says, appearing unconcerned.

"This isn't Talyton Manor, though," I say,

but I'm not sure I'm winning. Frances has the same rather glazed expression as Robbie the ex–police dog did just after he'd been hit by that tractor. "I'd appreciate it if you called this Gloria person straight back, please, and tell her to make an appointment to see me if her dog—"

"It's a cat," Frances interrupts, "one of her ferals. It's pretty wild."

"Okay, but that's no reason for me not to see it." I let Miff off the lead.

"It bit right through Emma's thumb last time—she was on antibiotics for weeks."

"Frances, just ring her." I'm not going to be intimidated by anything, be it feline or human. "I'm going to get changed. I'll be back in five."

"Take your time." Frances's reading glasses rest via a chain on the shelf of her bosom. She slips them onto her nose and taps at the keyboard in front of her with the end of a pen as if she's afraid of making direct contact with it. "There's hardly anyone booked in for you."

I go and change my shoes, and return to Reception, fastening the snaps on my paw-print top.

"Did you get hold of Gloria?" I ask Frances, who's reading a newspaper now, the *Talyton Chronicle*.

"She says she won't see a strange vet. She's going to wait until Emma's back."

"Didn't you explain the situation?" I'm smarting a little. I know it's nothing personal—I'd probably be just as choosy if I had pets of my own—but you would have thought that Emma's clients would have trusted her judgment.

"I told her Ginge could be dead by then, but she wouldn't budge. What else can I do? I can't force her."

I don't pursue it any further, and I refrain from asking her to put the newspaper away. It doesn't do to fall out with your receptionist on your first day.

"Here's your nine-thirty," Frances says, looking past me. "Mrs. Moss and her daughter, Sinead. They've not been to us before."

I look at my first customers. Mrs. Moss is wearing a green tentlike dress, and Sinead's dark hair has been scraped back into a Croydon face-lift. She's holding an open-topped cardboard box with THIS WAY UP and PERISHABLE GOODS stamped on the side. I cautiously show them into the consulting room where Izzy's waiting to assist me.

While Mrs. Moss keeps a tissue pressed firmly to her nose, Sinead keeps the box at arm's length and lowers it carefully onto the table. The stench makes me retch. Steeling myself, I look inside. A tricolor Border collie pup with an air of desperation in its eyes sits cowed in the bottom, its mouth set in a squiggle, reminding me of Snoopy from the Peanuts cartoon strips. Glistening strings of saliva stretch from its lips to the fringe of a bloodstained baby blanket.

Mrs. Moss informs me that the puppy's name is Freddie; he's eleven weeks old and they bought him from a farm while they were on holiday in Wales.

"Has he had his first vaccination yet?" I ask.

Sinead stands beside her mother, chewing gum and fiddling with her enormous gold earrings. I repeat the question, but the Mosses remain silent, their expressions blank.

"It's really important," I say, at which Mrs. Moss finds her tongue at last.

"He had some of those homeophobic drops—the breeder showed me."

"You mean homeopathic," I suggest gently, yet inside I'm churning with anger on Freddie's behalf, at both the breeder and Mrs. Moss for believing this would be enough to protect him from some of the nastier puppyhood diseases. "He has parvo—a viral infection." I hold back from angrily adding, *Which we could have prevented with a course of conventional, tested vaccine.*

Izzy hands me a pair of disposable gloves and disappears, rolling her eyes.

"I told you." Sinead turns to her mother. "I told you we should've had him checked out."

"He was fit enough when we got him."

I lift the puppy out of the box. "Come on, Freddie, let's have a look at you."

He shivers and moans when I press his belly very gently to check for anything that might suggest an alternative diagnosis.

"He's been passing blood from both ends," says Sinead. "It's bad, innit." I leave the Mosses in no doubt as to exactly how bad it is and admit him. I can't perform miracles though—it's up to Freddie.

"Give us a call later and I'll let you know how he's getting on."

"Leave it," says Mrs. Moss, as her daughter makes to pick up the box. Neither of them looks back. The door into Reception closes after them and, like magic, the door behind me opens from the corridor that links the consulting room with the pharmacy, Kennels, prep room, and operating theater. Izzy comes bustling in with a tray of equipment.

"Izzy, anyone would think you were listening at the door."

"I was," she says with a wicked twinkle in her eye, and I'm relieved that her initial shyness with me has already worn off. She takes a close look at Freddie. "Poor little scrap. There's no way he's eleven weeks—he can't be more than six. And the label on the box is apt—he looks highly perishable to me."

We put Freddie on a drip, dose him with antibiotics, and clean him up, then leave him in the isolation cage under the stairs in the corridor on the way to the laundry.

"Oops, I'm sorry," Izzy says when she bumps me with her elbow while hanging her plastic apron on the hook outside the cage.

"Not your fault," I say. "There's hardly room to swing a cat."

"Of course, we'd have had a separate ward for patients with infectious diseases if it hadn't been for Talyton Manor Vets. They called meetings and organized petitions to stop Emma getting planning permission for an extension at the back of the practice. Old Fox-Gifford spent a fortune on whiskey—for bribes, allegedly—but why he bothered, I don't know. A few extra square meters of floor space wouldn't have hurt anyone."

Not for the first time, I admire Emma's determination in setting this place up. Otter House used to be her family home. Her father ran a dental practice here before he died prematurely, struck by lightning on the golf course at Talysands when Emma was thirteen. Her mother passed away here, almost four years ago now, her body ravaged by a particularly aggressive form of pancreatic cancer. It was her dying wish that Emma should have the house converted so she could run a successful vet practice in her hometown.

"I'm sure Emma's told you I'm more than happy for you to call on me if you need a hand out of hours," Izzy says, changing the subject. "Do you—oh, perhaps I shouldn't ask—"

"No, go ahead."

"Do you have a boyfriend, or a significant other? Only, if you want to go out for the evening, I'll take the phones for you."

I shake my head, trying to suppress the image of Mike that appears in my mind—my Mike, not the one who screwed me over with his ex-wife but the one I fell in love with, the man who made me feel special and loved.

"The nightlife in Talyton won't be what you're used to—it's more bats and owls than clubs, but if you want to meet up and make friends, you could take up rambling, or join the Women's Institute, or there's an ad in the *Chronicle* for the Countrylovers Dating Agency, if you're looking for someone special," Izzy goes on brightly.

I swallow hard against the tide of embarrassment and hurt that rises inside me. "I'm definitely not in the market for a lonesome farmer," I say lightly.

"But you are in the market?"

"No," I say firmly. Definitely not. I couldn't go through all that rejection again. I've been there, done that, not once but twice in my life, and that's enough for me. I give Freddie one last stroke, then discard my gloves. "Er, have you seen my stethoscope anywhere?"

Izzy stares at me. "It's hanging from your neck." She grins. "Emma did warn me you were a bit dippy."

"Did she?" I say, a little upset by her comment. It's a bit personal coming from someone I hardly know.

"I didn't mean to offend you," Izzy says hastily.

"It's all right," I tell her. It's true, after all.

"I guess you can blame the odd blond moment on the color of your hair. Is it natural, that peculiar shade of golden retriever?" Izzy's hand flies to her mouth. "I've done it again, haven't I?" She giggles. "When will I ever learn to keep my trap shut?"

Izzy's like Marmite, I muse a while later when I'm in the consulting room, checking through the yellow Post-it notes Emma's left on the drawers and cupboards to show me where everything is. With Izzy, there's no middle way. You either love her or hate her. Luckily, considering I'm going to be working closely with her for the next six months, I suspect it's going to be the former.

I smile to myself. Emma did tell me Izzy was frank and straightforward. It isn't surprising then that she had a chat with Izzy about me. And as for the golden retriever remark, I suppose it is rather amusing.

As Izzy tops up the vaccine supply in the fridge, I check my computer, and the screen flashes to life:

Cadbury. Chocolate Labrador. 21 weeks. Entirely male. Vaccination status? Owner: Mrs. L. Pitt of Barton Farm ***

"Have you any idea what these asterisks mean, Izzy?" I ask.

She looks over my shoulder. "It must be some private code. At the practice where I did my training, we used them all the time. NGOR was my favorite."

"What's that?"

"No grip on reality." Izzy grins. "TPNN was another—take payment now, or never. I'll ask Frances to come through."

Frances joins us, slamming the door behind her and leaning back against it.

"How I wish Old Mr. Fox-Gifford was

here." Her lipstick is bleeding into the fine lines around her mouth. "One look from him could silence the most unruly child."

"What's wrong?" Izzy asks.

"One of Lynsey's is eating a sample pack of rabbit food like it's a bag of crisps, and another is scribbling on the notices on the board. I've threatened them all with a spell on the naughty chair, but will they listen?" Frances waits as if she's expecting Izzy or me to go and sort them out.

"I'm not good with children," Izzy says quickly.

"Leave it to me," I say. "First though, Frances, do these asterisks mean anything, or are they down to a slip of the mouse?"

"Alex Fox-Gifford says that it's a universal code, something every vet learns at vet school." The tone of her voice rises, as if she's questioning my competence. "The number of asterisks corresponds with the saying 'This year, next year, sometime, never.'"

Izzy and I look blank.

"It's a warning to take payment at the time of consultation. The Pitts have always been rather slow at settling their account." Frances stares at me. "Before you say anything, Maz, I've checked that the puppy isn't registered with Talyton Manor Vets." She glances toward the door. "I'm sending them in before they wreck the place."

"Go ahead," I say, and the boys—six of them, including a set of twins securely strapped into a stroller—traipse in with their mother, who has a sandy shoulder-length bob and shades on top of her head. Clearly an expert in the art of multitasking, she has one hand on the buggy and the other clasping to her breast a puppy—a chocolate Labrador with hazel eyes, and skin that falls in wrinkles over its belly.

"I'm Lynsey. I rang the surgery about worms not so long ago." She lowers the puppy onto the table, where he pads about on oversize paws, wagging his body as well as his tail. He's gorgeous.

"We had worms once," says the oldest boy, who must be about eight.

"Thank you for that, Sam." Lynsey's jacket is Puffa, her jeans are Next mater-nity, and her wellies Overdown Farmers, local wholesalers of farm supplies. "Boys, please be good," she says, looking a bit fraught as two of the boys crawl under the table, one starts investigating the contents of the fridge, and the remaining boy on the loose, Sam, mauls Cadbury affectionately about the head. I turn to the one who's now pulling boxes of vaccines out of the fridge. He reminds me of my brother when he was about four years old, taking eggs out of the fridge and dropping them one by one on the kitchen floor while my mother was out at work and I was in charge.

"Will you stop doing that, please." I use my best it's-me or-the-dog voice, one guaranteed to stop the most aggressive hound in its tracks. (Well, almost.) The boy stares at me, his cheeks glistening with snail trails of snot. "Now, put them away and close the door."

He hesitates.

"Didn't you see the notice on the board in Reception?" I ask him. "The one that says, WARNING, THIS VET BITES?"

He shakes his head, flicking his hair so that blond strands catch and stick to the snail trails. Keeping his eyes on me, he bends down, picks up the boxes, and puts them back in the fridge.

"Thank you. What's your name?"

"Ryan," he whispers contritely.

"Okay, Ryan, you can come and help me find out what's wrong with your dog."

"He's been very quiet for the past couple of days," Lynsey says, although Cadbury looks pretty bright to me, bouncing up and down and slobbering across the table. "He's hungry, but he can't keep anything down."

Cadbury doesn't make it easy for me to examine him. He thinks it's a game, but suddenly he stands quietly, his expression mournful.

"It's probably something he's eaten," I say, at which he retches and throws up a sausage of foamy, dark fabric onto the table in front of us. The boys stare, fascinated.

"Mummy, that's my sock," says Ryan.

I give Cadbury an injection to settle his stomach, then stick on a pair of gloves and rinse the offending object out in the sink. It is indeed a sock. Thomas the Tank Engine beams at us, unharmed.

"Mum's been sick like Cadbury," Sam observes.

"I can assure you that it isn't because I've been eating socks." Lynsey smiles. I like her. She's friendly and warm, and not in the least bit fazed by seeing me rather than Emma.

"Number seven's on its way—all I have to do is look at Stewart and I'm pregnant, but if it isn't a girl this time, I'm going to send it straight back. Thanks—Maz, wasn't it?" she goes on after I've murmured my congratulations, uncertain whether congratulations are in order or not. "It's marvelous having this practice on our doorstep. I can't believe how smart it is."

"It's cleaner than our house, Mum," Sam cuts in.

"Can't you keep anything to yourself?" Lynsey sighs. "What was I saying? Oh yes, you and Emma have a much nicer bedside manner than Old Fox-Gifford—he scares the living daylights out of the boys. Ryan's only just stopped wetting the bed since Fox-Gifford last came out to the farm."

"Barton Farm?" I say. "I spent a few weeks there with Mr. Pitt—"

"That would be my father-in-law. Stewart never calls himself that," Lynsey interrupts.

"It was when I was a student, doing my preclinical studies. Emma's mum put me in touch with them—I stayed here at Otter House with her for the summer." I remember Stewart—he was quite a bit older than I. I also remember that he had a bit of a reputation with the ladies—not that he tried anything on with me, probably because most of the time on the farm I went around in an unflattering green coverall and smelled of cows.

"That must have been before my time. Stewart's parents have retired, thank goodness. His dad, bless him, he's one of those people who's always right, even when he's wrong," Lynsey says. "Thanks again."

"It's nothing. It's my job." I love my work, the uncertainty of what you're going to see next, the adrenaline rush of tackling an emergency, the highs and even some of the lows.

"One other thing," I say. "Have you thought about castration at all?"

She looks around at her sons and laughs. "I think about it pretty often, but Stewart isn't too keen on the idea. As for Cadbury, I'll see how it goes. How much do I owe you?"

I check on the computer in the consulting room. Emma has everything itemized, so all I have to do is type in what I've done, press Enter, and wait. That's the theory anyway.

The screen flickers and goes black, then a message box pops up:

Fatal Exception at 00000xxxt2zzx

"It didn't like that, did it?" says Lynsey.

I head out to Reception with her and the boys to find out what's happened.

"I didn't touch it, Maz." Frances is on her feet, flapping. "Really, I didn't."

"Can't you reboot it, or something?"

Frances sticks her specs on the end of her nose, leans her hands on the desk, and peers at the keyboard.

"Try the power button," I suggest. "Switch it off and on again."

"Are you sure about that?"

"No, but I can't think of anything else to do, and Lynsey's waiting for her bill." I hesitate. "Emma said you were familiar with computers."

"I can Google like the best of them, but Old Mr. Fox-Gifford preferred me not to interfere with anything electrical. 'Frances,' he used to say, 'don't you dare, on pain of a lingering death, lay a finger on the equipment.'"

"All right, I'll ask Nigel to sort it out later." I tell Lynsey that we'll send her an invoice.

"That's great," she says. "I'm a little short this week—I could do with a bit of free credit."

I help her load Cadbury and the boys into the Land Rover parked outside. Not the most successful start. So far, I've taken no money, seen hardly any clients, and the computer's crashed. The responsibility of running my best friend's practice is beginning to weigh far more heavily on my shoulders than I imagined it would.

I'm missing Crossways, the comforting sounds of the city, the constant swish of traffic, the jets flying in and out of Heathrow, and the rumble and whir of the trains, and it's even quieter here in Otter House at night than it is in the daytime. You can hear the house breathing: the creak of a door upstairs as it rocks on its hinges; the intermittent firing up of the boiler; and from out the back, the higher-pitched hum of the freezer (for dead animal bodies, not your Ben & Jerry's).

I turn the radio on for company; then,

having checked on Freddie under the stairs, I head back up to the flat as quickly as I can, just in time to grab my mobile, which is ringing out the theme to *House* (one of the nurses I used to work with downloaded it for a bit of a laugh) from beneath a copy of *Vet News*.

It's Emma.

"Hi, how's it going?" she says.

"Where are you?"

"Dubai . . . ," she says, and I remember that she and Ben were planning to visit one of Ben's doctor friends who's living out there. "Is everything okay? Have you remembered to feed Miff?"

"Yes, of course. I even took her for a walk before work." I tell Emma about the man on the horse, but I don't mention the ditch. Neither do I mention Miff slipping her collar or the muddy tummy prints she's left on the carpet in the flat. "He was so rude. I don't know who the hell he thinks he is," I go on.

"God's gift," Emma says. "That has to be Alex, son of Old Fox-Gifford."

"From Talyton Manor? The other practice? So he's one of the vets there?" I take a deep breath. "He said his father would have had us shot if he'd found us. Me and the dog!"

"I wouldn't put it past him," Emma goes on. "I've told you before, the Fox-Giffords don't behave like normal people. They're like the triads of Talyton St. George. Oh, I hope they aren't going to give you grief."

"Stop worrying, Emma—you're supposed to be destressing. I'll cope. It's so quiet here, it'll be a complete doddle."

"Quiet?" she says, sounding a little hurt.

"I mean it's quiet compared to Crossways," I say quickly, not wanting to offend her, although I've been wondering how on earth she makes a living out of the practice.

"Actually, things have been a bit slow recently," she admits. "Talyton Manor Vets introduced discount microchipping and a vaccination amnesty, and a load of my clients left to take advantage of it. I guess some of them will drift back eventually." She changes the subject abruptly. "How are you getting on with Frances?"

"All right," I say noncommittally, but I can tell Emma doesn't believe me.

"I should have treated taking on a new receptionist more like buying a horse." She sighs. "I should have vetted her more thoroughly—checked her teeth, at least."

"Are you going to keep checking up on me," I ask, smiling to myself, "only you're supposed to be on holiday?"

"I didn't realize it would be so difficult to let go," Emma admits.

"Let's make a deal then. Don't call me again. Go and make the most of your time off." I take it from Emma's silence that she isn't convinced. It must be difficult for her: she's invested everything in Otter House—time, energy, money, and emotion. "I promise I'll ring you in the event of an emergency—fire or flood, that's all."

"Oh, I don't know . . ."

"Yes, you do, Em. Now, have a fantastic time. Give Ben my love. And don't worry about Otter House." You have me to do that, I think. "I've told you—I'll take care of everything. Trust me," I add, "I'm a vet."

CHAPTER 4

Kittens

I'M ALWAYS A LITTLE ON EDGE WHEN I'M ON DUTY, never sure exactly what I'll be called upon to do, or when. At Crossways I saw everything from an urban fox cub abandoned by its mum to a very sick marmoset. I also treated a puppy who'd snaffled up his owner's splifs and a cat who'd been shot with an air gun. However, Emma says it's pretty quiet here in Talyton St. George. Nothing much happens after nine o'clock at night.

I settle down in front of the television to catch up with the news, and it can't be more than ten minutes later when the phone rings. I grab the handset.

"Hello?" It takes me a moment to re-member where I am. "Otter House Vets."

"Is that Emma?"

"It's Maz, Maz Harwood. Emma's away. I'm the relief vet."

"It's Cheryl here—I served you a cream tea at the Copper Kettle a couple of weeks ago. Anyway, one of my queens is kitten-ing. She's in terrible distress—I need some-one to look at her straightaway. I can't get hold of Alex, my usual vet. I've phoned several times in the past hour, and driven up to the manor. The dogs are there, but there are no lights on."

I recall Emma's warning about getting involved with Talyton Manor Vets, then dismiss it. This is about the welfare of an animal, not unfair competition.

"You'd better bring her straight round."

"You're an angel. I'll be with you in five minutes."

I call Izzy to warn her there's a heavily pregnant cat on the way to the surgery, fling on a grubby T-shirt and jeans (I seem to have mislaid some of my clothes on the way from the car to the flat when moving in), shut Miff in the flat, and head downstairs. I hesitate when I hear noises coming from Reception. I push the door open.

"Who's there?" I call sharply.

"It's me, Nigel." A man with a tidy ginger mustache, a waistcoat, and a bow tie looks up from the innards of the computer. "You must be Maz." He smiles. "I'm sorry if I frightened you. I let myself in."

"I'd rather you'd let me know you were here." I don't like the idea of people I don't know creeping around the building while I'm upstairs. So much for Miff being a good watchdog, I think. "Do you think you'll get that computer back up and running by tomorrow?"

"I'm pretty sure I know what the problem is." Nigel taps the box with a miniature screwdriver. "It's the loose hair—it clogs the hardware."

I hope he's right. I don't want to deal with a whole day without access to my patients' case notes.

"Oh, while I remember, I hope you don't mind, but I've ordered a new trolley," I say. "The brakes aren't working on the old one. It isn't safe."

"I've canceled the order." Nigel gazes at

me with shifty gray eyes. "Frances contacted me to let me know. It isn't a case of
while the cat's away, the mice can play.
There's no money in the budget for new
equipment."

I can't say I'm entirely happy about Frances going behind my back and Nigel can-
celing my order.

"Who's in charge here?" I say. It's a
rhetorical question, considering Emma's
given me the responsibility for the running of the practice, but Nigel doesn't see
it that way.

"Me, *au naturel*. I'm practice manager,
in all but title anyway. You're the locum,
temporary staff."

How does he justify his naked ambi-
tion? I wonder. He seems to have given
himself a promotion in Emma's absence. I
don't think Nigel and I will get on if he's going to throw his weight around and make a
fuss about the cost of a trolley, although—my
conscience pricks me like a large-bore hy-
podermic needle—he does have a point. I
haven't even brought in enough fee income yet to cover it.

The doorbell rings, cutting my conversation with Nigel short and announcing

Cheryl's arrival. I take her through to the consulting room.

"This is Saffy, one of our precious babies." Cheryl lifts a Persian cat out of a carrier and puts her on the table. She has a smoke blue coat, apprehensive amber eyes, and a flat face, which makes her look like a cartoon cat that's walked into a wall. Cheryl holds her firmly by the shoulders and haunches. "This is her first litter and her last, because I'm not going to let our darling girl go through this again."

Saffy—which Cheryl tells me is short for Cheriam Sapphira, Cheriam being the breeders' prefix, a combination of her own and her sister Miriam's names—strains feebly, leaking a pool of dark fluid from beneath her tail, suggesting that her kittens are in imminent danger, if they aren't already dead.

"I need your permission to do a cesarean," I say gently, aware of how worried Cheryl must be.

"Is that really necessary?" Cheryl's earrings, black cats dangling from silver chains, tremble just above the neckline of her purple turtleneck. "My vet always tries the injection first."

"There's no time," I explain, but I'm not sure I've really convinced her, although she does sign the consent form.

"She's going to be all right, isn't she?"

I wish I could, but I can't and don't make any promises. Cheryl looks at me pleadingly.

"Alex always gives me some idea . . ."

I stick to my guns. All I'm prepared to guarantee is that every single one of my patients will die—eventually.

"She wanted to stay," I tell Izzy, who arrived soon after Cheryl left. We're now in the operating theater with Saffy between us. "I told her she couldn't."

"I bet she didn't take that very well," Izzy says cheerfully, checking the resuscitation kits ready for the imminent arrival of Saffy's kittens. "What did you say?"

"I said it was down to health and safety. For my health and her safety. I know she adores her cats, but even so, she's a bit pushy, isn't she?"

"I call her the She-devil," Izzy says with a wicked glint in her eye. "I can't believe she had the nerve to bring one of her cats here. She helped Old Fox-Gifford organize the petition to try and stop Emma setting up the practice in Talyton. Emma's forgiven her—you know what she's like, a real softy—but I haven't."

"It's lucky for Cheryl that it didn't succeed," I observe. "Where did you used to work?"

"Talymouth, and before that a practice in Exeter."

"So you haven't moved very far."

"I wouldn't want to live anywhere else." Izzy smiles. "You just wait—when you've been here a few months, you'll find that you'll never want to leave."

"I doubt that very much." This place is too quiet, too out of the way, and far too muddy for me. "By the way, I brought a couple of bags in from my car when I arrived the other day. Have you seen them? I thought I left them in the staff room."

"What kind of bags?"

"Yellow ones."

"The clinical waste went out this morning." Izzy glances at the watch pinned to her breast. "Eight o'clock on the dot."

"All of it?" I say, aghast.

"Of course."

"But that was my stuff—my clothes, some shoes, my iPod. Didn't you notice the stickers?"

"RADIATION HAZARD? I thought it was your idea of a joke."

"Not mine. The staff from my last practice's idea of giving me a good send-off."

"You should have mentioned it," Izzy says sheepishly.

"Don't worry. It gives me an excuse to go out and buy a whole new wardrobe next time I'm in London."

"You don't have to go all the way to London. You can get some really nice clothes at the garden center."

"What, macs and gardening gloves? Not quite my style," I say, smiling. "Here, have a kitten."

Within an hour Saffy has come round from the anesthetic, her days as a breeding queen over. There are three kittens. Only one has survived, and it's taking milk while Saffy licks frantically at its blue-cream fur, raising it up into tiny spikes.

It's adorable. I love kittens.

I must have been about twelve years old when I found a litter of them in the stairwell in the block of flats in Battersea where I lived with my parents and younger brother. They looked like the nightmarish Rat King of one of my father's poems, a mass of tangled tails and tiny bodies, but they weren't writhing and wriggling about. They weren't moving at all.

I never cried, but when thoughts of what they must have gone through, and how much they'd suffered, flashed across my mind, my throat tightened and my eyelids pricked. When I knelt down beside them, a tear dropped onto one of the kittens' faces and trickled into its ear. It shook its head and opened its mouth, a blink of pink. It was alive, the sole survivor.

"The kindest thing for it would be to knock it on the head." My father, who was sitting at the kitchen table in a work jacket that reeked of booze and cigs, hardly looked when I took it out from under my sweater to show him. He topped up his glass from the bottle in front of him. "Put it out of its misery, 'Manda."

"You can put me out of mine by going out and looking for a bloody job," Mum cut in from the sink, where she was in her rubber gloves, up to her elbows in bubbles. She was thirty then—a young mum. Her face was already toughened by frequent trips to the tanning salon, her hair in frizzy blond ringlets, and her bra straps, exposed by her sleeveless blouse, fell in loops down her strong, wiry arms, those of a woman used to manual work.

"I'm always working, even when I'm sitting here." My father, who was ten years older than she with a lean face, bright blue eyes, and crow's-feet, drained his glass and thumped it back down on the table. "Especially when I'm sitting here."

"Can't Pat give you a couple more shifts down at the Feathers," Mum said, "and get you out from under my feet?"

"How do I know?" My father yawned, reinforcing the message that my mother was boring him with her constant nagging, and stretched out his long legs. "I haven't seen him for weeks."

"Go and ask him. No, crawl round on your knees and beg him. Otherwise I'm going to have to sell the kids to pay the electric."

I left them to it. (I used to fantasize that my real parents would turn up out of the blue one day and take me away, reclaiming me from this mismatched pair, who were constantly at each other's throats.) I took the kitten, a tiny scrap of black and white fur with its eyes stuck closed, in a shoe box on the bus as far as the stop outside the parade of shops that I passed every day on my way to school.

Tucked between Tatchell's Bespoke Tailors and Gita's Saris was the Ark. To the right of the entrance was a brass plaque, engraved J. B. WILSON with some letters after it. The sign on the door read CLOSED. With the shoe box tucked under one arm, I reached up and pressed the doorbell. Eventually, a nurse—I guessed that's what she was from the silver buckle on her belt—opened the door.

"Can't you read?" she snapped.

"This is an emergency," I stammered, then, realizing that she was about to shut the door on me, I took the lid off the box. "Look."

"Oh, it's just a baby. . . . You'd better come in," the nurse said more kindly. "I'll ask the vet to have a look at him."

"I don't know if it's a boy or a girl," I said as I followed her through a door on the other side of the waiting area into a small room where the air smelled fiercely clean and chemical.

"Don't touch anything," she said curtly, and she left me there in the company of the kitten and a poster of a giant flea before returning with a man in gray trousers and a tunic that fastened across one shoulder. He seemed very tall and very old to me, although looking back, I imagine he was probably only just fifty at the time.

He introduced himself as Jack, the vet, and the nurse as Chrissie.

"I'm Amanda," I said as he lifted the kitten out of the box and glanced at its undercarriage.

"It's a boy," he announced. "I'd say he can't be more than a week old because his eyes haven't opened yet. What's his name?"

I thought of the Rat King and the tangle of tails. "King. He's called King."

"This little chap, as you've probably guessed, should still be with his mum, but as he isn't, he needs to be fed with a special milk substitute every two hours."

"I can do it," I declared immediately. I'd

bonded with the kitten as soon as I realized he was alive and depending on me for his survival. I felt responsible. I felt needed.

"Don't you have to go to school?"

"I can skip school for a few days. I don't mind."

"I'm sure you don't," Jack said gravely, "but I'd hate for you to get into any trouble, so what I suggest is that I keep King here for a while."

I gazed around the room, at the bottles and pots on the shelves, at the reassuringly long names printed on the labels, as if the longer the name, the more effective the medicine. I wasn't sure about Chrissie, but I liked Jack's quiet and reassuring manner. I trusted his opinion. King would be safer at the Ark than at home, but my chest ached at the thought of having to leave him behind. For the first time in my life, I was in love.

"Do you live far away?" Jack asked.

"I have to catch a bus. Does that count?"

"Oh, most definitely. Why don't you drop by after school tomorrow?"

My heart leapt. "Can I?"

Jack nodded. "It's almost time for evening surgery—you can help Chrissie give the kitten his first bottle before you head home."

"How much will it all cost?" I was thinking of my bus fare.

"Don't worry about it now." I wonder what Jack thought of me, a skinny blond girl in a grubby blouse with the top button missing and a skirt with a hemline halfway up her thighs. Perhaps he guessed from the state of my shoes that I wasn't from a particularly well-heeled family. "We'll see how it goes . . ."

I bit my lip. I knew what he meant: King might not make it. I had to be realistic, but whatever happened to him now, the path of my life was set. I was going to be a vet like Jack Wilson, and nothing was going to stop me.

"I CAN'T BELIEVE the Fox-Giffords would leave their practice unmanned without good reason," says Cheryl when she turns up to collect Saffy and the new arrival later the same night. (I like to send new mums home as soon as they're round from the anesthetic so they can feed their babies in peace.)

"I'm sure there's a good reason Alex

wasn't answering the phone." I don't want to bad-mouth Emma's rivals—I don't want to stoop to their level, for a start. "Perhaps he was called out to another emergency." I change the subject. "Look, I'll e-mail all the details of the surgery to Talyton Manor Vets tomorrow, and you can arrange to see them for aftercare."

"And that's a checkup in ten days' time, you say?"

"Maz! Phone!" Izzy calls out.

"Oh, listen to me going on," says Cheryl.

"I have to go. Good night, and good luck to Saffy and her baby." I push the door closed and turn the key in the lock before I go and find Izzy. Nigel is long gone.

"Who's on the phone now?"

"Oh, nobody." Izzy grins. "I thought I'd provide you with a means of escape from the She-devil." She looks down at my feet. "Did you know you're still wearing your slippers?"

"Am I?" I glance down at the pair of fluffy dogs with lewd pink tongues. The nurses at Crossways gave them to me last Christmas. I'm not sure I've done my image any good by having them on down here, but at

least I won't be seeing Cheryl in a professional capacity again. She isn't Otter
House's client.

Izzy continues to stare at me.

"Is there something else?"

"You know, in my twenty years of nurs-
ing, I've never met a vet who kisses their
patients."

I'd given the newborn kitten a little cuddle
before handing her over to Cheryl.

"Only the cute ones that don't bite. I do
draw the line at kissing snakes, though I
have kissed a lot of other reptiles in my
lifetime." Well, not that many, I think. There
have been two significant reptiles in my
life: Mike, and my first boyfriend from my
student days, Ian Michelson.

"I'm going home, if you're all right here,"
Izzy says. She lives alone, I know that much
from Emma. She owns one of the tiny ter-
raced houses on the road out to Talymouth,
sharing it with two rabbits, eight guinea
pigs, three tortoises, and a corn snake,
which someone found under the hood of
their car. I guess it must be pretty daunting
for a man to share Izzy with all that lot.

"I'm fine, thanks," I say, although I'm
feeling pretty shattered from having been

on my feet for most of the day. "I'm off to bed." I wish Izzy good night, and on my way back to the flat I check on Freddie. He's lying very still at the front of the cage, his head tipped back and his body pressed up against the bars. Is he sleeping? His eyes are open and staring. I tiptoe forward, looking anxiously for the telltale rise and fall of his chest. Nothing.

In a blur of tears, I go out to fetch a bag so I can put him in the freezer. Poor little guy. A life over almost before it began.

When I return, I slide the catch on the door, at which Freddie's body twitches, making me leap out of my skin.

"Freddie?" I lean over him, holding my breath. One of his eyes swivels in its socket. "You nearly gave me a heart attack," I chide him softly. "That's a very risky game to play." I restart his drip and cover him with a blanket, feeling very alone in the harsh glare of the light in Isolation. Only five months and twenty-eight days to go.

CHAPTER 5

Handle with Care

THERE'S A PUSH-BUTTON BELL AT RECEPTION for clients to use if there's no one behind the desk. Some give it the slightest touch, so all you hear is a faint *ting* if you're out the back. Others are less restrained.

Izzy rolls her eyes at me as the bell rings out loud and clear, and keeps on ringing.

"We've got our hands full here," she grumbles as Freddie makes an attempt to leap out of her arms while I untangle his drip. "Where's Frances?"

"Perhaps it's the Mosses." We haven't been able to contact Freddie's owners since they left him with us three days ago, and they haven't contacted us. The phone numbers they left turned out to be false, and the address they gave was for a plot on the new housing estate on the edge of Talyton St. George, as yet unsold. I reckon they've dumped him on us. Let's face it, his chances aren't great, and who wants to pay for a dead dog when they could put the money toward a new one? All right, call me a cynic, but I've learned that people aren't always what they seem.

"I'll go," I say. "I've finished here. If he hasn't been sick again by coffee time, you can try him with some fluid by mouth."

It isn't the Mosses. It's Cheryl—I might have known from the way she was pressing that bell—and she's holding a cat carrier.

"I didn't think you'd mind me popping in like this, seeing as you did the surgery the other night. Call me a fussy mummy if you like, but I'm worried about Saffy."

I don't mind at all. I'm always happy to help, and it isn't as if I'm rushed off my feet.

"How's she doing?" I ask as, once in the consulting room, Cheryl extracts a reluctant Saffy from the carrier and turns her on her back so I can examine her.

"Okay, I suppose, but I was wondering

about the wound." There is a note of complaint in Cheryl's voice. "It's much longer than Alex would have made it."

The wound looks fine to me. It's healing nicely, and it's no longer than average. What did she want me to do? I wonder. Cut the kitten into pieces to get it out of a smaller hole?

"Everything's as I'd expect at this stage," I say calmly.

"Are you sure?" She twists up her necklace of oversize beads the same color as her red shift dress.

"Absolutely." It's obvious that Cheryl adores her cats, but her concern seems a little over the top to me. "Why don't you make an appointment with Talyton Manor Vets for five days' time—they'll be able to take Saffy's stitches out then."

"You can't whip them out now, while I'm here?"

"No, definitely not." I hesitate. "Does Alex—?"

Cheryl shakes her head. "He says it's too risky. 'Cheryl,' he says, 'taking stitches out too early is like playing Russian roulette with your cat's life.'"

I'd love to be able to put one over on the

Fox-Giffords by saying he's wrong, but I have to tell Cheryl that he's quite right.

"In that case, I'll wait. Vet's orders." Cheryl points back into the carrier, where a scrap of blue-cream fluff lies curled up, half covered with a piece of purple fleece. "By the way, we've decided to call Saffy's baby after you because you saved her and her mummy's life. She's called Cheriam Maz."

"I'm—er, flattered." I stumble over my words, trying to accept this honor gracefully and without an attack of giggles. I've never had a cat named after me.

"Oh, I almost forgot—I've left you some Belgian buns at Reception."

"Thanks, that's very kind of you."

I open the door on the carrier to let Saffy back in with her kitten as Cheryl goes on, "Miriam and I always want the best for our babies. The Fox-Giffords are jacks-of-all-trades, but you are a specialist."

I can guess what's coming. "Are you sure?" I say, preempting her. Although I admit it would be great to win over a few more clients for Emma's business, I have a suspicion that Cheryl, with her particular brand of fussiness, could end up as the Client from Hell.

"I've never been more sure about anything," she says dramatically.

"If you want to register with us, I'll have to contact Talyton Manor Vets for your records."

That stops her in her tracks, but not for long.

"Do you have to? Only, we've had our babies with the Fox-Giffords for a long time and I'm a bit embarrassed about leaving them."

"It's important we have the records for your cats' safety, as well as being a professional courtesy," I point out as I open the door into Reception to make it clear the consultation is over. It'll also give me the opportunity to introduce myself, which won't be a bad thing. If I'm going to be here for six months, I'm bound to run into one or other of the Fox-Giffords at some time.

However, when I ring the Talyton Manor practice, the person at the end of the line is far from courteous as I explain who I am and what I'm after.

"Maz! What kind of name is that?" Snort. "Bloody hell! I knew this was going to happen, but would anyone listen to me?"

Izzy looks on, eyebrows raised, as I hold

the handset away from my ear. I can still hear Old Mr. Fox-Gifford's deep and angry breathing as I continue. "It's Cheryl's prerogative. It's up to her."

"The middle of town's no place for a vet practice. Problems with parking, barking, and dog shit everywhere. It's a complete menace, and I've said so all along."

"I beg your pardon," I say. I'm not sure what he's ranting on about.

"You gave our receptionist delusions of grandeur and lured her away, and now you're poaching our clients."

"It's nothing of the sort," I protest. (I always find it easier to argue when I'm not personally responsible.)

"What did you say to her, eh? Eh? Did you make out you were better than us because you specialize in small animals? Did you offer her free samples of that dried-out, processed crap that passes as pet food?"

"It *is* pet food," I say.

"Our cats and dogs should be eating what nature intended."

"Which is, in your not so humble opinion?"

"Raw meat and bones!"

"This is the twenty-first century, in case

you hadn't noticed." I'm not sure why I'm wasting my breath, because Old Mr. Fox-Gifford isn't listening to me.

"I don't know what the profession's coming to, but make no mistake about it, I'll be dealing with this. In my own way."

"Which is?" I say, realizing I'd be in a better position to cope if I knew what he was proposing, but he doesn't enlighten me. There's a loud bang, as if he's thrown the handset to the floor, and a humming tone before the connection cuts out altogether. I doubt very much that I'm ever going to see any sign of those records. I doubt very much that his phone will ever work again either.

I guess they're empty threats. I mean, there isn't anything he can do, is there? I've come across plenty of grumpy old men like him, and their barks usually turn out to be worse than their bites. No, Old Fox-Gifford doesn't scare me.

Frances doesn't scare me either when, during my lunch break, she calls me downstairs to see another client who's dropped by without an appointment.

"It's Mr. Gilbert with a dog called Arnie. I took the liberty of sending him to wait in the consulting room while Izzy finds the dogcatcher in the storeroom."

Dogcatcher? I can't imagine that Izzy resorts to that too often.

"Are you sure you aren't winding me up, Frances?" I say lightly as I approach the consulting room door, at which a low, visceral growl stops me in my tracks, providing me with the definitive answer. I push the door open and walk in, my heart beating faster.

Arnie is a black and tan mixed-breed dog, a bit of Doberman, a bit of Rottie, maybe some pit bull terrier and mastiff thrown in too. He must weigh in at well over fifty kilos. He staggers away from me like a drunk, bumping into the leg of the table, his eyes glazed over and froth dripping from his mouth. I back off, pressing my palms against the door behind me.

"He's gone mad, like," says a man's voice.

I don't dare take my eyes off the dog, but I'm vaguely aware that there's a man on the table, squatting on his heels. I'm guessing that it's Mr. Gilbert.

"I don't know what's got into him," he goes on. "Normally he's a complete pussycat."

Arnie turns, sways from side to side, stares at me for a moment, then gathers himself together and throws himself toward me. As I dodge to one side, he keeps going, crashing headfirst into the door. Within a heartbeat, he regains his feet, blood pouring from his nose, and staggers back in my direction.

There's only one thing for it. I make a flying jump for the table and join Arnie's owner. He's bald, tattooed with a spider's web on the side of his neck, and built like a boxer—that's the profession, not the dog—and I don't think he's taken refuge here in expectation of receiving a full clinical exam.

We cling together like the last two survivors on the *Titanic* and watch Arnie flounder. His muscles start to twitch, he growls, and then he goes berserk, running up the wall before throwing himself backward onto the floor with a hideous crash. He remains where he landed, lying flat out on his side, his legs paddling full pelt.

Mr. Gilbert is close to tears. "What the hell's wrong with him?"

"He's having a fit, but don't think about

that right now. We have to get you out of here before he gets up again." The last thing I want is anyone getting hurt. Imagine the headline in the *Chronicle*: KILLER DOG MASSACRE. I grab at Mr. Gilbert's arm, help him down from the table and, steering well clear of Arnie, lead him out to Reception, closing the door firmly behind me.

"Take a seat," I tell him, but he declines. He must be in his late twenties, fond of the gym, and I'd guess a family man, judging by the white, malodorous stains on his black vest, which could be baby sick.

"My wife called me at work, told me to come straight home because the dog'd gone mad and she was afraid for the kids." He worries at his lip. "He's only a puppy himself. Eleven months old." He pauses. "Do you think it's something he's eaten?"

"I don't know what's going on just yet," I say, "and I won't until I've had the chance to examine him."

"He'll rip your throat out," Mr. Gilbert says apprehensively.

"I'll be fine," I tell him. I'm used to handling difficult and aggressive dogs, but even so I suppress a quiver of fear at the thought of what lies behind that consulting room door. "Frances will get you a cup of tea." I give her a hard stare. "Won't you, Frances?"

"Leave it to me. I like a good crisis." She looks past my shoulder as I hear the door open. "Here comes the cavalry. It's young Mr. Fox-Gifford. What a stroke of luck, him turning up out of the blue like this just when we need him. Maz, help is at hand."

I turn to find myself face-to-face (well, almost, considering he's a few inches taller than I am) with the man I met down by the river. This time, he isn't riding his horse. He has his keys in one hand and a bundle of notes in the other.

"Hi," he says.

"Er, hi," I stammer, ducking the gaze of his fiercely blue eyes and focusing instead on the way his hair, dark and curling at the ends, is ruffled and adorned with strands of hay. It actually looks as if he's just tumbled out of a haystack.

"Oh, Alex, I'm so relieved," Frances begins, touching her chest as if she's about to swoon.

Not half so relieved as I am that he shows no sign of recognizing me. I suspect he's already marked me down as a fool by my mere presence here, and he doesn't seem like the kind of man to suffer fools gladly.

Frances fills him in on Arnie, twittering on like an awestruck fan. "It's just chased poor Maz and Mr. Gilbert out of the consulting room. It's foaming at the mouth. There you go"—she's positively glowing with triumph suddenly—"I've made the diagnosis for you—it's got rabies."

"Thanks for that, Frances," I say crossly, trying to regain some control of the situation. There are two kinds of rabies—dumb and furious—and at this precise moment, I'm pretty furious with Frances. "It isn't rabies. Arnie's having an epileptic fit. He doesn't know what he's doing."

Frances merely looks at me as if I don't know what I'm doing either. I'll have to have another word with her later about the dangers of making her own diagnoses and giving out advice.

"I'll deal with it," Alex says, making to step past me.

"Excuse me," I cut in. "You can't do that." And he stares at me with an expression that reads "I can do anything I like," and I can feel myself growing hot and angry with him for striding in and attempting to take over. Alex hesitates, stopping to listen as Arnie begins yelping and scrabbling as if he's trying to dig himself out. It doesn't last long, and in the ensuing silence Alex heads for the door and pushes it open.

"This has nothing to do with you," I say, following him. "This isn't your practice, in case you haven't noticed. Arnie's my patient."

"There's no need to make a drama out of it," he says, shutting the door in my face.

"All right then," I yell at the door, my cheeks burning with fury. Not only is it none of his business but I'm responsible for the safety of everyone on the premises and, unfortunately, that includes him. "On your head be it! See if I care."

"I've found it." Izzy rushes into Reception with the dogcatcher, an adjustable wire noose on the end of a metal pole. "It was tucked behind the bins. I can't remember when we last used it." She stops short. "What's up? Am I too late?"

"Sadly, you're not," I say sarcastically, my voice drowned out by the sound of shouting. Suddenly, Alex Fox-Gifford comes flying out of the consulting room, slamming the door behind him. He clutches his thigh where a triangle of material has come away from his trousers, then looks up, his cheeks pale and damp.

"He got me," he says, eyes wide with astonishment.

"Serves you right," I say without sympathy, but he looks past me, toward Izzy.

"I'll have that." He snatches the dogcatcher and heads back in.

Izzy turns to me.

"Don't ask."

"You might need this." Izzy hands me three small syringes of anesthetic. "I'm sorry—I couldn't find any bigger ones. We must've run out."

"I'll manage," I say. "Would you bring a couple of extra vials through, please?" I'm pretty sure I'm going to need them.

"I can't, Maz," Izzy says. "This is all we've got, and the new order still isn't in yet."

I gingerly open the consulting room door, hoping that I can make do with what we've got. Arnie is lying on his side in the far corner, thrashing all four legs around as if he's running for his life. The air is hot with his breath.

"I'll have the dogcatcher," I say quietly to Alex. "You look after the anesthetic." As

Alex opens his mouth to protest, I shut him up with a glare.

"Arnie's my patient. I'm in charge," I say, and Alex hands me the dogcatcher in exchange for the syringes, not meekly but with a snatch of resentment that I'm not going to let him do the heroics.

"Thank you." I approach Arnie, one slow step at a time, aware of my heart knocking against my ribs. I keep the dogcatcher in front of me, just in case. "There's a good boy," I murmur, but Arnie doesn't give any indication that he can hear me.

Standing well back behind him, I reach out with the noose, letting it touch his nose before I slip it onto his muzzle and tug it back over his ears, where I secure it tightly. I hang on to the pole so that Alex can move safely round beside me. He squats down, steadies one of Arnie's back legs, and shoots a dose of anesthetic straight into a vein.

Gradually, Arnie stops paddling. I loosen the noose and take a couple of steps closer so I can check on his airway and reflexes. There are three stages of anesthesia— awake, asleep, and dead—and I'm praying for the second one. It looks promising:

Arnie's uppermost eye is half-closed and his tongue is slack. I bend down and . . . snap! His head flies up and he's grabbing for me, for the pole, for anything within his reach.

I yank at the wire, tightening the noose hard until it's choking him. Alex injects more anesthetic, and Arnie begins to relax again. I loosen the noose once more, and gradually his tongue turns from deep purple back to pink. We watch him for a minute, maybe two, then Arnie raises his lip, and his throat vibrates with a warning growl.

"I'll make damn certain he's out for the count this time," Alex says, topping up the anesthetic again.

I really hope so, I think, counting the syringes sticking out of Alex's back pocket, because there isn't any more . . .

"I'll have a chat with Mr. Gilbert," I say. "Send him in, will you?"

Alex looks up at me, his eyes wide with concern. I'm not sure whether he's being chivalrous or he thinks I'm incapable of dealing with the situation. "I think I should stay . . ."

"I didn't ask for your help in the first place, and I don't need it now. Please leave," I say sternly. Alex doesn't move, and I've

got a dog coming round on the floor and
no more anesthetic . . . What language
does he understand? I wonder. I'm obviously being far too polite. "Just go!" I say in
desperation. "Get the hell out of my consulting room!"

"Is HE STILL HERE?" I ask Frances once I've
brought the Arnie-Gilbert episode to a
conclusion.
    "If you mean Alex, he's out the back."
    "What did you let him go out there for?"
    "I didn't," Frances says. "Izzy showed him
through."
    "Oh, fantastic." I stomp off down the
corridor, following the scent of hot, damp
cotton to where Izzy is unloading steril-
ized drapes from the autoclave. Emma
would go ballistic if she knew a Fox-Gifford
was snooping around her practice. "Where
is he?"
    "That way." Izzy points to the door into
the operating theater. "I wouldn't—"
    I shove the door open.
    "Too late," she sighs.
    There in front of me is Alex Fox-Gifford,
trousers in one hand, needle and nylon

thread from one of the suture dispensers in the other.

"Oh, er, sorry." Embarrassed, I start backing out, then change my mind. What have I got to apologize for? I'm allowed to be here.

"We haven't been introduced," Alex says as he stares at me, one eyebrow raised, his expression quizzical. "It is you." He grins. "I don't believe it, you're the bog snorkeler?"

I can't deny it. Suddenly it seems extraordinarily hot, and it isn't just because Izzy has left the autoclave open next door.

Alex sticks the needle into the fabric of his trousers, then holds out his hand to shake mine. "I'm sorry I was sharp with you the other day."

I hesitate, but his grip is firm and confident. His fingers are stained purple, his nails cut short but engrained with mud—no, blood. Definitely blood.

"I was angry with myself for letting the horse get the upper hand and spin away like that. I didn't have enough leg, as my mother would say."

I can't stop my eyes drifting downward.

He has more than enough leg in my opinion. There is a small puncture wound on
the inside of his thigh and, oh my God,
he's wearing a contour-enhancing pair of
pants, red ones with a logo reading SUPER-
DAD. Superdad? It hadn't occurred to me
that this man might have kids. I force myself to look up to where his shirt has fallen
away at the base of his neck, revealing the
line of his collarbone and a smattering of
dark hairs on his chest, and try to focus
my gaze on the tufts of white thread that
are all that remain of the top two buttons.

"Where's the dog?" he asks.

"In the freezer. It wasn't a difficult decision." It seems a pity to have had to put
down such a young dog, a much-loved
family friend, and kill off one of the patients
Emma has registered at Otter House, but I
had no choice.

"Another fit like that, and he could have
killed someone," Alex agrees. "I wasn't trying to take over before, you know." He
stops studying the tear in his trousers and
looks up at me, his eyes wide and appeal-
ing for forgiveness, and I find my resolve
to hate him because of who he is and what

he's done to Emma thawing slightly. "I didn't want anyone getting hurt."

"Thanks," I say quietly, and then he has to go and wreck the beginnings of what could eventually become a frost-free relationship between the two practices in Talyton by holding up his trousers and asking me, "What stitch do you think I should use?"

"I hope you're not asking that because I'm a girl," I say, outraged.

A flush spreads up his neck and covers his cheeks like a rash. I've obviously hit a nerve.

"I didn't mean that at all. I'm not like that. I might be a bastard sometimes, but I'm not a sexist bastard." He ties a knot in the end of the nylon and starts sewing furiously, running a continuous suture from one end of the tear to the other, then tying it off. "Could I possibly borrow a pair of scissors, please?" he adds.

"If you must." I dart out to the prep room and take a pair from beside the sink. When I return, Alex holds the thread up and I snip.

"Thank you, Nurse," he says, and when I respond with a glare he gazes at me, a smile playing on his lips. "Lighten up, will you—that was a joke. The responsibility of looking after Otter House must be getting to you, or are you always so fierce?"

Maybe I'm looking fierce because I'm trying not to think about kissing those beautiful lips . . . I can't believe I'm even thinking such a thing when I am so, most definitely, off men.

When I caught Mike and his ex-wife—in our bed—it was like receiving a shot of a particularly nasty virus. It laid me low but in the process triggered protection against further attack. I became immune to men. At least, I thought I did.

Alex gets back into his trousers, which makes conversation a little easier.

"You haven't told me why you're here," I say. "How come you turned up when you did?"

"Well, I'm not here to spy on you," he says lightly. "No, my father mentioned that you'd phoned for Cheryl Thorne's records. I thought I'd drop them in as I was passing."

"Oh, thanks. Thank you."

"You know I've never had the guided tour," he says, tilting his head. "Emma's never offered."

"What do you expect?" I say bluntly. "I

can't imagine she likes the idea of you snooping around her business."

"I don't blame her," Alex says. "My father's been a pain in the backside ever since he found out she was setting up in practice in Talyton St. George. In fact, it wouldn't surprise me if he's plotting something right now. I promise you, though, Maz, all the aggravation Emma's had has nothing to do with me."

"You could have had a word with your father, asked him to back off."

"Ah, you haven't met him yet, have you?" Alex smiles—fondly, I think. "He's a bit of a tyrant."

"We've spoken on the phone," I say.

"So you know what he's like then." Alex pauses. "About this tour?"

"All right," I say, finding myself softening toward him once more on discovering he isn't quite as bad as Emma makes out, and pleased to have the opportunity to show off her fantastic practice to another vet.

I start exactly where we are, in the state-of-the-art operating theater. I show Alex the piped-oxygen installation, the wall-mounted anesthetic machine, and the scavenging system, which removes waste gases from the atmosphere. I demonstrate the heated operating table and pulse oximeter. (Think Monty Python and the machine that goes *ping*.)

"I prefer to do my bitch spays on the kitchen table," Alex remarks.

"You what?"

"Without anesthetic. It keeps the costs down."

I shake my head. I hope he's pulling my leg.

"How much do you charge for a bitch spay?" he goes on.

"I'm not telling you that." In spite of myself, I'm smiling. "You'll only go and undercut us."

"I can always ring up and find out— Frances will tell me." Alex laughs. "Maz, I'm teasing you. I've dragged my practice out of the Dark Ages, against my father's resistance, particularly regarding the expense. There are people in Talyton who still practice the dark arts though. There's Mrs. Wall, for example, who wishes warts away. One or two of my farmers swear by her—it's cheaper than calling a vet out. All it costs is the price of a phone call, less if you go and see her face-to-face."

"Do you have to take the cow with you?" I have to ask.

"No, it's far more convenient than that. You just have to describe the size and position of the wart," Alex says, deadpan. "Apparently, it works for humans too."

I try hard not to giggle at the thought, but I fail.

Alex looks at me, bemused. "Is there anything else you'd like to show me, Maz?"

"Er, Kennels. This way," I say quickly, but before we can continue, Frances calls us through to Reception, where she's laid out a tray with mugs of tea, Cheryl's Belgian buns, and a few Jammie Dodgers.

"It's my emergency treatment for vets," she says happily when Alex thanks her. "I always keep a supply of biscuits tucked away."

"So, Frances," he begins, "is the grass really greener on the other side of the fence?"

"It's patchy," she says with neither tact nor diplomacy, which makes me cringe because she sounds as if she's being disloyal to Emma. "I'm paid on time, and I don't have to dodge Old Mr. Fox-Gifford's missiles anymore."

"Yeah—I'm in the firing line now. Pens, phones, notebooks. If it isn't nailed down, he throws it." Alex turns back to me. "Oh, that reminds me. I brought another set of notes along with Cheryl's. They're for a dog called Pippin. Mr. Brown asked to change practice as well—I didn't think you'd mind."

"Do *you* mind?" Considering how Emma has described Talyton Manor Vets to me, Alex isn't at all what I expected. He's easy to talk to, and not without a sense of humor. He also seems remarkably chilled about handing over his clients to Otter House, and I'm not complaining. We need them—the more the merrier, as far as I'm concerned right now.

"Pippin's been on our books for a long time, but no, I wish him well." Alex hands me a sheaf of papers sticking out of a tatty brown envelope, which he'd left on the desk at Reception when he first turned up. Thankful to have something less compelling to look at, I scan the first couple of lines of the top page. The writing is indecipherable. "I said I'd make an appointment for him."

"That's a bit beyond the call of duty, isn't it?"

"I've known the Browns for some years now—the wife is housebound and he's her full-time carer. Life isn't easy for them. The dog suffers from bouts of diarrhea, which we've never got to the bottom of, so to speak. I thought perhaps someone with a fresh eye . . ."

"Why don't we do it as a second opinion?"

"You're the small-animal vet," Alex says, "and it's easier for him to walk down here rather than drive out to us." He hesitates. "I can give you a translation, if you like—my handwriting's rubbish."

"I'll look at the notes later."

"You're busy. I understand."

But for the empty cages in Kennels and the empty seats in Reception, I'd big it up and say, "Yes, can't you see I'm rushed off my feet?" because I don't want the Talyton Manor Vets to know that Otter House is struggling.

"I'm sure it'll pick up soon . . ." The way Alex holds my gaze, as if he knows exactly what's going through my mind, makes me feel uncomfortable. "I'm sorry about the other night," he adds. "I was called to an emergency, switched off my phone, and forgot to put the calls through to my father, not that he would have been up to a cesarean on a cat, especially one of Cheryl's precious Persians." He smiles ruefully. "The doctor's prescribed him sleeping tablets— I'm not sure whether they're for the pain or for the stress he's been under since Emma set up here."

"That was over three years ago," I point out.

"He doesn't forgive or forget easily." Alex pauses. "Anyway, it won't happen again. My mother had called me out to one of her ponies, one I used to ride, in fact. He was pretty ancient."

"Was?"

"Yeah." Alex rubs the back of his neck. "He died. Poor old Topper."

"I'm sorry." Now I feel really bad.

"You win some, you lose some," Alex says softly. A phone rings from his pocket. He pulls it out, checks the number on the screen, and excuses himself. "I guess I'll be seeing you two weeks on Saturday, Maz."

"Saturday?"

"At the Country Show. Emma put your name down to judge the Best Pet class with my father." Alex tips his head to one side, clearly amused. "Didn't she mention it to you before she left?"

She didn't. I wonder why. There seem to be quite a few useful pieces of info she didn't mention to me before she left.

"It's the highlight of the social calendar," Alex goes on. "Thanks for the tea, Frances. Good-bye, all." He heads outside, crossing the car park to his four-by-four.

"Such a hero." Frances sighs. "They don't make them like that nowadays."

"Thank goodness," I say. "He shouldn't have done what he did. There was no need."

Lacking any patients to see, with a heavy sigh, I idly flick through the notes Alex left. I just about had everything under control, apart from my emotions. Why does Alex Fox-Gifford's presence disturb me so much? He isn't my kind of man at all. He's arrogant, pushy, well-spoken, fit . . . Stop right there, Maz Harwood. That's enough. You'll be falling in lust with him next, and look what happened last time you fell for someone . . .

I force my attention back to work-related matters. First, there's the matter of the missing order—I've seen what you can carry out on a farm with a bottle of brandy and some baling twine, but I'm not going to make do. However, Izzy's ahead of me. She holds the phone at arm's length, her complexion suddenly pale beneath her freckles.

"There must be some mistake," she says. "They're saying they've suspended deliveries to Otter House."

"Let me have a word." I take the phone. There's no mistake. Emma hasn't paid last month's bill, or the three months before that. I don't understand how this could have happened, but I head out the back and settle the account using my credit card.

"It's sorted," I tell Izzy a short while later. "Normal deliveries resume tomorrow."

"Thank goodness for that," she says. "I thought we were going to have to cancel tomorrow's ops." She hesitates, raises one eyebrow. "Is everything all right?"

"Yeah, I think so," I say. And then I realize there's no point in trying to hide anything from Izzy—she was probably listening at the door. "That must have been one loose end Emma forgot to tie up before she went away." Privately, I find it hard to believe that it slipped Emma's mind—there must have been reminders, warnings, and a final demand.

"If you speak to Nigel, he'll reimburse you," Izzy says, ever practical. "Oh, and Freddie's not looking so good—he's passed a lot of blood."

I check up on Freddie—he utters a low groan when I murmur his name. I run through the treatment we've given him. I wish there was something else he could have, but I'm all out of options. I'll give him another few hours, but if he continues to deteriorate, I'll have to consider whether it's fair to carry on.

It's pretty depressing when I've already had to put Arnie down today, but that's how it goes sometimes. It can be difficult to remain positive. The best I can say about Arnie's demise is at least it wasn't rabies, as Frances suggested, which reminds me that I need to have a word with her.

I join her in Reception.

"I know you mean well and you're only trying to help, but you could be putting animals' lives at risk by giving out advice and making up your own diagnoses," I say. If I'm honest, I'm more miffed about her under-mining my authority and making me look incompetent in front of Alex Fox-Gifford.

Frances stares at me, her mouth pursed like a cat's bottom.

"You'll put me out of a job," I add, more gently.

"I hear what you're saying" is all she's willing to say on the matter. I only hope she'll act on it. I fear there's some truth in the proverb "You can't teach an old dog new tricks."

"Do you know anything about this Country Show?" I ask her, changing the subject.

"Of course. Everyone knows about the show. I've won first prize for my chutney five years running." She flicks through the diary and runs her finger down the page for a Saturday in two weeks' time, where there's a note in Emma's handwriting. "Yes, you are indeed expected. What an honor it is to be invited to judge at Old Mr. Fox-Gifford's side, especially when you've only been in town for two minutes."

An honor? It's a pretty dubious one, in my opinion, although the Country Show sounds as if it could be fun, and I'd be looking forward to it if it wasn't for the Fox-Gifford factor.

"Promise me you'll drop in to the WI's marquee," Frances says. "I'll introduce you to some of our members. Don't look so worried, Maz, they're a friendly bunch."

I'm not worried about meeting Talyton's Women's Institute. It's everything else that is getting on top of me.

Waiting for the start of afternoon surgery, I type a brief summary of Cheryl's notes into the computer, then add my own code for Cheryl herself: S for Scary. If she ever asks to look at her notes, I'll tell her it's S for Special.

What code would I give Alex Fox-Gifford? I muse. How about "Handle with Care"?

CHAPTER 6

Muck Sticks

THE KENNELS ARE EMPTY, APART FROM FREDDIE and a ruffled pigeon, which, according to Frances's note on the card, has been brought in by a member of the public in a dazed and confused state. (Whether it was the pigeon or the member of the public who was dazed and confused isn't clear.)

Izzy and I stop beside Freddie's cage—we moved him out of Isolation a couple of days ago, considering him no longer infectious.

"It's a miracle, isn't it?" I say. "Freddie was so sick, I didn't think he'd make it."

"Neither did I. Oh, what's this?" Izzy scans the front of his notes, across which

I've scribbled, "Freeloader—for rehoming."
She lets him chase her fingers along the
bars before she picks up the tin of food
I've left open on the shelf beside the cage
and turns out a couple of forkfuls onto a
dish. She offers it to Freddie, who gulps it
down. "Can't you keep him?" she goes on.

"If I took on all the animals I meet needing homes, I'd end up like Doctor Dolittle. I
like looking after Miff, and I'll miss Freddie,
but I have to think of the future." It's too
uncertain. "I don't know where I'll go or
what I'll do after Emma comes back."

"Aren't you going to stay on?"

"No, whatever gave you that idea?"

"I just thought," Izzy mumbles. "I got the
impression . . . something Emma said . . .
Oh, I don't know."

"Yes, you do." I smile. "She's told you,
hasn't she? She's always wanted us to
end up working together."

I can remember when we first talked
about it. It was Emma's idea, hatched on a
snowy winter's day, the kind of day when it
was impossible to ride a bicycle, and believe me I tried. I ended up in a ditch at the
side of the Madingley Road on the outskirts
of Cambridge, my knees badly scraped

and both my bike's front wheel and my pride rather dented.

Emma abandoned her bike next to mine and we walked, struggling through the snowdrifts on our way to one of the university farms to take our turn on the student rota for some hands-on experience of lambing.

"You look as if you're on your way to a football match, Em." I was teasing her, trying to cheer her up. "That hat makes you look like a Cambridge United supporter."

"Thanks a lot. Some friend you are," she grumbled lightly, pulling her knitted hat down over her ears and gazing (enviously, I hoped) at my waterproof cap and college scarf, on which I'd blown the rest of my budget for the term.

"At least I'm honest," I said, grinning as I gave her a gentle nudge. "Is that the barn over there? Beyond the gate."

"I guess so." Emma sighed. "You know, I can think of a hundred and one things I'd rather be doing than practicing my midwifery skills on a day like this."

"Such as?"

"Curling up indoors, toasting marshmallows on the fire, and watching TV," she replied as we trudged closer to the barn in the cathedral-like silence of the falling snow, and I had to admit, as I buried my hands deep into my pockets, it did sound tempting.

It took all our strength combined to slide the barn door open before we could get inside, where the uproar of bleating and trampling feet assaulted our ears. We slid the door closed behind us, then I found the switch for the strip lights. I bashed the snow off my boots, sending the ewes in the pen nearest us stampeding off to the far corner for safety. One was left behind, a single black-faced Suffolk in a flock of mules. A translucent green bag dangled from the wet, matted wool at her rear end. She strained a couple of times, but nothing happened.

"Dibs not do the Herriot thing," Emma said. "I'll hang on to her for you, Maz, while you strip to the waist."

"You are joking?"

Emma giggled for the first time that day. "Of course."

I stripped down to three layers, then washed my hands in the soft light in the shepherd's den, a cubicle divided from the rest of the barn and supplied with hot water. I returned to the pen with lubricant dripping stiffly from the fingers of my plastic gloves and knelt to examine the ewe.

"Do you think we should call someone?" Emma asked, as I groped around blindly, finding first a head, then a neck and shoulders, but no legs: a lamb stuck on its way out through the birth canal.

"By the time anyone gets here, it'll be too late," I said. In spite of the cold, I was beginning to sweat. It was up to me. I closed my eyes, picturing my lecture notes annotated with sketchy cartoons of lambs trapped inside their mothers' wombs with speech bubbles saying, "Help me." "If I push it back, I should be able to catch its feet and bring them through first. What do you think?"

"Sounds good to me. I'm glad you know what you're doing—all I know about lambing is written on a couple of sides of A4 paper."

"Same here." I glanced at the ewe's face, her expression anxious, waiting for the next contraction. I had to do something for her sake.

Act confident, I told myself, and don't fiddle.

After five minutes, my confidence ebbed and I got fiddling. The ewe bellowed and heaved. The lamb's head and shoulders, and then the rest of its body, slid out in a rush of fluid and landed in a bloodstained heap.

Emma and I stared at it.

"Is it breathing?" Emma said.

"I'm not sure . . ."

"I don't think it's breathing," Emma said urgently.

I tore the membrane from its nostrils and mouth, picked it up and swung it by the hind legs, then lowered it down again and rubbed its steaming, close-curled coat with a handful of straw. Suddenly, it shook its head and took its first breath, by which time the ewe had given birth to a second lamb. Emma revived that one, and I dealt with a third, which arrived shortly afterward.

"Poor cow," I observed. "Fancy having to look after this lot."

"Call yourself a vet student, Maz." Emma grinned. "In case you hadn't noticed, it's a sheep."

The firstborn lamb made an attempt to struggle to its feet, then nosedived back into the straw. At the second attempt, it sat on its haunches. At the third, it walked shakily to its mother's udder, nudged at one of the teats, and latched on, sucking and wiggling its tail.

Emma and I watched our babies fondly for a while, sitting on bales of straw and drinking mugs of hot chocolate, the scent of lanolin on our hands.

"If we ever get out of vet school alive, we'll set up practice together," Emma said.

"Really?" I was touched that she included me in her vision for the future.

"Small animals only. Absolutely no sheep."

"We'll have lots of toys to play with and a coffeemaker," I said, fired up by her enthusiasm and picturing us doing a ward round in our own hospital together, checking up on our patients—lots of them, all with exotic and obscure conditions. (I was a student then, and even though I'd spent plenty of time with Jack Wilson at the Ark, I still thought vet practice would be a series of challenging cases every day, not yet realizing that much of the joy of the job comes with seeing the more mundane, routine cases and getting to know the patients.) As far as I could tell, it was the perfect plan, and I wished I'd been the one to have thought of it. What could be more fun than working alongside Emma?

"We'll have blue uniforms," Emma said cheerfully. "Green doesn't suit me at all."

"I don't care as long as we have central heating," I offered. I couldn't feel my toes. I slipped my feet out of my wellies and wrapped them around my mug in an attempt to restore the circulation. "How long have we got left?"

"A couple of hours." Emma checked her watch, scuffling under her multiple cuffs to find it. "This is a very slow night—the ram must have had an off day. I mean it, Maz, about the practice."

"I hadn't really thought about what happens after vet school," I told her. I guess I'd been so focused on getting a place at university and passing exams that I hadn't made plans for anything beyond my finals. I suppose I'd always seen myself becoming a single-handed vet in a practice just like the Ark. Meeting Emma and Ian had complicated matters, and I felt a twinge of regret that soon the excitement and camaraderie of vet school would be over and real life would begin. "What about Ian? I'm practically living with him, aren't I?"

"I'm not sure I could work with Ian," Emma said.

"You're right." Although I adored him, I wasn't blind to his failings. "He'd want everything his own way."

"He'll go on to do a Ph.D. and become a professor," Emma said. "I can't see him doing the routine stuff like vaccinations and clipping claws, can you?"

I shook my head. Ian had already talked of spending a year as an intern at a vet school abroad, making a career in academia. Where did that leave me? Us? We'd been together for over four years. Was it love? I plucked at the bale I was sitting on, scattering pieces of straw on the ground. Was it forever? I hoped so.

Emma returned the mugs to the den and arrived back with the elastrator, the kind of implement a torturer might have designed to extract a confession from the most stubborn prisoner way back in the Middle Ages. She sat down and stretched a thick latex band across its metal teeth.

Something rustled in the corner of the barn, near the door.

"Did you hear that?" I slipped my wellies back on and stood up.

Emma scanned the barn. "Rats, I expect," she said, and a tiny shiver ran down my spine.

"They must be very big rats," I said hesitantly.

Emma tipped her head to one side and grinned. "I expect they've escaped from one of the labs around here. Come on. Let's go and castrate some lambs."

"If there are any," I said, accompanying Emma to where the ewes with lambs at foot were penned. I was right. There were six or seven male lambs, and they had all been thoroughly emasculated before we could get to them.

The sheep bleated and the wind rattled the roof of the barn, ripping at the sheets of corrugated iron above our heads, so we could hardly hear the sound of a big diesel engine rumbling up through the snow outside.

"Who's that?" Emma said.

"I don't know. The shepherd? The next shift?"

"They're not due to start for another hour."

"Emma! Maz!" Two voices. Ian and Ben appeared, closing the door behind them. Ian was tall and sandy blond; Ben was shorter, chunkier, and dark-haired. (I imagine that's one of the reasons Emma and I never fell out—we had completely different tastes in men.)

Ben came jogging up to us, swinging his arms as if trying to catch hold of any stray warmth in the air. He grabbed Emma and pulled her to him, taking the end of his scarf and wrapping it around her neck. "We came to find you," he said, turning to me. "Ian." He waved. "They're over here."

Ian joined us, clapping his gloved hands together and exhaling lungfuls of mist.

"Hello there, kitten." He leaned down and pressed his face to my cheek, the contact making my heart skip a beat.

"You have a cold, wet nose," I whispered.

"Means I'm healthy." He might have pinched my bum just then, but I was too well-padded to be sure.

"We found your bikes abandoned in a snowdrift," Ben said.

"Why didn't you try our mobiles?"

"We did."

Emma pulled a mobile from her pocket. "I have mine with me, but there's no signal out here."

"I left a message on yours, Maz," said Ian.

I patted my pockets. "I must have left it back at the house."

"Typical." Ian sighed.

"Well," I said lightly, a little annoyed by his implied criticism of my forgetfulness, "you're just in time. We were looking for something to practice on."

Emma held the elastrator above her head. Both Ian and Ben backed off.

"That looks like a nasty piece of work," Ben said.

"You were on the shift before last, weren't you, Ian?" Emma said. "Only you didn't save us any lambs."

Ian held his hands up. "I'm sorry—I'm not great at counting sheep."

"You know the rules," I said. If there were cows with feet to be trimmed, we did one foot each. When there was a horse to shoot, we drew straws for it.

"Can we take you home now?" Ben asked.

"It's too early yet," said Emma.

"We'll wait so we can give you a lift back." Ian always joked that he was a man of dependent means, dependent on his businessman-father's generosity. His father gave Ian a monthly allowance, and paid his bar bills at the end of each term. To be fair, Ian was equally generous in his turn.

"Is there anywhere we can make tea?" Ian took my hand and lifted the flap on the pocket of his tweed jacket, revealing the silver top of a hip flask. "I've brought some Earl Grey too."

"You think of everything." I smiled.

"Attention to detail," he said.

"Attention to detail" was one of Ian's favorite phrases. He carried it through to the tea making, a bizarre and somewhat unnecessary ritual, I thought, as someone who was used to chucking a tea bag in a mug.

Suddenly there was a gust of wind and a burst of hail; the lights in the barn went out, and we had to make our way outside to Ian's Land Rover, following the feeble beam of his torch. I didn't mind—at the time, I think I'd have followed him anywhere.

Ian? Why is it I always go for confident, charismatic, and charming men? A small voice inside me tells me it's because I wouldn't be happy if they were otherwise. What it can't tell me is why they love me and leave me. I don't feel like a victim, although I do wonder whether I don't fight hard enough to keep them, whether I give up too soon.

"I should have given up on men after Ian," I tell Izzy. "I did for a long time. . . . Well, I did go out on a few dates now and then before Mike, but nothing serious."

Izzy stares at me. "You were a bit of a goer then," she says.

I don't take offense. I'm beginning to get used to Izzy's straight talking.

"What about you?" I ask, knowing from Emma that Izzy lives alone but in hope of meeting that someone special.

"There aren't that many eligible bachelors in Talyton." Before I can mention the name of the obviously single man attached to Otter House, she rushes on. "Nigel was keen on me at one point, but I made it clear that wasn't on. I couldn't stand his fussiness." Izzy puts a bowl of food down for Miff and another into Freddie's cage. "If you didn't marry Ian, what stopped you from going into partnership with Emma?"

"It's a long story. Emma and Ben got married and settled in Southampton—Ben was working at the hospital. I ended up working in various practices in London. It wasn't until I came down for Celia's funeral . . ." My voice falters as I remember Emma's mum, who showed me so much kindness when I was a student, offering me a place to stay during the holidays and bailing me out when I was on the verge of quitting vet school because I'd gotten myself into financial difficulties.

Even holding down two part-time jobs and living on lentils and economy cornflakes, I couldn't pay my credit card bills or put a deposit down on accommodation for the following term. It was my fault. The dress that I bought for the May Ball, for example, was an extravagance, but how could I have let Ian down by turning up in front of his friends in jeans and a calving gown?

I paid Celia back though, every penny.

"You were saying . . . ," Izzy prompts.

"It was just after the funeral when Emma suggested I joined her as a partner in Otter House."

"So why didn't you? I know," Izzy goes

on, excitedly. "There was a man. There's always a man."

"Mike, my boss at Crossways. It was very early days back then, but I always hoped things would go further, and they did . . ." I'm not sure who sighs the deepest, me or Freddie. Each time I think of Mike, the wound I thought was healing weeps a little. I change the subject. "Isn't there a local rescue center who'll take Freddie? What about the RSPCA?"

"No way," Izzy says. "I can't bear the thought of him being dragged from pillar to post, not after what he's been through. Give me time—a week, maybe two—and I'll find him a good home."

"Maz, you have one waiting," Frances calls through.

Consulting room, here I come . . .

Pippin. Shih tzu. Gray and white.
   Four years old.
Neutered male.
Problem: has the runs something
   chronic.

"So," says the client, Mr. Brown, "Alex suggested we come to see you."

"I thought you'd asked to swap practices." I'm confused. Alex seemed so gen-
uine, leading me to believe it was Mr.
Brown's idea to change from the Talyton
Manor Vets to Otter House.

"Oh no, not at all. In fact, it's much easier to park up at the manor than here." Mr.
Brown fidgets on the opposite side of the
table. His shirt crackles with static, his
trousers rustle, and his shoes break wind.
"Listen to me rambling on. You must have
Pippin's personal information already."

It's true. Every detail, apart from some
attempts to blot out the most disrespectful
comments in Talyton Manor Vets' notes
with correction fluid: "Motionless for 24
hours. Hoorah! Much wind. Diarrhea—esp.
verbal."

Where are Pippin's test results? A plan
of action for making a better diagnosis than
"dodgy tummy"? I realize I'm sounding a bit
prissy here, but if Alex couldn't handle the
case, he should have done a basic workup,
then sent it to one of the referral centers. I
don't think Alex's motives for handing this
case over to me were entirely altruistic.

"Have you had a look at the notes from
our previous vet?" Mr. Brown inquires.

"Perhaps you'd like to explain the problems you're having with Pippin yourself," I suggest. The notes are thicker than a Jeffrey Archer novel—I'd need at least a week on a beach to get through them. "Briefly."

"Well, let me see. . . . On some days, he passes three motions. Sometimes it's two, sometimes six or seven."

I try not to giggle in the face of such diligent explanation, a feat Pippin makes far more difficult, tipping his head from side to side and peering through his fringe like a Muppet.

"Yesterday"—Mr. Brown rattles his keys in one of the many pockets on his outdoor trousers—"the first one was what I would call normal." He goes on to describe the exact consistency and color, from shades of umber to burnt sienna.

"What do you feed him?" I cut in eventually because, although I have plenty of time until my next appointment, I can see this consultation running on all day.

"Whatever my wife and I are having—good-quality meat and veg, lightly cooked without added salt. He doesn't pick up rubbish outside," Mr. Brown continues, "and he hasn't got worms. I treated him last month

with a multipurpose wormer from Mr. Fox-
Gifford."

Pippin looks remarkably well, and I wonder if we have a problem here with the
owner rather than the dog. I decide that the
bringing in of a sample before starting him
on something to settle his tummy will buy
me time to decide on the best approach to
Pippin's case.

First, find your sample pot.

Emma's Post-it notes have all but disappeared, dislodged by the waving tails of
passing dogs. I give up hunting along
shelves and rifling through cupboards, and
ask Izzy, who's unpacking the latest drug
delivery at Reception. At least, that's what
she's supposed to be doing, but her mind
seems to be elsewhere, her gaze fixed on
the window that overlooks the road at the
front.

I can hear a heavy vehicle rumbling
along Fore Street, nothing unusual in that,
followed by a pitter-pat like rain, which is
odd, because I caught the forecast on TV
this morning and it was supposed to remain dry all day.

The pitter-pat turns to a splatter. There
are bird droppings, giant brown ones, land-

ing on the window, more and more of them, converging and blocking out the sky, blocking out the view entirely.

An air horn blares, an engine growls, then fades into the distance. The spattering noise stops, and a pungent countryside aroma drifts into my nostrils.

Izzy wrinkles her nose as Mr. Brown and Pippin join us in Reception to see what's going on.

"What a mess," Izzy breathes.

"What happened?" says Mr. Brown.

Shit, I think, and in more ways than one. Feeling slightly sick with apprehension over what I'm going to find, I run out to the road. It's worse than I could have imagined. The front of Otter House is dripping with slurry. It slides down the windows, drips off the window ledges, pools on the steps, and seeps across the pavement like chocolate from a fountain.

Shocked, I stand with my hand on my throat, staring at Emma's lovely practice. How long will it take to clean up? Will there be any lasting damage? Will I be able to keep the business open?

I can hardly breathe for the stench, and my revulsion soon turns to anger.

How did this happen? Who could have been so careless? Then it crosses my mind that this might not have been an accident.

Problems with parking, barking, and dog shit everywhere. I recall Old Fox-Gifford's words and what I thought were empty threats to deal with Otter House in his own way. Could he have put someone up to this? I wouldn't put it past him. In fact, the more I think about it, the hotter and crosser, and more convinced that Old Fox-Gifford's behind this incident, I become.

I head back inside and send Pippin on his way with a sample pot before running my theory past Izzy.

"What do you think?" I ask her. "Do you believe Old Fox-Gifford could have had a hand in this?"

"I shouldn't be at all surprised, considering how he's behaved toward Emma. He didn't want another practice on his doorstep in the first place, and now he's miffed because his clients—Cheryl, for example—want to come to us. This is the kind of situation—whether it's an accident or not—that'll have him chortling with delight." Izzy pauses. "What are you going to do now, Maz?"

"I think I should ring the police and report it, don't you?" I say, but I'm not sure. I've never been in the position of having to deal with a practice drenched in slurry before. It certainly wouldn't have happened at Crossways.

"It would be a good idea to report for the insurance, if nothing else," Izzy says. "I'll get Nigel to check the policy and start organizing the clear-up."

I dial 999, and within ten minutes Talyton's top, and probably only, crime-buster appears on the scene, wobbling up the hill toward Otter House on a bicycle as if his dad's just taken off his training wheels. The policeman steers his bike through the slurry, parks it, and introduces himself as P.C. Kevin Phillips. He must be about twenty but, with his uniform hanging in loose folds around his shoulders, could pass for ten. How is this man going to stand up to the Fox-Giffords when he looks as if he couldn't say boo to a goose?

He pulls a notebook and pen from his pocket and begins writing notes, the tip of his tongue sticking out from between his lips as he concentrates on forming his letters.

"There's no evidence I can see that this is a result of anything more than a careless mistake," he says eventually. "The slurry wasn't specifically targeted at Otter House. It hit your neighbors as well, the Copper Kettle included."

"Exactly. Old Fox-Gifford has a grudge against Cheryl too."

P.C. Phillips slips his pen and notebook back into his pocket, and I try again.

"Can't you question the driver of the tractor or something?"

"Can you identify him?"

"I didn't see the driver exactly, but the tractor was a red one."

P.C. Phillips restrains a smile. "Have you any idea how many red tractors there are in this neck of the woods?"

"You must have CCTV somewhere along the route," I say, in desperation.

"There are a couple of cameras on Market Square." He pauses. "I suppose I could take a look at them."

At last . . . "Thank you," I say.

P.C. Phillips returns to his bike, mounts it, and proceeds to steer it into the shoulder of the road. He looks back, not once but three times, like a boy taking his cycling proficiency test, before he wobbles off again into the traffic.

I take another look at the front of Otter House, at the slurry sticking to the plaster and staining the beautiful façade. I'm glad Emma isn't here—she'd be heartbroken if she could see it.

I return inside.

Frances is in Reception with a pained look on her face and a canister of air freshener in each hand. The air is thick with the smell of slurry and lemon sherbet, and I'm pleased to have an excuse to escape to the rooms at the back, where the odors of pet food and disinfectant take over.

I check out today's op, one Emma booked in before she left. Yep, there is only one, which is frustrating when I'm used to having a list of seven or eight. It's a dachshund called Poppy: biopsy and excise mass. I give her a pre-med and a kiss, and slip her back into her kennel. Half an hour later, and I'm in the operating theater, with Izzy there to monitor the anesthetic. A kind of peace descends as I concentrate on removing the lump from Poppy's flank. (It's all relative, mind, as the radio burbles on and the phone rings in the background.)

"Looking at the size of that," Izzy comments, "it's more a case of removing the dog from the lump than the lump from the dog. It's a lipoma, isn't it?"

"Yep," I say, "completely benign." I pick up a pre-threaded needle and forceps and start closing Poppy's wound.

"That's great news—her owner was petrified it was going to turn out to be something really nasty." Izzy drops a fresh batch of swabs onto the instrument tray, then looks toward the door at the sound of footsteps: clipped, precise, and metallic.

"Nigel," Izzy says when he appears in the doorway, twiddling his bow tie. It's maroon with cream dots, like a diseased liver. "I hope you're not traipsing wet slurry across my clean floors."

Nigel's response is drowned out by the sound of water spray of paint-stripping ferocity, accompanied by the dull *thud-thud-thud* of falling masonry.

"What the—?" The bin rattles at my feet. It sounds like Talyton's been hit by an earthquake.

"It's Chris, the chap I rent my cottage from," Nigel says as the echo dies down. "He's brought along a tanker truck and a couple of hoses. That plaster needs some attention. I'll ask him to turn the pressure down." He clicks his heels and marches away as a cheap but cheerful jingle introduces the traffic news on the radio. There are reports of severe delays through Talyton St. George, where Fore Street is closed because of an incident and is likely to remain so for the rest of the day.

"That's us," Izzy says. "I'll be okay here now, if you want to go and find out what's happening."

I snip the threads on the last stitch. "I'm not sure that I do."

"Are you going to get in contact with Emma?"

"I said I'd only get in touch in case of emergency, fire, or flood," I say. I listen nervously to the gallons of water rushing down the drains outside. "That doesn't count as a flood, does it?"

Six months running Emma's practice for her in the quiet market town of Talyton St. George? It'll be a doddle. Did I really say that?

CHAPTER 7

Smack That Pony

GIVE ME A DAY OUT IN LONDON ANY TIME. IN THE city you can be anonymous and wear decent heels. I feel out of place and rather vulnerable in my cheeky red coupe when I join the queue of four-by-fours and horse trailers heading out of Talyton for the Country Show.

P.C. Phillips, dressed in a fluorescent bib, directs the lines of traffic onto the showground. The Land Rover in front of me shoots past, sending showers of mud across my windscreen. I lower my window.

"Hi. Have you got hold of those tapes yet? The CCTV?" I ask him.

"Ah, I was hoping I'd see you," he says in a manner that suggests quite the opposite. "The cameras weren't working—not that it matters now. Didn't you see last week's *Chronicle*?"

I nod, recalling the headline—MUCK STICKS—in the rushed late edition in which their roving reporter interviewed the man responsible for releasing the slurry, an employee of the Fox-Giffords who stated that it was down to mechanical error. There was also a quote from P.C. Phillips saying that any suggestion of tit-for-tat rivalry between Talyton's vet practices was pure speculation. In my opinion, the whole piece was pure fiction.

There are warning signs and safety cones directing pedestrians off the pavement and into the path of oncoming traffic outside Otter House this morning, and Nigel's arranging for scaffolding to be put up next week. The heavy rain overnight has brought more pieces of plaster off and somehow soaked through into the living room of the flat on the top floor. I don't know how much it will cost to get fixed, and whether Emma's building insurance will pay for it. It doesn't seem fair, accident or not, that the Fox-Giffords should get away scot-free.

"Which way?" I ask. "I'm supposed to be judging the pets."

"You'll have to park in the area for the general public as you haven't got a badge." P.C. Phillips points to the right, across a swath of rust-colored mud.

Great. I put the car into first gear and let it creep forward, keeping as many wheels as possible on undamaged turf, but after a couple of hundred meters the wheels begin to slip. I put my foot down a touch harder, the tires spin, and I'm well and truly stuck. As I get out, my beautiful lime green pumps disappear into the mud, and just as I'm wondering if I'll have to wait in the middle of this godforsaken field until it dries out, help rolls up in the form of a knight in a shining tractor.

There's a sign in the side window reading YOUNG FARMERS DO IT IN WELLIES, but it's a very old farmer who looks down at me from the cab.

"Morning. Dickie Pommel, ex-M.F.H., pleased to be at your service." He doffs his cap, then jumps down, remarkably nimble for someone in his seventies.

"Um, what's an M.F.H.?" I ask.

"Master of Foxhounds. I was master of the Talyton Hunt for many years." His weather-beaten face creases into a grin as he examines my car, studies me as if I'm an exotic beast that's escaped from a zoo, then shrugs. "I see you didn't have room for your wellies, my lover."

He unclips a rope from around the waist of the faded pink hunting coat that he wears with waterproof trousers, attaches it to the tractor and my poor car, and then hops back into the cab of his tractor. Minutes later my car has been dragged, its chassis groaning in protest, to the end of a row of four-by-fours.

I thank him, silently dreading having to get out of the field later, and head across the mud to the ticket booths. When I explain who I am, the woman selling tickets gives me a badge with JUDGE on it, a pass for a free lunch in the officials' marquee, and a program.

"Isn't this a year out of date?" I ask, checking the front cover.

"Ah, it's a printing error," she says, peering at her pile of programs through half-moon glasses, "not that it matters in the slightest. The program's pretty well the same every year: Dexy's Dancing Diggers, the Heavy Horse Display, and Ferret Racing. Talyton Country Show has something for everyone. There's a great choice of food: an oyster bar, a whole tent dedicated to cheese, Mr. Rock's fish and chip van. There's plenty for the shopaholic too."

Shopaholic? A vision of acres of department store devoted to the latest fashions and designer shoes enters my mind, only to be replaced by acres of muddy field and canvas marquees as I hear the ticket seller say, "You can buy anything from a riding jacket to sand art. I guarantee you'll love it."

"I imagine it'll be quite an experience," I say drily.

"I'm glad Talyton has another vet," the woman says. "My Colin—that's my cat— he's scared of Old Mr. Fox-Gifford, especially when he's waving his thermometer about. Colin's very sensitive about his rear end." She proceeds to review her cat's history in full before giving me directions to Pets' Corner. "The judging's due to start in half an hour," she tells me.

Recalling Frances's talk of her prize-winning chutney and introducing me to some of the WI, I pop into their marquee on the way. It's stifling inside, stuffed with the scents of dahlias, crushed grass, and strawberry jam. The tent is crowded. There are trestle tables laden with plates of scones oozing with cream and jam, jars of chutney, some dressed up with gingham caps, others open, their contents dished out on plates with cubes of cheese stabbed with cocktail sticks.

Pushing my way through the gaggle of women, I catch sight of Frances. Bathed in the white glare of camera flashlights and polite applause, Frances holds up a jar and a red rosette marked FIRST PRIZE. When she sees me, she offers to introduce me to her friends. She holds out her hand to an elderly woman who's bowed almost double.

"This is Gloria, Gloria Brambles. Gloria, this is Maz, the vet I told you about."

As Gloria eyes me up and down, she reminds me of a tortoise peering out from its shell. Her skin is very pale, the type that easily burns.

"You're a strange creature," she observes. "You'll catch your death in those flimsy shoes." I don't know how to respond to this, but she goes on. "I've followed Frances's advice to the letter, but my Ginge is still out of sorts. I wonder if there's anything else I can give him to settle his tummy." The tousled white ringlets of Gloria's hair release a small puff of powder. Her face is powdered too, and her mouth a gash of pink lipstick. Her eyes are the lightest blue I've ever seen.

"I really should see him," I say. "It's been going on for a while now, hasn't it?"

"I'd prefer to see Emma, but I guess you'll have to do," she says grudgingly.

"This is Fifi Green, president of Talyton Animal Rescue and lady mayoress." Frances introduces a woman in robes and a chain, and an enormous hat swathed with netting and decorated with artificial flowers. If Gloria Brambles reminds me of a tortoise, Fifi Green reminds me of a Yorkshire terrier: sweet-looking with big brown eyes and long lashes, but full of attitude.

"She's also treasurer to the WI, in other words a professional busybody," Gloria says rather tartly. Her voice rings with money, and the black pearls around her neck must be worth a fortune, yet her clothes, which are more Jaeger than Next, seem shabby. The waist of her skirt is pinned with a diamond brooch—to keep it up, I assume. She smells vaguely unpleasant, of cat and sour milk. "I'll remind you that as one of the founder members of Talyton Animal Re—"

"You no longer have anything to do with TAR," Fifi interrupts. "The committee voted you off at the last Annual General Meeting for breaking the rules."

"Rules! Pah!" spits Gloria. "I've never turned an animal away."

I feel as if I've walked into a long-standing argument. Neither Gloria nor Fifi seems prepared to back down.

"We can't foster out to you anymore because you won't give them up to our adopters," Fifi says.

"They were unsuitable, Fifi, and you know it."

"We vetted them all. You wouldn't let my son have those two cats because he didn't have a cat door. And you refused to let my niece and her husband have the goldfish because they were out at work all day."

"They didn't have the right temperament for those fish. They're very quiet, peace-loving fish . . ."

Before I have a chance to voice my professional opinion that I don't think fish care who they live with as long as they have food and plenty of space for swimming, Fifi comes back with "I wish you'd be honest, Gloria. The truth is that you can't bear to let them go. You're under some delusion that no one can look after those rescues as well as you." The lady mayoress rests one hand on her well-upholstered hip as if convinced she's scored a point, but Gloria isn't about to give up.

"You don't care about animal welfare," Gloria accuses as she takes a swing with her handbag, which looks as if it's from the 1920s and made of crocodile skin. I don't know whether Gloria means to hit her or not, but Fifi totters a couple of steps backward, out of range. "All you're bothered about is your image."

"Ladies, please." Frances takes Gloria's arm. "I'd like a closer look at the winning flower arrangements. Connie misread the brief—for 'Exotica' she read 'Erotica—'"

"I'm due to officiate at the pet show in a few minutes," Fifi interrupts. "I'm glad we've been introduced, Maz. I can take you to meet Old Fox-Gifford." She looks me up and down, her gaze, like Gloria's, lingering on my feet. "Have you met before?"

"No, but I've had words with him."

"Then you know what a charmer he is." Fifi sighs, apparently oblivious to the exact meaning of what I've said. "Come with me. It's this way."

It is with some trepidation that I follow her to the next tent, a marquee that opens at the side into a small arena, marked out with posts and rope.

"Fox-Gifford," Fifi calls toward a gray-haired man with a bent back and bowlegs, who turns on his stick and touches the brim of his bowler hat. Alex is about forty, so I don't know why I'm surprised that his father's easily in his seventies. "I've brought Maz, Emma's relief from Otter House, along with me."

"So I get to meet one of the mad cows at last," I hear him mutter. The lapel of his tweed jacket is covered with badges: SHOW COMMITTEE, JUDGE, and VET ON CALL. His corduroy trousers are baggy and a bilious shade of mustard. His sideburns are unkempt.

"Oh, Fox-Gifford, you are a wag," Fifi says, looking a little embarrassed on my behalf.

"Do you see me wagging?" He hobbles toward me, stops and stares with eyes very much like Alex's, then sniffs at the air. "I hear you've been getting used to some nasty countryside odors." His lip curls—I'm not sure whether he's smirking or snarling.

"No thanks to you," I say, standing my ground as he moves closer. "You've got some nerve," I say, then I wish I hadn't put it like that, because he seems to take it as a compliment. "That was no accident."

"Maybe, maybe not. You can't prove it. My people won't say anything—they're as loyal as my old Lab—and anyhow, I don't understand why you can't see the funny side." He clears his throat. "Mind you, Emma's always been a bit of a sourpuss too."

The back of my neck prickles with irritation as he goes on. "I see you're offended—well, I call a spade a spade, and I can't help it if people don't like it. Still, you came out of the slurry smelling of roses, didn't you? All that free advertising on the front page of the *Chronicle*." He turns to Fifi. "Let's get on with this, shall we? We don't want to be late for luncheon. Elsa's doing the food."

A steward unfastens the rope, allowing the queue of competitors for the Best Pet competition into the ring, where they place their baskets, carriers, and cages on straw bales lined up across the center. I wait with Fifi and Old Fox-Gifford, watching a woman in a short skirt and long boots flash the length of her tanned thighs as she trots up and down with a black standard poodle—one of the tall ones, not the kind you can easily stick on your lap.

"She's one of our clients," says Old Fox-Gifford.

"Aurora owns the boutique in town, Aurora's Cave," Fifi says for my benefit.

I've seen it. The mannequin in the window wears a red T-shirt with BITCH splashed across it in silver.

"That's one of the Pitt boys with the Labrador pup," Old Fox-Gifford goes on.

"One of ours, I believe," I say. "Oh, and Cheryl's here too."

"She was one of ours until you brainwashed her."

"You start one end, Fox-Gifford. Maz can start at the other," Fifi says hastily. "The steward and I will record your scores for each pet—points out of ten, please. The one with the highest combined score wins."

It seems fair, I think, thankful that I won't have to make small talk with Old Fox-Gifford.

I adore the rabbit, an Angora with long, floppy ears and a harness covered with bling. It sits on a silk cushion sparkling with sequins. A boy stands with him, ducking in now and again with a hairbrush to straighten out its extravagant fur.

"What's his name?" I ask the boy.

"Dobby. I called him Dobby after the house elf in Harry Potter."

"If it wasn't for Dobby, my Paul would be dead." I assume that it is the boy's mother who's calling out from the ringside. "He was diagnosed with leukemia last year."

"I'm so sorry."

"He's cured now, aren't you, Paul?"

"I'm much better now," says the boy, and I give him the full ten points.

"Are you sure?" whispers Fifi when she comes to record his score on her sheet. "He won last year."

"It's such a sad story," I say. "He's had leukemia."

Fifi laughs. "You don't want to go listening to the Ashfields—it was a kidney transplant last year."

"So the boy isn't ill?" What's wrong with these people? It's only a country show. "I thought this was supposed to be a bit of fun."

"It's a sideshow," says Old Fox-Gifford from beside me, "just like the Otter House Vets. We're the main event in this town." He rubs his hands together. "Are we done?"

Fifi looks down the score sheet on her clipboard.

"The Ashfields' rabbit has the most points," she says.

"A rabbit?" Old Fox-Gifford grinds the end of his stick into the mud. "Vermin. We shoot the bloody things on the estate."

"Shh," warns Fifi, but he doesn't make any effort to lower his voice.

"Call in Aurora first. A lovely bitch that is." He points his stick. "Look at the legs on that."

"What about the rabbit?" I stick to my

guns, an inappropriate term in the circumstances, but I don't see why Old Fox-Gifford
should get his own way on this. It's supposed to be a joint decision.

"What about a compromise?" Fifi suggests. "How about Cheryl's cat?"

"Absolutely no way," says Old Fox-
Gifford. "It's cross-eyed, like all her bloody
cats."

"All right, it'll have to be the cat, the
tabby one." Fifi touches the steward's arm.
"We'll announce the result and give out
the rosettes, then we'll take you off to
lunch, Maz. And after that, you must pop
along to Talyton Animal Rescue's stall and
have a go at the raffle. There are some
fantastic prizes—bottles of wine, bubble
bath, oh, and a foot spa. Perfect for someone like you who's on her feet all day."

What is the point of me being here, I
wonder, when it's Fifi who gets to choose
the winner? It's kind of her to make me
feel welcome, but she does rather take
over.

I wonder too about making an excuse to
dash back to Otter House to let the dogs
out but decide that might be considered

letting the side down, and in any case, Fifi won't let me.

"You can't possibly leave just yet." She grabs on to my arm after the presentation, letting Old Fox-Gifford limp on ahead of us, apparently intent on making the most of his free lunch. "I wanted to have a quiet word . . ." I wait for her to go on. "Talyton Animal Rescue have been associated with Talyton Manor Vets for a long time, but it's all getting rather expensive, and I wondered if you could see your way to giving us a better discount."

It's a bit of a cheek, I think, to ask me, not Emma.

"I'll be straight with you, Maz. Old Fox-Gifford gives us twenty percent off across the board."

"Twenty percent?"

"We do have a lot of animals passing through our foster homes, and vets' fees are our biggest expense."

Fifi has a point, I muse. I want to help. I tell her I'll speak to Nigel. I need to have a word with him in any case about the check he gave me that was drawn on the practice account. It bounced.

"Oh?" she says. "Frances gave me to understand that Emma had left you holding the reins."

"Yes, the reins, but not the key to the safe, so to speak," I say firmly. Fifi doesn't say any more about it, because we join a long queue inside yet another marquee along with Old Fox-Gifford and a woman I guess to be his wife. She holds herself straight and tall in a tweed jacket and skirt, and green wellies. I chose my outfit of skinny white cropped trousers and a beaded halter top thinking it would look up-to-date and not too over the top, but I now realize it's completely out of place in a veritable ocean of tweed. I feel conspicuous—naked, almost.

"Sophia is joining us at the manger," Old Fox-Gifford says, nodding at his wife. "As district commissioner of the Talyton branch of the Pony Club, she's running the Mounted Games in the main arena this afternoon."

"Are you holding the camp at the manor again this year?" Fifi enquires.

"Against my better judgment," says Old Fox-Gifford. "Three of the little buggers left hoof prints all over the lawn last time, put paid to a decent game of croquet for months."

Somehow, I can't imagine him playing croquet. It's far too civilized a pastime.

"You will do your usual talk on worms after lunch on the second day, won't you, darling?" Sophia pats the stiff waves of her gray hair.

"Can't you ask Alexander?" Old Fox-Gifford twists a button hanging by a thread from the sleeve of his jacket, tugs it off, and sticks it in his pocket.

"You know how busy he is." Sophia is accompanied by a strong smell of antibiotic and Cheval No. 5. She picks a curl of wood shaving from her silk scarf and lets it fall to the ground before turning to Fifi. "The practice has been pretty quiet recently, which isn't such a bad thing. It's given us time to find a girl we like and our son approves of. Her family connections leave a little to be desired, but I can forgive her that—she has such lovely soft hands."

"That filly has a good bit of flesh on her too," says Old Fox-Gifford, hooking his stick over his arm and entering the fray for plates and cutlery.

I can hardly believe what I'm hearing. Do the Fox-Giffords still cling to the aristocratic tradition of arranged marriages? I'm confused as an image of Alex's Superdad pants and his long, muscular thighs flashes into my mind. Is this Alex's second marriage, or did he have his child or children out of wedlock?

"Are you all right, Maz?" Fifi asks. "You look as if you're burning up."

"It's the heat," I say, fanning my face with my program. "I'll be all right in a minute." I gaze at the queue ahead, which is moving at snail's pace, wishing everyone would hurry up so I can get some food and make my escape from these terrible people.

"You aren't local," says Sophia, bringing me back into the conversation.

Is it that obvious? I think, half smiling to myself.

"I was born in London," I say.

"We keep a small pied-à-terre in Knightsbridge, although Sophia and I don't get away from the manor as often as we used to," says Old Fox-Gifford, returning with plates and cutlery, which he hands out.

"Such a gentleman," Fifi whispers in my

ear. "They don't make them like that now-adays."

Thank goodness, I think as Old Fox-Gifford goes on. "Ascot hasn't been the same since they started letting the yobs in."

"Whereabouts in London?" Sophia inquires, in a tone that makes me feel this is more of an interrogation than a social chat.

"I spent my childhood in Battersea, near the dogs' home, south of the river."

"Oh, I am sorry," Sophia says.

"There's nothing to be sorry about. I liked it."

"Yes, but it's hardly West Ken, is it, Madge?" she says.

"It's Maz. My name is Maz." I'm not sure whether Sophia hears me over the general hubbub in the marquee or whether she's deliberately ignoring my reply.

"So, you're an out-and-out townie." Old Fox-Gifford shakes his head in disapproval. "Ever been blooded?" he asks, moving closer so I can see the whites of his eyes.

"Um, I don't know what you mean," I say, finding myself unable to step back from him for the crush behind me.

"He's referring to the custom of smearing the cheeks of new followers with blood from the kill at the end of a hunt," Fifi enlightens me, which is a relief because it crossed my mind that Old Fox-Gifford could be referring to some bizarre initiation ceremony for people new to Talyton St. George.

"Have you ever ridden to hounds?" he says impatiently.

"I can't ride."

The Fox-Giffords' mouths drop open, and I wonder what I've said. Not being able to ride isn't a crime, is it?

"I beg your pardon," Sophia says, touching her throat in apparent disbelief.

"You don't see all that many horses in Battersea," I say.

"I hope you aren't planning to stay on in Talyton once Emma returns from her jaunt," Old Fox-Gifford says.

"I don't think that's any of your business." I feel as if I'm being attacked from all sides.

"There aren't enough pet owners in Talyton to keep two vets occupied full-time, even when the new estate's finished," Sophia says.

"Estate?" says Old Fox-Gifford. "I wouldn't let my dogs live there."

"No, dear."

"I'm not staying," I say, but they aren't listening. Sophia, Fifi, and Old Fox-Gifford are talking among themselves again. I might as well not be here.

"We can't all choose to live in the country. Just imagine how unbearably crowded it would become," Sophia says, rolling her eyes.

"It's bad enough already—look at the traffic jams on Sunday mornings when the plebs go off to have breakfast at Fifi's garden center," says Old Fox-Gifford.

"That's a bit harsh when they're the very same people who turn up at your surgery during the week. Really, Fox-Gifford, you must never bite the hand that feeds you," Fifi says coyly.

"Talyton Manor has to support two families," says Sophia, apparently unconcerned that Fifi's flirting with her husband. "There's us and Alex, who has to provide for his children and ex-wife."

"And she's the very definition of high maintenance," Fox-Gifford cuts in.

"That isn't entirely fair—Astra's trying to do her bit," Sophia says.

"By selling herself to the highest bidder and cheapening the family name,"

Fox-Gifford says. "Why oh why did she talk to that cheap rag *Hello!* and not *Tatler*? Scandalous!"

I glance at Fifi, who shakes her head almost imperceptibly. Perhaps she'll give me the goss later on . . .

"Are you going to deny our grandchildren the right to a decent living?" Sophia says, turning back to me.

"I'm not staying," I repeat.

"We'll have to sell more land, or turn our home over to the National Trust, or have a roller coaster built out in the park," says Sophia. "Talyton Towers. Just imagine. How awfully awful."

"I'm not staying," I repeat for the third time, but Sophia and Fifi are counting out paper napkins, and Old Fox-Gifford is talking to the woman managing the buffet. She's curvaceous, blond, and expensively dressed.

"Elsa, how's the old boar? Is he showing any more interest in the ladies?"

"Hardly." The blonde giggles. "Oh, I thought you meant the old b-o-r-e."

"Not Charles," Old Fox-Gifford guffaws. "The pig!"

"Oh, him. He's got until the end of the

month and then he's bacon. If you can't cure him, Fox-Gifford, I will." I notice that no one addresses Old Fox-Gifford by his first name. Is he keeping it secret, like Inspector Morse, I wonder, or hasn't he got one?

"I'll pop out and see him again later in the week, give him a good talking-to."

"Elsa rears rare-breed pigs," Sophia explains.

"Happy pigs," Elsa says before she excuses herself. "I'll be in touch."

Like father, like son, I think. Old Fox-Gifford seems to have plenty of female admirers.

"Cold beef or ham?" one of the servers behind the buffet asks me.

"Er, I'll have the veggie option, please," I say, spotting something resembling asparagus quiche farther along the table.

"One vegetarian," the server calls along to his colleague.

"Vegetarian?" growls Old Fox-Gifford. His eyebrows form a single fuzzy caterpillar, which bristles above the bridge of his nose. All conversation stops, everyone's eyes turn on me, and I feel as if they're about to serve me up on a plate.

"Pale, spineless creatures!" Old Fox-Gifford goes on. "Is it any wonder farming's in such a state?"

Noticing a spare seat at a table on the other side of the marquee, I grab my plate of quiche, add some salad, and make my escape, trying to ignore Old Fox-Gifford's rant about how he holds me solely responsible for the demise of British agriculture as we know it.

"Absolutely no breeding, eh . . . calls herself a vet when she can't even ride a horse . . . should never have been admitted to the register . . ."

It's no wonder Alex turned out how he did with parents like that, I think. They're worse than mine. Both nature and nurture conspired against him.

Even from where I sit, I can't help hearing snippets of conversation provoked by Old Fox-Gifford's outburst. I can hardly taste the food, and I'm sure my face is pinker than the ham being served up to the people of Talyton St. George. I can't wait to get away. If I could jump in my car and drive straight back to London, I'd do it, but I promised Emma I'd look after Otter House, and I don't break my promises.

I cheer myself up at the Talyton Animal Rescue stall, gambling a few pounds on the raffle and walking away with a jar of body scrub, which appears to have been opened before, and a watercolor print of the Taly Valley at sunset.

I stroll back in the vague direction of the car park, keeping to the gravel path alongside the practice area where several riders are jumping their horses. Sophia is there too, lunging a small pony with a child on top, the pony trotting around in circles so fast you can hardly see its legs. The child, who can't be more than five, is wearing jodhpurs, a red tunic, and ribbons in her hair. She sets her mouth in a determined straight line, hauls back on the reins, and digs in her heels.

"Legs. More legs, Lucie."

The child flaps her legs, and the pony bucks and throws her up its neck, from where she slides slowly onto the ground.

"Whoa, Tinky." Sophia pulls the pony up to a halt. It lowers its head and starts pulling at the grass. The child begins to bawl. Sophia helps her up, brushes her off, gives her a smack on the bottom, and sticks her straight back in the saddle.

"That was your fault," Sophia scolds. "You let Tinky get her head down."

The child wipes her face with the cuff of her shirt.

"Does that mean I'm a rider now, Humpy?"

"How many times have you fallen off now?"

The child counts on her fingers. "Five."

"Two more to go," says Sophia. "It's seven times before you can call yourself a proper rider." I find myself thanking my lucky stars I never took up horse riding if that's the case.

I walk on past the Lace Makers' Guild and the beer tent. It really is a different world from the one I'm used to. In fact, I wonder whether I might have slipped through a gap in the space-time continuum into a parallel universe. I mean, who on earth thought of making a competition out of shearing sheep?

I stop before a stage that is set up in front of the sheep pens. Two men stand waiting.

"Get set, go." How I missed Nigel and his stopwatch up until now, I don't know. He's wearing a dazzling white shirt with ruffles, breeches, and long woolen socks with bells attached.

The men spring into action, each letting a sheep out of the pens behind them, turning it over, and grabbing a set of clippers that are plugged into a frame above their heads. The clippers whir. A generator throbs. The fleeces fall away from the sheep's skin. The sheepshearers sweat, and I mean that in the nicest possible way. The one on the left, the one with blond curls and flushed cheeks, is particularly fit. What country maiden could possibly fail to be moved by the sight of his taut, tanned torso as his undershirt parts from the belt of his filthy jeans? What city girl too?

And the one on the right? He has perfect pecs, although when he bows over his sheep, you can see that his hair is thinning on top. I recognize him, in fact. He's Stewart Pitt—Lynsey's husband and father of all those children.

"Maz, you made it." Izzy, looking very demure in a crocheted top, safari shorts, and wellies, strolls over from the edge of the stage to join me.

"What's Nigel wearing?" I ask.

"He's taken up morris dancing." She smiles. "It's a tradition here. Any excuse for a pub crawl."

"Nige, I've finished," the blond man shouts as he lets his sheep go. It scuttles about the stage, naked and fearful. "Switch the clock off, will you?"

"Who is that?" I ask.

"Chris," Izzy says.

"I didn't recognize him from the other day. We weren't properly introduced." I saw him only briefly at the practice when he was there cleaning up the slurry. He must be about forty, maybe a couple of years younger; his skin is flushed with exertion and exposure to the sun, and he isn't as tall as I thought he was, no taller than I am.

Izzy claps and cheers when Nigel declares Chris the winner. In the distance, a roar goes up from the direction of the main arena.

"I could do with a nurse, Izzy"—Chris jumps down from the stage and gazes longingly at her—"someone to rub some liniment into my poor back."

"Oh, I couldn't possibly." Izzy blushes furiously, and I wonder if her problem with finding Mr. Right is that she's shy with men. "Chris, this is Maz, the vet from Otter House. You know, Emma's relief."

"Hi, Maz." Chris smiles. "I would shake your hand," he adds, looking down at his grubby fingers.

"That's okay," I say, backing off a little. "Thanks for helping with the cleanup."

"It was no trouble," Chris says. "I'm sorry for bringing those pieces of plaster down."

"I'm sure it can be fixed," I say.

"It has to be repaired before Emma gets back. I'd hate her to think we haven't been looking after the place properly," Izzy says, glancing at me in a way that makes me realize she still doesn't have much confidence in me. "Um, Chris," she goes on, changing the subject, "I wonder if I could ask you something. It's a favor really."

"You know I'd do anything for you," Chris says lightly.

"We've got a dog in at the surgery, a Border collie pup, that needs a home."

"I could do with another dog. Meg's getting a bit old to chase sheep now. Alex has given her some pills for her arthritis, but she wears out easily." Chris scratches his blond stubble, leaving red marks on his cheek. "Why don't I drop by and have a look at this pup?"

"Or I could bring him over to the farm," Izzy says.

"Give us your number," he says. "I'll be in touch." He enters Izzy's mobile number into his phone, then bids us both good-bye. "I've got to go now. Stewart and I are going to load the sheep onto the lorry so I can get them back to the farm."

Izzy looks disappointed. "What about you, Maz?"

"I was just going," I say, deciding to leave the subject of the check until I see Nigel at work. He's due into the practice again on Tuesday or Wednesday—I'm not sure which. Nigel's working week seems to depend on his other commitments. He has his own business troubleshooting prob-lems with home computers and is keen to learn how to fish—as well as how to mor-ris dance, it seems.

"Oh no, you must stay," says Izzy. "Come and be sociable."

Thinking I might fall further in Izzy's es-timation if I don't, I decide to join her. She seems pleased.

"You never know who you might meet," she says brightly.

It is a case of renewing former acquaintances, I discover. Inside the beer tent, Izzy introduces me to the big man with a shaved head who is behind the makeshift bar. He wears a shirt and tie, and seems vaguely familiar.

"This is Clive—do you remember?" Izzy says. "You and Emma operated on Robbie when you were down for the weekend. Clive, this is Maz."

"I didn't have a chance to thank you for helping to save the old boy's life," Clive says. He glances over his shoulder toward Robbie, the German shepherd, who lies on a piece of sheepskin, alternately panting and sloshing his nose about in a bowl of water. A couple of marrowbone treats lie untouched beside it. "I didn't think I'd be taking him home again. Actually, you couldn't have a quick look at him now, could you?" Clive begins. "Drinks on the house?"

Why not? I think. I've never consulted in a beer tent before. "What's the problem?"

"He's having trouble getting up in the mornings." Clive's smiling, but there's an edge to his voice. "He's like me—too much beer the night before . . . Seriously though, he's started knuckling over on his back feet."

I join Robbie, squatting down beside the dog. I stroke his head, then run my hands back along his shoulders, rediscovering the scar on his chest.

"How did he get this?" I ask, tracing the line of the scar with my fingers.

"We're a matching pair." Clive lifts the front of his shirt and points to a jagged scar that bisects his paunch from his breastbone and disappears below the waist of his boxers. "I was a dog handler in the Met."

"The Metropolitan Police?"

"That's right." He covers up again. "Robbie and I were searching an old factory site for two men after an incident at a petrol station. One turned on me with a knife, slit me down the middle. Robbie went in before he could finish the job off." Clive bends down and ruffles the shepherd's coat, his voice cracking with emotion. "He saved my life."

I don't know what it is about this pair,

but at this moment I couldn't speak if I needed to save mine . . .

"We went back on duty afterward, but I couldn't take it anymore. I opted for early retirement, Edie—she's my wife—resigned from her job, and we came down here. We always wanted to retire to Devon to run a pub. It's been our dream." He smiles ruefully. "A dream turned nightmare, as it turns out. It's cost more than double what we expected to restore the mill to its former glory, and it's bloody hard work."

"I think I'll stick with being a vet."

"It's getting better," Clive says. "It's just a matter of pulling the punters in now."

Tell me about it, I muse, as he goes on in a low voice, "I don't know about you, but I've found that it takes a while to get used to the pace of life and the people here in Talyton. We only got to run the beer tent this year because it was our pub's turn. The landlord at the Duck and Dragon, who looks as if he's been there a hundred years, tried to get the rule overturned at the last town hall meeting, on the basis that Edie and I weren't born within twenty miles of Talyton." He grins. "I don't know what they did—consulted the runes, perhaps—but the ancient tradition decrees that it's the pub that counts, not the people running it."

I find myself chuckling at the idea of the runes. I wouldn't be at all surprised. I like Clive. I guess it's because he understands what it's like to be an outsider.

I give Robbie a quick once-over, checking his reflexes and pulling him about. I feel sick to the pit of my stomach. I could suggest X-rays and scans to rule out arthritis and other spinal disorders, but from the evidence in front of me—the muscle wastage and weakness—I'd say the diagnosis is pretty conclusive. I'm 99 percent certain that Robbie has a degenerative disease that results in a gradual paralysis of the back end. It's merely a matter of time.

"Well?" Clive says.

I shake my head.

"I know the score, Maz. I've seen it before," Clive goes on. "How long?"

"I don't know. I'm sorry." I tell him he can pick up some anti-inflammatories from the surgery to see if they help Robbie's mobility at all, but I'm not optimistic.

Clive turns away, picks up a cloth, and

takes a moment to wipe down the bar. His shoulders slump, and I notice him glance a moment too long at Robbie before turning back.

"What are you having?" he says with a barman's practiced cheeriness.

He serves up a Diet Coke for me and a shandy for Izzy. We take our drinks and sit at a table in the corner of the tent where someone has lifted a flap of canvas to allow in a slight breeze.

"How did the pet show go?" Izzy asks.

"Old Fox-Gifford and I couldn't agree, so Fifi chose the winner in the end. Izzy, what happened to Alex's father?"

"You mean the limp? He was gored by the bull up at Barton Farm. It was some years ago. He nearly died. They said he'd never work again, but he's a stubborn old stick." Izzy smiles. "Stewart had the bull shot. Lucifer, it was called. The Pitts had to employ the services of the AI man instead. His conception rates were the best in the county—the farmers used to lock up their daughters when he was around."

"I thought people like the Fox-Giffords became extinct with the dinosaurs."

"What makes you say that?"

"Alex's parents said they'd chosen a girl for him, someone they approved of." Izzy's brow furrows, and I continue. "A girlfriend with lovely soft hands."

"Alex is more than capable of choosing his girlfriends himself. He's always linked with some woman or another. According to the gossip, his latest squeeze is one of our drug reps. Eloise, she's called. She visited Otter House not so long ago, bringing lunch for us in return for watching some video about the company's latest product, something new for diarrhea. It went down well with pizza."

"I bet it did . . ." It's none of my business, but I don't like to think of Alex with another woman.

"I reckon Sophia was talking about their new groom. The reference to her hands means she's a good rider, that she doesn't pull on the horses' mouths." Izzy laughs. "I expect Alex has a woman to do for him as well."

"To do what?" My imagination is running away with me.

"A housekeeper. Someone who cooks, washes, and tidies up."

"I see . . . What's all this about the ex-wife and *Hello!* magazine?"

"It wasn't *Hello!* magazine. It was one of those celebrity gossip mags that you can pick up for fifty p. Astra had a brief but lucrative affair with some boy toy of a professional footballer after she left Alex, much to the Fox-Giffords' chagrin. She did a photo shoot with him, modeling some designer dresses. She also made out that the Fox-Giffords were snobbish, intolerant, old-money types"—Izzy grins—"which isn't all that far wrong, but it was a bit tactless of her to allow it to go into print when she wanted a decent settlement on her divorce." She leans back in her chair. "Oh, here come the boys."

Nigel and Stewart join us.

"It's Maz, isn't it?" Stewart greets me. "Friend of Emma's?"

"I'm doing her a favor, looking after Otter House while she's away."

"I'd heard a rumor, but I didn't realize it was you. Long time no see. How are you?" He looks past me. "Hey, Alex, come over and meet the new vet."

Alex strolls across. One eyebrow flickers

up, just briefly but long enough for me to realize that he's clocked the state of my shoes.

"I've already had the pleasure," he says—rather grimly, I think. His top buttons are undone, revealing a V of lightly tanned skin, and . . . I can't stop my gaze following straight down to where his shirt is tucked into the waistband of a pair of cream jodhpurs, which are ridiculously snug. You'd have thought he could afford to buy a pair that fits.

"I'm looking for my father," Alex adds. He seems a bit tense.

"I thought that would be the last thing you'd want to do," Stewart teases.

"He has my kids with him, and Mother wants to get them back to the manor in time for tea."

"He's probably still in the hospitality tent." Stewart turns back to me. "Let's hope Maz knows more about dogs than she does about cattle. I'll always remember the first day you turned up on the farm."

Not in front of Alex, I think, cringing, as Stewart blabs on. "You didn't know the difference between bullocks and steers."

"What is the difference?" Clive stacks our empty glasses on a tray.

"Bullocks have bollocks," says Stewart. "Steers don't."

"I wish I hadn't asked," Clive says, wincing.

"And then"—Stewart laughs and slaps his thigh—"when I was teaching you to drive the tractor, you reversed the ruddy trailer into the barn and brought half the wall down."

"That was a very long time ago," I say hotly, "and the wall was falling down anyway."

"I can't imagine you as a driving instructor, Stewart. I seem to recall you rolling your parents' car off the end of Elm Hill once." Alex steps up beside me. (Emma's taken me to Elm Hill before—it's on the north edge of the escarpment on the way to Talymouth.) "Stewart forgot to put the hand brake on when he was, let us say, entertaining one of his young ladies."

Alex's comment on Stewart's past indiscretions reminds me why I'm so off men, although Stewart does have the grace to blush. He drains his pint and changes the subject.

"It's a pity you had that last fence down, Alex," Stewart says. "I saw your last round."

"Yes, that was my own bloody fault, and don't I know it. I'm never going to hear the end of it from my mother," Alex says crossly. "That little mare—"

"You mean the horse, not your mother," Stewart cuts in, in a vain attempt to lighten Alex's mood.

"She's a fantastic jumper, the best I've ever had," Alex goes on, not smiling, "and I went and messed it up for her. I could kick myself, missing that stride at the planks."

"Well, I'm sure we'll see you on the British team one day, if your mother has anything to do with it." Stewart gives Alex a friendly shove.

"Pushy mothers—who'd have them?" Alex grimaces. He's not anywhere near so good-looking when he does that, and I find myself thinking that my first opinion of him was right. He's arrogant, self-obsessed, and he probably is the womanizer everyone paints him to be. In fact, I'm embarrassed that I asked Izzy about him.

"I shouldn't criticize," Alex says, his voice softening. "If it wasn't for Mother,

I wouldn't have a horse to ride, and I'd struggle to look after the kids."

"Talking of kids," Stewart says, "I'd better go and find mine." He checks his watch. "I said I'd meet Lynsey at the bouncy castle at four—she's going to kill me."

"What's new?" says Alex. "If you see my father, tell him I'm on the warpath."

"I'll see you on the farm on Monday," says Stewart. "Cheers, all. I'm off."

"I must go too," says Nigel. "We're dancing in the main arena in fifteen minutes. Are you coming along to watch, Izzy?"

"I can't, Nigel. I promised Fifi I'd do a stint on the Talyton Animal Rescue stall."

"Oh. How about you, Maz?"

"I really have to get back to the surgery to check on the inpatients," I say, not wanting to be left alone with Alex Fox-Gifford. I'm finding it difficult to be civil after the slurry incident, and he seems to be in a foul mood.

"Have you got many in then?" Alex asks as Nigel strolls off, the bells on his socks tinkling, "or is it an excuse to get away from here? It's all right. You don't have to lie. I loathe these events." He pauses. "Oh, how was Pippin?"

"Why did I get the distinct impression you were passing the buck?"

"All right." He taps the end of his whip sharply against his long leather boots. "Probably because I was. Sometimes these chronic cases need a fresh approach, and Mr. Brown has got this habit of turning a ten-minute appointment into a marathon."

"Well, thanks a lot for warning me," I say sarcastically.

"I apologize." Alex makes as if to move a step closer, then changes his mind. "I must get going. . . . I look forward to seeing you again soon, Maz."

I watch him duck out under the canvas at the tent entrance into the sunshine. The feeling isn't necessarily mutual.

CHAPTER 8

In the Event of Emergency

WHEN I GET BACK TO OTTER HOUSE AFTER THE show, I take Miff out for a walk along the river. I stop on the footbridge and drop sticks into the fast-flowing, muddy water, but it isn't much fun playing Pooh sticks alone, and Miff refuses to get her paws wet. She refuses to retrieve too. When I throw a stick (okay, I know I shouldn't), Miff picks it up, crunches it, and spits out the bits.

"Miff, that's rubbish," I tell her, and she looks at me, her eyes filled with hurt, as if to say, "What do you expect? I'm not a retriever."

"I'm sorry." Sometimes I expect too much of people—and dogs. More than that, I expect too much of myself. Miff wags her tail as if to say, "Apology accepted," and we stroll on along the right path this time, straying wide of it only where the bank has fallen away into a bend in the river.

There's no one else down here, yet I feel less alone than I did at the show, where I was the outsider, watching everyone living their lives. I was going to say "their quiet, rather boring country lives," but I've realized that living in the country isn't quite as dull as I'd imagined.

A pair of swans glide silently down the river. One spreads its wings, then tucks them in again.

Still, country life isn't for me—I'm quite sure of that. Whatever it is I'm looking for, I'm not going to find it here in Talyton St. George.

"I'LL GIVE YOU the number for Talyton Manor Vets . . ." Frances, who's wearing a dress so brightly patterned it could be on some sort of hallucinogenic drug, opens a new screen on the monitor at Reception on Monday morning. "The Fox-Giffords know everything there is to know about every kind of animal."

I wave at her urgently, mouthing no. She puts the call on hold.

"Maz, it's a farm animal, a sick chicken that's gone off lay," she says, looking at me over the rims of her glasses. "I don't think you'll be able to deal with it."

"I can cope with a chicken. Please don't send potential clients off to Talyton Manor Vets without talking to me first." I have a feeling I'm going to need all the patients I can get. "Here, let me speak to the owner."

The chicken turns out to be a pet—Duffy. I can hear her clucking in the background. She sounds like she's trying to lay a football. According to her owner, Duffy stays indoors to watch the soaps every evening, and eats chips and ice cream. A picture of a chicken lounging on a sofa with a tub of Häagen-Dazs comes to mind as the chicken's frantic clucking subsides.

"She's done it," says the owner with obvious relief. "I don't need to bring her after all. . . . Sorry for bothering you."

All's well that ends well, I think, except—I hate to sound mercenary—it didn't bring in a fee.

"It's going to be rather busier than of late, Maz," Frances says. I notice she's pinned her red rosette up on the notice board. "I've booked Gloria in to see you, and there are three—no, four—ops." As I congratulate myself on the fact that I must be winning some of Talyton's pet owners over, she goes on, "Oh, the clippers you ordered have turned up—Izzy's got them out the back. And there's a letter for you." She hands me an envelope.

"You've opened it," I say.

"I always open the post for Emma."

"I'd prefer you not to open mine in future, thank you."

"Oh, that's a pity," she says. "It saves so much time—and you vets are always so busy. Perhaps you'll change your mind."

"I won't," I say sharply. I don't want anyone reading my personal stuff, and from the handwriting on the envelope, I know this is personal. In spite of everything that's happened, my heart leaps into my throat and my knees turn to jelly as I pull out the letter. He's realized how much I meant to him, he can't sleep, can't eat, can't live without me . . . and it serves him bloody well right!

I escape into the consulting room, where I scan the letter in private—it doesn't take long because it's just a compliments slip headed with the Crossways logo.

Maz, you left some books. Let Carol know if you want them sent on. Mike.

I feel slightly sick as I picture Mike scribbling that note, making it clear I'm to contact one of the receptionists, not him, if I want my kit back. Scolding myself for my moment of weakness, I screw the paper up and aim it at the bin behind the desk.

"News from your old practice?" Frances inquires from where she's crept up to the consulting room door, her expression one of deep concern.

"Just some junk mail," I say, knowing that she knows that I know that she knows very well what it says.

Frances's lips form a silent O, and I wonder if she's miffed because I haven't chosen to confide in her. Well, there's no way. I've seen how gossip spreads in this town—it's faster than an outbreak of foot-and-mouth. I think of the woman at the checkout at the garden center and talk of

Emma's "pregnancy"—it's like foot-in-mouth as well.

Frances looks past me. "Leave it outside, Gloria."

Gloria struggles to push an old sit-up-and-beg bicycle, one with high handlebars that you can ride with your back straight, through the double doors into Reception. It has a wicker basket balanced on the handlebars.

"I'd rather you kept an eye on it." Catching her breath, Gloria props it against the desk. I notice how her clothes are hanging off her bones, as if there's no flesh between. She isn't wearing her black pearls today; instead she has on a piece of amber on a silver chain.

"Maz, you're going to need gauntlets," she says with glee. "Ginge is in one of his moods." She lifts the wicker basket all tied up with string, and the bottom falls out, along with a streak of ginger tabby, which springs over the reception desk before disappearing beneath the shelves of pet food.

Now what? The general rule in the event of emergency is keep calm, but the idea of chasing a wild cat through town makes the adrenaline kick in.

"Lock the doors!" I order and slip the top bolt on the doors on the way in. "Patient on the loose!"

"I thought he was supposed to be sick," Frances observes. "I'll call Izzy through to help you catch him."

I squat down beside the units. "Come here, little cat," I coax.

He answers me with a furious hiss and a gusty aroma of rotten fish. I put my hand out just in front of the gap between the bottom shelf and the floor, wondering how on earth he squeezed himself in there. A pink nose and a fine set of whiskers emerge very slowly, followed by the strike of a paw.

"Ow, ow, ow." Unsheathed claws snag on my skin as I pull my hand away.

"He got you then. I knew he would." I breathe through the pain, watching the bobbles of blood well up and coalesce on the back of my hand, as Gloria goes on. "Emma always has the gauntlets ready."

I fetch them, a pair of leather gloves that reach up to my elbows, and a thick towel, and then I do a commando crawl along the floor, trying to wheedle Ginge out. Eventually, he darts out toward the window, which is firmly closed. I make a tackle Jonny

Wilkinson would be proud of, grab the cat, and take him, growling and wriggling inside the towel, into the consulting room.

Izzy joins me and Gloria, shutting the door firmly behind us.

"My Ginge is a little on the skinny side," Gloria says.

That's an understatement. If Ginge was a supermodel, he'd be a size zero, a bit like Gloria in fact. He's so thin that I can see the apex of his heart beating against his chest as he sits hunched on the table like a stroppy stegosaur, but there's something about him that tugs on my heartstrings. He's feisty, bright, and independent, and in spite of the fact that Gloria's supposed to be looking after him, he appears in need of some TLC.

"I can't understand it," says Gloria. "He eats like a horse."

It doesn't take long to discover Ginge's problem: he's hyperthyroid. His metabolism is in overdrive, making him restless and wild-eyed. I explain the tests I need to run before I can advise on the best option for treatment: tablets to reduce the level of thyroid hormone in his blood, surgery, or radiation therapy at a specialist center.

"That all sounds terribly expensive." Gloria fingers the piece of amber around her neck with knobbly fingers marked with liver spots. I notice that there's an insect trapped inside, some prehistoric bug, which seems an odd choice of material for jewelry. "What happens if I let nature run its course?"

"He'll die."

"You're very blunt, young woman." Her teeth slip about on her gums. "Emma wouldn't have put it like that. I think I'll wait till she's back and have a chat with her. I've known Emma since she was a baby. I trust her to tell me what's what."

"I trained at vet school with her. We learned exactly the same stuff," I say. I do have my pride. "Emma won't tell you anything different, and I'm guessing if Ginge carries on without treatment, he'll be long gone by the time she returns."

"Well, I really don't know what to do for the best."

"Do you care about what happens to Ginge?" I'm beginning to lose my patience with Gloria. She's come here for my advice, yet she won't take it. "If you're unable or unwilling to commit to looking after Ginge properly, maybe it's fairer to put him down sooner rather than later, so he doesn't have to suffer."

"Oh no, I couldn't possibly . . ." Gloria's icy expression starts to defrost, and a tear trickles across her cheek, streaking through the powder. "How much will it cost for the tests you mentioned?"

I soften a little. She isn't completely heartless after all. I suspect that her reluctance to make an appointment, her defensive attitude, and her desire to delay Ginge's treatment are all down to money, or the lack of it.

"I want to do what's best for all my animals." She reaches out to touch Ginge's head but thinks better of it when he opens his mouth to hiss at her too.

"How many do you have now?" I ask, at which Gloria seems to shrink back into her protective shell.

"More than most people," she says. "Mainly cats and a few dogs."

"Okay, why don't I take the blood today anyway?" I say, deciding not to push her. "We can worry about the bill later." I think of Nigel's cash flow and Emma's profits. I look at Ginge. I look at Gloria's frayed cardigan, the runs in her double-layered tights, and the holes in her shoes. What else can I do?

It's a challenge taking blood from a cat so on edge, but Izzy and I manage at the third attempt to get a reasonable volume for the lab. I send Ginge home in a loaned wire basket with an appointment to return before his course of tablets runs out. When Gloria has finally left, I check through the computer records and ask Izzy to dig out the notes that came from Talyton Manor Vets to see if I can find out how many animals she's responsible for. I'm not sure about her. If you care for your pets as much as Gloria makes out, why do you wait so long before you bring one as sick as Ginge in to see a vet? His weight loss didn't happen overnight.

"The records aren't terribly informative, I'm afraid," Izzy says, handing them over to me in Kennels. Gloria's animals are listed under the general headings of "dog" and "cat" so you can't count them up, and, unsurprisingly, the notes are covered with red NOT PAID stamps. "There was a time when she was caring for forty or fifty animals over at Buttercross Cottage." Izzy looks at me. "Not all in the cottage at once.

Talyton Animal Rescue raised funds to build a cattery and kennel block in the garden. They called it the Sanctuary and ran it with Gloria and Fifi Green's band of volunteers."

"Gloria was arguing with Fifi at the show," I tell Izzy, pleased that she seems to have warmed to me a little more over our shared desire to do what's best for Ginge. "Talyton Animal Rescue have withdrawn their support—I assume that much of that was financial, as well as practical."

"Those two have never really got on," Izzy says. "Fifi had a fling with Gloria's husband—it was some years ago, and she was much younger than him. It was the talk of Talyton for a while."

"I didn't realize Gloria had been married."

"She's a widow. He died from a stroke, I think. He was some big-shot lawyer in the city. Gloria might look as if she hasn't got two pennies to rub together, but she's loaded."

It's certainly possible. Once, I offered to take an elderly woman with her Peke from a charity clinic to the main hospital before discovering that her chauffeur had parked the Bentley around the back. However, I still feel uneasy. Even if Gloria is coping with looking after herself and her pets, can she really get tablets down a semi-wild cat if required? I make a mental note to keep a close eye on Ginge's progress.

"If you don't need me for anything else, I'm going to give Freddie a bath," Izzy says. "I'm taking him up to the farm tonight. I haven't told you yet, have I? Chris has agreed to give him a home. And a job," she adds, chuckling. "He's going to be a sheep-dog." Her expression grows sad.

"That's brilliant news, but you're going to miss him, aren't you?" I say.

"Yes, but Chris has said I can visit him anytime I like," Izzy says as she takes Freddie from his kennel and hugs him to her chest. He licks her nose and wags his tail.

"I think he likes you."

Izzy grimaces, holds Freddie away from her, and gazes down at the dark trails forming on her scrubs. "He has a funny way of showing it—he's just weed on me."

"You know very well that I'm talking about Chris." Izzy's complexion pinks up. "I saw the way he looked at you on Saturday."

"No. No way." She hugs Freddie close again.

"You do like him, don't you? I mean, I can see the attractions—those sheepshearer's muscles, and a hefty acreage, I should imagine."

Izzy giggles, then her expression grows serious. "Do you really think he likes me? I mean, I've always thought . . . Well, I don't get to see him very often. He's busy on the farm, and I'm always here, at Otter House."

I look at Freddie, his head pressed to Izzy's chest and one ear being caressed by her thumb. I can hear him almost purring, like a cat. I hope—for Izzy's sake—that there's truth in the idea that animals can bring people together.

I head back to Reception and call my next client through to the consulting room, noting that there are three more waiting and I'm running about twenty minutes behind, thanks to Gloria and Ginge.

Harriet. Small furry. Brownish.
Reason for consultation: Lump.

Harriet's owner introduces herself as Ally Jackson, roving reporter for the *Taly-*

ton Chronicle—yes, the one who created the MUCK STICKS headline. Her suit is cut too small, the jacket creasing up into her armpits, the trousers ending an inch above her ankles, and it seems to have absorbed several eons of body odor, which it's reemitting into the tight confines of the consulting room. Ally hands me a shoe box, skewered with holes and stuck down with Scotch tape.

"We should have called her Houdini—my husband had to take the kitchen units apart to find her the other day." Ally's eyes start to fill with tears. "I don't know what I shall tell the children if it's cancer."

I offer her a tissue from the box I keep handy on top of the computer monitor. She takes several and blows her nose.

"I never thought I'd get so fond of a hamster."

It is indeed difficult to comprehend, I think, looking into the box. A pair of eyes like black pinheads stare back. An impressive set of whiskers twitch in a highly threatening manner.

"She's very friendly," Ally goes on.

Almost reassured, I reach out to pick her up, making sure I've scruffed up all the loose skin at her neck, so she can't twist round and clamp her jaws around my finger.

"She's only drawn blood once," Ally adds as I lift Harriet onto the palm of my hand. "Can you see the lump? It's under her tail. Is it . . . ?"

I can see two lumps, not one.

"It isn't cancer. Harriet's having a problem with her gender identity. Those lumps are supposed to be there. She's a boy."

"A boy?" Ally blushes. "You'd have thought I'd have known the difference by now—I've had three children."

I lower the hamster into the box, release it, and put the lid back on very quickly.

"I'll settle up at Reception, shall I?" Ally says.

"There's no charge."

"Are you sure?"

"Really."

"Thank you. You're all so very kind here."

"That's the second consultation you haven't taken any money for," Frances says in a low voice, once Ally has gone. "Emma would have charged for it."

"All I did was sex a hamster. It took two seconds."

"We'll have every Tom, Dick, and Harry coming in, expecting a freebie."

"We'll only have Tom and Dick," I say lightly. "I've just seen Harry," and try as I might, I couldn't justify charging a fee for what I did. However, I realize Frances has a point. I'm running Emma's business, not a charity. I turn to the waiting clients and call in the next one, a middle-aged woman who's red-faced with embarrassment because her spaniel has just cocked his leg against one of the chairs.

"Don't worry," I say. "These things happen. We're used to it."

"I'll fetch Izzy," Frances says.

"She'll be in the middle of bathing Freddie," I say. "I don't mind clearing up. It'll only take me two minutes."

ON BALANCE, IT'S been a pretty good day, I think when I've seen my last appointment and dealt with the last message in the daybook. I reckon Emma would be proud of me.

"Good night, Maz," Izzy says on her way out. Frances has already left. "I hope it's a quiet one."

It is quiet. The phone remains silent for

the rest of the evening, giving me the chance to eat dinner uninterrupted, watch a bit of television, and skim through *Vet News* before I shower, change, and fall into bed at eleven.

An hour or so later, I'm woken by a thumping sound and shouting from outside. Wrapped in my duvet, I crawl out of bed and peer out the side window. There's a four-by-four in the car park and a figure standing in the shadows at the entrance. Yawning, and slightly annoyed at someone turning up without phoning first, I pull a sweatshirt over my pajamas and head downstairs, switching all the lights on as I go.

When I reach Reception, I can see a man standing on the porch with a jacket or something similar bundled up against his chest. As I move closer, I can make out his features and the color of his hair. It's Alex Fox-Gifford. All I can think is, What the hell is he doing here?

"I'm sorry to disturb you, Maz," he says as I hurry him straight through to the consulting room, having ascertained from the tail that sticks out from the bundle in his arms that he's bringing a potential patient with him. Blood trickles down Alex's wrists from scratches on his hands, and his face is pale beneath the bright artificial light as he places the bundle ever so gently on the table.

"Don't you have your own practice to go to?" I ask flippantly, then wish I hadn't. This isn't the time.

"I hit the poor sod in Market Square." Alex unwraps the rest of what turns out to be a black-and-white jigsaw puzzle of a cat. Its ears are flattened against its skull. Its mouth is wide open as it struggles to breathe. "It shot out in front of my car, and I'm not carrying any drugs," he continues. "Otherwise I'd have finished it off myself."

"Hang on a mo." Did I hear him right? "What did you say? Finish him off?" The cat gazes up at me, helpless yet trusting, and my hackles rise with resentment at Alex's lack of initiative. If I'd run the cat over, I'd be doing my utmost to restore him to health. "Let's not be too hasty."

"I had a quick look before I wrapped him up. He's lost most of one leg and he's in a lot of pain. I thought it would be quicker to stop by here than drive up to the manor . . ." Alex looks up, his lips curving into a weak smile. "I did say I hoped to see you again soon."

"You could have just rung me, you know—you didn't have to half kill a cat," I say, feeling sorry now for Alex as well as the cat. They both appear to be in shock.

I touch the cat's head—his chunky cheeks are scarred, and he stinks of pee, confirming that he's an entire tom. "He looks a bit scruffy and unloved."

"Like me," Alex says, but he isn't smiling any longer.

I take a couple of quick chest X-rays—the machine's new, all-singing, all-dancing, and it's taken me a while to learn how to use it—and check with the scanner for a microchip. As I suspected, there isn't one. There's nothing to identify the poor cat's owner, if he even has one. I check the X-rays once Alex has put the films through the automatic processor—there's no evidence of a chest injury at least.

"Good news." I show Alex the cat's jaw. "I can wire that, and I'll amputate what's left of the leg."

The cat utters a barely audible meow, reminding me I should get on with the surgery.

"Are you staying?" I ask.

"You're going to do it now?"

"There'll be less risk of complications, osteomyelitis, septicemia . . ."

"It's all right—you don't have to give me a lecture."

Biting back my irritation at Alex's rather dismissive attitude, which suggests—to me anyway—that he doesn't really care about what happens to our patient, I pick up the cat and take him through to the prep area.

"You can't have qualified all that long after I did," Alex says, following close behind.

"Ten years," I say and then I wish I'd kept that piece of knowledge to myself too. A flush of heat creeps up my neck as I confess, "I looked you up in the register."

"So you know that I didn't go to Cambridge . . ." He pauses. "I looked you up too. I hated the idea of being accused of nepotism, of relying on the old boy network. My father's old college did offer me a place, but I turned it down."

I take a quick guilt trip around the prep area, collecting up the equipment I'm going to need. I like to pretend that I got into Cambridge on merit, but it was Jack Wilson who opened the door for me. In a way, I relied on the very same network of privilege that Alex avoided.

"What can I do?" Alex offers.

"There's no need. I'll call Izzy."

"No, don't disturb her." A smile plays on his lips as he goes on. "I'll be nurse."

"Okay, you can set up the drip"—I hand him a plastic pinny, thinking, What on earth is he doing, flirting with me when he's dating the drug rep?—"while I draw up some anesthetic."

Pretty soon, the cat is out for the count, shaved and prepped, picked up by the spotlight in the operating theater like an actor onstage. I'm gowned, masked, and gloved, and Alex is perched on a stool on the opposite side of the table, checking and rechecking the cat's condition. I notice how gentle he is. Somehow I imagined him treating a cat as if it were a horse or cow. It's only now that I notice how subdued he is compared with the last time I saw him. His eyes are ringed with shadows, his hair is messed up, and his skin looks sallow.

"Ready to go?" I ask, returning to the task in hand.

Alex nods.

I slip a blade onto a scalpel handle, pick up a swab, and gaze at the mangled limb in front of me, working out how best to tackle it.

"I thought this would give me an excuse to get Emma's Erector set out, but it's too far gone to repair," I say.

"I never got to play with construction toys when I was a boy."

"What did you used to play with then?" I look up from the cat, wishing I hadn't put it like that, because Alex has a wicked, unsettling grin on his face. I smile back. I can't help it.

"I used to have a rocking horse. My mother tells me that she caught me with my hand up its rear end when I was about four—I'd been out on calls with my father, I hasten to add."

"Is that why you wanted to be a vet?"

"I was expected to follow in my father's— and my grandfather's—footsteps, and take over the practice."

"You make it sound as if you have regrets."

Alex shakes his head. "It has its moments, but on the whole I love being out and about. I love my job.

"I was driving too fast," he begins again as I start the first cut. "Tonight. I've been to see my ex-wife."

"Oh?" I say, wondering why he's chosen to confide in me.

"She's getting married again," he goes on morosely.

Keeping my eyes fixed on the cat, I cut through a block of muscle and an artery, which starts to spurt pulses of blood. I clamp it off, clamping down my emotions at the same time, because Alex has confused me now. It's difficult to remain cool and professional when one minute he's gentle and teasing and the next he's deadly serious.

"As far as I'm concerned," Alex goes on, "she can marry whoever she likes, as long as it doesn't affect the children, but she wants to drag them off to Australia with this . . ." He swears. "She knows how to pick them. When will I see them if they're on the other side of the world? What about my weekends? What about my rights as a dad?" The table shudders as Alex thumps it with his fist.

"Hey, careful."

"I'm sorry. It's just—well, she knows exactly how to wind me up, the selfish bitch."

"How old are your children?" I ask, feeling quite smug at the thought that Alex Fox-Gifford is human after all.

"Lucie's five and Sebastian's three, so I'll miss all their growing up." Alex stands. "They'll forget me, they'll forget they ever had a real dad."

"That's terrible." I carry on cutting and picking out fragments of bone, then I look up and our eyes meet. I know exactly what it's like to be a child without a parent.

"My father walked out on me and my brother when I was twelve." I still find it difficult to talk about it. "I've never forgotten him."

"Yes, but how many times did you see him after that? Every week? Once a month?"

"Never." I look up to find Alex gazing at me with disbelief.

One Saturday, my mother and I took the bus to the Ark—we got off one stop early and walked the rest of the way so she could give the impression she'd parked the car in one of the side roads. We didn't have a car, but if we'd had one, Mum said we'd have had a Porsche with pop-up head-lights for weekdays and a camper van for weekends down at the coast.

I followed her as she flounced into Jack Wilson's consulting room in a purple tie-dyed skirt, sequined top, and red patent boots, her hair very short and freshly bleached. Jack looked up from where King was curled up in a basket on the table.

"I'm sorry for dragging you all the way over here, Mrs. Harwood—"

"It's Ms., not Mrs.," my mother inter-rupted brusquely, and my heart clenched into a ball as I prayed she hadn't blown it for me and King.

"You look so much like Amanda," Jack went on smoothly, oozing charm as he did with the majority of his female clients. (I think that's one of the reasons he had such a loyal following. As well as being a good vet, of course.) "In fact, I can hardly be-lieve you aren't sisters."

"Flattery will get you everywhere, Mr. Wilson," Mum said and smiled, tilted her head, and popped her eyes at him. I wanted to hide away under the table because I knew—and she didn't—that he was only humoring her.

"Do call me Jack."

"If you'll call me Trish."

"Well, Trish, let me first say that your daughter is an enthusiastic, intelligent, and compassionate girl." My face burned as I watched my mother glowing in my reflected glory, and Jack went on, "And I'm sure she'd make a great owner for King, but—"

But? My heart sank. I turned away and whispered King's name. He raised his head and stretched out one paw. The ruff of fur covering his throat began to vibrate—his purr seemed too loud for such a small cat. He was only about six weeks old, and I wondered if he'd ever grow into it.

"I need to be sure that you're happy to take him on. I'd hate to think of him ending up back on the street."

"Well, why don't you come and vet our home?" My mother stood straight, one hand on her hip, her stomach sucked in and her breasts thrust out.

"Oh, I don't think that'll be necessary." Jack backed off hurriedly to the opposite side of the table, and I wondered momentarily if he was about to press the panic button he'd had installed since he'd been threatened by a druggie with a knife afterhours one evening. "Er, you do have some idea yourself of what's involved?" He flashed her another of his winning smiles. "Looking after a pet can bring a lot of pleasure, but it also means making a long-term commitment."

"I know all about that," Mum said. "I've had pets before."

I thought of the two pets I could remember: the school goldfish and a budgie. Both had died. I willed her to shut up.

"Does that mean I can take King home?" I cut in. "Please, Mum."

She pursed her lips, and I thought, She's changed her mind. She could be cruel like that. Capricious.

"The only concern I have," she said after some deliberation, "is the cost—"

"I have money for cat food," I said desperately.

"What about the vet's bills?" my mother said.

"Amanda can work here," said John. "I could do with a Saturday girl to help Chrissie out. It won't be anything terribly exciting—cleaning kennels, sweeping floors, that kind of thing, in return for a small wage."

My mother couldn't argue with that.

"We'd better take him home then." My hand flew to the handle on top of the basket, then hovered above it as Mum went on. "On a week's trial."

"Oh, you won't be able to let him go once he gets his paws under the table." Jack glanced at me and, when Mum's back was turned, pretended to wipe his brow with the back of his hand.

Stony-faced Chrissie cried as we left. Mum and I took King home on the bus, and I felt like a celebrity because everyone wanted to pet him and talk to us.

King settled in well—in fact, from the day he arrived, he padded about the place as if he owned it. He chased shadows, dived into the laundry basket and curled up in our clothes; he patrolled the kitchen worktops and stole the remains of the Christmas turkey—which was great because we didn't have to eat leftovers for days afterward. (I wasn't vegetarian back then.) We all adored him—apart from my father, that is.

In my opinion, not liking animals is a particularly unattractive trait in a man. I'm not sure how fond he was of children either, and he certainly didn't like my mother much at the end. Ultimately, the only living thing he truly cared about was himself.

The last row my parents had was over the cat. My mum accused Dad of kicking King out onto the balcony. My father, who retreated to the sofa, falling back into its sagging embrace as if he'd had a few too many, said he had merely nudged him out of the way with the toe of his boot.

"You love that bloody creature more than you've ever loved me," Dad said, clenching and unclenching his fists.

"At least it's grateful," Mum said coldly.

I grabbed King and hugged him to my chest. He licked my hands, his tongue rasping against my skin and his breath smelling of fish. My heart was pounding almost as fast as his. My parents argued all the time, but this was different.

"That cat's a waste of space. All it does is eat and shit, and eat and shit again."

"Sounds like the pot calling the kettle black," my mother said, her face flushing to match the scarlet shine of her nails. I could see the jerky rise and fall of her chest as she struggled to go on. "I work my guts out to support this family, and what do you do?"

My father put his hands together, fingertip to fingertip. They were trembling. He couldn't keep them still. He swore and clasped them tightly.

"I'm a poet. I write poetry. I write poetry and live among philistines." He paused, his brows coming together. "Give us a few quid for a drink, will you?"

"I spent it," Mum said defiantly, "on fish fingers and feather toys for the cat."

"You . . . you . . ." My dad struggled to his feet. "That's it—it's me or the cat."

"Then there's no fucking contest."

I'm not sure what happened next. My brother, perhaps hearing the sound of raised voices, came running into the room, howling. At the same time, there was a sharp smacking sound and a cry. I caught sight of my father's foot, a black sock and battered roach-killer shoe with a pointed toe, disappearing out through the door, before the scene froze, my brother on his knees, clinging to my legs, my mother with her hand pressed to her cheek and King heavy in my arms.

In spite of all her flirting with other men and fighting with my father, my mother was devastated when she realized he'd left for good. She walked miles over the next few months searching the bars and pubs for him, and when she came home I sometimes found her lying on the bed they used to share, sobbing into King's fur. I'd creep away, knowing that if she saw me watching her, she'd yell and throw her alarm clock or hairbrush at me, anything that was to hand.

I believe King helped us all—me, my mother, and my brother—through our grief in one way or another. He didn't judge anyone. He didn't spout platitudes. He just was, and that was the greatest comfort of all.

"You must keep in some kind of contact with your father," Alex says.

"I would if I knew where he was," I replied. I start to close the skin, avoiding Alex's compassionate gaze. "Actually, I wouldn't. It's too late now. I spent a long time trying to track him down, but it never came to anything." I don't know how I'd feel if I ran into my father again now. Angry? Relieved to know that I'd no longer have to keep looking out for him, because that's what I do? What I am certain of is that I'd never be able to forgive him.

"What did he do? As a career, I mean."

"Sod all." I smile at a memory of my dad sprawled on the couch, can in one hand and a scrap of paper in the other, reading some doggerel he'd created on the way back from the pub in the name of performance art. "He was a poet, a street poet— more McGonagall than Keats. Before you ask, I didn't inherit his way with words, or his work ethic."

"What did he think about you wanting to be a vet?"

"He disapproved, especially when he realized I'd have to go on to further education. He used to say, 'Maz, what's wrong with the University of Life?'" The regret and pain combine like a hair ball in the back of my throat. In spite of everything, I did love my dad. I loved him, and hated him for abandoning us.

I force myself to concentrate on the cat, and when I've finished there's a line of neat stitches across the stump of the amputation site and a tiny trickle of blood across the shaved, gray skin.

"Leave him on the gas for a little longer, Alex. After I've wired his jaw, I'm going to castrate him to save knocking him out for a second time."

"I hope you're not planning to chop anything else off," Alex says lightly. "If you don't mind, I'll stand back a bit in case your scalpel slips."

"Are you casting aspersions on my surgical technique?" I say, feeling more cheerful.

"I wouldn't dare." He smiles as I brandish the knife.

"So where did you end up training then?" I ask.

"Bristol," he says, and he carries on chatting as I finish off the surgery.

A little while after Alex cuts the anesthetic, the cat gives a small cough and swallows. Alex sees to the ET tube and unkinks the drip tubing, which has twisted up on itself.

"What shall we call him? He has to have a name," I say as I pull off my gloves.

Alex ponders for a moment. "How about Tripod? It's apt, and you wouldn't feel too much of a prat yelling it across the garden in earshot of your neighbors."

"Tripod it is." I stroke the cat's head. He purrs gamely in response. "I'm going to sit up with him for a while. Would you like a coffee?"

"Please. Black, four sugars."

"Four?" I say, as Alex picks Tripod up. "Aren't you sweet enough already?"

"What do you think?" he says, grinning, and I back off, my face warm with embarrassment at having been so forward. "Where do you want him?" Alex sticks the drip bag between his teeth.

"Over there." I point to the empty cage in Kennels where I've rigged up a heated pad and disappear to make two coffees, which we drink while we sleepily watch Tripod snoozing.

He reminds me of King. I did work at the Ark as a Saturday girl, and then every day after school. It was Jack who encouraged me to apply to vet school, and it was Jack who took King in when I left for university. In fact, he was the kind of man I'd have liked my father to be.

I clear my throat and take a sip of coffee. "I wonder if he did ever have a home."

"I'll ask around," Alex says. "He could be one of Gloria's."

"I saw one of her cats today." I show him my scars.

"Did she use the it's-one-of-my-ferals line?" Alex raises an eyebrow. "She did that once too often when she was with us, pretending the cat wasn't hers so we'd waive the fee. You do know she's a bad payer? That's why we gave her her marching orders. I'm sorry, we should have told Emma when we sent the notes over, but you know what my father's like."

"I've just sent a load of blood off to the lab," I say, thinking of Emma's profits.

"Oh well. I expect she'll pay up in the end."

I hope so, I muse, thinking of my bounced check as I say, "What about Fifi Green? Do you really give her a twenty percent discount?"

"Not likely." He grins. "Is that what she told you?" Alex sticks his empty mug in the cage alongside Tripod's, drops his hands to his sides, and takes a step back. "I don't know about you, but I'm fit for bed. Thanks for tonight, Maz," he goes on. "I shouldn't have disturbed you—I'm sorry."

"I'm glad I could help." I smile ruefully. Alex's presence disturbs me deeply, and in places that I had decided to forget.

I let him out through the side door and watch him drive away in the dark and pouring rain. Not so long ago Alex Fox-Gifford was not the kind of man I felt inclined to like. Now, I'm not sure what kind of man he is.

CHAPTER 9

A Close Shave

THE GIRL BEHIND RECEPTION CAN'T BE MORE than three or four. She stares at me through big blue eyes and plays with the ringlets of her blond hair.

"Who are you?" I ask.

"I'm Ruby," she murmurs.

I turn to Frances, hoping for some explanation.

"What else can I do?" she says sharply. "My daughter-in-law is supposed to be at work today and the nursery have turned Ruby away because she's got a rash, and the doctor doesn't have a clue what it is."

"I got spotty spots." Ruby lifts the hem of her sweatpants.

"This isn't a day care, Frances," I say sternly. How's she going to look after Reception and a child as well?

"Look." Ruby points to her shin. "Spotty spots."

I squat beside her and take a closer look.

"Are they itchy?" I ask, and Ruby bends down to give them a good scratch. "Do you have a cat at home?"

Ruby nods. "He's called Chuckle and he's big and brown and stripy."

"Frances, Ruby isn't infectious. Those are flea bites."

"Oh, how embarrassing," Frances shrieks. "I told her"—I assume from the tone of her voice, the tone she uses when talking down to certain Otter House clients, that there's no love lost between her and her daughter-in-law—"to take that cat to see a vet about its constant scratching, but would she listen?"

"You can take her to nursery now," I say.

"I'll drop her round at lunchtime. It's all right, Maz. I won't let her run around unsupervised." Frances looks at me dis-approvingly. "You know, Old Fox-Gifford was more than happy to let her stay in the office and play with his dogs, and dear young Alex used to bring her toys and sweets."

"I don't care what Talyton Manor Vets did," I say, exasperated.

"Izzy tells me Alex brought a cat in here last night," Frances says. "She's rather put out that you didn't call her in to help with the op."

"I thought she'd be pleased I didn't wake her." I hope I haven't upset her.

"Eloise won't be too happy when she finds out," Frances says.

"You mean the drug rep."

"Alex's girlfriend, that's right."

"I can't see why she'd be the slightest bit bothered," I say. "Alex dropped by with the cat, we operated, he went home. End of story, Frances."

"Do I hear my name being taken in vain?"

"Alex?" I spin round to find him letting the door into Reception swing back behind him. "What are you doing here?"

"I've come to see the cat." He looks

weary. He's nicked himself shaving, and I find myself wanting to offer him a swab.

"How's the lovely Eloise?" Frances cuts in, apparently determined to extract the latest gossip straight from the horse's mouth. "I thought I saw you two going into the Barnscote for dinner when I was driving past the other day."

"It was her treat." Alex smiles. "The company's promoted her to regional head of sales."

"How marvelous," says Frances. "You must give her my congratulations."

"Will do," Alex says. "Of course, I always knew she'd go far. Eloise is the complete package—bright, funny, and ambitious."

"And beautiful," Frances adds. "She always manages to look glamorous."

"Come on through, Alex," I say, feeling rather nauseous at the thought of this paragon of a girlfriend.

In the corridor, Alex slips past me and holds the next door open.

"Thank you," I say, taking him through to Kennels.

"How's Frances getting on?" he says on the way.

"I hope you're not gloating because you've managed to off-load your receptionist as well as your more difficult clients," I say, stiffening my resolve not to get too friendly with the competition by reminding myself exactly who he is.

"Not at all," he says smoothly. "It was Emma who poached Frances from us. We weren't unhappy with her—we were used to her foibles."

"Then we'd better agree to disagree."

"That's what we've been doing for these past three years, Otter House and Talyton Manor," Alex says when we reach Tripod's cage. "How are you, little chap?" Alex opens the door. In spite of the wires in his jaw, the cat is trying to balance on his three legs while licking his rear end. He has no sense of loyalty—he purrs and writhes in ecstasy as Alex tickles him under the chin, then plays with his paws. "I missed that last night. He's got extra toes—look, six on each."

"He'll be good at touch typing then," I say drily. "Let's get him out and fix this drip. It's stopped completely."

Alex holds Tripod on the bench while I try to insert a fresh cannula into the vein in the cat's front leg. I miss it. Twice.

"Your thumb's in the way," I complain to Alex, the back of my neck growing hot with a mixture of embarrassment and confusion. I feel uncomfortable with him standing so close to me.

"Sorry," he says, shifting his grip.

"Maz, there's a phone call for you." I glance up at the sound of Izzy's voice. "Oh," she says, stopping in her tracks.

"Alex is helping me with Tripod's drip," I say quickly in case she's jumped to the wrong conclusion.

"I see," Izzy says.

"You don't have to stay," I say when she shows no sign of leaving us to it. I don't need a chaperone. I don't need another set of eyes watching me either. It's making me nervous.

I rip another cannula from its sterile pack. It goes in on the third attempt. I tape it in and attach a new drip bag.

Poor Tripod. I pick him up and kiss him before putting him back in the cage.

"Lucky cat," Alex observes quietly.

What does he mean by that? I wonder. Did he come to see me as well as the cat?

I'm tired, a bit miffed with Alex for flirting with me when he's going out with Eloise, and angry at myself for my clumsiness—I thought I'd overcome all that when I was at vet school. And I blame Alex for everything.

"I wish you'd stop messing about, pretending you like me," I say. "For all I know, it's just another stunt to wind me up."

"Stunt?" Alex frowns. "What do you mean?"

"You and your family, always trying to bring Otter House down. You made life hell for Emma, and now you're doing the same for me."

Alex's eyes darken, and I wish I hadn't spoken out so forcefully.

"You mean the slurry? My father didn't have anything to do with that. He might have offered a bottle of malt here and there to help people come to the right decision on certain planning issues, but criminal damage? Absolutely not." He paces a tight circle, his hands in his pockets, and for a moment, I think he's going to walk straight out, but he stops and faces me.

"It's a difficult time for us right now. Many of our farmers—families who've been working the land here for years—have sold up, while others can't afford to call the vet out every five minutes. They skimp on the routine stuff and use us as a last resort. It isn't just a problem for us at the manor, it's an animal welfare issue and a personal disaster for many."

"I see." I hadn't thought about it like that. I feel rather inadequate.

"My father's a sick man. The practice isn't merely a business to him. It's his life, and he'll do anything to protect it." Alex gazes at me as if he thinks I'm a bit dense. "Your lack of understanding of the issues affecting the countryside is exactly what I expect from you city types."

"I'm sorry," I say. Embarrassed? I'm mortified. "I really am sorry."

"Don't apologize. I rather like it when you're arsey with me," Alex says with a flash of humor. He turns away and opens Tripod's cage again. "Going back to the subject of this cat, I called Gloria Brambles first thing. She doesn't recognize the description I gave her. He isn't one of hers." He hesitates. "You assumed that I'd forget, didn't you? In spite of everything Emma's told you, I'm not all bad."

"If you're really the kindhearted person you claim to be, why don't you offer Tripod a home?" I suggest.

"We have too many cats on the estate already. Mother took on a couple of kittens as a favor to a friend. Two females. You can guess the rest. By the time I got around to spaying them, there was a litter of kittens in the shed among the croquet hoops, and another in the top of the trunk where my mother stores her old horse blankets.

"We kept a couple of the kittens and handed the rest in to Talyton Animal Rescue, along with vouchers for free neutering." Alex gives Tripod one last caress and closes the door. (I hate to admit it, but he has a great bedside manner, not that I'd want him anywhere near my bed, you understand.)

"I'd better go home and let the hounds out." Alex coughs—not a honking cough like a dog let out of kennels but a nervous kind. "By the way, there's a talk on tonight at one of the hotels on the way into Exeter. It's an update on the management of failing hearts, so it should be useful. I could give you a lift as you aren't familiar with the area."

"It's all right, thanks. I've got GPS." I pause. "Won't you be taking Eloise?"

Alex frowns briefly. "No, she'll be there

already," he says. "The drug company's sponsoring the talk—Eloise is hosting it. Come on, Maz. I insist."

Go for it, I think. It isn't a big deal. It isn't like it's a date or anything, and I'm beginning to see what Emma means—that it's impossible to argue with a Fox-Gifford.

And that's the last thing I'm going to say about Alex and his father, because life is too short, and I've got Emma's practice to worry about. I'm going to draw a line underneath it, like this:

I HOPE I DIDN'T hurt Izzy's feelings a second time by letting Alex help me with Tripod and not asking her. She's a little cool with me this morning, but it doesn't last. By the time we've had coffee and started on the ops, she seems more cheerful.

She opens Tripod's cage to remove his food dish, sending him scuffling back into the corner, wary perhaps that he's about to lose another body part.

"I thought you were having me on when you said Alex Fox-Gifford had brought him here," she says.

"I didn't send him an invite. He kind of gate-crashed my night duty."

"Why didn't he take him back to his own practice?"

"He thought the cat needed putting down and we were nearer."

"So it isn't Alex's cat?" Izzy sounds surprised. "He seems rather fond of it."

"I reckon he feels guilty because he was the one who ran it over. It's a stray, so there's no one to pay the bills." I pause. "I'll get Frances to put a notice up in Reception. Someone might claim him," I say as Izzy brings a Persian cat, a blue one like Saffy, with orange eyes, to the bench.

"Here's your chance to try out the new clippers," she says. "You did clear the cost with Nigel, didn't you?"

"Er, no. No, I didn't." I watch how Izzy rolls her eyes at me and quickly add, "I'll sort it."

"Please do, because I don't want to be the one to have to face him," Izzy says sternly. "This is Cheryl's stud cat for a tidy-up," she goes on. "I can't see what the girls see in you, Blueboy."

I have to agree. He's cross-eyed, one of his teeth sticks out, and his coat is decidedly disheveled. In fact, it's so matted it's difficult to find the cat underneath, which I find surprising since Cheryl professes to be so fond of her babies.

We give him a shot of sedative and wait a few minutes for it to take effect.

"Did I hear right when you said you were going to the talk with Alex?" Izzy says in a disapproving tone. "Emma wouldn't condone all this fraternizing with the enemy."

"He offered me a lift, that's all. It seemed churlish not to accept it." I change the subject. "How did Freddie get on last night? Did he pass muster?"

"Chris hasn't introduced him to the sheep yet. Meg, his other dog, tried to savage him, and Freddie didn't settle down until about ten, but apart from that it all went well."

"Are you going to see him again?"

"Chris invited me to the farm for dinner tonight—he doesn't want to go out and leave Freddie alone with Meg just yet."

"Is romance in the air?" I ask, but Izzy plugs in the clippers and hands them to me, switching them on at the same time to avoid giving me an answer. I press them against the fur on Blueboy's belly. The old clippers chuntered and snagged. These purr. The matted coat falls away from the skin in one piece, like a sheep's fleece. It's quite therapeutic, and very quickly Blueboy is parted from most of his fur.

"What do you think, Izzy?" I stroke the soft, velvety pile that's left on Blueboy's flanks. He looks like a lion, a blue one with a sleek body, a ruff of mane around his neck, and four fluffy paws. I cover him in a towel in case he should feel the cold as he comes round.

"He looks great. Less like Bob Geldof, more like George Clooney." Izzy combs out the last few knots from Blueboy's tail until it looks like a rather splendid bottle-brush and clips his claws.

Unfortunately, Cheryl doesn't share our opinion of Blueboy's haircut when she comes to collect him.

"Oh, what have they done to you, my darling boy?" She sweeps him up into her arms, and he lashes out at one of her earrings, sending it swinging from her earlobe while its partner trembles with fury; and, I confess, my knees are almost trembling with fright now that I study Blueboy more closely: my handiwork isn't quite as great as I thought. Bloody awful, in fact. Decidedly ragged. His look-at-me attitude has been binned with his hair and the masculine assets under his tail revealed in all their glory.

Cheryl stares at me, her eyes flashing across the room. "I trusted you!"

"His coat will be far easier to manage now," I say, as optimistically as I can.

"He hasn't got a coat anymore. And why does he look all spaced out?"

"That's just the sedation—it'll wear off in the next couple of hours."

"You gave him a sedative? Old Fox-Gifford always managed without knocking him out."

What did he use then? A straitjacket? I bite my tongue.

Cheryl glares at me, and I take a step back. There's a nasty smell of entire tom suffusing the air.

"I'm sorry if Blueboy's tidy-up isn't what you were expecting, but the hair will grow back," I say defensively.

"In the meantime, he'll be the laughing-stock of the Cat Fancy," Cheryl says as she stuffs him back into his carrier. "I'm beginning to doubt if you're really a vet at all."

"Of course I am. It's just that I didn't spend six years at vet school learning how to be a hairdresser."

"I wonder whether you learned anything. I showed Saffy's scar to one of our friends who's been in Persians for over fifty years, and she said she'd never seen anything like it. It looks as if you slashed her from end to end."

"It didn't look unusual to me," Izzy says, coming in to back me up, but Cheryl isn't taking any notice.

"It hasn't healed at all well—it's still red and lumpy."

"It isn't as if Saffy's going to have any hang-ups about her bikini line," I say, then wish I hadn't. Cheryl's like a stroppy cat— she needs careful handling because you can't be sure when she'll strike next. "You're welcome to bring her back and I'll have another look at her."

"There's no way I'm setting foot in this place again!" Cheryl storms out into Reception in front of a crowded waiting room (yes, it's what I've wanted to see since I arrived at Otter House, but why, oh why, did it have to be right now?) and stares at Frances. "Where's that form, the one I signed before I left here this morning, before your vet ruined my poor cat's life? You've as good as killed"—a gasp of horror goes up from the waiting clients—"his career. We were going to enter him for the National this year. I know one of the judges, and she said he'd easily make champion of champions and really put Cheriam Persians on the map!"

Frances shuffles through some papers beside the computer, mostly drawings of stick people and stick dogs, I notice. Ruby is strapped into a buggy behind the desk, alternately sucking on a breadstick and a pencil.

"Where is it, Frances? Where's the consent form?" The back of my neck starts to prick, as if a tarantula is slowly creeping across my skin. "I don't remember seeing it." I haven't got a good feeling about this.

"I signed it," Cheryl insists in an ultra-loud voice. "But I did not give you permission to drug him and hack all his fur off."

"Frances?" I say.

She clears her throat, puts her glasses on, then takes them off again. "There's been a bit of a muddle-up," she says finally. "I let Ruby help me shred some of the junk mail, and the next thing I knew, she was using the shredder all by herself. I promise it won't happen again. It was an exceptional circumstance."

Sure, I think, wanting to believe her. However, I've had enough experience of human nature to know that exceptional circumstances have a habit of repeating themselves.

"Let me get this right," Cheryl interrupts. "You made a mistake and now you've shredded the evidence. I'm not paying for the appalling service I've received here today. You—yes, you, Maz—are totally incompetent. I'll be going straight back to Talyton Manor—the vets there know exactly what they're doing." She takes a breath, then continues, "I'll be in touch with my solicitor for the way you've treated my babies. I'll have you struck off, and what's more I'll make sure everyone in this town knows." She gives the door a hard shove. It doesn't budge.

I point to the sign above the handle. "You have to pull it."

I return to Kennels to find Izzy for moral support. She's stuck cut-out eyes and a tongue on the mat of Blueboy's hair she's dragged out of the bin and put back on the table.

"I heard what was going on out there, so I came back to find this—I thought you might need to keep it as evidence," Izzy informs me. "I should have chased up the consent form when it didn't come through with the cat. I just assumed—"

"So did I. It's my fault." I take a deep breath. "Well, it isn't all that serious. Nobody's died."

"If Cheryl takes her complaint to the Royal College, you could be in big trouble though, Maz." Izzy stares at me, arms folded, giving me the distinct impression she isn't on my side.

"I know," I say, picturing myself in front of the disciplinary committee.

"Emma makes a point of checking the consent form before she ever touches a patient," Izzy says critically, making me feel as if it's going to take a very long time to redeem myself.

I should have been more careful, especially knowing how protective Cheryl is of her "babies." Even when she came in to pick Blueboy up, it wasn't too late to turn things around. Emma would have warned her before she saw the cat, and apologized gracefully.

I wish Emma was here, but she isn't, and it's down to me to sort it out, swiftly and quietly, before the whole of Talyton gets to hear of it. I resolve to go and see Cheryl first thing with an offer of compensation—a check drawn on my own account—to make amends. I don't like the thought of facing her again though—I'd rather have all my teeth pulled out without anesthetic.

CHAPTER 10

Eating Horses Is Wrong

"I'M SORRY I'M LATE." ALEX REVS THE ENGINE of his car as I settle myself in the passenger seat, surveying the chaos of sweet wrappers and apple cores on the dash and the mud in the footwell. There's a book, *Dear Zoo*, and a handful of pens in the pocket of the passenger door. "I've been fitting heels to a cow."

"It doesn't matter," I say—magnanimously, I think, considering I've been on tenterhooks for the past hour, wondering if he'd forgotten to pick me up. I brush a stray white hair off my trousers—I should have known better than to wear black—and feel a little miffed that the scent of farmyard has managed to overwhelm my extravagant use of Armani.

"It does if we've missed out on the buffet." He grins. "I'm starving, aren't you?" He doesn't wait for my answer, continuing, "I hear you gave Blueboy a short back and sides today. Cheryl called my father out to treat him for post-traumatic stress."

"That's all I need." Groaning, I shrink into the seat, embarrassed and ashamed at being made to look a complete idiot in front of Alex Fox-Gifford.

"It's all right, Maz—he told her to pull herself together." Alex brakes momentarily. "Hold your tummies."

"I beg your pardon?"

"It's what I say to the kids. We're coming up to the humpback bridge at Balls Cross—it's a local landmark. They like me to drive fast over it."

"Oh? Not too fast, I hope."

"I'll go slowly just for you . . . but not too slowly. Legend has it that if you drive across it at midnight, you won't make it to the other side without being strangled by the Hairy Hands of Talyton."

It's impossible to believe in malign magic

on an evening when the hedgerows are filled with flowers and bathed in sunlight.

I can't help laughing. "That sounds like wishing warts away to me. You must have driven along this stretch hundreds of times."

"Ah, but never on the stroke of twelve." He adjusts the rearview mirror as if he's checking for those monstrous appendages, hirsute with evil intent, and drives on, joining the main road, which takes us to an industrial estate on the outskirts of Exeter, where we turn off, following signs for a conference center and park.

Inside the lobby we meet a scene of devastation: tables laid with glaring white cloths, fallen wineglasses, and empty plates strewn with crumbs and soggy lettuce leaves.

"Don't panic, Alex." A woman in a green silk dress and heels glides toward us like a man-eating crocodile. Her hair is yellow Lab on top and chocolate underneath. She snaps her fingers. "This way—I've saved something for you."

"Eloise, you are an angel." I watch Alex kiss her on both cheeks in a just-good-friends kind of way, but then that might be because they're in public, I think, my lungs suddenly tight with envy. Alex is attentive,

Eloise adoring, her big blue eyes fixed on his face, her hand hovering as if she's about to grab his arm.

"This is Maz," Alex says, and Eloise turns to me, touching the gold chain around her long, slender neck.

"It's lovely to meet you," she says. "I'm organizing this evening on behalf of the sponsors, for my sins." She laughs lightly.

"I'm the relief vet at Otter House," I say, pretty certain now that Eloise is one of the many women I imagine has sinned with Alex. Frances was right—Alex's girlfriend is both beautiful and glamorous.

"You're very brave turning up here with Alex then," Eloise says. "There's no way you'd see Emma getting into bed with the competition."

Me neither, I think wryly.

"Now, now, Eloise, you know I don't bite," says Alex. "It's my father who's the old bear. I know I wasn't happy about Emma setting up Otter House in the first place, but I've discovered the advantages of having another practice on our doorstep." He tips his head to one side, teasing. "For one, it's great to have somewhere to off-load our difficult clients."

I smile ruefully, thinking of Cheryl and Mr. Brown.

"I've been hearing rumors about Otter House," says Eloise slyly, "about how the wholesalers have refused to make any more deliveries."

"Oh, that's sorted now," I say, trying to think quickly. "It was a mix-up, that's all."

"I'd heard that the practice is about to go bankrupt because Emma overstretched herself when she set the place up and there aren't enough clients willing to pay her rather exorbitant fees . . ." Eloise raises her perfectly shaped eyebrows, waiting for me to respond, while Alex fiddles with his mobile, politely pretending he hasn't heard.

"Oh, they're just rumors," I say, trying to brush her off, but her opinion is like a giant tick embedding in my skin, draining my blood and my confidence in equal measure.

"I've heard them from more than one source. I get to visit lots of the local practices," Eloise goes on.

I force a smile and say, "It's professional jealousy, I expect. You get that wherever you go."

Eloise doesn't look convinced, but before she can continue, Alex interrupts.

"No one takes on a relief if they can't afford it," he says, putting his phone back into his pocket. "That's why I never get to go on holiday."

"That's because your father's tight, not because you can't afford it," Eloise jokes. Alex smiles again, and I'm grateful for the change of conversation. She glances at her Rolex, and I wonder if Alex bought it for her. "I must love you and leave you, I'm afraid. I have to keep to my schedule if this talk's going to start promptly at eight."

"Where's this grub then?" Alex says.

"Along the corridor and left." Eloise touches his arm briefly. "I'll catch up with you later."

"What do you think of Eloise?" Alex says on our way to find the food. "First impressions?"

"She seems very efficient. And charming," I say, picking my words carefully. I don't want to offend Alex by being less than complimentary about his girlfriend. She comes across as rather hard, but maybe that's because she sees me as

some kind of threat, which is utterly ridiculous of course.

We find drinks and a couple of plates of
food on a table in a side corridor that leads
toward the kitchens.

I decline the sandwiches—they're all
meat and I couldn't eat a thing for worrying that there might be an element of truth
in what Eloise has said. I pick up a glass
of wine instead.

"Don't tell me you're on a diet," Alex
says and then takes an enormous bite out
of a beef sandwich.

"No . . ." I don't like the way his eyes
rake up and down my figure.

"I remember now—you're vegetarian.
Dad told me, several times over. I don't
think he appreciates your ethical stance.
We wouldn't have many clients left if everyone decided to turn veggie." He pours
himself a glass of orange juice. "So you
definitely don't eat horses then?"

"Horses?" I take two steps back.

"Dad's old hunters can be a bit tough."
Alex grins again. "You should see your
face. Of course we don't eat them. We turn
them out to grass, and I always sign the

not-for-human-consumption section in their passports. It's how I was brought up—I think my mother would have loved me more if I'd been born brown and furry with four long, gangly legs."

Ten minutes later, Alex and I find seats near the back of the main conference room. Eloise steps up to the front, fiddles with the lights, then turns to the audience of about forty—maybe fifty—people.

"A very warm welcome to tonight's talk on the subject of management of the failing heart," she says. "Unfortunately, our guest speaker is unable to join us. However"— there's a breathy pause, and a shadow steps through from the dark doorway at the front of the room—"please, put your hands together for . . ."

Eloise doesn't have to introduce him. I know who he is from the tread of his feet and the slope of his shoulders, then, as he steps into the light, the wave of his hair and the angle of his jaw.

"Dr. Mike Schofield," Eloise continues.

His eyes sweep the room. I slide down the chair, hiding behind the person in front of me.

"Can you see all right?" Alex whispers.

"Yep, I'm fine." I'm in denial. I'm not fine at all. In fact, the talk may be too late for me—my heart is failing as memories of my time with Mike flash by on fast-forward in my head.

I feel sick, angry, hurt all over again. It's the shock of it, of seeing him again, of hearing his voice. If I'd known he was going to be here, I could have prepared myself, I think as he takes charge of the stage.

I try to concentrate on the talk, not the speaker. Gradually, the room grows stuffy with the odors of surgical scrub, horseradish sauce, and alcohol. While Mike discusses exercise intolerance and circulatory collapse, Alex snores quietly, eyes closed and chin dropping toward his chest. When Mike winds up the talk, I give Alex a gentle nudge, at which he looks up and turns toward me, his eyes dark and soft. A tiny shiver runs down my spine. Then he yawns.

"Am I boring you?" I say softly.

He shakes his head. "No, but this chap is."

"Shh!" I say, but it's unlikely that Mike will hear him now because half the audience is clapping and the other half shuffling about ready to make a quick escape with the freebie pens and certificates of attendance.

Alex stands up and stretches his long, taut body, revealing a flash of toned stomach where his shirt has come untucked from his jeans.

"The best place for you to be is in bed," I say, then, realizing that I could have put it better, I add, "from the look of you, I mean." Alex cocks his head and grins. Why do I get the impression he's always laughing at me? "I don't mind not hanging around if you want to get back," he says. In fact, I'd rather not hang around, I think. The longer I stay, the more chance there is of my running into Mike.

"I promised Eloise I'd have a word before we go," Alex says, and he disappears in the direction of the bar, leaving me stranded. I join the crowd of people leaving the conference room, hoping to blend in, but as I reach the door I hear a voice behind me, calling my name.

"Hey, Maz. It *is* you . . ."

Reluctantly, I turn back.

"Hi, Mike," I say.

"I wasn't sure at first . . ." He looks me up and down, and I think, How can you not be sure when you've lived with me, seen me naked?

I had no doubts that it was him. He looks good in a checked shirt and tie, cords and polished shoes, but the pink of his scalp is beginning to show through his hair. Age is catching up with him and not being all that kind.

"That was a . . . er, great talk," I say. "Very informative."

"Thanks," he says. "How's it going?"

"Oh, not bad."

"How much longer have you got?"

"Until Ben and Emma get back from their holiday. Well, it's a bit more than a holiday. A six-month round-the-world trip." I'm gabbling, trying to think up an excuse to walk away. "A kind of late gap year, but done with money and style, and without a backpack. How's everyone at Crossways?"

"Janine's pregnant," he says casually.

"Right. Good." I'm assuming he's pleased from the smug expression on his face. In fact, now I think about it, I recall his reaction not long after we moved in together when I said I could see us living there forever, just the two of us. "And a baby, a little girl with blond hair like yours," he'd said, and I'd said, "No children." We were in bed, and I remember how his hand, which had been caressing my thigh, seemed to freeze, how he had then rolled away from me.

"Why not?" he'd said, and I'd tried to explain about looking after my brother when I was much younger, that, although I'd loved him to pieces, I knew about the frustrations of keeping a small child out of trouble and occupied. I knew I didn't want one. A fantastic boyfriend and a great career—that was enough for me.

"Congratulations," I say.

Mike nods. "I'd better make a move, say good-bye to Eloise. I've got to rewrite one of my papers—one of my fellow academics, who hasn't a clue what he's talking about, asked for some pretty major changes. You've probably seen the latest one—last week, in the *Vet Record*."

I shake my head, and he looks a little offended.

"I must catch up with my lift," I say and step past Mike, crossing the corridor to the bar while he walks along at my elbow. "He's with Eloise, look."

"Are you and him—?"

"Absolutely not," I blurt out quickly, and then wish I'd said, "Yes, we're having a fling with lots of passionate sex."

"I'll see you around then," Mike says, tugging at his collar where it's rubbed a red mark on his neck.

I don't say anything as he moves away.

"How do you know Mike, the speaker chap?" Alex says on the way home. "Bit of a robot, isn't he?"

I look out at the road, at the dark shadows of the trees and the hedges pressing in on us, at the star-pricked sky above.

"I used to work for him. In London." I glance toward the silhouette of Alex's face. Why can't I admit it? That Mike and I used to be an item? "He was my boss."

"I should think he was sorry to lose you," Alex says.

"Oh, he had his eye on a suitable replacement way before I left," I say, wondering if Alex is paying me a compliment.

"You must find it pretty quiet here."

"Not at all," I say. "It's rather hectic."

We continue chatting until Alex stops the car outside Otter House, its damaged façade hidden by a mask of scaffolding.

"Well, thanks for the lift. Would you like to come in for coffee?" I ask, surprised at how much I'm enjoying Alex's company.

"Not tonight, Maz."

"Is it the way I make it?" I say lightly.

"It isn't that . . . I might sound like a wuss, but I've been called out three nights in a row, and then there was Tripod last night. I'm completely knackered." I notice Alex's hand moving toward me before settling on the gear stick between us. "Another time?"

"Another time," I murmur, uncertain now whether inviting him in for coffee was the right thing to do.

"You do understand?"

"Of course I do," I say regretfully. Eloise. Eloise wouldn't like it, and who can blame her? I shouldn't have asked. "Good night." I open the door and jump out.

"See you around," Alex calls after me.

On my way back inside the house, I hesitate at Reception. There are lights on in the corridor beyond and footsteps coming toward me. It's Nigel, and from the expression on his face, I'm not sure he's all that pleased to see me.

"I'm glad I've caught you," I say. "That check—it bounced."

"Aha," he says. "I was going to talk to you about that."

Still, his relief is almost palpable when we're interrupted by a call on my mobile from a client who says her fish is drowning and she's on her way in. A couple of minutes later, I'm in the consulting room with Mrs. Finnegan and Nigel looking over my shoulder, watching a goldfish gasping to death in the bottom of a Pyrex casserole dish.

"There's a piece of gravel in its mouth," Nigel points out.

"Yes, I have noticed . . ."

"How are you going to get it out?" Mrs. Finnegan asks.

"I'm thinking." How indeed? My heart races and my skin grows clammy, which is ridiculous because it's only a fish . . .

"The children like to give them names," says Mrs. Finnegan. "I think this is Mickey—he has the white mark on his tail."

Great, the goldfish is no longer anonymous. I picture the young Finnegans anxiously awaiting his safe return. What goes in, though, must come out. I decide to take Mickey to Kennels, parking him on the draining board beside the sink while I find a kidney dish and tweezers. I tip him into the smaller dish, grab him behind the gills, fit the tweezers around the stone, and pull it out. It's all too much for him— when I pour him back into the casserole dish, he sinks to the bottom. It doesn't look good.

"I fear that Mickey will be sushi by midnight," I say when Nigel joins me to find out if I need a hand. "This check—"

"Ah yes," Nigel says, with the slightest tremor of his mustache.

"Look, I admire your loyalty to Emma and the practice, but you can tell me what's going on. We're on the same side." I continue watching Mickey's apparent lack of response to conservative treatment—all right, I confess, that's a euphemism for doing nothing. "I need to know the truth."

Nigel sighs dramatically and finally relents.

"I guessed Emma was having some financial difficulties," he says, "but I didn't realize how serious they were until I took over the accounts."

That isn't like the Emma I know, I think. She's always been so careful with money. I was the spendthrift.

"In my opinion, she's in denial," Nigel goes on. "She overstretched herself in the beginning—the work to convert Otter House cost far more than she budgeted for, and she bought all the kit from new. I don't think she compromised on anything, and I can understand why. She always wants the best for her patients. She's a great vet, but not such a great businesswoman. Talyton Manor Vets haven't helped the situation of course—the competition was fiercer than Emma expected. You have to admire the Fox-Giffords for their tenacity."

I look down to see that Mickey is showing surprising tenacity too—he's started swimming about and nudging the sides of the casserole dish.

"I'd better reunite Mickey with Mrs. Finnegan," I say. "How much does Emma usually charge for seeing a fish out of hours?" I'm teasing—I shouldn't think she's ever seen a fish out of hours before.

However, Nigel is perfectly serious when he answers, "That will be a small-animal consult, plus the after-midnight out-of-hours supplement, and half an hour of your time."

"No way," I say. "Mrs. Finnegan could go out and buy twenty goldfish for that."

"But she didn't," says Nigel, "because she wants to hang on to this one."

I can't do it. Back in Reception, I suggest a donation to an animal charity, and a delighted Mrs. Finnegan posts a fiver into the collection box on the desk and carries Mickey out to her car. I know Nigel's been listening—I heard his sharp intake of breath and his disapproving tut-tut-tuts.

"Let me show you something, Maz." Nigel reaches over the desk and presses a button on the printer, and out churn several sheets of figures. Numbers? I can feel my eyes glazing over already. Nigel highlights some of them with a neon yellow marker from his pocket. "I expected a temporary decrease in turnover when you started here—clients don't like change—but this is excessive. Free credit, free consults . . . Your generosity is almost as reckless as your spending. For example, did you really need to buy new clippers when sending the blades off to be sharpened would have sufficed?" I don't try to defend myself as he goes on. "And then there's Cheryl. Izzy told me," he adds quietly.

I don't blame Izzy. It's in the nature of small businesses that everyone knows everyone else's business.

"It takes years to build a reputation, and minutes to shatter it," Nigel says. "If takings haven't gone up this month, I'm not going to be able to pay everyone's wages . . ."

"Okay, okay," I say. I need to think, but my head aches. "How bad is it? What's the bottom line?"

"Another three, four months and the business goes bankrupt," Nigel says. "Otter House will be no more."

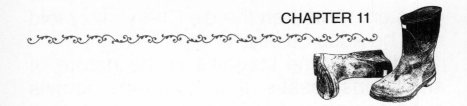

CHAPTER 11

Dark Horse

I DON'T SLEEP. LIKE THE TAILS ON A RAT KING, my thoughts become tangled and tied in knots. I pull the duvet up around my ears, force my eyes closed, and start counting sheep. Dorset Horn or Texel? I settle on curly-coated Devon and Cornwall Long-wools, but it doesn't work.

How am I going to turn Otter House's fortunes around? Is it possible to set the practice's finances back on track before Emma returns? I know it isn't my fault—they were already in a mess—but I certainly haven't helped.

I make plans, the first of which is to pay

Cheryl a visit to persuade her to keep quiet about Blueboy's haircut; the second is to offer to Nigel not to take any wages myself until things pick up. Should I call Emma? I decide against it. What purpose would it serve? Better to give things a little more time to improve—they certainly can't get much worse than they are now.

In the morning I head downstairs, toast in one hand, phone in the other. I have one text message.

> Maz—wd like to take u up on that coffee sometime.
> Can I drop by later? Alex

It takes me a while to compose a suitable response. Is this just a friendly gesture, or is it something more?

I know I said I'd never go out with anyone again, but I'm beginning to waver. Alex isn't as bad as everyone makes out, and *if* he ever did turn out to be interested in me and *if* Eloise wasn't on the scene, then who knows? I suppress a ridiculous pang of regret. The idea of any romance between me and Alex Fox-Gifford is beyond the realms of fantasy.

Hi Alex—you're welcome any time. Maz

I press Send just as I push through the door into Reception.

I work all morning. It's slow but steady, and I make sure everyone pays at the time of consultation, and charge for every bandage and every milliliter of antibiotic I use. When I've finished, I brace myself to visit Cheryl. That way, I can start putting everything right—for Emma and Otter House.

When I reach the Copper Kettle, I pause outside to collect myself. There are several posters stuck to the window, partly obscured by runnels of condensation. On closer inspection I realize that they're all the same, a full frontal view of a cat, two hands holding it up by its chest so that its back legs dangle off the ground. Its eyes are wide, the pupils huge and black. Its tongue sticks out, and its hair sticks up as if it's been plugged into the mains.

"The Otter House Vets Did This to Me" reads the jagged script at the bottom of each poster. "For further information, apply within."

It isn't some antivivisection propaganda— it's Blueboy—and my feelings of contrition are replaced by a wave of anger and hurt that Cheryl could even imagine I'd deliberately harm an animal. I spend my life trying to relieve suffering, not inflict it. I take a deep breath, reach out for the door handle with trembling fingers, and throw the door open with such force that I send the bell jangling to the floor. Inside, a wall of humidity hits me in the face and an ominous hush assaults my ears. When a spoon clatters, one of the women at the table closest to me hisses, "Shh!"

Cheryl stops cutting a sleekly iced cake.

"What do you think you're doing, darkening my door?" she demands.

I came in a spirit of truce, but it's clear Cheryl's in no mood for compromise.

"Is there anywhere we can talk?" I ask, trying to take control of the situation, but this isn't my consulting room. Cheryl's on home territory, and like a furious wildcat, she's on guard.

"I'm not sure I have anything to say to you—unless you're willing to offer us compensation."

"I'm willing to do that," I say, feeling for the checkbook in my bag, "but it has to be on condition that you take those posters down." It crosses my mind to tear them down myself, but I have a feeling I might get lynched by a gang of women with shopping trolleys and walking sticks.

"I'm not doing any such thing." Cheryl bares her teeth in a mocking smile. "The posters stay. How else are we supposed to protect the innocent animals of Talyton?"

A knife taps against a plate, and someone murmurs, "Hear, hear," at which I retreat to Otter House, where the building is still masked by scaffolding and the pavement cut off by railings and tape.

It's a mess, and I have a feeling we'll be waiting for a builder for some time—the insurance company says they'll pay for one, but they're all tied up with the new development on the edge of town.

Nothing ever happens in a hurry in Talyton St. George.

LYNSEY PITT WADDLES IN half an hour late for the urgent appointment Frances made for her at the end of the morning, her bump swathed in a floral cotton that matches her sun hat. She's accompanied by—I do a quick head count—just three of her boys, two of whom are restrained in the double buggy. Cadbury follows on the end of a long lead, his head down and tail between his legs.

"As you can see, he isn't his normal self," Lynsey says. "We're really worried about him. I could do without this right now, Maz." She takes a deep breath and strokes her belly. "I can't wait till I've popped this one out. I'm shattered."

"When's it due?" I ask, helping the oldest boy—Sam, if I remember rightly—lift Cadbury onto the table.

"Yesterday."

"Now you've made me nervous."

"Don't worry, I'm not planning to have this one anywhere but in the hospital. None of those six-hour stays for me. I'm having five days away from home, a holiday from the rest of my little ruffians."

Laughing, I decide to give Cadbury a break from them too and admit him for X-rays. The images suggest that he's eaten something he shouldn't have (again), and I decide to go in without delay.

I open him up in the operating theater and search through the snaking loops of bowel, finding a solid blockage. I cut down over the top and open out the tube of gut to reveal a tiny hand, raised up as if calling for help.

"Guess what—I've found a body," I exclaim.

"Isn't that what you were looking for, a foreign body?" Izzy says.

I tug gently on the tiny plastic hand, pulling it out from the green ooze of gut contents. "It's Spider-Man." I drop him into the kidney dish Izzy's holding, then check that no other superheroes or baddies accompanied him on his journey along Cadbury's gut. There is something else though, something soft, like a piece of rag or a sock. I milk it out through the incision and drop the wad of discolored material into the kidney dish alongside Spider-Man so Izzy can take my finds away to the prep area for a thorough rinse while I close up.

I hear her chuckling at the sink.

"Lynsey's a dark horse. Look at these." She unfurls a pair of pants at the porthole window in the door. "These are no ordinary knickers—she must have bought them from somewhere like Aurora's Cave. They're very tiny." Izzy squeals with shock. "Gosh, Cadbury has chewed out the gusset."

"Izzy, they're crotchless."

"Yes, I know."

"They're meant to be."

"Oh?" she says. "Oh . . . I get it now." She chuckles. "I think I'm getting a little overheated."

I don't know about Izzy, but I'm pretty overheated myself—the radio is on in the background, warning of the risk of sunstroke and telling of queues of almost stationary traffic on the roads to Talymouth and Talysands, and I can feel the perspiration trickling down the bridge of my nose and soaking into my mask.

The radio burbles on in the background—I'm only half listening, but the word *vet* catches my attention.

"Would you mind turning it up, please, Izzy?"

"The dog's doing fine . . ."

"Not the anesthetic. The radio . . ."

Izzy tears a piece of paper towel from the dispenser on the wall and wipes my sweaty forehead before turning up the volume.

"Once again, it's *Vet's Corner* on Megadrive FM. Now, Mr. Fox-Gifford, you were saying . . ."

I listen for Alex's voice, but it's Old Mr. Fox-Gifford who's on air.

"When you're choosing a practice for little Fido or Kitty, it's the vet that counts, not shiny gadgets and toys. Let me tell you a story, a true story. . . . One of my clients made the mistake of allowing herself to be seduced by some slick-talking smart-aleck young vet recently." My needle snags as I pull it through Cadbury's skin. I start again. So does Old Fox-Gifford. "As a result, she has one cat who's scarred for life, and another who's having to see a psychologist for counseling."

"Slimy toad," says Izzy. "He's talking about Cheryl. That's appalling! He can't do that, can he?"

"I think he just has." I bow my head, crushed.

"Remember, no vet worth his salt kisses his patients and gives them treats after every consultation. Good behavior should be expected, not rewarded."

"Everyone will know he's talking about you," Izzy says, "about us."

"Switch it off, Izzy," I groan. "Switch it off."

"Everyone in Talyton listens to Megadrive FM," Izzy says, reaching out and turning it off. "I told you the Fox-Giffords were trouble." She looks at me accusingly, as if

I'm to blame for their outrageous behavior. "There's the son, taking advantage of your generosity and our facilities, bringing injured strays in at all hours of the night, and then there's the father, stabbing us in the back. And then there's the son's girlfriend. She can be pretty noxious too."

What Izzy's saying makes perfect sense. Alex was too good to be true. Suddenly, I feel utterly drained.

"I bet we'll lose a load more clients after that," Izzy goes on. "Emma will be absolutely livid. Otter House's reputation is in tatters."

"Not if I can help it," I say, rallying. "I'm not going to let that family ruin everything."

My mood lifts a little when Cadbury's safely round from the anesthetic and settled on a heated pad in a kennel. Even Izzy seems more cheerful.

"I meant to ask, how was the talk the other night?" she says.

"It was certainly interesting. The original speaker canceled, and my last boss gave the talk instead. My ex."

"That's an unfortunate coincidence," Izzy says, raising an eyebrow at me. "What did you do?"

"I tried to hide, but it didn't work."

"How did you feel?"

"I wish I hadn't gone—seeing him again brought it all back," I say. What I don't add, however, is that in a small way, during the restless hours of last night, I realized seeing him again helped. Now I know I've done the right thing, leaving Crossways. Even if coming here is proving to be a mistake.

"Chris and I introduced Freddie to a flock of sheep for the first time last night," Izzy says, tactfully filling my silence as she washes up the instruments. "I walked him up to them on a lead and said, 'Hey, sheep, meet Freddie.'"

"Were they suitably impressed?"

"They just stood there, glaring at him and stamping their feet. I don't think he has any idea what he's supposed to do."

"I thought it was supposed to be instinctive."

"So did I."

Izzy and I take Tripod into the staff room to wander about and stretch his remaining three legs while we have a tea break. Miff is about too—I must have forgotten to shut her in the flat. As soon as she sets eyes on

Tripod, she comes trotting over, wagging her tail. Tripod arches his back and hisses. Miff backs off, then returns, at which Tripod decides that discretion is the better part of valor and scrambles up the arm of the sofa, tugging loops out of the chenille. He settles himself and sits blinking at us.

"No one's called to claim him," says Izzy.

"He can't go to the Fox-Giffords," I say quickly. "They don't want him, and I wouldn't let them anywhere near him now if they did."

"I think he'll have to join Otter House Vets as practice cat. I know Emma won't like it, but we can't possibly bump him, not after all he's been through."

"I wasn't planning to bump him."

"We'll have to fit a cat door."

"Where will—I mean, where would he sleep, if he stayed?"

Izzy looks at me as if I'm an alien. "In the flat, of course."

"So he'll need a stair lift as well!" At which Izzy laughs, but I realize all of a sudden that she's talking as if Otter House Vets are going to go on and on. I watch her smiling as she tickles Tripod under his chin. I'm wondering how much she knows when her smile drops and she looks at me seriously.

"Nigel told me about the problem with the accounts." She hesitates. "I'd guessed there was some kind of hitch. Emma hasn't been herself recently, as if there's been something preying on her mind. I thought she might have talked to you about it . . ."

"I wish she had," I say. I don't like to tell half-truths and lies, but I don't want to betray a confidence. I guess the problems in the practice probably stem from Emma's preoccupation with her failure to fall pregnant.

"She wouldn't open up to me. She kept making out that everything was hunky-dory." Izzy sighs. "The practice has to survive—I can't afford to lose my job."

The phone starts ringing, and I reach out to answer it. "Well, don't worry about it. I'm going to keep this practice going if it kills me," I tell her. I'm not sure exactly how, but I'm working on it. "What's up, Frances?"

"There's a man for you." Frances sounds somewhat breathless on the other end of the line.

"I don't need a man," I say flippantly. "Send him away."

"It's young Mr. Fox-Gifford."

"Send him through," I say. "It's Alex," I add, turning to Izzy. "I'm going to give him a piece of my mind."

"I'll go," Izzy says.

"No, stay," I say, eager to prove to Izzy where my loyalties lie, in case she still has doubts.

"Hi, Maz. Izzy. Have you got the coffee on?" Alex appears at the doorway, smiling. Izzy goes over to the coffee machine to top up the water.

"Don't bother, Izzy," I say. "He isn't staying."

Alex frowns, pulling his mobile from his pocket and answering its ring. "Hi. Speaking. How's Satan?" He pauses. "I'll be out to check up on him tonight. Yes, it sounds as though we've put the devil back into him." Alex chuckles. "Cheers, Eloise.

"Sorry about that, Maz," he says. "I couldn't leave it in case it was urgent, but then you know all about that . . ." His voice trails off. "Have I come at a bad time?"

"You aren't welcome here," I say.

"But I thought?"

"You thought wrong," I say curtly. "You gave me the impression you wanted to be friends, but I reckon you're only here to gloat. Oh, stop pretending you don't know anything about it. Your father. On the radio. I've never heard anything so unprofessional. It's appalling."

"I'm sorry." Alex's face flushes. "I heard what he said. It was wrong, but I can't be held responsible for my father's actions."

"He was speaking on behalf of your practice, and he said some terrible things." I'm spitting with anger. "Emma was right about your family. I can't trust any of you."

"Well, you aren't so perfect yourself," Alex says reproachfully, "telling me the robot was your boss. He was a bit more than that, wasn't he?" Before I can answer him, he goes on, "Eloise told me. He's your ex-boyfriend."

"How does she know?" I say, confused. I don't know why I'm so embarrassed. I didn't lie, I think. I just didn't tell Alex the whole truth.

"They had a cozy tête-à-tête after the meeting," he says. "Eloise can't keep anything to herself."

"Look," I say, "I don't care about Eloise, or you, or your father. I want you to leave."

"I'll go then," Alex says after a moment's hesitation.

"That's right. Go. I don't know why you came here in the first place."

"Because you invited me, remember?" he answers with an infuriating smirk, as if he thinks he's had the last word. "Good-bye."

All I can do when he turns and marches back down the corridor is call after him, "Why don't you go running back to Eloise?"

I'm aware that Izzy is staring at me.

"I didn't think you had it in you, Maz," she says—admiringly, I think. However, the fact I seem to have done something right in Izzy's eyes for once doesn't make me feel any less upset. Emma warned me about the Fox-Giffords, yet Alex somehow misled me into giving him the benefit of the doubt. I was wrong, and I'm still fuming when I head back to Kennels.

I try to look on the bright side. At least I've done something good today. I've saved Cadbury's life.

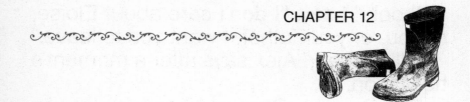

CHAPTER 12

Baby Baby

WHEN I WAKE UP IN THE MORNING ON FRIDAY, I find Nigel has slipped a letter under the door of the flat—Miff has left her teeth marks in it, but it's just about decipherable.

Dear Maz,
Re: the chat we had the other night about ways to save money.
Working on the principle last in, first out, it is with great regret that I must ask you to give Frances notice to leave the practice with immediate

**effect. I know I can rely on your
discretion.**

Yours sincerely, Nigel.
**P.S.: Any questions, feel free to
call me.**

I head down to Reception to unlock the doors, and pick up the phone, checking no one is around to listen in.

"Nigel," I say, once I get hold of him. "Where are you?"

"I'm having a fishing lesson," he says. "I assume this call is about my letter?"

"It's a bit drastic, isn't it? How's Izzy going to cope? We need a receptionist to greet clients and answer the phone."

"We'll have to manage. There aren't all that many clients anyway, especially after Old Fox-Gifford's radio broadcast. Frances told me we had three more transfer to Talyton Manor yesterday."

It's pretty worrying, I think, as I go on. "Why do I have to speak to Frances? Isn't it the practice manager's role?"

"It's better if it comes from you. I'd hate Frances to hold it against me—I mean, I'm going to be living in this town long after you've gone. I'd rather she held it against you."

"Thanks a lot." I pause, catching sight of Frances drawing up in the car park in her battered Morris Minor. "How am I going to tell her?"

"I'm delegating the whole process to you, Maz." There's a splash, and Nigel's voice fades out, then back in again. "I've got to go—I think I've got a bite."

A bite? I'm not sure what he's talking about, but then I remember that he's gone fishing. I don't approve. I can't see what fun there is to be had in sticking a hook through the mouth of a living creature, but then I won't eat anything that has eyes, potatoes excepted.

"Good morning, Maz." Frances walks in with a spring in her step. "It's such a lovely day."

It seems a shame to spoil her mood straightaway.

"Erm, if you're okay here, I'll go and give Izzy a hand in Kennels."

"Of course I'm okay here—it's like my second home," she says and beams, and my heart sinks to the very soles of my Crocs as I retreat.

"Izzy, did you know about this?" I wave Nigel's note at her. She looks up from where she's cleaning out Cadbury's kennel. "About Nigel asking me to fire Frances," I go on when she stares at me uncomprehendingly.

"Get rid of Frances? Well, don't expect me to do extra hours." She is not happy. "I have got a life outside Otter House."

"I know you have, but if we can't cut costs there won't be a job for you either."

Izzy sits back on her heels, thinking. "All right, when are you going to tell her?"

"Later," I say. "Tonight, at the end of evening surgery."

"Good luck," Izzy says. "I can't see her going without a fight."

That's what I'm worried about.

I take Cadbury out of the kennel next door and give him a thorough checkup. It's two days after his surgery, and he really should be picking up by now.

"He's getting wise to this," I say, as he wiggles his bottom away from my thermometer.

"I'll hang on to him for you," Izzy says, snapping off her yellow rubber gloves.

"Thanks."

"He threw up bile a couple of times last night."

"Mmm, I'm not sure he's quite right." I ruffle his coat with my free hand, and a shower of white flakes settles on the bench. "He could do with some Head & Shoulders for his dandruff."

"He's very thin," Izzy observes. "Emma usually takes some blood to make sure there's nothing odd going on," she adds pointedly, which makes me wonder if she trusts my judgment after Blueboy.

As a new graduate, I soon learned that when a nurse makes a tactful observation, it's worth following it up.

I check the thermometer. Cadbury's temperature is just a touch high, but it has been since his op.

"I've kept him in long enough—I'm going to send him home today to see if he's happier there. I'll ask Lynsey for permission to take some blood when she comes to pick him up." I pause. "You did count the swabs after the op, didn't you?"

Izzy looks at me, shocked. "Of course I did." She gazes at Cadbury, pointing toward his belly. "You don't think I'd have let you leave one behind, do you?"

"I didn't mean to offend you—I just have to be sure I haven't missed anything." I'm going to worry now. My dreams will be haunted by a hot chocolate Lab until I'm sure he's okay. He should be okay. There's no reason why not. "I'll make appointments for him to come back every day till he's better, if necessary."

"I'm not sure Lynsey is going to appreciate that in her condition," Izzy says.

I'm not being difficult. I'm thinking of how Lynsey will manage to cover the cost if Cadbury stays much longer.

"Perhaps she can find someone else to bring him in," I say. I kiss the top of Cadbury's head, wishing I had someone to brainstorm his case with. I don't know how Emma copes with it—it's far more stressful working solo than in a multi-vet practice. "It's important."

There are occasions when I wonder what else I could do. Retrain to be a driving school instructor? Deliver leaflets? Be something in the city? (By which I mean something that isn't in the country, not a stockbroker or fund manager.) If I hold my hands out in front of me, it's an effort to stop them shaking at the moment. Too much caffeine. Too much stress.

"ARE YOU OKAY?" I ask Lynsey when she struggles in toward the end of the day with one hand on her back and the other on her bump. "Would you like a seat?"

"No, I'm fine." She forces a smile. "Really."

"No boys today," I observe.

"My mother's looking after them. They'll be over the moon to see Cadbury again. We've missed him."

Izzy brings the foreign bodies to show off to Lynsey before bringing Cadbury through. Lynsey doesn't seem all that interested in superheroes. She's more interested in the pants. She picks them up, catching at the lace trimming with the ragged edges of her fingernails.

"They have been through the wash, as well as the dog," Izzy says.

Lynsey examines them slowly, stretching the waistband as if testing its elasticity, then fingering the label.

"Size eight?" she says eventually. "I have

never been a size eight in my life." Her cheeks acquire a deep red hue. "I'll kill the bastard!"

I glance nervously toward Izzy.

"I expect Cadbury snaffled them up on a walk," she says.

"Oh, I know exactly where he picked them up from: the back of my husband's bloody Land Rover." There's an odd popping noise, and suddenly the color drains from Lynsey's face. She clutches the edge of the consulting room table, bows forward, and groans.

I grab her arm. "Izzy, fetch a chair, will you?" I say.

"I can't sit down," Lynsey gasps. Sweat droplets bubble across her forehead. "My waters have broken. The baby's on its way." She tries to smile through a twisted grimace. "At least I'm in the right place."

"You aren't!" I start to panic.

"I had a couple of contractions on my way here, but they weren't all that strong," she says. "I thought I'd have a few hours yet."

"You should be in a hospital." I think back to my obstetrics notes on delivering kittens, foals, and calves. "With a midwife."

Izzy returns with a chair from Reception.

"Forget the chair. Call an ambulance. Quick!" I tell her. I don't know what else to do. I keep hold of Lynsey's arm. She starts panting, then moans, then pants again. What do we need? Buckets of hot water and towels, bottles of obstetrical lubricant, and copious amounts of tea?

"The ambulance is on its way." Izzy reappears for a second time.

Frances pushes in beside her. "Lynsey, dear, I'll call Stewart and your mother."

"Nooo . . ." Lynsey howls like a lone wolf, then recovers enough to say, "I won't have that two-timing bastard anywhere near me. Ever. Again."

"Oh?" says Frances. "Well, let's sort you out first. I'll walk you along to the staff room, where you can make yourself comfortable. Do you think you can manage that?"

Lynsey nods, biting her lip.

"Let's go quickly then, before you have another contraction." Frances holds her by the hand and rubs the small of her back. "How often are they coming?"

"I don't know. I'm losing track."

"Every ten minutes? Five? Three?" Frances asks patiently.

"I'd say they're about two minutes apart," Lynsey says.

"Oh dear," says Frances.

"The ambulance will be here any moment." I glance anxiously at my watch. How long has it been?

"This baby isn't going to wait for an ambulance—it has to come up from Talymouth." Frances looks at me. "This baby isn't going to wait for anyone. Lynsey's contractions are already too close."

"Frances," I say in desperation, "it has to . . ."

Less than a minute later Lynsey is in the staff room, hanging on to the back of the sofa, with Frances in attendance. Izzy waits in Reception for the ambulance. I fetch clean towels, a damp flannel, and ice cubes from the flat at Frances's request, but Lynsey doesn't want them.

"I feel like I want to push . . . ," she gasps. The ensuing wail cuts through me like a scalpel blade. I never want a baby. Never.

"Just breathe—in and out," Frances says very calmly.

"I have to push . . ."

There's a knock on the door, and a man

strolls in, as if he has all the time in the world. Typical!

"Thank goodness for the NHS," I say, looking from the man, who's short and swarthy, to the big black hairy dog at his heels. "You're just in time!"

He frowns, glances past me, then backs out very quickly as Lynsey's voice rises to a high-pitched scream.

"The baby's on its way," I say urgently. "You can't just leave."

"It's nothing to do with me, my lover. I'm the builder—your practice manager asked me to call in."

"Oh, I'm sorry. Nigel isn't here at the moment. Would you mind waiting in Reception for a few minutes?"

"Not at all," he says, his eyes darting about as he tries to take it all in. I show him back along the corridor, where he starts looking at the collars and leads that are on display. "How long do you think you'll be?" he asks me.

"Not long, I hope." I glance at my watch again. "I don't know where that ambulance has got to." On tenterhooks, I look out of the window. Izzy's pacing up and down the pavement. She catches my eye and shakes her head, and my heart sinks. I start running through various scenarios in my head. What if the baby needs life support when it arrives? We've got oxygen in the operating theater. We've got a tiny incubator in Kennels. We've got sterile clamps for the cord if necessary. The trouble is, I'm not all that confident about using them on a human baby.

I'm panicking like mad, until I detect the sound of a distant siren.

I catch sight of flashing blue lights further along the street, but because of the traffic it's another couple of minutes before the ambulance arrives outside Otter House.

"Thank goodness," I breathe as Izzy shows two paramedics with their paraphernalia into Reception and out through the corridor, following Lynsey's screams. I head after them and wait outside the staff room with Izzy, my hands over my ears.

"Maz." Eventually Izzy grabs my hands and pulls them away. "It's over. Listen!"

I hold my breath and listen to the baby's cry and Frances's happy shout of "It's a girl!"

To my chagrin, my eyes prick with tears, tears of relief and joy.

"Lynsey . . ." Stewart comes running along the corridor, his work boots clicking on the floor. "Where is she?"

I show him to the door.

"I need to see my wife." Stewart tries to push past Frances, but she's like Fluffy, the three-headed dog, guarding the philosopher's stone. "I want to see her."

"She doesn't want to see you," Frances says coldly.

"Why not?" Stewart raises his eyebrows. "What am I supposed to have done this time?"

"There's no supposed about it. You've been at it again." Lynsey's voice comes belting out, slightly hoarse now, like an aged rock star's. "You've been up lovers' lane with one of your floozies. Who is it this time? Let me guess."

"Please, Lynsey, d-d-don't upset yourself . . . not now . . . ," Stewart stammers.

"I'm not upset. I'm very calm"—Lynsey's voice trails off, then explodes—"for a woman who's just given birth and found out that her husband's been screwing around. You told me you'd been in Aurora's Cave to buy me a present."

"There's no need to bring Aurora into it."

"So it is her."

"At least let me see the baby."

"Over my dead body!" Lynsey's voice again. "I'll look after my daughter. You can take care of the bloody dog."

When the paramedics take Lynsey, who's draped in one blanket, and the baby, who's swaddled in another, to the hospital for checks, she stops briefly to show off her new offspring.

"Look." She pushes the edge of the blanket away from the baby's face. Her skin is red and wrinkled, her features are squished up, and her skull is pointed, like an elf's hat. Just for a moment my heart tightens with, dare I admit it, yearning and envy.

"She looks angry," I say tentatively.

Lynsey smiles. "Like mother, like daughter. A chip off the old block."

Block?

"I'm glad you said that." I touch Lynsey's arm. "Congratulations."

Block. Building blocks. It reminds me that I've left the builder waiting with his dog. I hurry along to Reception.

"I'm sorry to keep you. Is that your pickup on the road outside?" I glance toward the window and past the scaffold poles. The ambulance pulls away, followed by Stewart's tractor. Cadbury stands inside the cab beside Stewart, looking out with his ears flipping back in the wind.

"That's mine." He stands up and introduces himself, handing over a business card that reads: "D. J. Appleyard & Co., Quality Builders. We don't make promises we can't keep." "I brought Magic in with me—I didn't like to leave her in the van in this weather."

"You do know you're parked on double yellow lines?" I ask anxiously. I've learned the hard way back in London that parking attendants lie in wait to slap tickets on your windscreen within seconds.

"You don't want to worry about that, my lover. You have to be stopped for at least two days before anyone takes any notice around here." DJ grins. He has nicotine-stained teeth and a nervous tic of the right eyelid that makes him look as if he's winking all the time. "The pace of life around here is naturally slow."

"Oh. Well, let me show you the work," I say, and he follows me at a snail's pace round to the front of the house, making me wonder if your metabolism slows down more the longer you live in Talyton. Some people might like it. I find it excruciating.

"How much will all that cost?" I ask eventually, as DJ ruminates, chewing on gum like a cow chewing cud. "I need a rough idea for the insurance company."

He gazes up at the deep scars in the plaster. "As much as it costs," he says.

"And how long? A rough idea?"

"You can't hurry a proper job, my lover." He looks at me and winks again. "It'll take as long as it takes."

"Are you going to join us?" Izzy waves a greasy paper bag in our direction. "Doughnuts and tea all round to wet the baby's head."

"I can't stop," DJ says.

"But you will be back?" The thought crosses my mind that I might kidnap him and hold him in a kennel until he agrees to start work immediately.

"I'll be back."

"When exactly?"

"Tomorrow. Maybe Monday. Definitely no later than the end of next week." He squints at the sky. "Them clouds are mares' tails—could mean rain, which will add another couple of days—but don't you worry, I'll have it finished before your friend gets back. I did the renovations on the Talymill Inn—did you know? I told Clive my team'd get the mill ready in time for opening, and we did. Trust me. I'll see you as soon as I can."

We shake on it. What else can I do? I watch him go, his dog at his heels, then join Izzy and Frances in the staff room.

"There, clean as a whistle," says Frances. "You'd never know this had been a labor ward, would you?"

"Thank you, Frances." How can I sack her now? "You were amazing."

"I was birth partner for my daughter-in-law when Ruby was born," she says, blushing. "Indispensable's my middle name."

"Well, I don't know how we would've coped without you."

"Chris would have known what to do." Izzy gazes out of the window. "He's going to let me help him with the lambing next spring."

"I've never heard a ewe screaming out for an epidural," I observe.

"Or that she's going to shoot the ram for getting her into that situation," Frances says. "Oh, today's been so exciting—I do so love a good crisis."

"I'm hoping there won't be too many more." Izzy looks up from where she's stirring milk into three mugs of tea. "Oh, Maz, before I forget, Tripod's due his second lot of jabs. He's asleep on the pile of clean bedding in the laundry whenever you're ready for him. Oh, and I couldn't find Cadbury's blood sample to send off."

"That's because I forgot to take one in all the panic." I swear inwardly, Izzy staring at me as if she thinks I'm completely useless. "I'll take it when he comes back tomorrow—I don't suppose one more day will hurt."

Izzy passes round the tea and doughnuts. Frances chooses the one with the hole—for the sake of her figure, she says.

"I noticed that the posters have gone from the window of the Copper Kettle when I was on the way to the baker's," Izzy says. "Cheryl must have taken them down."

"I don't think it was out of consideration for your feelings, Maz," Frances points out. "It hinted at unpleasant goings-on and cats' hairs in the scones."

"Just like here." I pick a hair—one of

Tripod's, I suspect, and a side effect of having a practice cat—out of my tea.

"I wonder when Emma and Ben will start a family. She's devoted herself to the practice," Izzy says. "I only hope that she doesn't regret it later, if she should decide not to have children."

"Do you regret it?" Frances cuts in rather tactlessly.

"I did briefly, when I turned forty, and then I thought, What the hell. It wasn't meant to be."

I bite through my doughnut, avoiding eye contact with the others. Lynsey's baby has opened my ears to the ticking of my biological clock. I didn't know I had one until now.

"Poor Lynsey," Frances pipes up. "She's been through labor, been humiliated by that husband of hers—mind you, I always said he was trouble—and now her hormones are going to kick in."

"Yes, poor thing," Izzy agrees.

I keep silent. The only thing worse than washing your dirty linen in public is having someone else do it for you.

I glance toward Frances, who's pouring more tea. She belongs at Otter House. Like a slightly worn but colorful sofa, she's part of the furniture. I can't imagine her working anywhere else now, and I can't see Talyton Manor Vets offering her her old job back either. In fact, if it wasn't for those dreadful Fox-Giffords, I wouldn't be in this position.

"Frances," I begin. My palms grow clammy as the memory comes flooding back to me of when Mike suggested I hand in my resignation and leave Crossways. It was one of the worst days of my life because, although I knew it was personal, I couldn't help suspecting that he'd have found a way of keeping me on if he thought I'd really been going places in my career.

"Yes, Maz?" Frances says.

"No, it's all right." It will be better to wait until after the weekend, give her the bad news first thing on Monday morning. "It'll keep."

CHAPTER 13

Death by Spider-Man

"STEWART HASN'T KEPT HIS APPOINTMENT WITH Cadbury today. Would you ring him and ask him to make another one ASAP?" I ask Izzy. I'm chickening out of talking to him myself because I feel partially responsible for the marital discord. I should have been more careful. By no stretch of either the imagination or the elastic would those pants ever have fitted Lynsey.

"For Monday?" Izzy says, picking up the phone in Reception while I tidy up after my last appointment of the Saturday morning surgery.

"Today, preferably. Even tomorrow—I

don't mind opening up on a Sunday." It's important, possibly more for my peace of mind than for Cadbury. A few more days of worrying about Cadbury, what Cheryl might do next, and how I might persuade a few more clients into the practice, and I'll be a nervous wreck. However, when Izzy does finally get hold of Stewart, he's tied up on the farm and the cowman is off sick, so it has to be Monday. I guess it's all right—Stewart knows his animals.

"Nigel wants to see you," Izzy says. "He's in the office."

"Thanks," I say, sighing inwardly. I was looking forward to some time to myself.

"I hope you don't mind me saying, Maz, but you look whacked," Izzy says. "Why don't I take the phones for you tomorrow night? You could walk Miff along the river to the Talymill Inn, have a bite to eat, and watch Nigel and his morris troupe dancing."

"That's very kind of you," I say, a little surprised.

"You don't seem to be coping with the pressure, and we don't want clients complaining because the vet's half asleep."

Although put out by her lack of faith in me, I decide that a couple of hours without the phone sounds too tempting an offer to refuse.

"What about you though, Izzy?"

"I'll be at Chris's. I'm going to do dinner while he's out on his tractor. I can't believe how much there is to do on a farm on a summer's evening."

"So you and him?"

"We're friends," she says coyly.

"Well, if you really don't mind," I say. I can see why Emma has come to depend on Izzy. I hope she doesn't start looking for another job because of the situation here.

She smiles. "You'd better catch up with Nigel quick—he doesn't like to be kept waiting. Don't mention the butterflies though—he's got butterfly strips on his cheek." She giggles. "He caught himself with his fishing hook, would you believe. He says he's going to be the compleat angler by Christmas. Complete idiot, more like."

"Now he knows what it's like to be a fish," I say drily.

"And he's strained the ligaments in his knee, morris dancing. I told him he really shouldn't take up such dangerous sports."

Cheered up a little, I find Nigel is in the

office, and of course my eyes are immediately drawn to the sticky strips on his cheek, and then to the pile of papers in front of him on the desk.

"Bills," he says. "I've been dealing with them in order of priority. I'm going to have to interrupt Emma's holiday." There's a funny smell in the office, the sickly scent of hot lavender and moldy grain. Nigel rolls up one trouser leg to reveal a shiny white calf covered with sparse gingery fuzz before placing a heat pad across his knee. "She'll have to come straight back—I can't see any other way." He picks up a piece of paper and waves it at me. "Do you have any idea what this is?"

I shake my head. There's a strangulating pressure on my throat, like someone's fingers, Cheryl's maybe . . .

"This is a letter from Cheryl's solicitor, threatening legal action against us unless we agree to settle for Blueboy's loss of earnings and his post-traumatic stress, as well as a manicure for Cheryl after she tore her nail on the front door as she left, and her solicitor's costs, of course. It has to be the most expensive haircut in history—we could have had Vidal Sassoon himself." Nigel stabs at the paper halfway down with his finger to show me the figure.

"That much?" My pulse flutters with panic. Where am I going to find that kind of money? Will my indemnity insurance pay out, considering the circumstances? If the Fox-Giffords find out how much she's asking for, they'll have a field day. They'll make sure it reaches the national press as well as the *Chronicle.*

"There's also another piece of correspondence that I took the liberty of opening—a letter from the Royal College asking you to comment on Cheryl's complaint against you. If I'm not very much mistaken, she intends to have you hung out to dry."

"It isn't as if I did any harm." My mouth feels tacky, as if I've just woken with a hangover. "In a way, I was doing the cat a favor."

"If you can prove that, you're in the clear. Can you prove it without the consent form?" Nigel removes the handkerchief that's neatly folded in his shirt pocket with a morris man's practiced flourish and blows his nose. "I'm inclined to make her an offer."

"I've already tried. It didn't work." Nigel's mustache begins to twitch, and I shut him up quickly. "It's all right. It was my own money."

"Did things go better with Frances?" he asks, changing the subject. "You have done the deed?"

"I couldn't bring myself to tell her," I admit. "I'm going to do it on Monday. In the meantime I've got some ideas to improve the practice income, so there's no need to bother Emma just yet. I mean, she must have known what was going on before she left . . ." It's almost as if she wanted someone to find out. "There's still time to turn Otter House Vets around before she gets back—all we need to do is get the clients back through the door."

"Wow, you should have been a rocket scientist. Brilliant." Nigel tries to stand but fails. (I don't know about man flu, but he seems to have acquired a serious case of man knee, and I can't see how he's going to be able to dance later.) "What exactly do you suggest?"

"How about some free clinics: a slimming club, puppy parties, and checkups for our senior citizens. The consultation would be free, but they'd pay for any extras—blood tests, vaccinations, and diet food."

"I've got a better idea," Nigel says sarcastically, "a sign reading 'Talyton Manor Vets, branch surgery.'"

BY SUNDAY EVENING I'm feeling a little more relaxed and looking forward to my night out. I haven't heard anything from Stewart, so I assume Cadbury's on the mend.

Down by the river I stop on the footbridge to let Miff off the lead. This time she doesn't run away. She waits beside me as I watch the water flowing beneath my feet, gazing at me with those soft brown eyes of hers as if to say, "Don't do it, Maz. It can't be all that bad." And now that I'm outside, away from Otter House, it isn't.

It's a lovely evening. The sun burns orange in the west, silhouetting the hills with neon halos, and the trees cast lengthening shadows across our path as I stroll on with Miff at my heels. A duck skims the water ahead of us, sending up bright splashes, as if it's showing us the break in the line of trees beyond, where we turn off to enter the garden of the Talymill Inn.

Back in my student days, when I was working at Barton Farm, the pub was done up with a flashing floor, piped music, and a pink elephant slide to attract the tourists. Since then, Clive's taken it from trashy plastic to smart rustic.

I tie Miff to a picnic table outside and head for the bar, where Clive refuses to take my money.

"Would you like me to have another look at Robbie?" I ask.

"If you wouldn't mind. Only if it's not too much trouble." He glances around at the busy pub. "I don't seem to have the time to bring him to you."

"It's all right. I don't mind making pub calls." I glance over the bar to where Robbie's sitting up on an enormous cushion. "How is he?"

"He isn't so good, are you, son?"

Robbie gazes in the direction of his master's voice—I'd guess his vision has deteriorated since I last saw him, along with everything else—and beats the cushion with his tail.

"There are things you could try," I say. "Hydrotherapy, physio, lifting aids, trolleys . . ."

"A trolley?" Clive grimaces. "What kind of life would that be for a dog?"

"It would save your back." A woman joins Clive behind the bar. She's very striking, taller than Clive, with dark eyes, a slightly hooked nose, and long black hair lightened by silver streaks. "I'm Edie," she says. She holds out her hand to shake mine. The sleeve of her purple dress falls away, revealing a slender white wrist. "You must be Maz, the vet." She turns back to Clive. "Don't make the poor girl talk shop while she's here."

"Maz doesn't mind . . ."

"I expect you're like us, Maz. You can rarely get away," Edie says. "And when you do, you have people like my husband going on about their dogs. He's obsessed with old Robbie. In fact, I'm convinced he loves him more than he loves me."

"Is it surprising?" Clive teases. "Robbie doesn't boss me about."

Edie grows serious. "Robbie's been messing himself—I don't suppose Clive's mentioned that."

"I clear up after him," Clive says, his voice defensive. "Everyone has the odd accident when they get to that age, but you don't put them down because they're an embarrassment."

"I'm thinking of Robbie, how he feels losing his dignity," Edie says quietly. "What do you think, Maz?" she adds, putting me on the spot as I sense the tension between husband and wife. What would I do if Robbie was my dog? At what point does a life become not worth living?

I look toward Robbie, who's picked up a toy and is holding it hopefully in his mouth, waiting for someone to play.

"I wouldn't say he's suffering yet," I say tactfully, "but you both know Robbie better than I do. You'll know when it's time."

"Thanks, Maz." I can almost hear Clive's sigh of relief, although I'm a little afraid that I've offended Edie by taking his side when she's probably really fed up with the mess, especially when they're running a busy pub. A smelly old dog—I'm sorry, Robbie—is the last thing they need.

"I can hear bells—the morris men are here." Edie throws Clive a towel. "I'll have to get back to the kitchen. You'd better get on and change that barrel."

I return outside to rejoin Miff, who's delighted to see me, jumping up and squeaking and wagging her tail. If no one else has, at least she's forgiven me at last for not being Emma.

I sit down with my drink at the table on the lawned area that sweeps down to the river and watch the morris dancers, male and female, wandering about and exchanging rowdy greetings while what seem like hundreds of kids play on the jungle gym.

The morris band tunes up their fiddles to an old accordion, and Clive emerges from the pub with a tray of pint glasses slopping over with bitter. With a tapping of sticks and tinkling of bells, the dancing kicks off. Nigel gives me a little wave when he sees me, skipping back and forth as if there's nothing wrong with his knee, and twirling a handkerchief in each hand.

Is this really how people in Talyton like to spend their Sunday nights? I wonder.

I miss being able to pop out with friends—admittedly, most of them were staff from Crossways—for a meal. I miss being a student too. Emma used to be a real party animal. She'd throw a party at the drop of a hat. I gaze into the depths of my glass, recalling the time when the guests found knots of catgut in the punch. We'd been at home practicing our suturing techniques on oranges the day before, and Emma had chucked them in without checking them first.

I feel rather exposed, sitting on my own, knowing I've not had the best start here. Occasionally, a stranger casts a glance in my direction, and I wonder how many of them have seen Cheryl's posters, how many of them doubt my professionalism.

My phone rings. I grab it from my bag and check the caller display. It's Izzy, and before she even has time to explain I can tell from the tone of her voice that there's something very wrong.

"I'm sorry, Miff," I say, untying her from the table leg. "We have to go."

IZZY HAS EVERYTHING READY, including a consent form, which Stewart has signed, giving permission for any necessary procedure. Stewart himself is pacing up and down Reception, his lower jaw jutting forward, his mouth set in a grim, straight line, and his fists clenched at his sides.

"Er, hi," I say, sick with nerves.

Stewart doesn't speak.

"Maz." Izzy holds the door into the corridor open for me. "This way! Now!"

The light is out, and it feels as if I'm following her down a long, dark tunnel.

"The bulb's gone," Izzy says. "I haven't had a chance to change it. Quickly—we haven't got much time . . ."

She shoves open the door into the operating theater. The light sears the backs of my eyes, and it takes a moment for me to recover my sight. When it returns, everything is all too clear. Cadbury lies on the table with an IV drip up and running.

"He isn't going anywhere," Izzy says quietly. "It took me a couple of minutes to find a pulse. I assume you're going straight in." This is an order, not a statement of fact.

I give Cadbury the lightest touch of anesthetic and a quick scrub and open him up. The diagnosis is simple: peritonitis and septic shock.

"I'll need more fluids."

"They're warming in the sink," Izzy says curtly.

"And some soluble antibiotic."

"All ready—here on the crash trolley."

"Come on, Cads," I murmur. "You're going to make it. You have to."

"He's stopped breathing," Izzy says urgently.

I watch his rib cage. No movement.

"Bag him," I say.

"There's no pulse."

"Start massage."

"I'll have to put him on his side." Izzy rolls him over and immediately starts cardiac massage, pressing rhythmically on his chest. She pauses, gives him a breath of oxygen with the black rubber bag on the anesthetic machine. Pump-pump-pump-pump-pump. Breath. Pump-pump-pump-pump-pump. Breath.

Izzy's face grows scarlet with effort, but I can see that it's no use . . . It's too late.

Nothing concentrates the mind more than being up to your elbows inside a dead dog, particularly a puppy who should have had twelve to fourteen years of life ahead of him.

I stop fishing and watch the tears streaming down Izzy's face as she squeezes the bag, sending oxygen into lungs that will never take another breath.

"Izzy, you can stop now," I tell her. I take off my gloves. Izzy keeps on. Cadbury's chest lifts and falls repeatedly as she empties and fills the bag. I walk round the table and put my hand on her shoulder. "Izz, stop. He's gone." I give her a rough shake. "Izzy! You have to stop."

She stops. Uttering a sob, she tears off her apron, turns on her heels, and walks out, her apron trailing to the floor behind her. When I look down, I find I have one of Cadbury's soft, velvety ears between my fingers. My eyes burn, my throat tightens, and all I want to do is curl up into a ball and howl, but I have to speak to Stewart first. How on earth am I going to face him?

It's a very long way back down that dark corridor. When I step into Reception, Stewart spins round to face me.

"Well?" he mutters.

I hang my head. "He's gone," I whisper.

"He's dead?"

I nod.

"Fucking hell." Stewart runs his hands over his bald patch. "I knew I should have taken him straight up to the manor."

"I'm sorry." I don't think saying "sorry" is

the same as making an admission of fault, and even if it is, at the moment I don't care.

"Don't tell me it was one of those things. Don't put the blame on me for missing that appointment. This is your bloody fault." Stewart glances around Reception. "Old Fox-Gifford's right—what's the point of having all this fancy equipment when you can't even use it properly? Look at you— it's all about the money to people like you."

Keep calm, I tell myself.

"First of all," I say, "we need to find out exactly why he died."

Stewart looms toward me, his face crimson with fury. "He died because of your bloody negligence."

"I'd like to carry out a postmortem," I say, refusing to back off.

"I bet you would, but I'm not going to give you the chance to cover up your mistakes." Stewart pulls his mobile from his pocket. "I'm going to get Alex to do it."

I wait until he's arranged for Alex to meet him here as soon as he can. I offer him tea.

"No way," Stewart says. "It'd make me throw up."

"Would you like to see him?" My heart

knocks against my ribs with the hollow sound of a metronome.

Stewart fixes me with an icy stare. "What would I want to see him for? He's dead, isn't he? You fucking well killed him."

I'D ALREADY BEEN DREADING seeing Alex again, but these circumstances couldn't have been worse. I'm mortified.

"I came straightaway because I wanted to get it over with." Alex looks up from the cadaver on the bench in the prep room, a mask over his nose and mouth. "I've got a horse to vet for my mother tomorrow morning, a couple of farm calls, and a jumping clinic in the afternoon."

It was gone eleven by the time Alex arrived. He had a brief conversation with Stewart before Stewart left to go back to the farm to take over from his mother-in-law, whom he'd left looking after the boys.

"Is there anything else you need?" I ask curtly. I sent Izzy home as soon as I found her—she was hiding out in the dark on the old swing that hangs from the tree at the end of the garden.

Alex shakes his head.

"I'll leave you to it then . . ." I back away,

unfurling my hands and discovering the crescents of my nails imprinted in the flesh.

"You must stay," Alex says. "I don't want anyone accusing me of planting evidence."

"I'd never do that!" I exclaim, assuming he's referring to me in particular. Our eyes lock, and I wish that it wasn't like this. I wish I could rewind the past month and start again. No, make that the whole of my miserable life . . .

"You don't trust me," Alex says gruffly, and he returns to the task of removing the length of Cadbury's intestines from his body and spreading them across the bench. It isn't like *CSI*: it's far more messy.

Alex points at a section of gut. "There's no problem here where you made your original incision—it's healed well."

"I removed a plastic Spider-Man toy and a pair of pants," I say, as he keeps searching.

"Ah, here we are." I recognize the lift in Alex's voice at finding the answer—I don't blame him. I do the same myself. "There's a reaction in the gut wall here and here, and it's completely disintegrated here," he goes on. "That's allowed the gut contents to leak out and set up peritonitis. Once the infection got into the bloodstream, that was that."

"He must have died in agony." I can't even bring myself to look at Alex. Why didn't I see how ill Cadbury was? I try to dismiss a picture of the chocolate Lab bouncing into the consulting room on my first day at Otter House, how happy he was, how full of life . . . I can still feel the warmth in the skin he was supposed to grow into, and see the bright shine in his eyes.

"My theory is that Spider-Man is our murderer, so to speak," Alex says. "The plastic must have pierced the gut as he passed through." He drops his scalpel and forceps onto the bench. "I'd better make a record of what I've found, in case this goes any further."

"You mean, when Stewart sues me."

"I don't see why he should—there was nothing wrong with your surgery."

"I'd better call Stewart to give him the news," I say flatly.

"Let me handle it."

"I can do it."

"No, let me. He's a close friend of mine. I've known him since we were at school in

Talyton. We went to the primary school round the corner until my parents packed me off to boarding school." Alex glances toward the door. "I left my camera in Reception, along with my notebook. Would you fetch it, please?"

I return with his gear and stand back while he photographs Cadbury's remains, wincing as the flash from the camera lights the room like a scene from a black-and-white horror movie.

"He shouldn't have died"—my voice wavers as it catches in my throat—"I knew he wasn't well, but I didn't pursue it."

Alex slips his camera back in its case. "You can't blame yourself, Maz."

"But I do. When I sent him home, I was supposed to talk to Lynsey about taking some blood, but the baby came, and I completely forgot, and then Stewart was supposed to bring him back for a checkup . . . Oh, it's no use trying to find someone else to blame. It was my fault. I should have taken more care."

"Nobody's perfect. You can't get it right all of the time." Alex fishes about inside the empty cavity of the dog's belly—checking for missed swabs, I presume. "Stewart said you were out and about when he called this evening?" It's a question, not a statement.

"I went to see the morris dancing at the Talymill Inn, but I came straight back." I don't know why I feel I have to justify myself. "It took me no more than fifteen minutes, and Izzy was here before me to give first aid."

"Well, I can't find anything else here," Alex says. "Does Stewart want the body back?"

"I don't know. It was all so frantic, I didn't ask." I shrug. "Anyway, he wasn't in the mood to give me an answer."

"I'll tidy him up then, just in case."

I'm very grateful to Alex. I don't think I could bear it. I fetch a needle and some nylon so he can close up.

"I heard about the skimpy knickers, and that Frances practically delivered Lynsey's baby," Alex says.

"Almost. The paramedics arrived just in time." I try threading the needle to save Alex time, but I can't get the nylon through the eye.

"Allow me." Alex takes it from me, his fingers briefly touching mine. He threads it at the first attempt and starts on the task

of making Cadbury's body look present-
able.

"It's a bit of a cheek to ask," I begin after
a while, "but I was wondering if you would
consider taking Frances back."

"At the manor?" Alex frowns. "Why?"

I hesitate. Should I tell him? Why not?
He's going to know everything sooner or
later, I guess. Before I even realize, out it
all spills: my continuing conflict with Cheryl;
the state of Otter House's finances; having
to fire Frances; all the doubt, anxiety, and
pressure.

"I feel so isolated here," I say, near to
tears again.

"I'm sorry," Alex says.

"Sure," I say, and then I wish I hadn't
been so sharp.

"You should have said something
sooner. Contrary to popular opinion, I'm a
good listener."

"Thanks," I say grudgingly, because
somehow it's easier to deal with my feelings for Alex when I'm seeing him as a Fox-
Gifford and one of the Talyton Manor vets
than when I'm seeing him as he is now,
sounding thoughtful and kind. It's probably
all a front, part of a charm offensive to win

me round, then drop me in it, since I can't imagine he's going to keep this quiet.

"I try not to listen to gossip, but there have been rumors . . ." He pauses, thinking. "I can't give Frances her job back—we've managed remarkably well without her—but if I hear of anything suitable, I'll let you know."

"I don't know how I'm going to tell her . . ."

"Mmm," Alex says. "She's going to find life very hard—poor Frances. She practically supports her granddaughter—her son's a ne'er-do-well, always at the bookies. Her daughter-in-law does her best, but it's Frances who keeps them afloat." He sighs. "Oh dear, bit inappropriate of me to put it like that, considering how she lost her husband."

"How did she lose her husband?"

"He was a fisherman—his trawler went down in a storm. He drowned, along with his four crew." Alex shakes his head. "I'll never forget that night."

I remain silent, wondering how Frances must have felt when her husband didn't come home.

Alex ties and cuts the last knot, and rolls Cadbury onto his side, then—for my sake, perhaps—covers him over with a drape. He looks up, and I force myself to meet his gaze.

"Cheryl came crawling back to the manor," he says. "I thought you might like to know. I told her we weren't taking on any new clients."

"I suppose you saw the posters," I say, taken aback that Alex has been so quietly supportive. It's the last thing I thought he'd do.

"I couldn't miss them, could I? It's all right though—I made her take them down."

"How did you manage that?"

"We hold quite a few functions up at the manor every year." Alex strips off his gown and gloves and walks over to the sink to wash his hands. "I threatened not to order our cream teas from the Copper Kettle anymore, and she agreed to let the matter rest."

"Why did you do it? I mean, you didn't have to . . ."

"It's my duty to uphold the honor of the profession," Alex says with a glint in his eye, then, "Oh, Maz, I'm teasing. I did it for you."

"Me?"

"Yes, and I'm sorry about the other day," he goes on.

"I'm sorry too," I say. "I shouldn't have blamed you for what your father did."

Alex pulls some paper towels from the dispenser and walks back toward me, drying his hands. "Will you be okay?" he says softly.

I nod, not trusting myself to speak. If he keeps being nice to me right now, I'll burst into tears.

"I'll say good night then . . ." He moves closer, until I can clearly see the stubble on his cheeks and the shadows under his eyes. For someone who's always in such a hurry, he seems reluctant to leave.

"Good night, Alex," I say, mustering my emotions, "and thank you. For everything you've done."

He reaches out his hand and cups my chin.

"What are you doing?" I stammer as he leans down and presses his lips against mine, sending an unexpected jolt right through me. Trembling, I respond as he deepens the kiss, pulling me against him. Alex Fox-Gifford is kissing me. It's shocking, breathtaking, amazing. And, in spite of everything, I don't want him to stop.

Suddenly, though, he pulls away, his breathing ragged as he rests his forehead against mine.

"Good night, Maz," he says, stepping right back. "I'll see myself out."

CHAPTER 14

I Don't Like Mondays

I DON'T SLEEP. IF I'M NOT THINKING OF CAD-bury, I'm wondering about Alex and the kiss. Do I regret it? I think so, given that I suspect he's still with Eloise.

By morning, I have stomach cramps and my head aches. I don't feel up to facing anyone, but I have to. I'm the boss. It's up to me to rally Emma's team and keep Otter House going.

When I arrive downstairs, armed with a cup of strong coffee, I find Izzy in the prep room.

"Er, hi," I say. "How are you?"

She turns to me, her eyelids puffy from crying and lack of sleep. "How do you think?"

I nod, and thinking of Cadbury again, I realize that there's no sign of the body that I left on the bench last night, not knowing what else to do with it.

"Where's the, er, you know?" I ask, wondering—half hoping—that I've missed Stewart coming in to collect him.

"In the freezer."

"They haven't decided what they want to do with it," I point out gently.

"If they want him back, we'll have to put him outside to defrost. I can't have dead bodies littering up the practice." Izzy carries on with the clearing up, throwing instruments into the sink and slamming the autoclave door shut on the first load. I suspect her desire to hide the body has more to do with not wanting to be reminded of what happened. It also occurs to me that she blames me—in part, at least—for what happened.

"Can anyone join the party?" demands a voice from the prep room door.

Party? I turn. "Alex, hi . . ."

Behind me, Izzy starts swirling the instruments around the sink, sending up steam and tiny bubbles of detergent.

"You look terrible," Alex says.

"Thanks very much."

"I didn't mean it in a bad way, Maz. What I meant was . . ."

"It doesn't matter." I smile weakly. He's quite right. I've had no sleep. I have bags under my eyes the size of suitcases. On the other hand, lack of sleep seems to suit Alex. He doesn't appear to be having any regrets about kissing me when he's supposed to be going out with Eloise.

"It does." He rumples his hair, which is damp from a shower, I'd guess. "I was trying to pay you a compliment."

"I shouldn't worry if it's really that difficult." I step away from him, trying to keep my distance in front of Izzy, yet he moves in closer, keeping his gaze fixed on my face.

"Well"—he lowers his voice—"what I intended to say was that no matter how rough you look, you always look lovely to me."

I hear an instrument, a pair of scissors perhaps, clattering into the sink.

"Thank you," I say graciously, although I don't entirely believe him. "This way." I hurry Alex back into the corridor and along to the staff room, where we can talk out of Izzy's earshot.

"Did I embarrass you?" he asks.

"Yes, a bit."

"I'm sorry." He smiles and changes the subject. "Izzy's like a whirling dervish, isn't she? Chris Hunter was talking about her the other day—I was taking a look at a couple of his sheep and the new dog. Freddie, isn't it? According to Chris, you and Izzy saved Freddie's life."

"Yep." I know what he's doing—he's trying to make me feel better, but all it does is remind me of Cadbury and my role in his death. "Have you spoken to Stewart or Lynsey yet?"

"Yes, and I'm afraid Stewart isn't in the mood for any kind of reconciliation. He knows he's partly to blame, but he isn't ready to accept it."

I stare at the toes of my Crocs. What a bloody mess.

"He'll come round." Alex reaches out and strokes my arm. "I know you feel bad now, but it'll get better, Maz."

Thrilled by his touch and reluctant to do or say anything that would spoil the moment, I look up. Alex gazes at me, his gorgeous blue eyes wide with concern. My pulse kicks and leaps like a bucking donkey.

"I've done a lot worse," he says eventually, breaking the physical contact between us. "There was an occasion when I operated on the wrong leg."

"You what?" I can't believe it. Alex Fox-Gifford made a mistake?

"It was one of Fifi and Gloria's rescues—has no one told you this?"

I shake my head, and he continues, "I was supposed to be repairing a cruciate in a young crossbreed. I opened the joint to find the ligament intact."

"What did you do?" I say, surprised he got so far before realizing his error.

"Grovel, of course."

Try as I might, I can't see Alex groveling to anyone.

"I must have been distracted"—his lips curve into a grin—"must have been thinking about some girl."

I don't like to imagine him thinking about

some girl, not some girl other than me anyway, and especially if that girl's Eloise.

Alex glances at his watch. "I'd better be getting back to the manor."

"Thanks for dropping by," I say.

"That's okay. I had to pick up a prescription for my father anyway. He's laid up in bed. He isn't all bad," Alex goes on. "Since the bull got him, he's hardly been out of pain. He makes himself look busy, but the truth is he can't cope with the physical side of the job anymore. He isn't capable of much more than manning the phones, and putting his foot in it on the radio. Oh, and making a nuisance of himself. Much like yourself," he adds, smiling.

I smile back, feeling guilty that I've let Alex cheer me up when I've just lost a patient in such terrible circumstances.

I walk through to Reception with him, and he stops at the desk. "Good morning, Frances," he says.

"Hello, Alex." She touches the hollow at the base of her throat. "Such dreadful news about the Pitts' dog," she says, shaking her head.

"It could have happened to anyone,"

Alex says. He nods in my direction. "Good-bye, Maz."

"Alex, wait." I hasten after him toward the door. "Alex."

He hesitates. "What is it?" He drops his voice to a whisper. "I see you haven't plucked up the courage to fire Frances yet."

"I keep hoping that Nigel will find some extra money from somewhere, so we can afford to keep her on. I know she isn't the best receptionist in the world, but she means well." I pause. "Alex, did Stewart say what they wanted to do with the body?"

"They'd like cremation and the ashes back," he says. "If you don't mind, I'll leave that one with you. I'll see you around, Maz."

I wait until the door swings back behind him and then turn to Frances, hoping that I'll be saved from having to speak to her right now by a client turning up, or the phone ringing.

"I wonder if you'd mind coming to the office for a chat," I begin.

"Well, I'm not sure," Frances says. "Emma and Izzy don't like me to leave Reception when there's no one to cover for me."

"You're right," I say, looking around the empty waiting room. "We can talk here. It isn't exactly busy, is it? Which rather leads me into what I want to discuss with you."

"And what is that, Maz?" Frances gazes at me, her head tipped to one side like that of a dog expecting a juicy titbit. "I see young Mr. Fox-Gifford came to see you again. He seems to be spending rather a lot of time at Otter House."

"Frances, it's nothing to do with Alex," I say, slightly exasperated to find there's no way I can ease her gently into the idea that she's not going to be working here for much longer. "I'm so sorry, but I'm going to have to ask you to pack your things and leave the practice." I glance from the red rosette she's pinned on the notice board along with a photo of her and her winning chutney to the collection box for the families of fishermen lost at sea on her desk.

"Why?" she says, her expression grave in contrast with the joyful flowers on her tunic. "What for?"

"There's no money to pay your wages after this week. I really am sorry," I go on. To my horror, because I'd find it easier to handle the situation if she put up some kind of fight, she starts to weep, big tears rolling down her cheeks.

"I saw this coming," she says, and I'm just wondering how—whether she has supernatural powers—when I remember how she used to open the post. She must have seen the bills and the final demands. She grabs a tissue from the box she keeps for clients who are in distress.

"What am I going to do?" she sobs. "What are you going to do without me?"

"I don't know." I don't know anything about anything anymore.

BAD NEWS SPREADS FASTER than a tummy bug on a cruise ship in Talyton St. George. Stewart talks to everyone.

The driver who collects the milk from Barton Farm turns out to be married to the headmistress of Talyton Primary School, and the cowman has two sisters who are members of both the church and the WI. Within a week, the tale of Cadbury's fate has been repeated along the chain, twisted and elaborated, like a message in a game of Chinese whispers, until it is as if I had strung the poor dog up in front of a waiting room filled with people, taken a knife, and stabbed him directly through the heart.

A few days later, Mr. Brown drops by with Pippin.

"I haven't made an appointment," he says.

"That's all right," I tell him. I've plenty of time on my hands—I did have seven clients booked in, but five have canceled.

"I don't need one, as such. A word would do."

I show Mr. Brown and Pippin through to the consulting room, where Mr. Brown pats the table as if he expects the dog to jump the equivalent of the pole vault without a pole. I pick Pippin up, kiss him on his topknot, and stand him on the table myself.

"He's no better, Maz," Mr. Brown says mournfully.

"That's because we haven't put him on any treatment yet," I say brightly. "I've had the results from the sample we sent off, and they're all perfectly normal, so I suggest we put him on a course of anti-inflammatory medication."

"We've done all that before. Alex diagnosed inflammation without going to the trouble of taking samples. Do you know how long I had to wait in the rain the other morning for Pippin to spend his twopenny?"

I'm not omnipotent. I have no control over the weather. As for Pippin's bowels, I suggest a third opinion. "Mr. Brown," I say, "I've done all I can here. I suggest I refer Pippin to a specialist at one of the vet schools."

"Dear Pippin doesn't travel well. The motion . . ." Oh no, not more motions. I sigh inwardly as Mr. Brown goes on. "The motion of my vehicle, any vehicle, makes him bring up froth the color and consistency of a partially beaten egg." Mr. Brown stops to clear his throat. "Maz, I've been reading a book about homeopathy."

"I'm not sure . . . ," I begin. Not sure? Of course I'm sure. "I don't believe in homeopathy. I haven't seen any evidence to persuade me that it works."

"There has to be some truth in it," Mr. Brown says. "The library wouldn't stock books that aren't true, would they? It wouldn't be allowed."

"That seems a little naive, if you ask me."

"I'm not asking you," Mr. Brown says, ever so politely. "I'm telling you. For your information . . ." He takes a piece of paper out of his pocket, slips a pair of glasses on, and reads it aloud, every word. It's a

list of homeopathic remedies from pulsa-
tilla to sulfur. "I shall purchase these from
the pharmacy on the way home and start
Pippin on them at dinnertime, as long as
you think they'll do no harm."

I shrug my shoulders. "They'll certainly
do no harm." I give up. He's given up on
me. He's going to ignore my opinion and
buy them anyway.

"Thank you, Maz. You've been most
helpful." He slips his glasses off again, and
I breathe a sigh of relief that the "word" he
wanted with me is coming to an end. My
relief is short-lived.

"There is something else," he begins.

"Go on," I cut in.

"I've found a lump on Pippin's neck." He
fumbles through the dog's abundant coat.
"I tried to pull it off because I thought it
was a tick. Ah, here it is. I marked the hair
with a touch of my wife's nail polish so I
could find it again."

I take a look. "It's a wart, Mr. Brown,
nothing to worry about. I can remove it
surgically, if it bothers Pippin at all."

"I don't want to worry you with it, Maz.
My wife and I have discussed it at some
length, and we don't like the idea of Pippin

having surgery." He looks around the room and shudders as if imagining Cadbury's ghost. "We don't want to risk his life."

He doesn't trust me anymore, does he? He's lost faith.

"I'll phone Mrs. Wall—she'll wish it away for us," he goes on. "I assume you'll be leaving us when your colleague returns?"

"Yes." If not before, I muse, feeling sad that even Mr. Brown, whom I quite liked in spite of his long-windedness, seems to want to see the back of me as soon as possible. I watch him leave with Pippin at his side, thinking that there's nothing for me to stay for. For some reason a vision of Alex, scratched and weary, and holding Tripod in his arms, comes into my mind and refuses to budge.

The sooner I can leave Talyton St. George and return to civilization, the better. I'll be able to regain my sanity, and console myself with the thought that I won't have sold myself cheap. I shan't be responsible for another notch on Alex Fox-Gifford's bedpost. I shall be eligible for beatification: Saint Maz, the Unintentionally Virtuous.

Later I buy sandwiches, a Diet Coke, and a packet of custard creams in the Co-op, where I run into Gloria Brambles, struggling to put on a pair of fingerless gloves before she puts packets of frozen fish into a bicycle pannier.

"How's Ginge?" I ask. "He must be due to see me again very soon."

"Ah, I've put off bringing him because he hates the basket." I suspect it has more to do with what happened to Cadbury, I think, as she continues. "He seems so much better and I've got plenty of tablets left—the ones I collected after you rang me with the results of the blood tests."

"Are you sure you're giving him the right dose?" I say, pretty certain that the course of tablets should have finished by now.

"Quite sure," she says abruptly, and I back off, worried that she might just prod me with the end of her stick, which is laid across the belt beside the cash register. "I've had cats for more years than you've had hot breakfasts, young woman." She smiles, and her eyes turn to slits and her teeth slide forward. "I've heard a rumor you've had to give Frances the push."

I don't comment. I'm worried about Ginge, and if Gloria won't bring him to me, I'll have to go to her.

On the way back to Otter House, I pick up a paper in the newsagent's and join a queue of people trying to buy their way out of their ordinary lives with a pound on the lottery. Sarah, the woman behind the counter, snubs me. As I walk away, head down and feeling cut to the quick, I overhear one of the customers chatting with her husband.

"Serves them right for being greedy . . . milked Talyton's pet owners dry . . . outrageous . . . only a puppy he was . . ."

Clutching my burlap shopping bag— Talyton St. George is a plastic-bag-free zone—to my chest, I rush back to the practice. I look up at the scaffolding on the front of Otter House on which two of DJ's team are standing. (When DJ said he had a team of workers, I assumed he meant eleven men at least, but it's more like a fencing team: three max, including DJ, and only one ever works at a time.) Anyway, one wolf-whistles in my direction, and the other raises his National Pet Smile Week mug.

I don't wave back. I'm not in the mood for anything, even a little lighthearted flirting. It isn't just that Otter House Vets is on the verge of bankruptcy. No one trusts me with their pets. The town is against me. Izzy says we are mud in dog-walking circles. Old Fox-Gifford writes about professional negligence in purely hypothetical terms in his column in the *Vet News.*

What can I do? What difference will a couple of puppy parties make?

Sighing, I push the door open and enter Reception, where Izzy is on the phone. She looks up, covering the mouthpiece with her hand.

"It's Edie," she says. "Clive's digging the hole."

My heart sinks even further. That can mean only one thing. "Tell her we'll head over now."

"What about the phones?" Izzy says rather sharply. "I can't be in two places at once."

"We'll have to put them through to my mobile," I say, collecting my stethoscope and visit case. "Let's go."

"You have checked you've got enough of the blue juice?" Izzy says. "Emma always makes sure she has enough of everything before she leaves, so she doesn't have to dash back. It doesn't do to end up with a patient that's only half-dead."

Sighing inwardly, I open up the visit case. I was right. Izzy doesn't trust me. She tolerates me because I'm Emma's friend. It makes for an increasingly strained working relationship, one that I couldn't put up with forever.

I drive Izzy to the Talymill Inn, a little surprised that Edie and Clive didn't call Talyton Manor Vets instead. I can't believe they haven't heard about Blueboy, even if they haven't caught up with what happened to Cadbury yet, which must mean they still trust me to do my best for Robbie. It isn't fair that I'm being ostracized by the pet owners of Talyton St. George. I'm experienced, caring, and I put my patients first. I'm a good vet, and I'm going to make sure I prove to everyone that I don't deserve to be treated like this.

As I drive alongside the river, I glance at Izzy. Her eyes are fixed straight ahead. Every so often recently I've noticed a small smile playing on her lips. Not only that, she's started using mascara—not scary black but a soft touch of blue.

"How's Chris?" I ask gently.

"What do you mean?"

"You and him? Are you . . . ? You must

be. You aren't going round to the farm just to visit Freddie, are you?"

"He's really nice," she says.

"Nice?"

She touches her throat, her skin scarlet. "More than nice . . ."

I drive on. The sun is high in the sky on a perfect summer's day. Lucky Izzy, I think.

"Oh, I forgot to mention that Alex Fox-Gifford called in to ask for a couple of sets of notes," Izzy says. "I didn't think there'd be any need to worry about clearing it with you."

"He didn't, er"—my throat seems to have gone dry—"ask to speak to me at all?"

"No, although he did ask after Frances," Izzy says matter-of-factly, and I wonder if he's avoiding me.

"Have you heard from Frances at all?" I say.

"I ran into her in the Co-op the other day. She's looking for another job, but there isn't much out there." Izzy pauses. "She says she misses us."

"But she does have lots of friends in the WI and the church," I say hopefully, as I turn in to the car park at the Talymill Inn. I hate to think of Frances struggling on alone.

"I suppose she's got more time to spend with her granddaughter too."

"I guess so," Izzy says, unfastening her seat belt, "but I don't think it's the same."

When we get out of the car, I can hear the ominous ring of a shovel against hard ground, reminding me of why we are here. Edie shows us through to the private garden behind the pub.

"Clive, love," Edie calls across the lawn to where Clive stands in the shade of a tree, stripped to the waist and with his back to us. "Maz is here."

He tips a shovelful of earth onto the pile beside him, throws down the shovel, and slowly turns to face us. Robbie, I notice, lies beside him.

We walk over, joining them alongside a hole about three feet deep and one dog long. Robbie barks, lifts himself onto his front legs, then tries to haul himself up, but his back end slides along behind him. Panting with the effort, he collapses again. All he can do is raise his head and look up at Clive as if to say, "Do something," then, worse still, he looks at me as if he knows something's up, as if he knows what's coming . . .

I always tell my clients that they'll know when it's time. They might deliberate for days or weeks. They might make a decision, then waver, but there comes a time when they are certain. "It's time for him to go, Maz," they say, "It's time to cross the rainbow bridge," or "I'd like you to do the necessary, to put him to sleep, to put him out of his misery." Sometimes they don't say anything at all.

Clive faces me, his hands clasped together, shoulders sagging, and beads of sweat trickling down his forehead.

"Are you sure?" I ask quietly.

"His front end's still working, but his back end's useless. He's lost his dignity, lying in his own mess. I can't bear to see him struggle anymore." Clive turns to Edie.

"Come on, love." Edie touches her husband's shoulder. "You've made the decision—let's not keep Maz any longer . . ."

"Take as long as you need," I say. Whatever else has happened, I want this, more than anything, to be right.

A sob escapes Clive's lips. "I'm not sure I can go through with it."

"You don't have to stay . . ."

Clive stumbles to his knees, hugs Robbie's ears to his head, and buries his face in his fur. "I'll stay," he mutters. "I owe you that, son."

Izzy and I join Clive and his dog on the ground. Izzy hands me a swab and syringe from the visit case and, without speaking, she raises the vein in Robbie's front leg.

Murmuring his name, I slip the tip of the needle into the vein and pull back gently, bringing blood swirling into the syringe. We're in. I press the plunger, and Robbie gives out one last sigh before his breathing stops and his eyes go blank.

"He's gone," I say quietly, removing the needle at the same time as Izzy covers the injection site with cotton wool and sticky tape. Clive lays Robbie's head across his knees and removes his collar. His hands glisten in the shaft of sunlight that glances through the trees. A drift of rose petals falls across the lawn. One catches in Robbie's coat. A lump catches in my throat.

There's a long pause. A breeze rustles through the trees, the river laps at the timbers of a small landing stage at the end of the lawn, and a bee hovers above a clump of wild strawberry flowers. Robbie's struggle is over.

Izzy offers Edie a tissue, then takes one for herself and wipes her eyes. As for me, I swallow hard and blink a few times while I pretend to refit the shield onto the needle. I stand up and rejoin Edie. Clive keeps his head bowed over Robbie's muzzle.

I look from Robbie to the hole and back.

"Can we help, Edie?" I say.

"Clive'll deal with it. When he's ready. We'll go inside?"

Izzy and I stay for cold drinks, sitting with Edie at a table close to the bar. Above Izzy's head is a photo of a much younger, slimmer Clive with Robbie at his side, being presented with an award for bravery.

Edie follows my gaze as I look at it.

"I'll miss the old dog," she says, choking up, "but—I hate to admit it—I'm relieved it's all over and we don't have to watch him suffer anymore, whereas Clive . . . He and Robbie were best mates. I don't know how he's going to cope." She stares into what's left of her drink (vodka with a splash of orange juice, I'd guess) and swirls it around the bottom of her glass. "Don't get me wrong. I was very fond of Robbie, but for me he was always a dog, not a person."

"You can never tell how it'll hit you, losing a pet," I say.

"Clive'll never have another one," Edie goes on. "He's adamant."

"Maybe he'll change his mind eventually." I'm annoyed with myself for offering platitudes. Why should he change his mind? I haven't changed mine about never having another cat. Like Robbie, King was a one-off.

On the way back to Otter House, Izzy sits in the passenger seat, hugging the bottles of wine that Edie forced upon us in way of thanks.

"I hope Clive's going to be all right," I say.

"Of course he'll be all right. He'll have to get on with it—he has a pub to run."

"What kind of bereavement counselor would you make?"

"A practical one." Izzy reaches across and turns up the radio.

Recognizing the track, I tighten my grip on the wheel—it's the Killers.

CHAPTER 15

Sanctuary

I WORRY ABOUT CLIVE FOR THE NEXT COUPLE of days. Even in the short time that's passed, I feel as if Clive's become more of a friend than a client. I try to focus on work: an anorexic tortoise, a budgie with an overgrown beak, and a spaniel with a heart murmur who can no longer keep up with his master on their cross-country runs. It keeps me distracted, but it isn't enough to keep Otter House solvent.

I've just finished a cat spay when Izzy bursts back into the room. The look on her face tells me she has more bad news.

"Maz, that was Nigel on the phone. He

says to warn you that the bailiffs are coming in tomorrow to seize some of the kit." Izzy's voice falters. "The X-ray machine and the practice car . . ."

"They can't do that. Emma isn't here. Surely they have to speak to her first."

"I wonder if this is what she wanted all along, to be away when it all kicked off," Izzy says quietly. "She was a fantastic boss at first, really keen and enthusiastic, but over the past year or so she seemed to lose it. I don't know why. She seemed preoccupied, less in control, but I thought she was coping. Maz, I feel so let down."

"I don't believe she expected it to go pear-shaped while she was away." Emma's my best friend—she wouldn't have left me in the lurch like this either, not deliberately. "Izzy, it was a bad situation to begin with, but I've made it worse."

"Why didn't she ask Ben to help?" Izzy says. "He's a doctor—he must be loaded."

"Emma has her pride. There's nothing she can't do. At least, that's how it used to be." My instinct is to bail her out, but she's in debt to the tune of thousands of pounds, not hundreds, and I don't think even Ben could have helped. I make up my mind. I know I planned to stay to prove the pet owners of Talyton St. George wrong, to show them I really am a good vet, but it now seems impossible. We can manage to keep going without the car, but not the X-ray machine.

"We close the practice down tonight," I go on.

"Close Otter House?" Izzy stares at me, her expression one of desolation. "What about our patients? What will they do without us?"

"I have no choice, Izzy," I say firmly. "I'll contact Talyton Manor Vets and make sure they can take on more clients. If they can't, I'll check with practices further afield. Just as important, I'll make sure you receive your wages in full, and write you a great reference to help you find another job."

"What a complete and utter disaster," Izzy sighs.

"I'm really sorry, Izzy," I say. "I'll get in touch with Emma as soon as I can, and ask her to come back. In the meantime, I've got a couple of loose ends to tie up . . ."

I text Emma, asking her to call me ASAP, then behind Frances's desk—which, I have to remind myself, isn't Frances's desk anymore—I find the last of Emma's yellow Post-it notes: condolence cards. I take a card out of the drawer. There's a picture on it of a black Labrador, which doesn't seem appropriate, so I nab a piece of printer paper instead and write a short letter, stick it in an envelope, pick up some more of Ginge's tablets and my car keys, and head out again.

"Call me if you need me, Izzy," I tell her on my way out.

"Where are you going?"

"To the Talymill Inn."

"You're not taking to drink already?" she says. I think she's only half joking.

"Not yet. I'm going to see Clive."

The Talymill Inn is overrun with grockles—probably too late now to have picked up the local lingo—who've stopped on their way to the beach to wait for a break in the weather. I squeeze the car into a space be-tween a motor home and a minivan with a stripy windbreak and surfboards tied to the roof bars.

Inside, Edie looks up from behind the bar as I approach.

"Hi," she says, forcing a smile. "I as-

sume you're here to collect your stethoscope."

"I wondered where I'd left it—I've been
using one of Emma's." I pause. "Actually, I
came to see Clive."

"You'll be lucky to get anything out of
him—he's gone mad." Edie runs her hand
through her hair. "He's talking about packing it all in, just as the business is looking
up. Last month the pub broke even for the
very first time."

"He's bound to be depressed. Perhaps
he should speak to someone?"

"You mean a doctor?" Edie shakes her
head. "He won't even talk to me about it. I
can't see him talking to a stranger."

"Er, where is he?"

Edie lifts the board to let me behind the
bar and shows me along the corridor past
the kitchen and out to the private garden.
I stop on the back doorstep. Clive is arranging a blue tarpaulin over Robbie's
grave, weighing down the corners with
stones.

"Clive," I call softly.

He turns to face me, showing no surprise that I'm here.

"I couldn't bear the thought of him getting wet," he mutters. "Bloody stupid, isn't it?"

"I don't think so." What can I say? Sorry? It'll get better with time? I start to peel up the front of my T-shirt. "I'll show you my scar."

Clive raises his eyebrows. "Are you sure?"

"I've always believed in the principle that the showing of one scar deserves another." I reveal a couple of inches of my midriff.

"That isn't a scar," Clive says haltingly. "That's a tattoo." He tips his head slightly to one side. "Quite a fetching tattoo, at that."

"I had it done on impulse, the day I heard that my cat died."

Jack Wilson is retired now, but I visit him and his wife when I can. King passed away peacefully soon after my last visit, at the age of eighteen, under the apple tree Jack chose as his final resting place, which is why I decided to have an apple with an arrow through it tattooed on my belly.

"Did it hurt?" asks Clive.

"Yes, but I needed it to hurt."

He nods as if he understands. "And now?"

"It hurts if I think about it too much—it isn't just about King, it's about the memories I have when I think of him, family stuff . . ."

"I know what you mean—with Robbie, it's like the end of an era, the end of my old life up in London, the job."

"Edie says you're thinking of giving it all up."

Clive shrugs. "That's how I feel at the moment, but I guess it'll pass."

The wind takes a deep breath and catches one corner of the tarpaulin, raising it off the bare earth. I pick up a stray half brick from the path and hand it over to Clive. Silently, he places it on the tarpaulin, then turns to me. "Thanks, Maz. Thanks for coming."

As I leave, I think, Who am I to lecture anyone about not giving up?

Back in the car, I remember that I still have my condolence letter in my pocket. I take it out, tear it up, and drop the pieces in the glove box before making my way to Buttercross Cottage, Gloria's place.

I'm not ready to face Stewart yet, although I will call on him later today, or tomorrow, before I leave Talyton for good.

And it will be for good, because I don't want to be reminded of my failures. Actually, I'm lying to myself. What I mean is I don't want to be reminded of Alex and what might have been . . .

I find myself traveling down a particularly narrow and twisty lane, which peters out into no more than a farm track with grass growing along the middle of it. The ruts deepen, the hedgerows press in from either side, and the overhanging branches of trees grope at my car's paintwork until the track becomes impassable. I pull into a gateway and walk the rest of the way down a slope where the track opens out onto an expanse of rough lawn in front of a house. The rain has stopped again, leaving the fresh scent of bruised grass and wet earth in the air, and water droplets that sparkle like diamonds scattered through the hedges.

To my left is a wood, Longdogs Copse I assume, and to the right is a small paddock that contains a little grass, a tin bath of green soup, two cracked buckets on their sides, and two elderly donkeys, one wearing a head collar with FRISKY on it and the other with feet so overgrown that it looks as if he's wearing slippers.

The house is nothing like the cottages you see on the boxes of Devon fudge in the window of the gift shop. There's grass growing out of the dark, moldy thatch, and the chimney stack leans at an almost impossible angle. The walls have sloughed off their outer layers like dead skin, leaving earthy scars of cob and brick repairs. The small garden at the front is a tangle of honeysuckle, roses, raspberry canes, and brambles. One of the small windows upstairs has been carelessly boarded up, and splinters of glass glint like tears on the path below.

The front door can't have been painted for years, and when it was last done the job was left unfinished, as if the painter didn't care. The top half is a grimy white, the texture of crackled glaze, while the bottom half is scumbled blue, as if someone's taken a dry paintbrush to it. On the doorstep, beside a crate of empty milk bottles, an ancient feline, lying on its chest like the Sphinx, guards a stack of damp circulars, newspapers, and post. It isn't Ginge.

As soon as I rap at the door, there's a riot of barking and something repeatedly hurls itself at the other side. From the depths of the cottage, maybe from the buildings beyond, another dog joins in, howling, then another, and another.

I knock again. The barking continues, but no one answers. I can't believe that Gloria doesn't know I'm here with that racket going on. I step aside and press my nose to the window. Through a layer of dust and a shabby net curtain, I can see a small, ghostlike figure in pale robes approaching.

"Gloria," I call. "It's Maz, Maz the vet."

The hinges groan and the wood scrapes across the step as she opens the door a mere inch or two. Something snuffles about at her feet.

"I've brought Ginge's tablets." I hold out the packet. A gnarled hand reaches for them, but I snatch them back. "Gloria, I'd like to come in for a minute."

One eye gleams from the darkness beyond. "Another time. I'm not dressed."

"I can wait."

"Oh?"

"I've got some biscuits in the car." I flung

them in, thinking I might have them instead of lunch. "I'll fetch them while you sort yourself out, then perhaps we can share them over a coffee."

"I'm very busy . . . I haven't fed the dogs yet."

"Let me give you a hand." I pause. "Gloria, I really need to see Ginge. Today."

"Oh, all right. Go and fetch those biscuits. I'll put the kettle on," she says and slams the door shut.

Ten minutes later she's back at the door, dressed in a dark green housecoat with stains down the front, fleece-lined boots, and stockings the color and sheen of caramel, an outfit that is apparently satisfactory for receiving a visitor.

"Come in, young woman," she says grudgingly, eyeing the packet of custard creams I've fetched from the car. "I've shut the dogs out."

I take a step across the threshold. The stench is overwhelming. Even when I breathe through my mouth so I can't smell it, I can still taste it. Like a wine connoisseur, I can't help analyzing the flavor: cat's pee and dog's mess, talc, smoking coals, the vanilla scent of old books, undertones of mildew and dry rot, with an added hint of blocked drains. All in all, it's like licking out a pot of fish paste that's gone off.

I follow Gloria as she shuffles off down the hallway, passing a coat stand on which hangs a long coat and a bowler hat, both gray with dust.

"They belonged to my husband." She waves one hand toward them. "I don't like to get rid of anything."

The sitting room is stacked with piles of newspapers and books, some of which almost reach the low beamed ceiling like enormous stalagmites. There's a sofa, a couple of chairs, a log smoking in the grate—in spite of the fact it's summer—and a rug in front of the fire. Gradually, my eyes become accustomed to the gloomy conditions and I start to make out other shapes. The rug is moving. Everything is breathing and shifting about. The space is alive with cats: a black cat feeds her litter of kittens; a white cat sits on top of one of the stacks, washing its face; on the sofa, a silver tabby uncurls itself, stretches, then curls up again.

How many are there? Five? Ten? I lose count.

"Take a seat if you can find one." Gloria

clicks her tongue and mews, shooing the silver tabby off the sofa and pushing the papers and rubbish along to make me a space. When I don't move, she says, "Sit!" sharply, as if she's talking to a dog.

I sit down carefully and wait for Gloria to fetch the coffee, a little unnerved by the number of pairs of reflective eyes staring at me. The possessor of a particularly striking green pair, a black cat, moves closer and jumps lightly onto my lap. I tickle its chin and run my hand along its back. It's quite skinny and scabby, but I couldn't honestly say that it was a welfare case. I lean down and scratch my ankle. How do you define suffering anyway?

"I forgot to ask how you take your coffee," Gloria says, returning with a tray of cups and saucers and silver spoons.

"Black's fine. Black, no sugar." It doesn't really matter. I have no desire to drink it. I dread to imagine what state the kitchen is in.

Gloria puts the tray on the pile of old newspapers closest to me, hands me a cup, and takes the other for herself. She tips another two cats off the armchair nearest the fireplace and sits down.

I scratch my ankle again.

While Gloria concentrates on eating the biscuits, I take a surreptitious look at the carpet—it's literally jumping with fleas, and I'm being eaten alive, yet Gloria is oblivious.

I don't know where she puts the biscuits, but within minutes they've disappeared. She creases the packet, making careful folds as if she's doing origami, then, appearing to lose patience, crumples it into a ball, which she drops onto the floor at her feet. The black cat with the bright eyes pounces on it, picks it up, and carries it away, tail held high.

I feel as though I should start a conversation, but I don't know what to say. I can hardly say, "Nice place you have here," can I?

"That's Tom." Gloria nods toward a photograph on top of the mantelpiece, which is cluttered with ornaments. "That was taken on our wedding day. And these"—she pulls herself out of the chair and points to some urns—"these are the dogs we had together." She picks one up, rubs it on her sleeve, and peers at the plaque on the front. "I can't read it." She holds it in front of me. "What does that say?"

"Julius."

"Dear Julius. He was Tom's favorite, a handsome springer spaniel who had a penchant for chewing Tom's slippers." She puts Julius back and picks up another urn, but I'm more concerned with the living than with the dead. The more I see here, the more I want to see Ginge.

Without a by-your-leave, I collect up the cups and take them through to the kitchen. It looks like a scene from *How Clean Is Your House?* before Kim and Aggie get their rubber gloves on. There are cats on the cooktop, the work surfaces, and the windowsill. One licks at the fat congealed in a frying pan, and another investigates the fridge, the door of which is propped open by a dish that seethes with flies.

"How many cats do you have altogether, Gloria?"

She's right behind me and not looking too happy at my intrusion.

"Twenty-seven, not including the kittens," she says eventually. "That's just the house cats. There's a small cattery out the back. I have another eleven out there. And then there are the ferals—I've lost count of them."

"I'd like to see the cattery."

"There's no need for you to waste your time." Gloria's neck stiffens. "Why exactly are you here?"

"I told you—I've brought Ginge's tablets. I thought I'd save you a trip," I say lamely. I edge around the kitchen, wondering how I can get out through the back door to see what horrors lie behind it. It's very noble of Gloria to have rescued all these animals, but it's beginning to look as if they now need to be rescued from Gloria.

She blocks my way.

"Go back to your surgery, young woman!" Her voice rises to a plaintive wail, like that of a cat in distress. "I'll call the police."

"Not a good idea, Gloria. The first thing they'll do when they see the state of this place is call the RSPCA." It occurs to me that is exactly what I should do, but something in Gloria's eyes holds me back. It's heartbreaking, like the gaze of an animal caught in a snare. I notice that she's powdered not only her face and her hair but her earrings too. "I want to help you."

I push past her and open the back door, ignoring her appeals to leave her alone. Two terriers, a white Westie and a black Scottie, come flying at me from the other side of a small concrete yard, jumping up and barking. They're over the moon to see me, as if they know I hold the key to their escape.

"You're all mouth and no trousers, aren't you?" I squat down beside them. "Who are they?"

"Mac and Tosh." Gloria's voice is thick with resentment. "Boys, go to bed." Wagging the stumps of their tails, they retreat to a cardboard box filled with skanky newspaper. "You'll have to excuse the mess," she goes on. "I haven't had time to clean up after them yet today."

Not just today, I suspect, observing the scummy water bowl and heaps of dog dirt, skidded through here and there with paw prints. It's disgusting. Squalid.

"They've been here with me for about eighteen months. They came from a broken home. Terribly sad."

"You couldn't find new homes for them?" I say, my throat tightening with a different kind of sadness. The yard is like a prison. Their only contact with the outside world is

Gloria, an old woman who can't possibly give them the attention and walks they need. I've no doubt she loves them, but . . .

"Fifi—ugh, I can't stand that woman— she wanted to split them up, but I couldn't bear it. It would have broken their little hearts to be separated. You may mock, but they've been together since they were eight weeks old."

"I'm not mocking." I stand up again. "Now, where's the cattery?"

"That's it." Gloria waves her hand dismissively toward the wall of concrete blocks straight ahead of us. "There, you've got what you wanted. You've seen it."

"Gloria, I'm not stupid."

"I would show you around, but I seem to have mislaid the key"—she pats the pockets on her housecoat—"and you must be needed back at the surgery by now."

"You'd better un-mislay it," I tell her. "I'm going to fetch the visit case from the car. If nothing else, the little black cat needs treatment for its skin, Mac's claws could do with a trim, and we need to think of the best way to wipe out all those fleas."

"Fleas? I don't have fleas."

"You don't, but your carpets are alive

with them. I've seen kittens die from anemia with that level of infestation."

Alternately I bully and cajole her, and ten minutes later, after I've fetched the visit case, the key miraculously appears from the depths of her pocket. Gloria fiddles with the padlock on the bolt of the door into a long, low building behind the yard. The sound of howling crescendos. I try to look through the tiny window to the side, but the view's blocked by a bag of animal feed.

"I have to keep the dogs and cats in the same building at the moment because the roof of the old kennels leaks," Gloria explains. Finally, the padlock comes away and she pushes the door open. "Good morning, my darlings," she coos, and the dogs go quiet.

It's afternoon, I want to say, and it's a bit late for breakfast.

"How often do you feed them?"

"Every day. I go without so that my animals are fed." Gloria fumbles at the wall, and a light comes on. "Come inside, if you must."

"I must." If the smell in the house was bad, this is ten times worse. I run straight back outside and throw up in the grass by the door. Trying to hide my embarrassment and find a way to breathe through the stench, I tuck my nose into my top and head back in. Gloria seems oblivious to my struggle and the smell.

She shows me into the first small room off the main corridor.

"This is where I wash up and prepare the dinners." She waves vaguely at the sink, which is stacked with bowls; a sack of rubbish, which spews its foul contents across the floor; and a workbench crowded with tanks and cages, some on top of each other like slum tenements. Something inside one of the cages starts to rattle: a gerbil on a wheel. When I look closer, I discover that Gloria's retreat for small furries is running at 100 percent occupancy.

"You see," says Gloria. "They all have food and water."

It's true, although the water in the various bottles and dishes doesn't look too clean and there seem to be more husks than seeds in the various receptacles that she's using as food containers.

"I clean everyone out at least once a week, unless I'm not feeling up to it," Gloria goes on. "I haven't been so good recently."

"Don't you have help?"

"I don't need help. Fifi said I'd never man-age without her and Talyton Animal Res-cue, but I manage perfectly well—better, in fact, without her constant interference. And I can manage without your help too. I haven't asked for it."

"Let's take a look at the rest now," I say, ignoring her protests. Somewhat subdued, Gloria leads me back into the corridor, which is lined with walk-in cages on either side. The building is well-constructed, each cage having access to an outside run, but it's showing signs of neglect.

The occupant of the first cage stands on its hind legs and starts mewing and batting at the wire in the door. There's a bowl of water and a litter tray overflowing with wet clay. There's an empty washing-up bowl on the stage above its head, which I assume is where it sleeps.

The occupant of the next cage is less fortunate. It's a scrawny tortoiseshell cat lying flat out on her side, hardly breathing, her eyes staring into the corner where a shaft of sunlight enters the building through a gap between the walls and the roof. As I unbolt the door and enter, she utters the low howl of distress of an animal that's too far gone.

What a miserable way to end your life, I think as I turn to Gloria, my voice grating in my throat. "What's going on here?"

"That's my Molly." Her voice quavers. "She's been sick for a while, but she seemed so peaceful that I didn't want to disturb her. I knew what you'd say if I brought her to the surgery . . ."

"I think it's time to let Molly go, don't you?" I open the visit case. "Have you got a blanket or towel handy, Gloria?"

She fetches a rather grubby towel, and I pick Molly up and wrap her in it, leaving her head and front legs exposed. I hand her over to Gloria, who holds her while I give her the final injection and a merciful release.

"I wish they'd close their little eyes." Gloria tries to hold the cat's eyelids closed, but they won't stay.

"I'll take her back to the surgery with me."

"Not straightaway." Gloria nuzzles the dead cat, staring up at me as if I'm the madwoman around here. "I like to spend some time saying good-bye first. When I had help, I used to bury them in the garden." She covers the body with the towel and leaves it beside the cage, by which time I've ascertained that there are another fourteen cats imprisoned in the cattery and, beyond that, seven dogs. At least the rest are on all four paws, so to speak.

Five of the dogs come trotting up to the barriers to sniff me, wagging their tails. Two hang back, a beautiful white German shepherd and a big bully-boy of a boxer, who starts to move toward me then stops, slumps onto his bottom, and scratches furiously at his ear, crying out at the same time.

"Who's that, Gloria?"

"The German shepherd's called Petra."

"And the boxer?"

"Ugli-dog, I call him. I've had him here so long he's almost part of the furniture. He's on a herbal tincture for his skin condition—Mrs. Wall prescribes it."

I stare through the chicken wire. Ugli-dog is a mess. His skin is scarred and angry, and he's so thin you can make out the detail of his skeleton.

"Old Mr. Fox-Gifford said, 'Gloria, that dog's a hopeless case,'" she says, steadying herself against the cage. I realize Gloria looks as forlorn and underfed as Ugli-dog.

"The injections he gave him made him ill, so we stopped them altogether," she goes on.

"Doesn't Fox-Gifford ever ask how he is?" I put my fingers up to the wire. Ugli-dog sniffs at them, then gives them a friendly lick.

"I wouldn't expect anyone to remember to ask after all my animals," Gloria says. "Would you?"

"I would if he'd been in this state when I last saw him." As a vet, I'd feel some responsibility for his welfare.

"I don't recall him ever being quite as bad as this . . . Still, you can't put an animal down because they have bad skin, can you?"

"Gloria, we must have a proper talk—this situation can't go on. I'm going to take Ugli-dog back to the surgery so I can have a good look at him and treat him accordingly. He needs a bath and some food, if nothing else."

"You can't do that." She blinks back tears, and whereas when I first met her I found her a small but forbidding figure, she strikes me now as rather pathetic as she whines, "You can't take him away from me."

"I have no choice." I harden my heart. I can imagine what it's like to have your pets taken away—to many people pets are family. To some it would be like giving up their children, and I suspect that is how it seems to Gloria, who appears to have few friends.

"Maz, I thought you of all people would understand. I thought you were an animal lover."

"I am, which is why I can't stand by and watch things get any worse."

"You're planning to take them all away from me, aren't you? I'll never let them go," Gloria says, pushing her way between me and Ugli-dog. "Over my dead body."

"All I'm going to do today is take Ugli-dog for treatment and call Fifi to get you some help," I continue firmly. "You need someone to help fix your roof, walk the dogs, and clean up in here."

Gloria opens her mouth to argue with me, but I stop her before she can start. "You're an intelligent woman. Surely you can see you aren't coping?"

She stares at me. Mute. Humiliated. Defeated. In fact, I don't like to leave her on her own.

CATHY WOODMAN

"Is there someone who can come and sit with you?"

"There's no one left," she says weakly. "All I have is my animals."

"Why don't I help you feed this lot and tidy up a bit, then I'll be back tomorrow." I reach out my hand, but she shrinks away from my touch. "I promise you, we'll sort this out." I leave my stethoscope behind, deliberately this time.

"YOU'VE BEEN HOURS," Izzy says when I return to Otter House with Ugli-dog in tow. I sat him in the footwell of the passenger seat in my car—he didn't seem to mind.

Izzy looks at the dog. "What have we here?"

"A bit of a crisis, I think. I'm going to take some skin scrapings, hair pluckings, a biopsy, and blood, and then he'll need a bath." Ugli-dog wags his stump of a tail. "I'm going to need a bath too. I stink."

I describe the situation at Gloria's to Izzy as I take skin scrapings from various parts of Ugli-dog's anatomy: his thickened, crusted ears; his greasy, spotty back; and the red-raw webs between his toes.

"I didn't even get to see Ginge. Gloria

says he's always out in the fields, which means he only gets his medication when he turns up, and then she gives him extra to make up for the doses he's missed. I can't see how he's ever going to get better."

"What are you going to do?" Izzy takes the microscope out of the cupboard under the bench and sets it up on top. "I can call Andrea if you like—she's our local RSPCA inspector."

"No, not yet. I'm going to call Fifi first." It might be a little awkward seeing I wouldn't give her a better discount than Talyton Manor Vets, and I'm sure she's heard every detail of Blueboy's bad hair day and Cadbury's demise. But Fifi is Gloria's best hope of help without losing all her animals.

"Are you sure that's wise?"

"She and Talyton Animal Rescue must take some of the responsibility. They can't let their personal differences take precedence over the welfare of those animals." I pop Ugli-dog in a cage. "I've done what I can for now. None of them is in immediate danger. I'll arrange to meet Fifi and as many volunteers as she can round up tomorrow at Gloria's. That way, we can decide together which of the rescues can be rehomed and make arrangements to look after the rest."

"You mean you're going to leave some of them with Gloria?"

"One or two of the cats, maybe three, no more than she can care for properly."

"Maz, you're too soft." Suddenly, Izzy's face falls. "How on earth will she choose which ones to keep?"

"I want to give Gloria a chance, like she gave those rescues. I think it would kill her to lose them all."

"Look at poor Ugli-dog," Izzy says. "What kind of life has she given him?"

"What kind of life does Gloria have?" I counter. "She has no relatives, no friends, no one who cares whether she lives or dies. Imagine ending up like that." I have a quick look at Ugli-dog's skin and hair under the microscope, finding the mites that are causing his skin problem. "Ugh, it's mange. And I kissed him. I'm sure I kissed him."

"I'll get him started on the washes," Izzy says. "You go and phone Fifi."

"I DON'T SEE what I can do about it" is Fifi's immediate reaction. "Gloria's made it per-

fectly clear that I'm not welcome at Buttercross Cottage anymore."

"I'd hoped that Talyton Animal Rescue
would be able to help out, but if it's that
difficult, I'll have to speak to the RSPCA . . ."

"Oh?"

"It could reflect badly on you and your
committee, but I've run out of options."

"Oh no, there's no need to involve any
other organization," Fifi says quickly. "We're
more than able to handle any situation."

"It's a pity you didn't get a handle on
this one sooner," I point out.

"I admit that I should have kept an eye
on her. I should have insisted." Fifi pauses
for a millisecond. "I tell you what I'll do."

"No," I cut in, "I'll tell you what I want you
to do. Come over to Otter House tomorrow at eleven, and we'll go up to Gloria's
with Izzy and any other helpers you can
rustle up."

"I'll go up there now," Fifi says.

"Please don't rush in. Promise me . . ."

"All right. I'll wait." Her voice brightens
a little. "What about Talyton Manor Vets?
I'm sure they'd help us."

"No, there's no need to involve the Fox-

Giffords," I say. "There's plenty of room here at Otter House."

"Oh? All right then. Well, I'll concentrate on rallying the troops and organizing supplies."

"Thanks, Fifi." I return the phone to Reception, where Tripod joins me, winding himself around my calves.

"You had a lucky escape ending up here, not at Gloria's," I tell him, at which my demons come howling back, reminding me that Cadbury wasn't so lucky.

I promise myself that I'll make up for my perceived failures and make the pet owners of Talyton St. George proud to have me as their vet until Emma gets back. I'll ensure all those animals at Gloria's so-called sanctuary are found good homes and treated well. To do that, there can be no more thoughts of closing Otter House down. Emma has still not returned my frantic calls, so like it or not I'm going to have to stay on in Talyton for a while longer, which means I'll have to get hold of the bank and sort out the payments on the X-ray machine at least.

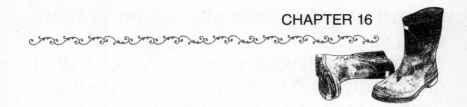

CHAPTER 16

It Really, Really Shouldn't Happen to a Vet

"I'M RUNNING OUT OF TIME, SO I'LL CUT TO THE chase." My heart leaps at the sound of Alex's voice. It's seven-thirty in the evening and the first time he's spoken to me since he kissed me. That was a whole week ago, and I want to give him a gentle telling-off for leaving it so long. However, there's something in his tone that makes me hesitate. "I've got a horse with colic, and I need to refer it to a hospital ASAP."

"I'm sorry, you've lost me . . ."

"Yeah, I guessed that some time ago. Listen, I need to ask you an enormous favor. I wouldn't normally dream of bothering you, but this is an emergency."

"I can take your calls for you," I offer grudgingly, "but I can't remember anything useful about cows and sheep."

I'm not sure Alex is really listening to me, because he continues, "My parents are up in London, I can't get hold of Lisa, my groom, and old Dickie Pommel is much the worse for wear in the Coach and Horses—"

"Well, can't Eloise help? She is your girlfriend after all," I interrupt.

"Eloise? My girlfriend?" I hear Alex make a half-choke, half-laugh snorting sound. "No way. It's nothing like that. She isn't my type at all; we're just good friends. We go back years. She's more like a sister. Now, I'm looking—no, begging—for someone to give me a hand getting Liberty over to the referral clinic at Westleigh."

"Liberty?"

"My horse."

"The show jumper?"

"Please, Maz. You're the only person left. You're my last resort."

I make up my mind. "Okay, put your phones through to us—Izzy will take the calls." At least, I'm pretty sure she will. She might not be my and Alex's biggest fan, but she'll do anything for an animal in distress.

"I'm up at the manor, in the yard."

"I'll be there in ten minutes."

"Thanks, Maz." Alex's voice seems to catch in his throat. "I owe you."

I PARK IN THE YARD beside the lorry that has TALYTON MANOR HORSES and a logo of a jumping horse printed in gold across its purple bodywork. The rear ramp is down, and there are lights on inside, in spite of the fact that it's only eight o'clock in the evening and the sun has yet to sink completely behind the hills that lie beyond the house.

I find Alex by the stable closest to the house. As I lean over the stable door to peer in, my hand brushes against his—it's the slightest touch, but it raises goose bumps over my skin and sends a tiny shiver of longing down my spine.

"How is she?" I ask.

"Not good." Alex opens the stable door and whistles quietly. "Steady there, girl," he murmurs, but the mare continues to pace tight circles in the straw, her coat dark with sweat, her nostrils flared with anxiety. She stops to paw at the ground and kick at her belly. "She's been down twice already—I can hardly bear to watch."

"What's the plan?" I ask.

"I'll stick some boots on her and load her up. As soon as she's in the lorry, you shut the gates behind her and fasten them quick. I don't want her throwing herself backward down the ramp."

"Have you given her anything?"

"An antispasmodic and a painkiller, but they aren't touching her."

I follow Alex into the stable. He clips a rope onto the mare's head collar and passes the other end to me. It feels odd to be holding a horse again—I'd forgotten how powerful they are.

"Keep her head up if you can," Alex says. "I don't want her going down again."

I hang on to the head collar. Gradually, Liberty lowers her head until her nose touches the straw. I lean against her shoulder, trying to haul her head up, and just as I think that I'm beaten, that she's going to go down, she tenses. A spasm grips her belly, and her front legs come up in a half rear, knocking me momentarily off-balance.

"Take care, Maz," Alex says, his voice gruff with concern.

"I'm okay." I stroke Liberty's neck, noting the dull expression in her eyes, and she calms down again, long enough for Alex to throw a set of travel boots—purple ones to match the livery of the horse trailer, I notice—on to protect her legs.

"I'll take her now." I pass Alex the rope, and he leads Liberty out of the stable and straight up into the lorry. Quickly, I shut the gates and the ramp behind her. So far, so good. I find myself able to breathe again until all hell breaks loose as Liberty starts throwing herself around and kicking out at the side of the lorry. I don't know what she's doing in there, but she manages to put a dent in the panel.

"I'd better get going before she demolishes the trailer," Alex says.

There's silence followed by another bang, which makes the whole lorry shake.

"I'm coming with you." I check the fastenings on the ramp. "I'll ride in the back."

"You shouldn't . . . ," Alex says hopefully.

"I know, but I can try to stop her going down and getting cast in the trailer," I point out. I gaze at him. His brow is furrowed with anxiety. I can see he's torn between protecting me and giving his horse the best chance of survival. He obviously cares for her very much, and I want to do this, because I care for him—and I can admit that now I know there's no Eloise. "Please, Alex."

"All right then, but make sure you keep the partition between you and the mare," he says. "I'll take it very slowly."

THE JOURNEY SEEMS to take forever, not only because I'm with a horse that's manic with fear and pain but also because I can't see out to get an idea of how far we've gone, how much longer it'll be until we get there.

Liberty leans back against the rope, which is fastened via a piece of baling twine to a metal ring set in the fabric of the lorry. Her head and neck are outstretched, as if one lurch of the vehicle might tear them apart. The veins stand out of her skin with the effort of bracing herself, front legs forward and hind legs underneath her belly.

I can see pools of sweat glistening on the rubber mats under her hooves. Her expression is desperate. She rolls her eyes, the whites gleaming in the artificial light, then utters a long, drawn-out groan.

"Hang on in there," I murmur as I try to keep my feet. I touch her ears—they're freezing—and make a quick check on her pulse. "It can't be far now."

The lorry slows right down and swings left. Liberty leaps forward in a panic and bashes her face against the partition.

"Steady there!" I'm all churned up inside. What if she goes down? Don't go there, I tell myself, dismissing an image of a dead horse being hoisted from the back of a lorry. Liberty pulls back on the rope again, blood pouring from her nostrils. Her limbs start to fold. Her back begins to sink.

"No! Get up, you stupid horse!" I bellow at her. "You have to stay up." I untie the rope and pull with all my weight on it to keep her head high. I pinch her nose and slap her neck. "You have to!"

Liberty rolls her eye in my direction. That's good. She knows I'm here.

It might be only ten more minutes, but it feels like ten hours before the lorry finally stops moving.

"Let's get her out of here," I hear Alex shout as he lowers the ramp. Two men, in jeans and green sweatshirts, open the gates and guide Liberty out with Alex at her head. I follow, my legs weak from the exertion of the journey, finding myself in a yard outside a modern building with a sign reading WESTLEIGH EQUINE HOSPITAL.

Immediately, we are surrounded. There are the two grooms, the vet with his stethoscope around his neck, his anesthetist, his houseman, and two nurses. Alex introduces me to the vet—he's called John and he's worked at Westleigh for the past four years. He has a firm, steady handshake; I hope it's the sign of a good surgeon.

"We have to go in. 'Watch and wait' is not an option," Alex says harshly, trying and failing to hide the fact that he's utterly distraught at the thought he might lose his special horse. "I don't think she'll make it, whatever we do."

"Our survival rates here at Westleigh are pretty good," John says. "Eighty percent of our surgical colics go on to make a full recovery."

I look at Alex, at the tension in the muscle in his cheek, and my throat tightens because I know he's thinking of the other one in five . . .

"I'll get you to fill in the paperwork, Alex," John says. "There's a viewing gallery in Theater One, if you'd like to stay and watch."

"I'm expecting to assist," Alex says.

"Oh, I don't know about that. I mean—"

"I won't interfere," Alex interrupts. He strokes Liberty's neck.

"It's our policy not to—"

"It's something I have to do."

"Okay," John says, apparently giving way to the steely determination in Alex's voice.

"Maz is coming too," Alex adds, in a tone that brooks no argument.

"All right. Let's take Liberty round to the stall and get her knocked out and prepped."

I check in with Izzy before I rejoin the team to scrub in for surgery. All's quiet at Otter House, and there's still no word from Emma.

The two grooms I saw earlier bring Liberty in on an automatic hoist, upside down with her legs hobbled together. The anesthetist attaches the ET tube onto the anesthetic machine and connects up the monitoring equipment. The grooms unfasten the hobbles and arrange Liberty on padded boxes and foam wedges, then the nurses clip the hair from her belly and clean her skin. Finally, John parades into the operating theater, tweaking the fingers of his surgical gloves. Alex follows, masked, gowned, and gloved, and wearing a surgical cap. All I can see are his eyes, dark with determination and focused on Liberty.

I stand aside, ready to help out if I'm needed. I can hardly bear to watch, yet as I stand at the edge of the circle cast by the surgery light above John's and Alex's heads, my eyes are drawn to the sight of the horse's gut ballooning out of her belly and the two men working together to unravel it.

I hear Alex's raised voice, see the taut movement of his hands as he makes a point rather forcefully during the operation. I don't know how long the surgery takes: two, maybe three hours. When I check the clock, it's gone eleven and John is closing the last layer, the mare's skin. I hear Alex finally exhale, and we step into the cool of the outer room.

"Allow me," Alex says, unfastening the tapes at the back of my gown and taking it from me.

"Thanks," I say.

He stands slightly to one side, his hands in his pockets, his face still etched with worry.

"The surgery went pretty well," I say, trying to cheer him up.

"Better than I'd expected," Alex says, but he doesn't sound terribly positive.

I guess he's right to be cautious. Nature didn't design horses to lie down for long periods of time under anesthetic. Liberty's made it through her operation, but there's still a chance that she'll never get up again.

ALEX AND I wait for a couple of hours outside the recovery stall where Liberty is thrashing about. I hate hearing the scuffle of her hooves on the matting that pads the floor and walls of the stall, and the hefty slap of her body as she falls back again, and so does Alex, I suspect.

"Would you prefer to wait in the lorry?" he asks, apparently noticing my distress, but I shake my head.

Eventually, the horse goes quiet. Alex opens the door to the stall and looks inside. Liberty is on her feet at last. We take a few minutes to watch her, then Alex turns to me, a smile of relief on his face.

"That's great to see, isn't it? I'm happy to leave her to John and his staff now."

"Are you sure you don't want to stay longer?" I ask.

"I think I should get you home. I've kept you up long enough," he says with a flash of humor.

Having thanked the team at the hospital, Alex and I return to the lorry. I clamber into the dark cab and take the seat next to the door, leaving the one between us vacant. As I fumble for the seat belt, I become aware that Alex is looking at me, his expression gentle and questioning. He reaches out his hand, letting it rest on the seat between us, and my heart starts thumping. Forgetting the seat belt, I slide my hand across the ripped velour until our fingertips touch. The contact sends delicious shivers of desire up and down my spine.

"Maz," Alex says, his voice hoarse and caressing. "Come here . . ."

I shift toward him, ending up with his arms around me and our lips locked together in an earth-shattering kiss.

I don't know how long it lasts, but it isn't

until lights come on at the front of the hospital that we recover ourselves.

"I think we should go somewhere quieter," Alex says with a low chuckle. "Does your offer of coffee still stand?"

"Of course." Smiling, I leave my hand on his thigh for a moment before moving away. There's nothing stopping us now, is there?

Alex switches on the engine and reverses out of the yard. As he drives us back toward Talyton, I phone Izzy to tell her that Alex and I will take the calls from now on.

"How's the horse?" she asks.

"So-so. She's on her feet. Thanks, Izzy. I owe you."

"Don't be silly, Maz. Night."

Alex pulls over to the side of the road to answer his mobile. "Mother? Yes. She's up, but it's going to be touch and go for a while. She's staying at Westleigh for now. Yes, we had to remove a section of her small bowel. Two meters." Alex pauses. "It's far too soon to worry about whether or not she'll ever jump again." He wishes his mother good night, drops the phone back onto the dash, and drives on through the darkness, then remarks, "What the hell is that?" Keeping his hands on the wheel, he points straight ahead, where the horizon glows orange.

It isn't a summer sunset, I know that much . . .

The horizon is flickering beneath a plume of smoke darker than the night sky and spiraling across the crescent moon.

"Who would light a bonfire at this time of night?" Alex asks as he cranes forward.

My heart sinks. "That's no bonfire. That's Buttercross Cottage, Gloria's place." I'm already dialing the emergency services. "Oh, God, quick, we have to help." Moments later we're outside the cottage, where the thatch at one end is already ablaze.

"Open the gate to the paddock, will you?" Alex says.

I don't need to be asked twice. I jump down and pull at the gate, but it's chained and padlocked.

"Open it," Alex shouts over the sound of the engine.

"I can't." I struggle with the chain. "It's locked."

"Stand back!" Alex puts the lorry into reverse, drives back a couple of meters, then roars forward straight through the gate, which cracks and splinters, and finally shatters under the wheels. The donkeys trot away hee-hawing into the night, the dogs howl, the fire spits and crackles, and a siren joins the cacophony.

Alex leaves the headlamps on. They cut swathes of light through the darkness toward the burning cottage.

"We can put the animals in the lorry when we get them out," he says, running across the paddock ahead of me.

"Gloria?" I catch up with Alex at the cottage, keeping a wary eye out for the pieces of flying debris that land flaming and smoking at our feet. "What about Gloria?"

Alex bangs at the front door with his fists. He turns the handle and pushes it. It doesn't budge. "It's locked from the inside."

"What are we going to do?" The sirens seem too far away. By the time they arrive, it'll be too late.

As if reading my mind, Alex takes a step back, then rams the door with his shoulder. It falls in with a crash, letting out a gust of intense heat and the smell of burning wood and hair. Several dark shapes fly out and disappear into the darkness of the garden, as if carried on will-o'-the-wisps of smoke.

I stand at Alex's side, looking through the haze and trying to make sense of the geography of the hallway: the coat stand, the bowler hat. The door into the sitting room beyond is dark against a halo of gold light, a ray of which extends from beneath the door to the runner on the hallway floor.

"We'll have to try another way in." Alex interlinks his fingers with mine.

"What if Gloria's in there? I can't leave her . . ."

"Maz."

I push past him.

"Maz, don't!"

I'm already at the inner door, choking on a lungful of filthy smoke.

"I know she's in here!" I lift the latch on the door, aware that it's almost too hot to touch. Keeping my hand over my face, I push the door open. Mistake! I might as well have unleashed a dragon.

A roaring gust of flames slams down the hallway, but through the smoke and the heat I can just make out a figure slumped across the sofa. Alex pulls me back and presses me against the wall with the weight of his body.

"Gloria. Gloria!" Eyes streaming, I fight my way out of Alex's restraint. I can hardly see him for the smoke, but I can feel his hands clawing at my arm and hear him yelling, "Maz, we've got to get out. This way!"

I glance both ways: at the flames and smoke on the one hand; at the smoke and the faint outline of the front door, beckoning me to safety, on the other. Can I live with the guilt? It's a split-second decision. I drop to my knees, take a breath, and crawl for it, keeping close to the wall to avoid the fire that has taken root at the base of the coat stand and sent runners of flame up to consume the long coat that hangs upon it.

I can't use the same strategy when I reach the sitting room, where the fire has really taken hold, the newspapers and books feeding its frenzy. At first, I'm driven back by the heat of the flames. At the second attempt, I take a different route. In a flash, I'm leaning over Gloria's inert body, trying to force my arms up under hers so I can drag her off the sofa. She's much heavier than I imagined.

Please make this easy for me, I urge her silently. You can be as awkward as you like later.

As I start to lift her, the skin on the back of my neck begins to prick with unease. Something has changed. It is as if someone has turned the volume up on the surround sound. There's a rumbling noise, a fresh surge of flames, screaming . . .

"Maz!" A pair of hands grabs me about the waist and throws me aside as the ceiling comes caving in above my head. Blackened beams fracture and fall, and an avalanche of masonry and plaster sends up showers of orange sparks and golden dust. The landscape has changed, making me feel disoriented. Where's the door? Where's Gloria? Where's Alex?

"Alex!" I yell out. "Alex!" I can't breathe. I can't see. I can't see Alex. I dig at the burning rubble. The fire bites back, searing my skin. "Alex! Where are you?" I keep digging, but all I can see in front of me is a throbbing mass of black circles that gradually coalesce. And then nothing . . .

I COME ROUND to the cool of the night air, hunched on a fallen log, breathing through a mask over my face and with the sound of running water in my ears.

"Is it raining?" I mutter.

"It's the hoses you can hear, love." A man holds a silver blanket tight around my shoulders while flashing blue lights strobe through the darkness. Floodlights focus on the smoldering ruins where emergency workers are damping down the fire. Now and then, a fresh surge of flames flickers up from the pyre of Buttercross Cottage.

"Come and lie down in the ambulance for me." The man gently removes the mask. "I'm Dave. I'm a paramedic. What's your name?"

"Maz. Maz Harwood." I can't stop shivering.

"It's all right, Maz. You've had a bit of a shock, but you're going to be okay." He holds me tighter. "Let's go."

"I can't go anywhere until I know what's happened to Alex. Where is he?"

"You mean the man who was in the house with you? They've got him out," Dave says.

"He is all right, isn't he?" I say, panicking as I watch the lights of an ambulance disappearing off down the lane.

"Let's concentrate on you, shall we?"

Dave says in a tone that suggests—to me anyway, in my state of confusion and shock—that he's holding something back.

"Alex!" I can hear my voice screaming in my ears, and I'm finding it difficult to breathe, and it's all Dave can do to restrain me from chasing after the ambulance.

"Hey, that's better," he says when I've calmed down a little.

"What about Gloria, the woman who lives here? She's one of my clients."

"No news yet. Come on, take it easy now . . ."

"Don't I know you from somewhere?" Dave says, as he leads me across to the back of a waiting ambulance. "I remember. It was the baby, the one we delivered at Otter House. You're the vet."

I nod. I'm the vet, I think, with a sense of desperation. If I can't be of any help to Alex, I should be helping to get the animals to safety.

"Has the fire reached the cattery?" I ask. "It's the building that backs onto the yard at the rear of the house."

"As far as I know, the fire's been contained, but it's nothing for you to worry about."

"There are at least fifty cats and dogs on the site—I'm the best person to deal with them," I tell him. Coughing, I try to discard the blanket. "Patch me up and let me go. Please."

Dave tips his head to one side, as if considering. "All right, but it's against my better judgment." He insists on bandaging my arms while I call Izzy to bring the visit case, cat carriers, collars and leads, and anything else she can lay her hands on.

"I'll bring Chris too," she says, once I've explained very briefly the scene at Gloria's place, and then the phone cuts out and I'm sitting there like an idiot with it pressed to my ear until Dave extricates it from my grasp and gently stretches out my right arm so he can bandage it to match my left. As my elbow straightens, a wave of pain shoots up from the ends of my fingers to my brain. It is as if it's ignited all the nerve endings between. I gasp. I can't stop myself.

"I really think you'd be better off in hospital," Dave says firmly.

"No," I snap. "I'm fine. Just leave my fingers free, otherwise I'll be worse than useless. Make it quick, will you?"

"What score—out of ten—would you

give me for my dressings, lady vet?" Dave unwinds the last turn of the self-adherent wrap from the roll and touches it to the layer underneath, making me wince.

"Ten and a half," I say, and summoning some superhuman strength, I force the pain to the back of my mind and jump down from the ambulance. "Thanks, but I've really got to go . . ."

I head out into the darkness, unsure where I'm going, and by chance run straight into Izzy, who's carrying the visit case and dogcatcher. Chris walks alongside her, a rolled-up stretcher under one arm.

"This is unbelievable. I've never seen so many fire engines in one place before," Izzy says, wide-eyed. "Are you all right, Maz?" she adds, looking at my bandages.

"I'm fine," I say.

"What about Gloria? And Alex?"

"Alex is on his way to hospital—that's all I know." Biting back tears, I force myself to concentrate on my mission to save Gloria's animals. "We have to hurry. This way." I grab Izzy's arm. "Did you bring a torch?"

"Everything but a torch and the kitchen sink," says Izzy, "and I'd have brought that with me, if you'd asked."

"I've got one in the truck," Chris says. "I'll get it." He hands me the stretcher and jogs away into the night, returning shortly after with a powerful lantern. "We'll have to be quick. If P.C. Phillips gets wind of this, he'll pull us back behind his cordon."

We cross the paddock, then skirt the hedge until we find a gate. Chris unfastens it, and we hasten through.

"You can get to the cattery this way, as far as I remember. I brought a couple of sheep up here for Gloria once to keep the grass down in the paddock. Trouble was, when it was time for me to collect them, she refused to let them go. Couldn't bear the thought of them going for meat." Chris aims the beam of his light at the door alongside us. "Is this it?"

"No, the animals are in the next building down, right behind the house, where all the howling's coming from." I don't like it. I don't like being so close to the fire. I can taste it, smell it, feel it tearing at my arms . . . Shuddering, I force myself to keep going.

Chris breaks the lock on the door into the cattery and pushes it open.

"I'll go first," I say. "I've got a rough idea of which animals live where."

We remove all the cages to the paddock, then release the cats, opening the doors to their pens and shooing them out in the hope that they'll head for the open fields or hide out in the copse. Finally we take the dogs, collaring all of them but Petra, the white German shepherd, with rope leads.

Petra won't come. She sits pressed against the wall at the back of her cage like a cornered wolf, her eyes dark with fear, her tongue hanging out, and her teeth glinting in the shadows. I imagine her heartbeat knocking against her ribs and the adrenaline surging through her blood, like mine. Flight or fight? There's nowhere to flee . . .

"Petra," I call softly as I step inside to join her with Chris behind me, making clicking noises in his throat. Petra growls, then lunges toward us. Chris flies back behind the wire door. I stand my ground.

"We'll have to leave her," he says. "It isn't safe."

"Here." Izzy hands me the dogcatcher, and I have a go at slipping the noose over Petra's nose, but she snaps at the wire, catching it on her teeth.

"Who's there? Is anybody there?" Heavy

footsteps come hurrying along the corridor toward us, and two firefighters appear from the gloom. "We're here to clear the building. We'll show you the way out."

"Give us a minute," I say, making another fruitless attempt to get the noose around Petra's neck.

"You can have half," says one of the firefighters.

"Last chance, Petra," I mutter through gritted teeth. I hold out the noose, and Chris approaches her from the front like bait to a shark. Just as she makes to spring toward him, I manage to slip the noose right over the back of her head and pull it tight. She fights back, scrabbling at it with her paws until they bleed and twisting her body, repeatedly backing off and running forward, while I cling on for grim death until Chris takes over, dragging her outside, where he allows a little give on the noose so as not to choke her. We cross the paddock to where P.C. Phillips and Stewart Pitt are waiting to help us load the animals into the back of Chris's truck. I have to admit that I'm relieved when Stewart starts talking to Chris, not me.

"I was getting the cows in for milking

when I saw the fire. You can see it for miles, although I'm surprised you noticed it from your place, seeing as you're on the other side of the hill."

"Ah," says Chris, "I wasn't at my place, but don't ask me now. It's a long story."

"I'll take the dogs up to the manor," Stewart says.

"You can't do that," I cut in.

"It's you, the one who let my dog die." He swears. "I don't think it's up to you to tell me what I can or can't do."

"We're taking them back to Otter House."

"No way." Stewart stares at me through narrowed eyes. "That's like condemning them to death."

"They can't go up to the manor. Old Fox-Gifford's up in London, and Alex . . ." His name catches in my throat.

Stewart steps toward me, his face menacingly close to mine. "Where is he?"

"In an ambulance on the way to hospital. We went inside. I thought there was time to get Gloria out, but the roof fell in, and Alex . . . he saved my life." Rubbing my eyes, I watch the last cinders drift and die on the wind. My arms, my lungs, my bones, everything hurts, and I guess from his expression that Stewart is hurting too. He'll never forgive me now.

"I don't know what it is about you, but I wish you'd do the right thing and push off back to London," he says harshly. "I never want to see your face around here again."

"Steady on, Stew." Chris touches his arm and draws him back. I don't know what he says to him, but they return a couple of minutes later and Stewart closes the tailgate on the dogs, who are now quiet and subdued on finding themselves outside the prison of the sanctuary.

"Stewart's going to catch the donkeys and take them to Barton Farm in Alex's lorry," Chris says as he drives away from the scene of the fire, and I notice how Izzy, who sits beside him, rests her head on his shoulder. I envy her. "I'll go back for the cages."

"What about the cats?" Izzy asks. "We've got lots of carriers and old baskets at Otter House—we'll have to go back and see how many we can catch."

I don't like to think about it, but I suspect that many of Gloria's animals, Mac and Tosh included, have perished in the fire. As for Ginge, who knows?

"Can I borrow your mobile, Izzy?" I ask in a small voice. "I seem to have lost mine—probably when I was grappling with Petra—and I have to find out what's happened to Alex."

"Yeah, sure," she says. "Let me call directory inquiries and find the number of the hospital. I'll speak to them—you're in no fit state."

Izzy contacts the hospital, but they won't give out any information about a patient unless she's a relative, and it's too late to claim that she's Alex's sister.

"Have you got Alex's mobile number on there?" I ask her, praying that not only has he got it with him and left it switched on but he's in a fit state to answer it.

"I think so." Izzy hands me the phone. "Try searching for 'Fox-Gifford.'"

I call Alex's mobile. When he answers, my heart jumps, but it's only his voice mail telling me to leave a message and he'll get back to me as soon as he can. I try Talyton Manor, but the phone redirects me back to Alex's mobile. I leave seven messages in all: please, Alex, please, answer your phone.

Intensive Care

WHAT HAVE I DONE? I DON'T BELIEVE IN GOD, or angels, but I'm praying like mad anyway.

By nine o'clock in the morning, the Kennels at Otter House are full—I must be hallucinating. The lights are too bright and the clank of the cage doors too noisy as Izzy, in her scrubs and clogs, bustles about feeding and watering the inpatients, adjusting the drips and changing soiled bedding and litter trays. Petra and Ugli-dog are in the two large dog cages, the other five dogs we brought back with us occupy the remaining dog cages, and there are eleven cats—one in each cat cage, two sharing the space under the stairs, and another in the cage the practice loans out for confining cats at home after major surgery.

Even Nigel is here, getting his hands dirty for once. He came in at six, hoping to intercept the bailiffs and not knowing that I'd settled the repayments on the car and the X-ray machine using my own account the day before. I should have told him, but unsurprisingly, considering all that's happened in the past twenty-four hours, it slipped my mind.

I stay with the sickest of the dogs, a cute little Heinz 57 with a long body, short legs, and a curly tail. Izzy's nicknamed him Raffles. He sits inside a cage that we've converted to an oxygen tent with a clear plastic sheet over the front. He's panting, his big brown eyes wide with fear as he fights for air. He's terribly thin, the ridge of his spine is black with flea dirts, and his wavy coat, which is a golden tan, is crawling with lice, but I can't think of dealing with these problems until his condition stabilizes and I can assess the level of damage the smoke has done to his lungs.

I slip my hand inside the cage and check his color—his gums are still an ominous blue. It's such a shame—he's only a baby, eighteen months old, if that.

"Maz." Izzy touches my shoulder. "Can you leave Raffles for a sec? I need a hand with a dressing. The silver tabby."

"Okay." I force myself to keep going—for the animals' sake. I perch on a stool at the prep bench and hang on to the cat for her while she applies a nonstick dressing to a superficial but extensive wound across his back, then fastens a clear plastic collar around his neck to stop him licking at it. Izzy sweeps the cat up and returns him to his cage. She fills in the inpatient card on the front—no name, number 7—then returns to me.

"You're leaking," she observes.

I'm not sure what she means, since I associate leaking with incontinence.

"Your bandages—I can change them, if you like."

"I'll do it," I say as I look down at my arms. The feeling is coming back to them, a constant stinging sensation, as if someone's holding them under a jet of boiling water. My fingers, which were only lightly seared, are beginning to throb as they swell, and the bandages are wet through and stained reddish brown, as if they've been dunked in the river Taly. "Later."

"Maz, you can't possibly. Let me do it."

I bite my lip as Izzy peels the dressings away, revealing weeping weals and cuts across my forearms that look just as bad as they feel.

"We have to get these checked out at hospital," she says.

"I'll be fine." I grimace. "They aren't infected."

"You're the vet." Izzy shrugs. I don't think she believes me. She fetches fresh dressings—blue self-adherent wrap with paw prints on it. "We're going to have to get hold of some more supplies—we're almost out of bandaging tape."

"I'll call the wholesaler's," I say. "They've got the number of my credit card."

"You know you shouldn't be here," Izzy says.

"I almost wasn't." Memories of the fire creep back into my head like tiny flames. They grow in intensity and surround me, the heat burning my lungs, the smoke, like a pair of arms, clutching my chest too tight, Alex's hands on my waist, the panic in his voice. I make to grab a tissue from the box at the end of the bench, but my hands are trembling and I can't bend my fingers.

"I didn't mean it like that," Izzy says. "You should take a break. Let me and Nigel clear up."

"There's loads to do." I look around at the muddle. There are animals to treat, Raffles needs a chest X-ray . . . "I'd rather keep going. It keeps my mind off . . . things . . ."

"I'll get that." Nigel hurries out of Kennels.

"What was that?" I ask Izzy.

"The bell. Didn't you hear it?"

I shake my head as Izzy goes on. "I think Nigel's pleased to have an excuse to take his rubber gloves off." She falls silent at the sound of Nigel's footsteps trip-trapping back along the corridor.

"This way, ladies," I hear him say, and he shows Frances and Fifi Green into Kennels. Proving Izzy wrong, he slips his rubber gloves back on and returns to the sink to continue washing up all the empty food and water bowls.

"We've heard the news." Fifi clutches a Louis Vuitton handbag to her chest, and it suddenly strikes me exactly how insulting it was of her to ask for a discount at Otter

House when she's swanning around in designer gear.

"The most dreadful news," echoes Frances. "We just had to come."

One of Izzy's eyebrows disappears into her hair.

"How awful. Poor Gloria." Fifi puts her bag down on the bench in a pool of fluid of questionable origin. Izzy rescues it, shifting it onto a piece of paper towel, yet Fifi scarcely notices.

"I've confessed to P.C. Phillips," she goes on. "I'm entirely responsible for what's happened—"

"I don't think so," I interrupt, but Fifi raises one hand to shut me up and keeps going. "After you called me, Maz, I went straight over to Gloria's. I know you said not to, but I was so angry I just had to. I told her a few home truths. Someone had to do it." Fifi shakes her head slowly. "I didn't think she'd do anything like this."

"It was an accident, one of the cats knocking a candle over, or a spark from the fire," I say, recalling the log Gloria had burning in the grate.

"My son's a firefighter," Fifi replies. "He says there were signs of an accelerant, kerosene, something like that. Gloria kept all kinds of chemicals in the old sheds. Tom, her husband, needed them for the tractor. That's when the place was looked after, the lawns mown and the fields kept harrowed and tidy."

"I can't believe that she'd dream of hurting those animals though. She adored them," Izzy says. "Have they found her?"

Fifi nods. "The ceiling came down on her—she didn't stand a chance."

"Stupid, stupid woman! What did she have to go and do that for?" Would I have gone in to try to save her if I'd known she'd set the fire deliberately? Would I have tried so hard?

"Alex Fox-Gifford is in hospital," Fifi continues.

"Have you heard how he is?" I ask quickly, my heart pounding with a mixture of hope and apprehension.

Fifi shakes her head. "My son says he's in Intensive Care. That's it."

"I'll take you up there, Maz," Izzy says.

"Now?" I glance toward the row of cages. I can't leave them.

"Raffles will be okay for an hour or two. We can go whenever you like."

"Now."

"Before you rush off," says Fifi, "I thought I'd let you know that I've called an emergency meeting of the Talyton Animal Rescue Society for tonight. You must come."

"Fifi, I can't," I say, a little irritated by her bossy attitude. "I'm needed here."

"I've told the trustees that you'll be there."

"Give them my apologies. They'll understand." I know Fifi means well, but she's trying to organize me, and I will not be organized.

"We'll see," says Fifi. "Anyway, now that we're here, you'd better make use of us. What can we do?"

"You can do some drying up, Fifi," Nigel says from his post at the sink.

"What's happening up at the manor?" Izzy asks, handing Fifi a tea towel.

"The surgery's closed," Fifi says. "The hospital at Westleigh is taking Talyton Manor's horsey clients, the farm animals are being looked after by the nearest large-animal practice, and as far as I know, Otter House is going to look after their small-animal side—if that's all right with you, Maz."

"Of course," I say.

"Are you sure you're up to it?" Izzy sighs. "Ask a silly question . . ."

"How can I contribute?" Frances asks. "Shall I take over in Reception?"

"We can't pay you," Nigel cuts in, rather ungraciously, I think.

"I know that. I'm doing this out of the goodness of my heart." Frances touches her chest. "I just love a crisis." She corrects herself quickly. "Well, not the really bad bits, like dear Alex getting hurt."

"I do hope he's going to get better," Fifi says, frowning pessimistically.

"Old Mr. Fox-Gifford was on death's door for weeks when the bull got him, but he pulled through," Frances says.

"I suppose he's lucky he comes from good stock—his father has the constitution of an ox," Fifi goes on.

As I stand listening to Fifi's and Frances's speculation about Alex's condition, my hands ball up into painful fists. Izzy hustles me away, her lips curving into a small smile.

"If those two old pantomime dames can't help themselves, they can make themselves useful and help us. And if that sounds disrespectful, it is. Separately they're not too bad, but together they're a right double act. I'm sorry, Maz. I can see that all their talk of Alex has upset you."

Nevertheless, I'm beginning to see the good side of Talyton gossip. As soon as they heard the news, Frances and Fifi rallied round to help, and looking at the state of Kennels, we need all the help we can get.

As soon as we arrive at the hospital, I leave Izzy sorting out the payment for the car park and head straight for the Intensive Care unit. There's a nurse at the desk on the way in. She's older than I am, in her forties, I'd guess, and she's wearing a uniform that's a couple of sizes too big for her, as if she's lost weight recently. Her hair is short, dark at the roots and blond at the tips.

"I'm looking for"—I can hardly keep my voice steady enough to say his name— "Alex Fox-Gifford."

"Are you next of kin?" she asks kindly, assessing me with calm gray eyes. When I don't respond, she goes on as if I'm one instrument short of a full set. "Are you a relative?"

I say the first thing that comes into my head. "I'm his fiancée."

"I'm Debbie," she says, apparently satisfied with my answer. "Go on through then," she continues, once she's warned me what to expect. "He's second on the left."

I hesitate a couple of feet from the bed, thinking that this person can't be Alex. He looks like Alex, but he's lying so still. I step closer. His lips are the same deathly pallor as his cheeks, his chin is pricked with dark stubble, and there's a bruise on his temple. His hands lie limp across the sheets.

"Oh, Alex . . . ," I whisper. I reach out and run the tips of my fingers down the side of his face. His skin is cool. There's no response, not even a flutter of the eyelids. He isn't even breathing for himself— a machine is doing it for him.

"You lazy sod," I accuse him lightly, my teeth aching with the effort of not breaking down and crying. "Can't you try a bit harder?" My hands tighten with a desire to thump him, to slap him across the face and dig him in the ribs to make him open his eyes and answer me back with some sarcastic remark. "Why didn't you listen? I would have been all right." I glance away at the series of images of Alex's skull that are up on a monitor on the wall. They blur and fuse. I wouldn't have been all right. It would have been me lying here, hovering somewhere between life and death. It *should* have been me.

I pull a chair to the side of the bed and sit down, and I don't know how long I stay, staring at his face, before I sense someone standing behind me. I turn to find Izzy, her expression grave.

"We should go," she says quietly.

"Give me a minute."

"We really should go now. We can come back later."

I strain forward, studying Alex's face again. Is that the tiniest flicker of those long dark lashes? I'm so tired I can't trust my eyes.

I take his hand, tangling with the cannula and drip tubing taped across the back, where the veins snake small and blue. There are freckles of silver nitrate stain on his thumb, and dried blood outlines one fingernail. I squeeze his fingers tight until the skin loses its mottled pattern.

"Alex!" His name catches in my throat. "Alex. Wake up!"

"Maz, stop. He can't hear you." Izzy

places her hand over mine. "I've been talk-ing to the nurse—they've put him to sleep."

"Put him to sleep?" I gasp. It is as if the ceiling and the whole world are falling in around me, and I can smell the smoke and feel the fierce heat of the flames.

"Maz?" Izzy's voice breaks through to me. "They're planning to let him wake up later. They'll know more then."

Tears streaming down my face, I glance out of the window at the sky, where the wind is teasing white strands from candy-floss clouds and spinning them away. "They'll know more then." What exactly will "they" know?

WHAT WOULD HAVE HAPPENED if I'd followed my head, not my heart? What if I'd done the right thing and called the RSPCA in straightaway? What if I hadn't tried to deal with everything myself, to make up for what happened to Cadbury?

All these thoughts and more flash through my brain as Izzy drives me back.

"I want to stop off at Buttercross Cottage on the way," I say.

"What on earth for?"

"I need to check. I want to be certain. I mean, Ginge might come back and find no one there."

"You're rambling," Izzy says gently. "Are you sure you're all right?"

"Will you stop asking me that?" I say irritably. "Yes, I've had a drink and something to eat." Two black coffees, half a cheese roll, and a double dose of painkillers. "Yes, I'm . . . ," I start, and then I give in. Delayed shock is kicking in. "No, I feel like crap."

"I've been wondering if we should contact Emma. I know you tried the other day, but I think we should try again. You're going to need some help—you won't be able to scrub up for a while."

It's true. My toes curl at the thought of taking a nailbrush to my hands and arms.

"I know she won't like it, but I'd like to ask her if we can take on a relief."

"A relief to cover for the relief," I say drily as Izzy hands me her mobile.

I leave a message on Emma's voice mail.

"You could try phoning Westleigh too— find out how Liberty is," Izzy says.

John the vet is tied up, but he rings me back five minutes later.

"I thought Alex would be in touch first

thing," he says. "Talk about fussy clients, he was completely over the top and now . . . ," he goes on lightly.

"Alex hasn't been in touch because he's been in an accident," I say. "There was a fire. He's unconscious. That's why I'm calling, not him."

"I'm sorry," says John, sounding contrite. "How bloody awful."

"How is the horse?" I ask, although it almost seems irrelevant now. Who knows if Alex will wake up, let alone ride again?

"She's doing well so far," John says. "She needs to stay with us for a while, so tell Alex not to worry about her." He pauses. "He is going to be okay, isn't he?"

"I don't know," I say, my voice sounding distant, as if it's coming out of someone else's mouth. I cut the call and stare at the mobile and then at the blood-tinged fluid seeping through the paw-print bandages on my arms. I just don't know.

Liberty isn't out of the woods yet, and neither is Ginge if he managed to flee the fire and hole up somewhere in Longdogs Copse.

Izzy parks just inside the paddock, not being as concerned about the paintwork of the practice car as I am about mine. We set out across the grass toward the remains of the cottage, which reminds me of the wreck of the *Mary Rose* when I visited it once with Emma and Ben: vapor rising from the glistening timbers, the atmosphere incredibly peaceful. And sad.

"Ginge," I call. "Ginge!"

"I don't think he'll come rushing over to greet us—we aren't exactly his favorite people," Izzy says.

"He can't live wild out here, not in his condition. I'll come back later and set up a trap. One of the squeeze cages at the practice will do."

Izzy puts her arm on mine. I tear it away, acutely aware of the pain and unable to bear any contact. "Maz, he's probably dead," she says gently.

"He's alive," I say, and I think of Alex again, his face pale against the pillow, and I can't speak anymore. If Alex dies, nothing will ever be the same again.

CHAPTER 18

Vet Rescue

"I'M A PRETTY BIRDIE, YES, I AM." AN INSUFFER-ably cheery cockatiel—a bird bigger than a budgie and smaller than a parrot, with gray and white plumage, a tuft of yellow feathers on the top of its head, and an or-ange circle behind its eye—greets me with a whistle as I walk through into Kennels the following morning. "I'm a pretty birdie, yes, I am."

"Hi, Izzy." I check the inpatient card on its cage. "Jude? What kind of name is that?"

"One of the firemen found him in the back of Gloria's barn," says Izzy. "I chose the name. He and Jude Law are both such pretty things." She smiles. "Oh, and the same chap brought the Siamese cat in." She points toward one of the high-rise cages, where a cross-eyed Siamese cat peers out from beneath a piece of vet bedding.

"I'm a pretty birdie, yes, I am." The cockatiel pipes up again. "I'm a pretty birdie, yes, I am."

I'm beginning to understand why Gloria didn't keep him in the house.

"Like certain other men I know, he has far too high an opinion of himself," Izzy says. "I'll cover him up for a while." She picks up an old towel and drops it over the cage. Jude falls silent. "Result."

"What are all those cages doing on the bench?" I ask, trying to concentrate on the animals and the practice instead of going frantic with worry about Alex, although I can hardly think about anything else.

"They're Gloria's small furries. The firemen found them unharmed when they were damping down after the fire. I've cleaned them out, and given them fresh sawdust and toilet-roll insides. Frances is going to print up labels for them all and make some posters to put up around town. There must be some families out there who can give a couple of mice and gerbils a good home."

"Where are we supposed to work though? It's complete chaos."

"It's organized chaos," Izzy says, ever the optimist. "I have a list." She pulls a clipboard out from under an empty cat carrier. "First, I'd like you to have a look at the Siamese. Second, I thought it would be a good idea to X-ray Raffles again, because yesterday's images were inconclusive. Then you can go and see your appointments—and there are quite a few today—while I give Petra a bath. If you like, I'll change your dressings too."

"What about Ginge? I don't want him stuck in that trap for any longer than necessary."

"If he falls for it," Izzy says. "I imagine he's too savvy for that. Anyway, there's no need for you to go—Fifi and some of her volunteers are going to the cottage this morning to see if they can catch any of the other cats. The firemen saw several about, but they all ran away, except for the Siamese." She takes him out of the cage, bringing the bedding with him attached to his claws. She puts him on the draining board, the only free surface left. "They'll bring Ginge back, if he's there."

Wincing as I straighten my arms, I run my hands over the Siamese. He's an elderly gentleman with long white whiskers and terrible breath. His teeth are dripping with pus, and his gums are yellow with ulcers, telltale signs of chronic kidney failure.

"Are you thinking what I'm thinking, Izz?"

She nods as he lies purring gamely but effortfully in her arms. "'Fraid so. I think he's too far gone."

"I'm not being mean, am I?"

"I'll fetch the juice," Izzy says, and five minutes later the old Siamese is at peace, with Izzy and me the only ones to mourn his passing.

Izzy wraps him up in an old blanket, and I head off to Reception, aware of the ache in my arms: it's there all the time, a constant throb made worse by any movement, however small. I don't feel so great this morning. After I did manage to get to sleep last night, I woke up with a raging thirst, and now I feel weak and sick and sweaty.

I turn in to the consulting room, where I remove the dressings. It's a slow process. I pick at the edge of the last nonstick pad, which is well stuck on, then, scolding my-self for being a wuss, I take a deep breath and rip it off in one go.

"Are you in there, Maz?" Frances comes bursting through anyway, waving a copy of the *Chronicle* with the headline VET RESCUE in one hand and a box of cat food in the other. Tripod accompanies her, I notice, his eyes fixed on the box.

"Is that brunch?" I shuffle around in one of Emma's cupboards for some more ban-dages; hot pink is the only color left.

"If you like beef in gravy. The residents of Talyton are rallying round, bringing us gifts of pet food and offers of homes, and the phone hasn't stopped ringing. I'm not sure I'll have enough appointments for ev-eryone today."

Worrying that I'll be too busy to visit Alex, I wind the bandage around my right arm first, then start on the left. I hope I'll be able to keep going.

"DJ would like a word," Frances adds. "He's in Reception."

"What's up?" I ask the builder a moment later. As always, Magic, his dog, is waiting patiently by his side.

"It's more about what's coming down,

my lover." He smiles. "I've noticed some cracks in the plaster at the side of the house. I'd hate it to come down on one of your clients, so I wondered if we could put up some extra scaffold and make a proper job of it, not a bodge."

"How much more is it going to cost?" I wish Emma was here—she'd know what to do for the best.

"A little more than the front—because," he quickly adds, "of the difficulty of working over and above the glass extension."

"How long will it take?"

"Ah, that, my lover, will be—"

"Let me guess," I interrupt, "as long as it takes."

"You're getting the idea. I'll go and get started." DJ sticks his hand in his pocket. "By the way, me and the lads had a whip-round this morning"—he pulls out a wad of notes and a few coins—"for the animals you saved from the fire."

"Thanks, DJ." I'm touched. Everyone's being so kind. It reminds me of Alex and his kindness to me when I lost Cadbury. I can hear his voice. *Maz, I did it for you* . . .

I close my eyes, trying to get a grip on my emotions when all I want to do is collapse in a sniveling heap. I can hear Magic's nails pattering across the floor toward the exit and the tap of DJ's boots; the clattering of stainless-steel bowls somewhere from out the back; a phone ringing; a dog barking, Petra perhaps. I can smell boiled chicken, fresh coffee, antiseptic wash, and greasy dog. It's comforting.

I open my eyes again. Alex was right. I didn't kill Cadbury. It was bad luck, and in spite of everything that's happened, I still love my job, and if it should ever turn out that I have nothing else left, at least I have that.

"Otter House Vets, how can I help?" Frances is on the phone behind the desk. I notice that she's repersonalized her workspace—the rosette is back, along with a photo of Ruby, and it reminds me that I must have a word with Nigel to see if there's any way we can find the money to pay her wages and take her back on. She's been wonderful, identifying those clients who really do need to bring their animals in, and those who want to see what's going on and be part of the event that is coming to be known as the Great Fire of Talyton.

I return to Kennels to catch up with some

notes. Izzy is at the far end of the room, brushing Petra in preparation for a bath in Emma's innovative dog-washing station, a shower cubicle with a sunken tray. There's a patter of dog claws, and Miff comes flying in, huffing and puffing as if she's trying to tell me something.

"Who let the dog out?" I call.

"I did." A perfumed shadow falls across my paperwork.

I look up. "Oh, Emma! Is it really you?" My heart lightens. "You're back." I stand and put my arms up to hug her, but the pain forces me to sit down again. "Am I pleased to see you! It's gone a bit mad here."

"So I see," she says drily. The break has done her good. Her hair is sleek and shiny, like something out of a Pantene ad, and she has a tan, set off by a red dress that shows off her curves.

"I'm sorry about the mess."

"There's no need to apologize, Maz."

"And I wish I hadn't cut your holiday short."

"I did get your texts," she says, "but we were on our way home anyway. Ben made the decision—I've had a dodgy tummy for a couple of weeks. He said he'd be happier if we came home early."

"Em," I start, but a drumroll of hammering from outside the building takes over.

"I told you there'd be trouble if you got involved with Talyton Manor Vets," Emma says over the noise, and I realize she knows about the slurry, as she goes on, "and I come back to discover that you've been fraternizing with the enemy. Frances caught me on the way in—she mentioned you just happened to be out and about with Alex when Gloria's cottage went up in smoke." She hesitates. "How is he?"

I shake my head, not daring to speak in case I dissolve into tears.

"I saw the headlines on the billboards outside the newsagent's." Emma doesn't say any more about it, either to save my feelings or so as not to offend the dying, perhaps both. Instead, she stares at my arms. "What about you?"

"I got out with superficial burns, that's all."

"Superficial hogwash," Emma says. "Let me have a look."

"I'm fine." I'd rather she didn't see my

wounds, the wet, raw welts where the skin was burned right through to the flesh underneath, but Emma takes both my hands and leads me to the sink, where she grabs a pair of scissors and starts to snip at the dressings. I can't argue with her anymore. I can't speak for the pain.

"I'm going to ring Ben," she says. "You'll be no use to anyone if you go down with some hideous infection. What's more, you won't be able to wear short sleeves at the wedding—those burns will scar if they're not looked after properly."

"The wedding? I'm not getting married."

"Not yours, unless there's something you're not telling me," Emma says lightly. "Izzy's."

"I didn't know she was getting married," I say, a little hurt she hasn't told me.

"Frances told me about the dog that brought Izzy and Chris together."

"Freddie," I cut in.

"That's right. The goss in Talyton is that they'll be married within the year."

"It's just talk," I say, but Emma tips her head to one side and goes on.

"Ah, but there's no smoke without fire."

"You're as bad as the rest of them," I tell her.

"Then you'd better give me the true version of events," she says.

"Oh, Emma, so much has happened, I hardly know where to start."

"I think it'll have to wait. We'll talk later," Emma says, as Fifi sweeps into Kennels with two of her volunteers, both weighed down with cat baskets. She certainly knows how to delegate.

Izzy looks up from the dog-washing station, where she's bathing Petra, who isn't having any of it. There's foam up the walls and in Izzy's hair—everywhere except on the dog.

"We've got another nine for you," Fifi says.

"We'll have to double them up," I say. "Even then I don't know how on earth we'll fit them all in."

"You're very busy," Fifi observes. "It's just like *ER*."

"Except there's no George Clooney," Izzy calls out.

"Did you find a ginger cat," I ask, "a skinny-looking thing?"

Fifi looks toward the volunteers, who shake their heads, then turns back to me. "Good news though, Maz. At last night's emergency meeting, the committee agreed to offer all the practical and financial support available to treat and rehome Gloria's animals. It was a unanimous decision."

I thank her.

"I let my personal feelings come between me and my duty to protect lost and abandoned animals. I shouldn't have done," Fifi continues. "I could have handled things very differently."

So could I, I think.

"Gloria and I used to be great friends." Fifi dashes a teardrop, like one of the diamonds on her necklace, from her cheek.

"I'm sorry, Fifi," Emma says, touching her hand to comfort her as she goes on.

"At least this way I can make amends."

"Maz, could you throw me another towel?" Izzy calls.

I fetch one from the cupboard under the sink.

"Make that two!"

"Is that Petra?" Fifi frowns. "I thought she'd gone to a family in Talymouth. I suppose that was another of Gloria's stories."

"Do you know where she came from?" I hand Izzy the towels. I'm not sure who's wetter, Izzy or the dog.

"A breeder gave her to us when she was a few months old because she didn't quite make the grade as a show dog. I can't understand why—she's so glamorous."

"She will be when she's had a blow-dry and pedicure," Izzy says.

"I'm sure we'll be able to rehome her several times over, but I think I shall have first refusal," Fifi goes on.

Fifi and Petra? In my opinion, they're completely unsuited.

"I've already found Petra a home," I say quickly. She needs a calm and experienced handler, and I know just the person. "I'm sorry, Fifi. There's another very cute little dog who needs a good home though." I show her Raffles, but I can see she isn't impressed.

"No," she says, "he isn't my kind of dog."

I'm glad. On second thoughts, I'm not sure that Fifi is Raffles's kind of person.

"Hi, all . . ." It's Ben, and he's wearing a bright yellow polo shirt and smart trousers. "Emma sent for me."

"It's a house call then?" Izzy cuts in.

"An Otter House call." Ben smiles. His hair is short and receding from his broad, tanned forehead, and his nose is crooked, evidence of his enthusiasm for rugby.

"Good to see you back," Izzy says, giving him a damp hug. "How was the holiday?"

"Fantastic—I've got hundreds of photos to bore you with later."

"Then it's a good thing you only got half-way round the world, not all the way," Izzy says.

"Dear Dr. Mackie"—Fifi joins the conversation—"promise you won't leave us to go flying off round the world again. I've been dying to have another word about my"—she glances down at her feet—"my little problem."

"Save me," Ben whispers; then, "Not now, Fifi. I'm taking Maz to the hospital."

"Oh? There's nothing seriously wrong, is there?"

"We won't know until we get there," Ben says, keeping a straight face. I don't know how he does it. He should have been an actor. "Come on, Maz. Let's go." His hand is on my back, steering me past her.

"Our lady mayoress treats me as if I'm her personal physician. I've told her the bunions would soon clear up if only she'd wear sensible shoes."

"No woman wants to be told to wear sensible shoes," I point out.

Ben chuckles, but in the car on the way to the hospital he goes all serious and lectures me on the stupidity of trying to self-medicate with antibiotics from the surgery shelf, and the correct doses for acetaminophen and ibuprofen—apparently, I've been overdoing it.

"I've made you an appointment with Richard—I play squash with him now and then," Ben says when we arrive at the hospital. "He agreed to fit you in straightaway. Hey, Maz, are you paying any attention to me at all?"

"I'm sorry. I did hear what you said." Some of it anyway—I was thinking about Alex. "Thanks, Ben. You're very kind, although all this fuss is completely unnecessary."

"We'll let Richard be the judge of that, shall we? You're obviously not going to take any notice of me," he adds wryly.

"I'm going to go and see how Alex is first."

"You are not," says Ben. "You're due to

see Richard in five minutes. You can see Alex afterward."

I hesitate.

"I promise," Ben says firmly. "Now, I'm going to chase up some lab results for one of my colleagues back at the surgery—I'll see you later."

After an hour, during which Richard inspects my burns and has a nurse redress them, I'm allowed home with the appropriate antibiotics and stronger painkillers, along with appointments to return for regular dressing changes and instructions not to go back to work. Not work? That's like asking the sun not to rise.

I find my way to Intensive Care.

Debbie, the nurse at the desk, is much friendlier now she knows who I am.

"Is there any change?" I hardly dare ask.

"Mr. Summerson, his consultant, may reduce the level of sedation later today. Alex is breathing without help and his condition is stable, that's all I can say at this point. As you well know, these things take time."

I bite back tears. I'd hoped the news would be better than this.

"Can I . . . ?"

"Go on through."

I hurry toward the unit, but before I reach Alex's bedside the sound of voices—like a town criers' convention let loose in a library—makes me hesitate. I turn to see the Fox-Giffords at the nurses' station I've just left. Quickly I step out of the line of sight through the doors between the corridor and the rest of the unit.

"His fiancée?" says Sophia. "Our son doesn't have a fiancée."

"He had his fingers badly burned when he last got hitched," Old Fox-Gifford observes, a rather inappropriate remark, I think, considering the present circumstances. "He'll never marry again."

"Besides," Sophia says, "he would run it past us first. She might be some gold digger, and we have to protect our estate."

"Oh?" Debbie sounds doubtful. "She was pretty convincing."

"So?" Old Fox-Gifford asks sharply. "Who exactly is she?"

"Maz, of course. The vet from the Otter House surgery. I didn't recognize her the first time she came in, but I remember her now. I took my cat there for his booster."

I feel a twinge of guilt that I don't recall either Debbie or her cat, but then I've seen lots of new people since I arrived in Talyton. I can't possibly remember them all.

"What!" Old Fox-Gifford growls like an injured cat. "The bitch who's put Alexander in this damned place! When I see her, I'll . . . I'll . . ."

"Do calm down, dear," says Sophia. "Not in front of the grandchildren. If it weren't for Madge, Alexander wouldn't have managed to get Liberty to the hospital in time."

"We must bring Liberty to see Daddy," pipes up a child's voice, and I feel ten times more guilty than before. I'm not the only person in the world who's suffering. If Alex dies, his parents will have lost a son, and his children will know what it's like, as I did, to grow up without a father. They'll probably lose contact with their grandparents too.

"I don't think Liberty would like it in here, darling," says Sophia. "She'd spook at just about everything."

"Can we go and see Daddy now?"

My sense of panic deepens. If the Fox-Giffords find me here, they'll have me escorted off the premises. I look for somewhere to hide—under a bed, behind one of the banks of life-support machines, on a chair behind a curtain? I'm just working out how I can scramble onto an empty trolley and cover myself with a sheet when I overhear Debbie saying, "Just a moment please, Mr. and Mrs. Fox-Gifford. If you wouldn't mind waiting out here for a couple of minutes while I check his vitals."

With her back straight and stiff she marches onto the unit, takes one scathing look at me, and points her finger in the direction of the washdown room.

"I'll tell them you're gone, that you must have slipped out past me while I was on the phone," she says.

It isn't the greatest place to wait, but I can look through the porthole window in the door and eavesdrop on some of the Fox-Giffords' conversation. There are two children, a girl—the one who fell off the pony at the show—and a boy, who's no more than a toddler, with black curls and green dungarees.

Sophia lifts the boy onto Alex's bed. "Say hello, Sebastian."

"Hello, Daddy." Sebastian puts out his hand to grab at the tube in Alex's nose.

Just in time Sophia catches his arm and hugs him to her chest. "Daddy 'sleep?" Sebastian asks with wide, curious eyes.

"He isn't asleep," the girl says. She's well-spoken and sounds quite mature for her age. "He's in a jug an' juice coma."

"It's a drug-induced coma," Sophia corrects as she touches the corner of her eye.

"Wake up, Daddy," the boy says happily, as if it's a game.

"He won't wake up just yet," Sophia explains.

"Will he wake up for dinner?" says the girl. I hear the tone of her voice change. "He'll die if he doesn't have any dinner, won't he?"

"We don't know what will happen . . ." Sophia's voice fades.

"He might never wake up," Old Fox-Gifford says bluntly. "He might never work again."

"Husband of mine, you are insufferable." Sophia's voice rises to a high-pitched wail. "No matter if he can't work again. What if he isn't able to ride?" She puts the boy down, and he comes toddling straight toward the door to my hiding place. Ducking down, I lean back against the door, bracing myself with my knees bent against the series of small pushes that follow. Go away. Please.

"Come here, Sebastian. Leave that door alone," Sophia calls. "Do as you're told, darling."

"We must be off. It's time to let the hounds out," says Old Fox-Gifford, "and the horses need their grub."

"We'll buy some sweeties on the way home," Sophia says, at which there's one last shove at the door.

"Sophia, you're too bloody soft with him," Old Fox-Gifford says. "That boy needs to feel the force of the rod to break his spirit."

"It didn't work with Alexander, did it?" Sophia's voice fades out again, along with the sound of footsteps, and I breathe a sigh of relief that they've gone. However, my relief is short-lived.

"You have some explaining to do," Debbie says, opening the door to the washdown room.

"I lied. I'm sorry, but . . ." I pull a piece of crumpled tissue from my pocket and blow my nose. "I'm responsible for what's happened to Alex. It's my fault."

Debbie takes a small step back, as if she's worried for her own safety.

"I thought I could get Gloria out in time. I almost got her . . . but the fire . . . Alex saved my life. He's a hero." I break down, sobbing. "Don't you understand? I couldn't bear not to see him. I couldn't bear it."

"I shouldn't do this, but Alex needs someone like you right now, a good friend, not that dreadful family of his." Debbie puts her arm around my waist and leads me over to the bed. "Come on. You can have five minutes."

"But what do I do?" I say, starting to panic. Last time I was overwhelmed by the unfamiliarity of the hospital and the sight of Alex lying helpless and surrounded by equipment and machines. Now it seems more familiar, and I feel I should be doing something. "Can he hear me?"

"Possibly," Debbie says. "Best to treat him as though he can."

"What shall I say?"

"I don't know." She gazes at me with those cool gray eyes of hers. "You know him a whole lot better than I do."

But I don't, I think, when I sit down beside Alex and slide my hand across the sheet that covers him and under the tubing of his drip, being careful not to dislodge it, so I can carefully interlink my fingers with his. Gently I tighten my fingers, but there's no answering pressure, no sign that he can feel my touch.

I don't know anything about this man. What music does he like? What's his favorite film? His favorite book? How have I got the nerve to let Debbie describe me as a good friend when I'm still very much a stranger?

"Hi," I whisper, leaning closer, so I can see the curve of his ear. "Hi," I repeat, a little louder this time, but all I can hear is the faint sound of his breathing. I can't hear his voice; I'm already unsure exactly how it sounded. His scent of aftershave, cows, and penicillin has disappeared too. Now his skin smells of disinfectant and alcohol, all too clean, as if even the little of Alex I did know, or thought I knew, has gone.

With every heartbeat a pain within me grows, a crushing ache in the center of my chest, as I realize too late why I'm here at his side and what compels me to stay for as long as I possibly can. I gulp back a sob, but it's too late. Tears track hot down my cheeks and drop onto the sheet.

It wasn't just lust, or the fact I was lonely in Talyton and on the rebound from Mike. It isn't because I'm grateful to him for looking after me when Cadbury died, and standing up for me against Cheryl. It isn't because I feel guilty for rushing in to try to save Gloria from the fire.

It's because I'm falling in love with him, and—I stare through a blur at the way his long, dark lashes curl against his pale skin—now he'll never know how much he means to me.

CHAPTER 19

Small Miracles

I CAN'T SLEEP. I'M SO WOUND UP, WHAT WITH RE-alizing too late my feelings for Alex, Emma coming back, worrying about the animals rescued from the fire, and coping with the searing pains in my arms, and the panic attacks that come upon me when my eyes close and the darkness takes over, and my mind fills with smoke and the roar of flames.

As I walk downstairs from the flat, I hold my hands out in front of me. They're shak-ing, and a layer of skin like tissue paper is peeling from my fingers.

"I thought you were told not to come back to work." Emma hands me a coffee and an open packet of biscuits as I sit down on the sofa in the staff room. "That's what Ben told me. He also said you spent a long time with Alex Fox-Gifford."

"Is there any news?" I ask, afraid that I've missed something in the past few hours when I've been lying awake, listening to the creaks and clunks that the house makes at night, as if, like me, it's shifting about, trying to find a comfortable position.

"About Alex?" Emma shakes her head. "Frances says that she's spoken to Fifi, who'd spoken to Sophia—she said there's no change."

"Oh."

"Maz, we need to have that talk, if you're up to it."

"What, about the inpatients?"

"Izzy and I came in early—we've dealt with them. They're doing well, even Ugli-dog and Raffles." Emma's expression is serious. I notice she's drinking fruit tea. She never drinks fruit tea. "You know, I never meant to leave you in the lurch. It was un-forgivable."

"But I've forgiven you . . ."

She goes on. "I've had some problems with cash flow recently—"

"Hey, that's my line," I cut in.

"You used it all the time at vet school—I remember it well." Emma's smile is brief, like the sun breaking through rain clouds. "Anyway, I thought I'd sorted it. I thought the takings would cover the bills as they came in, at least until I got back."

"Why didn't you say anything?"

"Oh, lots of reasons. Pride mainly, and I didn't want to put you off." Emma takes a sip of her tea, wrinkles her nose with disgust, and tips it away down the sink. "I hadn't even told Ben because I didn't want to worry him with it. I didn't want him subsidizing my business. We've sacrificed enough for Otter House already—quality time together, our marriage . . ." She turns toward me. "We're all right now though. We needed that time away. It's given me a sense of perspective."

"I don't understand—you always made out that the practice was a success."

"It's a girl thing. I wanted to prove I could do it myself." Her shoulders sag. "This only goes to prove that I can't."

"Don't talk rubbish—what you've done to get this far is amazing."

"But in the process I've come this close"—

she holds up one finger and thumb with the tiniest gap between them—"to losing the thing that's most important to me—my marriage. I'm so lucky to have Ben. He's stuck by me through this baby thing, even when I've been a moody old mare, which is most of the time. He deserves better than that."

"What will you do then? Will you give up the practice?"

Emma shrugs. "I don't know."

"You can't do that." Tripod, who's snoozing at the other end of the sofa, looks up at the sound of my raised voice.

"Why not?"

"It's your dream. Your life." Otter House Vets is the culmination of all she's worked for.

"It's a part of my life. As Ben has pointed out, it doesn't have to be the whole of it." Emma leans back against the counter.

"What about Izzy? What will she do? Where will she go? There aren't that many jobs around here. She'll have to travel."

"I know, I know." Emma chews on her lip, then turns back to me. "I don't know why you're so appalled. Izzy told me you were about to close the practice down the day before the fire. I did get your messages, but what you said didn't sink in somehow." I open my mouth to speak, but she goes on. "Nigel told me what you did— how you changed your mind and settled the outstanding bills out of your own pocket to stop the bailiffs turning up. He told me how you even had to sack Frances. I wish I hadn't put you in that situation."

"It was pretty awful," I say, smiling in spite of the tension.

"She can be rather scary."

"It isn't that." I've seen Frances's softer side. "She isn't working for fun—she needs the money. I felt so guilty."

"It wasn't your fault," Emma says, but it doesn't make me feel any better about it.

"I should have made sure I charged for the work I did, not let people get off without paying. I made that stupid mistake with Cheryl's cat. Worst of all, I killed Cadbury."

"You didn't kill him—Nigel told me what happened."

"Everyone thinks I did," I say, thinking especially of Izzy. "That's why you've got no clients left."

"That's a bit of an exaggeration," Emma says. "They're flooding back now anyway. It's all over town that we've taken Gloria's animals in and looked after them." She hesitates. "Friends?"

I nod. Nothing will ever change that.

"What are you going to do next?" I ask, referring to her long-term plans for Otter House, but Emma misunderstands me—deliberately, I think.

"I'm going to get back to work. There are a couple of consults left and three ops, so I'd better get a move on." Emma's gaze settles on the other end of the sofa, where Tripod is lying stretched out and belly-up. "What's that cat doing in here?"

"Er, sleeping."

"How did he get in?"

"Through the cat door."

"We haven't got a cat door."

"We have now. . . . Haven't you seen it?"

"I must have been too preoccupied to notice." Emma sighs. "What's its name?"

"He's called Tripod. I knew you wouldn't be keen on having a practice pet, but it's difficult to rehome a three-legged cat—most people want a whole one. I did try to resist, but once he'd got his paws under the table, I couldn't bring myself to evict him."

Emma tickles Tripod's chest. He opens one eye, mews, and closes it again.

"You fell on your feet, didn't you, the three you have left," she murmurs, and I think that's one problem solved. I'm worried though about the much larger one she's thrown up. I can't believe she's thinking of giving the practice up when it's meant everything to her. What about her loyal clients, and her patients? What will they do without her?

"I'll do the consults," I offer, remembering that my stethoscope went up in smoke in the fire.

Emma looks at me, a little pale and uncertain, then says, "All right then. Frances can run you up to the hospital afterward. You've got an appointment?"

I nod. I reckon the dressings on my arms would last another day, but who am I to argue? I'm just a vet, not a doctor, and anyway, it's a good excuse to visit Alex, to sit and watch over him, to hold his hand, to pull him through . . . I try to stay focused, positive.

CLIVE'S ARRIVAL CHEERS ME UP. He drops by first, dumping a large cardboard box on the table.

"It's always a worry when someone turns

up with a great big box like that—I'm never quite sure what I'm going to find inside it," I say.

"Our customers organized a collection," he explains, opening the lid to reveal a jumble of tins and boxes of pet food. He seems more cheerful than when I last saw him.

"I don't know how to thank you," I say, touched at the gesture. "It's great. Everyone's really pulling together to help."

"That's something I've learned about the good people of Talyton St. George this past week," Clive says. "They can behave like a bunch of mean bitches, prattling on about everybody's business but their own, but when someone's in trouble, they have hearts of gold." He pauses. "That's why I'm staying on. Edie thought I was going to do a runner—after Robbie . . ."

Don't cry, I urge him under my breath, otherwise you'll start me off, thinking of that beautiful day beside the river and the rose petals drifting across the lawn and catching in Robbie's coat.

Clive pulls a rumpled white handkerchief out of his pocket and blows his nose.

"I didn't think I'd be able to walk back in here, but I've done it," he says. "One day, one step at a time . . ."

"Why don't you come and have a look around Kennels as you're here?" I say, thinking of Petra.

"I'll never have another dog," Clive says, one step ahead of me. "Robbie was irreplaceable."

"I wasn't suggesting you replace him," I say, slightly hurt that he could think such a thing and wishing I hadn't introduced the idea quite so abruptly. I suppose it does look rather insensitive on my part, but Clive and Edie could offer one of those poor dogs out the back a wonderful home. "I was wondering if you'd be able to take one of the rescues."

"No. It's kind of you to think of me, Maz, but no. I've made up my mind. I'm busy with the pub. I've just started a new project to restore the wheel and the race, so we can get the mill working again. Another dog would be too much."

I'm disappointed. Petra isn't going to be the easiest dog to find a place for.

"I heard what happened to Stewart's

dog," Clive goes on. "You're a good vet, Maz, and I wouldn't have had anyone else look after Robbie. I just wanted you to know."

"Thanks, Clive." I watch him go, stopping for a word with Frances on the way. I wish other people had his faith in me.

Back in my room, I clean the table, wash my hands, and log in to the computer. There's no one waiting, according to the list, but there's definitely someone in Reception.

"Ooooh!" I hear a high-pitched howl that makes me think of werewolves. "Ooooh, what shall I tell the children?"

I rush out to take a look. Frances is holding a shoe box, Ally Jackson a box of tissues. Ally's hair is a mess, and her skirt is caught up at the back.

"There there, dear," Frances says. "Do you want to take him home with you?"

Ally grimaces. "I don't think I can bear it."

"I'll deal with it for you then." Frances glances toward me. "I'm afraid it's too late, Maz. Harry has"—she lowers her voice—"expired."

"Ooooh!" Ally starts howling again.

Frances reverses through the swing

doors, holding the shoe box out in front of her, then disappears up the corridor.

"What happened, Ally?" I ask.

"I opened the cage to give Harry his half a biscuit this morning—he soooo loves a digestive—and I found him at the bottom of the tube that leads up to his penthouse." She stuffs a ball of tissue between her lips and is unable to say any more.

Who declared him dead? I wonder. Ally or Frances?

"Frances!" I catch up with her in the laundry room, the shoe box sticking out of the rubbish bin, her finger on the button of the clinical waste compressor. "Stop!"

She straightens a little, her finger still on the button.

"I'll be back at my post in just a tick, Maz."

"Don't press that button. I want to check on Harry."

"Why? He's dead," she says, stepping aside so I can peer over her shoulder into the compressor. "Look."

Harry is curled up on a nest of kitchen roll.

"Excuse me." I reach past Frances,

catching the static on her polyester tunic with a crackle. I pick Harry out and hold him cupped in my palm. He's cool and smooth, like a beach pebble. But I'm pretty certain I can feel the tiniest lift of his rib cage and faintest beat of his heart. "He's alive. Just."

"You mean?" Frances recoils from the compressor, her face white with shock, as if she's seen a ghost, which I suppose, in a way, she has.

I'm beginning to understand why Ally is so attached to him—he has the cutest little nose and whiskers, and he's a fighter.

"I'll talk to Ally," I say, and Frances gets the incubator out of the cupboard, so I can pop Harry inside it on my way out.

I SUPPOSE YOU'D describe Harry as being in a state of suspended animation brought on by a drop in temperature. It's a natural, physiological response to ensure survival in the wild. I doubt it has the same benefit for hamsters in captivity—how many have been buried alive by their well-meaning owners?

I'm being morbid. It's not knowing about Alex, you see.

I check that Izzy's happy for me to leave Harry with her and Emma while Frances drops me at the hospital. Emma looks as if she's going down with some bug she's caught abroad, Delhi belly or malaria maybe. Gloria's animals need me. Otter House needs me. Keep strong! I think. I have no choice, and if I'm honest, I wouldn't have it any other way. It feels good to be needed.

Frances drops me off and goes shopping while I have my dressings changed and then head to see Alex, my body buzzing with nerves as I wonder what I'm going to find.

"Don't you have a home to go to?" I ask, finding Debbie at her workstation, a pen in one hand and a chocolate biscuit in the other.

"Hi, Maz," she says brightly.

"How is he?"

"You'll have to ask him yourself."

"He's awake?" My pulse flutters with hope. "Is he going to be all right?"

"Let's just say it's looking very promising, but—"

"It's early days, one step at a time, et cetera," I cut in.

Debbie smiles. "You could do my job."

"I am sure I couldn't. Animals can't tell me what's wrong with them, but at least they don't answer back." I pause. "Can I go through now?"

"You'll have to wait a few minutes." Debbie looks at me quizzically. "He has someone with him."

"His parents?"

"She didn't say exactly, but she's the third female visitor today. Our Alex is remarkably popular with the ladies." Debbie looks at the clock behind her. "She's had her fifteen minutes. I'll ask her to leave now—we mustn't wear him out."

It's Eloise. When we pass in the corridor I say hi, but she doesn't acknowledge me, which I suppose isn't surprising seeing as I've only met her once and I'm in a tearing hurry to reach Alex's bedside.

There's a figure lying on Alex's bed, very still and silent, and shrouded with rumpled white sheets, like a corpse.

Is he . . . ? I reach out my hand and pull the top of the sheet down to reveal his face. There are no tubes, no machines.

"I thought, I thought you'd woken up," I

whisper, wondering how Debbie has got it so wrong.

Biting my lip, I touch the curve of his cheek. It's cool and prickly with stubble. His complexion is pale, and the bruise on his temple has darkened to a grayish purple. His eyes are closed. However, there's the slightest movement of the sheet covering his body, and his lips part slightly, exhaling warm breath. Even then it takes me a moment to decide that it isn't wishful thinking on my part and he really is alive.

My shock at finding him like this is replaced by relief, then anxiety.

"Alex, please wake up . . ."

He doesn't respond, and I don't know what to do because I have so much I want to tell him, how I'm sorry for misjudging him, for assuming he was just like his father, for being sharp with him when he was only trying to help me out. I want to tell him how my heart beats faster whenever I'm with him, whenever I think about him, how much I . . .

"Alex," I say, "I love you." I lean down and press my lips against his. One moment I'm looking at his eyelids; the next,

I'm looking into his eyes. The pupils darken and dilate. The creases at the corners deepen. "Alex?"

I straighten up, gazing at him in wonder.

Alex's lips, the ones I've just brazenly kissed, curve into a smile, and my toes curl with embarrassment. Did he hear what I said?

"I thought you'd had a relapse," I say joyfully.

"I thought I was dreaming," he murmurs, and my heart soars, only to come crashing back to earth when he adds, "Eloise?"

If I were rigged up to a heart monitor right now, I would be flatlining. He told me he wasn't involved with her.

"I'm Maz." I stare at him, uncertain. He's had a knock on the head. He's been unconscious for some time. Am I speaking to the Alex I knew before, or a slightly different Alex, who's lost his memory? "Don't you remember me?"

"How could I forget?" he says wryly. He rolls onto one elbow and winces. "Has she gone?" He lies back down, massaging his forehead. "Thank goodness for that. Don't get me wrong, she's lovely, but her constant chattering on and on about her new horse was giving me a headache. I pretended to fall asleep. I'm sorry if I frightened you." He grins, and I realize that he hasn't changed at all. "I didn't think you cared . . ."

"Do you want me to get you something?" I say, trying to cover my confusion. It's all very well confessing true love to an unconscious man, but it's quite different when you discover he was awake at the time. He doesn't mention it, maybe out of respect for my feelings. I doubt very much that he feels the same way about me.

"Maz, I've had enough fuss for one day. I'll be fine." Alex sits up against the head of the bed and pats the mattress. "Sit down and fill me in on all the gossip. No one will tell me anything."

I perch on the end of the bed, facing him. He's wearing pajamas with a T-shirt-style top. A few dark hairs curl across the base of his neck.

"Don't spare me any gory details," he says. "All I know is that I had a knock on the head, and a touch of concussion."

"Concussion? You were out cold for hours—no, days. It felt like a lifetime. I've been worried sick." I lower my voice. "You saved my life."

Alex frowns. "Did I?"

"I behaved like a complete idiot, rushing in without thinking."

"What about you?" He looks at my bandages. "Your arms?"

"It looks worse than it is," I say.

"Gloria?" Alex says. "What happened to Gloria? I can't remember anything after . . ."

"She died in the fire," I say quietly. "She set the cottage alight herself." She took a load of pills—Ginge's included, it turns out, not that they would have had any effect on her—and lit several small fires with firelighters and kerosene. Even if I'd managed to get her out, they say she would probably have died from the overdose. "We saved most of her rescues, but the cottage was destroyed."

"Have they held the funeral yet?" Alex asks.

"I can find out."

"I'd like to go, if it hasn't happened already."

"I'll let you know," I say, feeling guilty that I hadn't thought of Gloria's funeral myself. Alex seems as upset as I was at Gloria's demise. She was quite a character, who touched both our lives in her own way.

"I think that's enough for now," Debbie interrupts. "You have to pace yourself, Alex—I'm worrying about how many more of your girlfriends will be calling in on you today."

"Maz isn't my girlfriend," Alex says. "She's my fiancée." He looks at me, chuckling. "That's what she told you, wasn't it, Debbie?" He's teasing me, I think, trying not to blush as he goes on. "Is it time for my bed bath?"

"You should be so lucky," Debbie teases. "You're big enough and ugly enough to use the shower yourself."

"When will you be back, Maz?" Alex asks, turning back to me.

"Um, I don't know," I stammer. "Do you want me to . . . ?"

"Of course I do." He's doing it again, I think. He's back to his old self. "The novelty of daytime TV wore off in half an hour, and I can't stand grapes."

"I hate to think we're boring you," Debbie says, with mock severity, "but you've had a head injury. You can't go home just yet."

"How long?" I ask.

"For as long as he behaves himself, and when he does go home, he won't be running around the countryside sticking his arm up cows' backsides and wrestling with sheep. He'll be grounded for a week or two at least."

Alex grasps my hand, interlinking his fingers through mine and giving them an affectionate squeeze. "Could you do me a favor?"

"Depends on what it is," I say.

"Don't listen to him, Maz," Debbie says. "I've already told him he can't have his horse brought in to see him."

"It isn't that," he says. "Would you run into town and buy me a new mobile? My mother won't let me have one. She doesn't want me getting overexcited."

"I'll bring it tomorrow." I hover at his bedside, not wanting to leave.

"Go on, off you go." Debbie shoos me out, and I finally tear myself away, turning to hide the tears of joy. I nip into the toilets to wash my face before I meet Frances out in the car park.

"Can I borrow your phone?" I ask as I get into her car. I want to let the whole world know that Alex is going to be all right, but I guess Emma and Izzy will do to start with.

"Go ahead," Frances says, nodding to

the outsize first- or second-generation brick of a mobile in the top of her handbag.

"I'll pay for the call," I say, remembering that poor Frances has been working the past three days without pay, a situation that I can't allow to continue for too much longer. "Hi, is that you, Izzy? Great news." I try to sound cool about it, but really it's the most fantastic, wonderful, and unbelievable result. "He's come round."

Izzy sounds confused. "How did you know?"

"Because I've just been talking to him."

"Harry?"

"Alex."

Izzy giggles. "I'm such an idiot sometimes. I'm so pleased. Harry's awake too and fighting fit. He's just tried to bite me, the little sod, I mean sausage."

I take Alex's recovery as a good omen, and on our way back I persuade Frances to stop by at Gloria's place to check on the trap. It's empty and there's no sign of Ginge, but I'm not going to give up until I know what's happened to him.

"VET'S MIRACLE RECOVERY—I can see the headline now," Ally says, handing me a bottle of wine. "Two miracles in one day. Words can't express how grateful I am," she goes on, which strikes me as a bit of a problem for someone whose livelihood depends on them. "I'm going to make sure everyone in town knows what you did. To think he could"—her eyes fill with tears—"have been crushed alive."

I hand her the shoe box across the consulting room table. Harry gives me the evil eye when I open the lid to prove to myself, more than to Ally, that he really is okay.

"Do I need to bring him back for a checkup?"

"Not unless you're worried about him."

"I'm always worried about him. I tell you, I shan't be leaving him in the garden shed overnight again. It must have been pretty chilly for June."

"What was he doing in the shed?" I can't believe someone as dotty about her hamster as Ally is would banish him from the house.

"My other half's threatening to divorce me. Harry keeps us awake all night, running on his wheel."

"Why don't you take the wheel out?" I suggest helpfully.

"I couldn't do that, poor thing. He loves his wheel. No, I'm going to buy a couple of pairs of earplugs." Ally smiles. "That way I'll save Harry and my marriage. Maz, how can I repay you? Can I help with the animals you've rescued from the fire? Raise money for their care? Anything?"

"You could adopt another hamster, or one of the other small furries."

"I don't think I could stand the stress. . . . No, Harry's more than enough for me to cope with. Isn't there anything else?"

"Actually," I say, thinking of all those animals, including Raffles, Ugli-dog, Petra, and Jude, who are out the back, desperately needing good homes, "there is something you can do."

THEY DON'T LIKE being confined. I do a last round of Kennels the same evening, taking each dog out into the garden in turn—well, Raffles and Ugli-dog are happy to go out together, but I don't risk taking Petra with any of the others. Now Emma's back, I rather miss having Miff's company in the flat. I'm tempted to let Raffles upstairs, especially when he looks at me with brown eyes filled with despair as I shut the kennel door on him, but that seems mean on the rest of them. I give them each a biscuit and leave the radio on low before I turn out the light.

"Good night, guys," I say softly. It's all quiet and I can relax at last, except for the persistent stinging sensation from the burns on my arms, and wondering how I'm going to persuade Emma to keep Otter House Vets open and what I'm going to do about Alex.

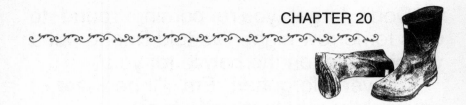

CHAPTER 20

A Breed Apart

"ARE YOU GOING TO SEE ALEX AGAIN?" EMMA says between consultations the next morning. She seems happier, I think. Perhaps she's changed her mind about closing the practice down.

"Can't you tell?" Izzy cuts in. "She's put her makeup on specially."

"Izzy! I said I'd drop a few bits and pieces in to him as I was going to be there anyway." You know that feeling you get when you're about to blush and you can't do anything about it? I've got it now. "I'm doing my bit for neighborly relations, that's all. I'll see you later."

"Don't forget you're coming round to ours tomorrow night. I've told Ben to put a veggie cutlet on the barbie for you."

"I haven't forgotten, Em. I'll be there." I pause. "Are you feeling better?"

"I am, thanks. I guess it's a touch of Delhi belly," she says. "Go on then, angel of mercy. What are you waiting for?"

WHEN I ARRIVE at the hospital, I check in with Debbie.

"Hello, Maz," she says. "I'm glad you're here—you might be able to knock some sense into him. No one else can."

Before I can ask her what she means, the phone on her workstation rings.

"Go on through," she says, picking it up.

I find Alex clean-shaven and dressed in jeans and a casual shirt. He sits on the edge of his bed with a sports bag beside him.

"Hi," he says, smiling.

I walk toward him, catching his scent of aftershave and mint toothpaste. The closer I get, the faster my heart beats.

"I've brought you your stuff," I begin. "I'm sorry I didn't get here sooner, but I've been tied up at Otter House since I saw you yesterday. I'm trying to stop Emma over-doing it—she hasn't been well."

"It's nothing serious, I hope."

"Ben was worried enough to suggest that they come home early."

"Emma's very lucky to have you around to share the workload. I don't know how my father's coping on his own. I dread to think what's been happening at the manor, and I can't sit here any longer, worrying about it, so"—he catches my hand—"I want you to help me make my escape."

Now I know what Debbie was getting at, I think, as he continues. "I can't stand it here any longer. I want to get out in the fresh air, eat some decent food, and sleep in my own bed."

He looks over my shoulder. I turn to find Debbie listening in.

"He shouldn't be alone for the next twenty-four hours," she says, "and I'm warn-ing you, he isn't the easiest of patients."

"Please, Maz."

"I thought you'd have a queue of people lined up to take you home."

"You mean Eloise?" He grins. "I didn't think you'd be in the slightest bit bothered."

"I'm not," I say sharply, and he laughs,

making me flush hot because he knows I'm lying.

"You know, if you were a chocolate, Maz, you'd be a hazelnut whirl, one of those with the nut in the center that you crack your teeth on."

"Thanks a lot." I try to sound arch and devil-may-care, but it comes out flat because I'm not really like that. I do have a soft center, but since Mike, I keep it buried deep inside.

"So you'll do it?" Alex says. "At least give me a lift home and stay with me until my parents get back from London."

I'll do it, but out of the purest of motives—because I owe him for saving my life.

"Okay then," I say, giving in. "I'm off for the rest of today."

"Great," Alex says, standing up. I notice how he puts out his hand momentarily to steady himself. "I've been lying down for too long," he says, when Debbie and I rush to help him, one on each side.

"Alex, I wish you'd change your mind," Debbie says. "Another day won't hurt."

"I'll be fine. Maz'll look after me."

I didn't make a very good job of it the last time, I think, when he picks up his bag. He links one arm through mine, and we walk side by side out through the corridors and into the sunlight.

"Did you get that mobile for me?" he asks as soon as we're clear of the hospital buildings. "I need to check up on Liberty."

I dig it out of my bag and hand it over. "I did call Westleigh, and she's doing well, according to John," I say, but Alex insists on phoning himself to find out every last detail on the way to my car.

I unlock it and open the doors, then watch Alex fold himself up and slide into the passenger seat.

"There isn't much room in here," he comments. "What do you do with all your kit?"

"There's space for a visit case—that's all I need. Anyway, it means I don't have to carry the hairy, incontinent, or bleeding in the back. Where are we going?"

"Up to the manor. I don't live in the main house—that's my father's domain. I live in the barn."

"A barn?" I have a vision of Alex and his horse eating breakfast over a bale of straw.

He grins. "It's a conversion. My mother sometimes threatens to take it back to store extra hay for the horses."

"Silly me," I say.

"Maz, it's one of the things I like about you, your ditsiness." He reaches out and runs his fingers lightly across my hand as I change gears. "That's a compliment, by the way."

"Thanks," I say, driving on.

"I'm sorry," Alex says suddenly. "I shouldn't have imposed on you."

"I don't mind."

"You must have far better things to do with your time."

"I promised Fifi I'd help her and her volunteers with some of the rehoming visits sometime, but it can wait. We want to make sure the rescues are going to good homes."

"That's a bit over the top, if you ask me."

"I'm not asking you," I say, grinning. "And I can understand why Fifi wants to do it—Gloria's animals need the best homes possible after what they've been through."

"Now you're making me feel really guilty."

"Don't be." Little does he know that it's no sacrifice. "I checked with Frances about the funeral—it's next week. I'll give you a lift."

"Would you?" At this moment I'd do anything for him, I think, as he goes on. "This is it. Turn left here."

I've seen the manor before, of course, but not up close. Traveling up the long drive, I realize that it's bigger than I recall, an elegant Regency house with white walls, a slate roof, and fluted pillars supporting the porch at the front. There's a cedar tree on the lawn and roses in the formal flower beds. Eat your heart out, Mr. Darcy.

In the field to the west is a herd of South Devon cattle. To the east and continuing round behind the house are paddocks divided by electric fencing tape for horses, and a riding arena set up with a course of show jumps.

"You can park around the back," Alex says, and I follow the left-hand sweep of the drive, turning in to the courtyard behind the house and stopping alongside some other vehicles, including a battered Range Rover with a broken brake light, the purple horse lorry, and a vintage Bentley, just as a pack of dogs—a mixture of Labs and spaniels—come racing toward the car, barking.

Alex flings open the passenger door, unfolds himself to get out, and then almost disappears into a flurry of flying dogs and thrashing tails. They're all over him, barking and tugging at his clothes.

"That's enough now," he says, holding up one hand, and immediately they settle down and start milling around instead.

"You don't want another dog, do you?" I say, joining him on the gravel, taking in the surroundings. The rear of the manor forms one side of the courtyard, a row of stables with a second story above forms a second side, and a barn made of brick and an oak frame with long windows forms the third.

"Probably not. Not unless you're desperate." Alex heads toward the stables.

"Where are you going?"

"I want to check up on a few things in the surgery. I left some stuff undone. It's been preying on my mind."

I reach for his arm to slow him down, but he strides on toward a sign reading SURGERY, with an arrow pointing vaguely skyward.

"Are you sure that's wise? You're supposed to be resting," I say, but he's already halfway way up the steps to a door at the end of a balcony above the row of brick stables, some of which are occupied, some closed up. Alex takes the steps two at a time, and I follow. He unlocks the door and pushes it open, letting me past.

I step inside, tripping over a cardboard box of yellowing paperwork on the way into a long, shadowy room. The shelves are overflowing with books, old leather-bound manuals with titles such as *Poultry Management* and *How to Physic a Horse,* and on the walls are photos of Old Fox-Gifford dressed in shooting gear with a gun slung over his shoulder, pheasants hanging from one hand and a Labrador at his feet; Sophia riding sidesaddle, rosettes pinned to her horse's bridle; and Alex jumping various ponies and Liberty. I smile to myself because it seems to me that the Fox-Giffords are a breed apart.

There's a desk too, a vast mahogany affair covered with diaries, notebooks, biscuit wrappers, and boxes of cattle antibiotic, and there's an all-pervasive odor of dog. I can see why Frances might have wanted to move from Talyton Manor to the more salubrious surroundings of Otter House.

Alex rifles through the papers on the desk and selects two.

"Lab reports," he says. "I don't suppose

my father's thought to phone the results through to the clients. He isn't a great believer in blood tests. He's more of the old school, like his father before him—if a cow's down, you chuck a cat on its back to see if it'll get up." He pauses to check the answerphone. A voice—I think it's Sophia's—gives out the numbers for Westleigh and another vet practice. Alex turns it off and deletes the message.

"What did you do that for?" I ask.

"I'm here—I can take the phones now." He silences me with one of his withering looks. "I don't want to risk all our clients deserting us for good. The sooner I'm back in harness the better." His expression softens. "I won't overdo it, Maz. I promise. One thing I learned, lying in that hospital, is that I've got too much to live for."

I guess he's referring to his family, especially his children.

"Let's go," he says, and we head for the barn. He opens up the double doors along the side and hooks them back to the wall. "After you." He follows me inside, where the air is cooler. "What do you think?"

I look around at the open-plan space downstairs, the contrast of old and new, and the galleried landing upstairs. There's a large brick fireplace, wooden floors, and a couple of leather sofas in chocolate. It's quite masculine. A bachelor pad.

"It's amazing," I say, taking in the vaulted ceiling, crisscrossed with beams, "like Dr. Who's TARDIS."

"It isn't all that big," Alex says seriously. "My parents had it converted when I got married, but Astra and I only lived here for a couple of years before the children came along. It wasn't spacious enough for her, so we moved out to a house a couple of miles north of here." He smiles ruefully. "I did my best, but it was never good enough for her."

"I'm sorry."

"Don't be. It's all in the past now. I married her because I liked her—as well as all the other stuff. I was devastated when she went off with someone else."

"The footballer . . ." I wish I hadn't said it, ashamed at myself for listening to gossip, the same tittle-tattle that made Alex out to be a womanizer, when he clearly isn't.

"Yeah," he continues. "The divorce nearly finished me off. I couldn't concentrate on anything, and if it hadn't been for Lucie and Seb, I'd have walked out on the practice,

Talyton"—he waves his hand—"everything."
As if reading my mind, he goes on. "We
might never have met. And I suppose, if
you hadn't split with the robot—"

"Mike, you mean?" I cut in, suddenly realizing that I no longer wince when I say
his name, which has a lot to do with the
man standing in front of me.

"Izzy told me a bit about him—when I
was up at Chris's. She was afraid she'd
ruined the course of true love with her rev-
elation, but I told her I already knew." Alex
moves a little closer. "Idle gossip is rife in
Talyton, but it does have its uses."

He's so close now I can feel his breath,
making the hairs on the back of my neck
stand on end. If he should take my hand
and lead me up the stairs to the gallery, I
wouldn't resist . . .

"I'll get the coffee on," he says, breaking
the spell.

"I'll do it," I say, but he insists.

"You look tired," he says, gazing at me.
"I'm fine—I've been in bed for days. Go
and sit down."

His hands are on my shoulders, turning
me toward the sofa closest to the long
window, where a shaft of sunlight slants

through, illuminating a child's plastic trike and an abandoned My Little Pony toy in the corner. I long for Alex to sit down with me, never to take his hands off me, but instead he wanders over to the kitchen area at the far end of the barn.

I'm not tired, but I tip my head back and close my eyes, feeling the heat from the sun on my face and listening to the sounds of Alex preparing coffee, of the pigeons cooing outside, and of the horses whickering and banging at their stable doors.

I WAKE TO the sensation of something warm and heavy leaning against me. The leather squeaks as the weight shifts further toward me. There's the briefest touch of something against my lips, the scent of coffee and mint. It isn't unpleasant. In fact—the contact returns for longer this time—it's amazing and reassuringly familiar. I open my eyes. Alex's gorgeous, smoky blue eyes smolder at me.

"I'm sorry," he tells me.

"Don't be," I say softly, reaching out and resting my hand on his shoulder.

"I couldn't resist," he whispers, touching the side of my face with his fingertips. "Sleeping Beauty."

"I'm supposed to be watching out for you . . ." I catch the edge of Alex's collar and pull him toward me, my pulse beating a chaotic rhythm of will I, won't I? Should we, shouldn't we?

Alex answers, pressing his lips to mine, his breathing ragged and matching mine, and I'm just about to lose my mind with desire when he pulls away.

"Don't stop," I murmur brazenly.

"I'm so happy," he says. "I'm so glad you've decided to stay here."

"Stay? To look after you, yes."

He frowns. "I meant in Talyton."

"I'm not," I say, unsure what I've said or done to give him that impression.

"I thought you'd decided to stay on at Otter House?" His eyes are dark with disappointment, and my heart aches because I feel as if I've let him down. "Perhaps I dreamed it," he goes on. "There have been some funny things going on in my head since, you know"—his voice grows husky— "the fire . . ."

Even as he mentions it, I can hear the terrifying roar of the flames and clatter of tumbling masonry all over again, and my heart beats even faster and I want him to hold me, to make love to me and obliterate those memories, and start all over again with new and happier memories of our own.

I begin to unfasten the buttons on my blouse as his fingers trace the curve of my jaw, down the side of my neck, and along the ridge of my collarbone, then hesitate.

"What's wrong?" I ask, aware that he's looking past me, over the back of the sofa, toward—I turn to see—the shelf on the wall behind us. Two children—Alex's children—gaze back from silver-framed photographs: Lucie from the back of a Shetland pony, grinning from ear to ear beneath a riding hat that appears far too big; Sebastian with a mop of curly hair cuddling a big old black Lab. I turn back to Alex and watch his pupils shrink as he withdraws, doing up my buttons as fast as I can undo them.

"No"—he tangles his fingers with mine—"stop. Maz, this is wrong."

I don't understand. "It feels right to me . . ." Confused and frustrated, I try to bring him back to me, but it's as if he's shut the door on his emotions and trapped them inside. "Alex, I'm—"

"Please don't say it," he cuts in, pressing his fingers to my lips. "Don't make this any more difficult than it already is." He pulls away and sits beside me, not touching. I grab a cushion and clutch it to my chest to cover what feels like a gaping hole, a crushing pain where he's as good as ripped my heart out. I think I love him, but he doesn't love me back.

"I know how you feel, Maz," he begins gruffly.

"No, you don't," I say sharply.

"I think I do . . ."

"It's all right anyway." I make to stand up. "I made a mistake. I read too much into . . . whatever it was we had."

"Sit down," he says firmly.

There's something in the tone of his voice that makes me settle back on the sofa, putting the cushion between us, like a barrier.

"I do like you, Maz. In fact, I'm very fond of you, but despite my reputation—due in part to my misspent youth, chasing girls around the countryside with Stewart—I don't go for one-night stands. In my experience, someone always gets hurt." He lowers his voice and adds softly, "I can't bear the thought of hurting you."

You've just hurt me by rejecting me, I

think, but the expression in his eyes is tender as he continues, "We'd both get in too deep."

"Oh, Alex . . ." His name catches in my throat as he reaches out and strokes my hand. He's right. There are so many reasons why we shouldn't take our friendship any further.

"I wish you weren't leaving Talyton," he says, and I almost say, "So do I . . ." This has to be the worst day of my life. I've fallen in with love with this man and now I'm walking out on him for good, and why?

But I know why. I'd never be happy in Talyton. It would never feel like home to me. I messed up with Cadbury, and I'll never be allowed to forget.

The horses start neighing and banging at their doors, and a car comes scrunching across the gravel to park alongside mine.

"That's the parents," Alex sighs.

"I should go." I stand up again. Alex won't let go of my hand.

"Don't leave Talyton without saying good-bye, will you?" His voice sounds small, as if it's taken all his effort to speak. "Promise me, Maz."

"I promise," I mutter, tearing myself away

from the intensity of his eyes, and his grasp, and under my breath I add, "Good-bye, Alex," so I don't have to break my promise in the future, and have him break my heart all over again.

WHEN I LET myself back into the practice, Tripod comes prup-prupping up on his three legs. He hops up the stairs with me, holding his tail at an angle to aid his balance, and then jumps onto the bed. "Push off," I say companionably. He takes no notice, of course.

I sink down on the edge of the bed, and he treads across the duvet and insinuates himself on my lap, butting his head against my chin and purring, as if to say, "It can't be as bad as you're making out." I put my arms around him. Sometimes I wish I were a cat.

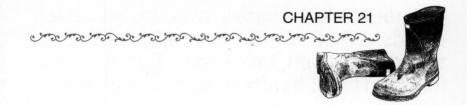

CHAPTER 21

Horses for Courses

"THE COUNTRY AIR SUITS YOU, MAZ. YOU'RE positively glowing, unlike my briquettes." Ben holds his palms toward me as I approach. "I wonder who's been lighting your fire. I could use him to get the barbie going."

Ben and Emma invited me for a barbie, and we're in the garden at the back of their house. I'd expected them to settle for a place with history, like Otter House, but this is a new-build on the housing estate Old Fox-Gifford considered to be beneath his dogs, if I remember correctly.

The house is a good size, but the garden is what estate agents describe as "manageable." There's a patio, on which stands a hot tub, and an area of freshly turfed lawn. Ben, dressed in T-shirt, shorts that don't suit him because he has what I call Popeye legs—bulging with muscle and covered with a wiry fuzz—and an apron with COME AND GET IT on the front, is tinkering with his barbecue on the decking at the far end, which overlooks a field of young maize plants. Miff, who was actually pleased to see me, sits in the flower bed, playing a game of risk with a bee.

Emma, looking cool in a long navy skirt and white vest top, hands me a glass of Pimm's and lemonade, mixed with crushed ice and slices of cucumber and orange, the way we always made it in Cambridge.

"Cheers," she says, clashing a glass of what looks like lemonade against mine.

"Cheers," I say in return.

"Perhaps it's Alex Fox-Gifford," Ben says.

"Hardly, Ben. Honestly, you're a hoot." Laughing, Emma turns to me. "I don't know why you've been doing him all these favors though. If it wasn't for Alex and his precious horse, you wouldn't have been anywhere near Buttercross Cottage on the night of the fire."

Suddenly, I find my loyalties torn between my best friend and a Fox-Gifford.

"If it wasn't for Alex," I say quietly, "I wouldn't be here now."

"So that's it." I can hear the relief in Emma's voice. "You've been looking after him because you feel somehow responsible for what happened?"

"I don't think it's that at all," Ben cuts in. "Can't you see? She's in love with him."

"Darling, do stop pulling poor Maz's leg," Emma says, and I turn aside to face the sun, which hangs like an orange fireball over the hills to the west, hoping she won't notice my burning cheeks. "That's ridiculous. He's a complete boor."

There was a time when I would have agreed with her, but I know differently now. I want to tell her how kind, sensitive, and thoughtful he is, but there's no point.

"It doesn't matter," I say. "I don't suppose I'll see him again."

"What about Gloria's funeral?"

I shrug. I assume he'll be there, but he hasn't been in touch about wanting a lift. I guess he's avoiding me. I mean, he did try to let me down gently when I threw myself at him like some old tart, like my mother does at anything in possession of a Y chromosome.

"Well, I'm more than happy for you to go as one of Otter House's representatives. I expect Izzy will go, and Frances wouldn't miss it for the world," Emma says. "I'll hold the fort."

"I'll be going," says Ben. "Gloria was one of my patients."

Emma puts her glass down on the table on the patio, walks up to me, and links her arm through mine. "Come inside and give me a hand with the salad."

In the kitchen, we chop tomatoes and cucumber. I don't get to do much cooking, and it's actually quite therapeutic.

"I have a confession to make," Emma begins as she starts mixing the dressing. "I'm not ill—I'm pregnant."

"You're what?" The sharp scent of balsamic vinegar hits my throat. "I thought you said . . . Oh, that's wonderful news!" I put the paring knife down and give her a hug.

"We kind of stopped trying so hard,

knowing that we were coming back to visit the fertility clinic for tests, and it just happened. Life's full of surprises, isn't it?" Emma says, her eyes shining brightly.

"When's the baby due?" I ask.

"It's very early days yet," Emma says, sobering up. "It's a souvenir from our holiday."

"Ben must be delighted," I say, watching him blowing onto the barbecue, tiny flames licking up through the rack.

"He's over the moon," Emma says softly. "We both are." Smiling, she touches her stomach, and I feel an unexpected tick of my biological clock. "So, we've been talking things over, and we've decided I should take on another vet on a permanent basis. And now you must be able to guess what I'm going to say, Maz. I want that vet to be you."

"M-m-me?" I stammer.

"I'm offering you an equal partnership in the business," she says, beaming at me like an overenthusiastic puppy. "Well? I wasn't expecting stunned silence."

"I thought you were thinking of closing the practice down."

"Ben wouldn't hear of it. He's still sure

that we can make a go of it." She pauses as if collecting herself. "It's what Mum would have wanted. Maz, it isn't just about money. I've known some of my clients for years. Some of them have known me since I was a baby. I'd like to be able to carry on looking after their pets."

My instinct is to say no, but why not? My thoughts meander back to our cozy chats at vet school, our plans to work together. A permanent job with my best friend. Only small animals. No sheep. And a coffee machine. It's all falling into place.

I gaze at Emma, at the disappointment that clouds her face when I don't respond.

"I've waited so long for this baby," she says, "I want to spend as much time as I can with him, or her. I'd like to be able to take maternity leave, knowing the practice is in safe hands. Please, Maz."

"It's all a bit of a surprise. I'm not sure . . ." I glance down at my "not-so-safe" hands and the bandages—lighter ones now—on my arms. Am I up to the job? Look at what happened to the practice when Emma left me in charge the last time.

"We'll have to go house hunting. You'll

need somewhere to live—you don't want to stay above the shop for the rest of your life." She pauses. "Maz, cheer up. You look as if I've just condemned you to death. Aren't you pleased?"

"I'm really pleased that you asked me . . ."

"What's the problem then?"

"I never planned to live in the country," I say. "It's too quiet for me." I think of how long it takes to buy a newspaper, of the mud and muck, of the gossip, of how the people of Talyton St. George don't like me . . . Well, a lot of them don't. They might be rallying round to help with the rescues, but they don't respect me as a vet. What about Izzy? I'd be her boss, yet she doesn't trust me. And then I think of Alex . . . "Emma, I need time to think it over."

"That's all right." Emma gazes at me as if she's searching for clues as to which way I'll decide. "Take all the time you need."

I pick up my glass and follow her back out to the garden, where Ben is carefully tweaking the steaks and burgers so they're equal distances apart on the grill. I smile to myself. He's going to have to change when he becomes a dad—there won't be time for such precision. I congratulate him on the baby.

"I've popped the question, Ben," Emma says, "and Maz says she isn't sure."

"I told you it was a bit much to expect an instant answer, darling," Ben says, turning fondly to his wife. "It's a huge decision."

"I know," Emma says, her eyes downcast.

"It's a lovely place to live, Maz," Ben says, waving his spatula toward the vista of green hills beyond the garden. "Look at that view."

He's right, I think. It is beautiful, but could I really put down roots in Talyton St. George? I know that if I don't, I'm back on the road, not knowing where life's journey will take me next.

As I'm watching the seagulls sweep across the sky, I notice a tiny plume of smoke rising from the barbecue behind Ben.

"Ben, something's burning," I say quickly.

"Oops," he says, turning back to salvage the food while Emma pops indoors and returns with a packet of veggie burgers.

"Don't burn those," she says, smiling, as

she gives them to Ben. "They're the only ones we've got." Emma returns to my side. "Now, Maz, why don't we talk this through? What's getting in the way?"

"There's Talyton Manor Vets?" I say after a pause. I can imagine Old Fox-Gifford's reaction if I should decide to stay.

"Yeah . . ." Emma looks at me through narrowed eyes. "They got to you too, didn't they?"

They did, I think, flushing slightly, but not in the way she's thinking of. I touch the cool glass in my hand briefly to my face.

"Damn them." Emma kicks at a clod of earth. "They're the bane of my life. They still want to ruin everything for me."

"Emma, they aren't all that bad. Large-animal work's in decline. Otter House and Talyton Manor Vets are after the same thing."

"Anyone would think you were on their side, Maz," Emma says dismissively. "Look, I've asked Frances to stay on. Is that part of the problem?"

"No, Frances isn't so bad when you get to know her." It's actually Izzy, I think, but I don't feel able to tell Emma about how I sometimes feel uncomfortable working with her. She doesn't trust me after what happened with Blueboy and Cadbury, and I don't see what I can do to regain her trust.

"Is it the money? I realize joining Otter House Vets as a partner doesn't look like the most attractive prospect at the moment, but that's my fault. I wanted the practice to be perfect when I set it up, and I spent too much on it. I'm sure we can get the finances back on track."

"You don't seem to have enough clients to make it work," I say.

"They're coming back," she says, "and there are more families moving into Talyton all the time."

"They're coming back because of you, Em. They prefer to see you, because they don't trust me."

"What about Ally and Mr. Brown? I haven't heard them complaining."

"I know, but . . ." I tail off as Emma finishes my sentence for me.

"The people who live here are perfectly capable of making up their own minds. They know you went overboard with Cheryl's cat, but they also know that Cheryl

can be a spiteful gossip. They know Cadbury died after you operated on him, but
they also understand that things can, and
do, go wrong. They're very forgiving, and I
wish you'd stop wallowing and start looking
on the positive side. You helped Clive Taylor through a tough time with Robbie, and
rescued Gloria's animals . . ." Emma falters, then glances at me, a spark of amuse-
ment in her eyes. "I'd better not start bossing
you around, had I? Otherwise I'll have no
chance of persuading you to work with me."

"Dinner's ready," Ben calls, interrupting
our conversation, and Emma excuses herself to fetch another bottle of Pimm's. "Are
we celebrating?" Ben asks as he comes
over with a plate of food from the barbecue. "Have you come to a decision?"

"Not yet, I'm afraid." Emma is right. I
have done some good since I've been
here, but I'm not sure it's enough to make
up for the bad.

"Of course," Ben says, "I've no objec-
tion to you going into partnership with my
wife, if that's what you're worried about, as
long as you don't live with us again." (He's
joking—we shared a house in our final

year at university, and poor Ben didn't understand that the only place suitable for
drying calving gowns was over the bath.)

"Oh, Ben, I know that," I say, touching
his arm in thanks.

"I'll let you in on a secret, Maz," he says,
lowering his voice. "I wouldn't have chosen
to settle in Talyton if it hadn't been for Emma
and her mum, but now I'm here, it isn't so
bad. The people are great"—he qualifies
that—"most of them. The pace of life isn't
as frantic as it is in London, and it's good to
be near the river and the beach." He hands
me a laden plate. "I don't want to put you
under any pressure to make up your mind,
but I have to think of Emma and the baby. I
really don't want her working full-time in her
condition."

"She could ask someone else," I say.

"Maz, she's asked you." Ben fixes his
eyes on mine. "The decision is entirely up
to you, of course. All I'm asking is that you
put Emma out of her misery very soon."
His face relaxes into a grin, and the tension dissipates. "It shouldn't be beyond
your capability—you're the vet, after all."

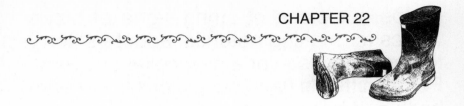

CHAPTER 22

Partners in Practice

"ALLY JACKSON DID A GREAT JOB THERE, MAZ." Clive grins as he throws a copy of the *Chronicle* onto the consulting room table. It bears the headline FIRE RESCUE ANIMALS NEED GOOD HOMES and a note reading, "See inside for photos of the many cats and dogs looking for a new start." "How could we resist Petra after this?"

I recall Ally's rather poetic description of Petra as a goddess of dogs, highly strung and very sensitive, in need of that extra-special home. Ally has turned out to be a decent wordsmith after all.

Izzy brings Petra through, and Clive

swaps our piece of string—one of Izzy's tactics for making potential adopters sorry for the animals—for a new collar and lead. Petra sniffs his hand suspiciously, her ears back and her body slung low.

My heart is in my mouth. Will she accept him, or will she reject him like she did Chris?

"Hello there, gorgeous." Clive rubs her head. Petra tenses. She's going to growl, I think, and what could have been a beautiful relationship will be over before it's begun, but Clive pulls a treat out of his pocket, shows it to her, and asks her to sit. Without faltering she obeys him, then takes the treat gently from his hand. "Good girl." Clive rubs her head again. She whines and wags her tail.

"She's such a beautiful dog," says Edie. "She looks even better than she did in the photo."

"She should have been a show dog—I can just see her in the final judging at Crufts." I mix an injection, her second jab. I assume Gloria never got round to having her vaccinations done. I inject it into the scruff of Petra's neck. There is a look in her eye. I don't know what it is, but I don't warm to her like I did to Robbie. I don't kiss her.

However, I think there's room for optimism. She's young and in good hands— Clive knows far more about training dogs than I do.

"We might see you later, Maz," he says before they leave with Petra. "We're holding the wake for Gloria up at the Talymill. We thought it was the right thing to do, as she has no relatives left to do it for her." He pauses. "You see, the good people of Talyton have accepted us at last."

I know what he's hinting at, that there's hope for me too.

"Bye, Maz," Edie says. "Let's get you to your new home, Petra, and show you your toys."

After they've gone, I check the waiting list on the computer. Petra was my last appointment and, as usual, I'm running late.

Emma pops her head round the door.

"Izzy and Frances have gone on ahead. It isn't good form to be late for a funeral, you know. Everyone'll talk."

"I'm coming," I say, untangling myself from my stethoscope and leaving it on the table.

Emma blocks my way out. "Have you decided yet?" she asks. "Should I get on with organizing your leaving do?" She's trying to make light of it, I think, but I know her better than that. It means a lot to her, and I shouldn't keep her in suspense, especially—I smile to myself, happy that it's worked out for her—in her condition.

"I'll let you know tonight," I say, taking off my tunic, which I threw on over a gray asymmetric top and black trousers this morning, and brushing past her. "I promise."

Ten minutes later and I'm parked on the road outside the church. It could be a cathedral. It could be a film set for a horror movie. I'm not sure which came first—the church or all those pubs in Talyton St. George—but you might speculate that a bishop had it built to punish his intemperate congregation. One night in the crypt and you'd soon dry out.

The gargoyles' rabid mouths are dribbling rainwater from an earlier shower, creating dark stains down the stonework; and the churchyard, bordered by toxic yews—toxic to horses anyway, I can remember that much about them from vet school—is chockablock with gravestones and memorials with the history of Talyton St. George written in their inscriptions.

If I stay, I'll become a small part of the town's history, as an Otter House vet. I'd be like Gillian of Petals, or Cheryl of the Copper Kettle, or Mr. Lacey of Lacey's Fine Wines. I would belong . . .

I glance at my watch, realizing that, as Emma predicted, I'm late. I duck inside the church and take a seat at the back, on one of the chairs behind the pews.

There are far more mourners than I expected. It looks as if the whole town is there. I can see Izzy and Chris, P.C. Phillips, Dave the paramedic, Fifi, Frances and her band of volunteers, along with a handful of elderly women dressed in black and scented with camphor and Je Reviens. I can see the Fox-Giffords in the pew at right angles to the rest, one that presumably separates the aristocracy from the common people. Alex is wearing a dark suit, which emphasizes the width of his shoulders, and a white shirt, which contrasts with his lightly tanned complexion. I've not seen him in a suit before. It gives him a brooding look.

He catches my eye and nods a greeting,

and a wave of embarrassment washes through me as I recall how I threw myself at him and he pushed me away.

Old Fox-Gifford, leaning on a stick, wears a navy blazer. Sophia sports a fox fur across her shoulders, a real one, its head still on, the face ghastly and glassy-eyed.

When the organ plays a piece—Bach's "Jesu, Joy of Man's Desiring," I think—signaling that the service is over, I bow my head as the coffin passes, and pay my respects.

Poor Gloria. I thought I'd be angry with her. I didn't see how I'd ever be able to forgive her, but now that Alex is out of danger—I glance toward him again—I am incredibly sorry that she felt driven to take her own life.

I join the throng of mourners and wait while they bury her in the far corner of the churchyard, where her husband, Tom, was laid to rest. There's space on the headstone for her name and epitaph, proving, I think, that she must have found it in her heart to forgive him his affair with Fifi, and I don't know if it's that or the handfuls of the earth clattering onto her coffin, or the seagulls' mournful cries as they swoop across the sky, but a lump rises in my throat, and Ben is at my side, touching my arm.

"Are you all right, Maz?" he asks.

I nod, not trusting myself to speak.

"You mustn't blame yourself," he says sternly. "Gloria was ill. What began as self-less charity became a compulsion, a behavior she couldn't control."

"She did love her animals," I say.

"Yes, I have no doubt, and she really believed she was the best person to look after them, but as Fifi says, she was deluding herself. When the money ran out and she grew more infirm, she couldn't cope." Ben hesitates. "We're all partly responsible for what happened."

I know he's right. Ben was in the position of knowing that there was a problem but didn't—or couldn't because of his professional ethics—communicate his suspicions to anyone else. Fifi and Talyton Animal Rescue gave up on Gloria too easily, and I put her in an impossible situation from which she could see no escape. The thought of living without her animals was worse than dying, so she tried to take them all with her by creating the inferno at the cottage. I think of the insect trapped in the amber on Gloria's silver chain. The sanctuary was a death trap.

"Dr. Mackie, you are coming to the wake?" Fifi sweeps toward us, a rather frightening vision of purple and black. "And you, Maz."

"I'm going straight back to Otter House," I say.

"Oh, you can't possibly," Fifi says. "You're one of us now. You have to come," she adds in a tone that brooks no argument.

I'm touched that Fifi at least wants me there, but—I glance down the path where Alex is walking along with his mother on his arm and his father in front—there are others who aren't so welcoming. However, there is a part of me, a big part, that persuades me to head to the Talymill Inn with everyone else, and it's all down to the thought of snatching a few more minutes in Alex's company.

"WHAT IS THIS STUFF?" Old Fox-Gifford eyes the canapé he's picked up from one of the trays on the bar.

"It's olive and anchovy toast, I believe," Fifi says. "We have these at some of the dos I have to attend in my capacity as lady mayoress."

Old Fox-Gifford wrinkles his nose. "It isn't vegetarian, is it?"

"Anchovy is a fish," Fifi says.

"Why on earth didn't they stick to good old-fashioned vol-au-vents?" Sophia says. "Everyone likes those."

"I don't know what this town's coming to," Old Fox-Gifford says. "People should leave their newfangled ways behind, or push off back to where they came from."

"Some would say that change is good," Fifi says, glancing toward Clive, who's serving drinks. I wonder about Fifi. Clive's married, and she must be at least ten years older, but it doesn't stop her flirting with him, I think, as I move across and pick up a glass of apple juice.

"Maz, wait right there," Fifi says, spotting me. "I'm going to say a few words."

I start to panic, wondering what I've said or done to offend her, but she taps her glass with a knife from the bar.

"Friends and fellow Talytonians," she says, commanding the room's attention. "I'd like to thank everyone for turning out to say their farewells to Gloria and sending her off in such style. Thank you, Clive and Edie, for putting on such a wonderful spread." There's a ripple of applause from the crowd of people in the bar, which include, I notice, DJ and his team of builders, here for the free lunch, and many of the shopkeepers from the town, along with a deputation from the garden center, including Margaret the cashier.

"There's one more person who deserves a special mention." Fifi turns to me. "I should like to thank Maz for all the work she's put in, helping with Gloria's animals, and always with a smile. Thank you, Maz."

"Hear, hear," I hear Clive murmur, and to my surprise, Fifi strikes up with "For She's a Jolly Good Fellow," and everyone joins in—apart from Alex's parents, I notice. Alex moves up beside me, slipping his hand behind my back, as if he's aware that I could do with some moral support. I'm not used to being center of attention, and I blush as the song draws to a close and Fifi calls on me to make a speech.

I take a deep breath, wondering what to say as I scan the crowd, and then I realize that it isn't all that difficult. I'm among friends.

"I couldn't have done it without your support," I say, tears pricking my eyes. "Everyone has helped in any way they can, from vetting new homes for the rescues, to getting their hands dirty and cleaning out kennels and cages, to bringing in pet food. I'd like to thank all of you . . ."

There's another round of applause, wolf whistles from DJ's team, and a sharp bark from Petra, who's in Robbie's old place behind the bar.

I check my watch. I ought to be getting back.

"Patients to see?" Alex asks.

"It's my turn to do the run up to Buttercross Cottage, or what's left of it. We've still got a couple of traps up there, although we haven't found any waifs and strays for a few days now."

"Oh?" His eyes are shadowed with weariness, and I wonder if he's been sleeping. "I guess you want to round up the rest of them before you . . ." His sentence hangs unfinished, his voice hopeful.

"Well, yes." I don't know what to say. My heart burns, a molten ball of regret, because I'm pretty sure now that he does have feelings for me, that he turned me down out of respect, not because he didn't want me.

I wish I could talk to him, tell him about Emma's offer and how my decision is balanced on a knife edge, because today, thanks to Fifi, I've realized I can belong here.

"I'll see you around, Alex," I say.

"Yeah," he says mournfully, and I walk away, thinking that there's one obstacle left, one problem that I don't know how to solve.

On my way back to the practice, I divert to Longdogs Copse, where someone has fenced off the ruin of Buttercross Cottage and put up signs reading KEEP OUT. I ignore them and walk to the site. Already green shoots are sprouting from the ashes. Cow parsley and wildflowers mingle with the few surviving rosebushes. There are rabbits nibbling the short grass in the paddock, and birds singing in the trees in the copse beyond. Despite the devastation that has occurred here, I feel a sense of calm.

Do I really want to go back to London? The stress of seeing forty patients all before lunchtime, the hassle of communicating with clients who are under pressure themselves, the traffic, the throngs of gray people scurrying about like rats across the greasy pavements, always chasing the clock?

I tramp toward the new fence to reset the trap, and there he is, a very sorry-looking ginger cat sitting hunched up on top of it. Momentarily, I wonder if I should have brought the gauntlets with me, but he doesn't appear to have much fight left in him. He hardly lifts his head when I call his name.

"Hi there, Ginge," I murmur, kneeling down beside the trap. "Izzy said you were too savvy to end up in there." Remembering what he did to me before, I reach out slowly to touch him. He turns and bares his teeth in a furious hiss, but he doesn't lash out. He's so scrawny I don't think he can anymore.

He lets me grasp him by the scruff of the neck and pick him up, a bundle of bones and matted hair. I hold him to my chest to take him to the car, where he lies unrestrained in the footwell, howling—it's a fearsome howl, as if he's calling to the cat gods on the other side of the grave—for what I'm afraid will be his final journey to Otter House.

Emma's at Reception.

"Everything okay?" she asks, looking up from the desk.

"Not really." I show her the cat in my arms. "One of Gloria's. Do you remember Ginge?"

"The one who bit through my thumb." Emma smiles ruefully. "He looks as if he's on his way out. Do you want me to give you a hand?"

"I'm going to give him twenty-four hours," I say.

"I'd say you were being wildly optimistic."

I take him through to Isolation, where Emma helps me put him on a drip, dose him up with a cocktail of drugs, and restart him on his antithyroid tablets. He growls when I put him on a fluffy bed and close the cage door.

"I don't know what we'll do with him if he does recover," Emma says.

He might hiss at me, he might hate me, but Gloria managed to find room for him in her heart, and if she could, I can too. I said I'd never have another cat after King, but if Ginge does make it, I shall keep him.

"I'll take care of him," I say.

"You? You haven't got a home to call your own, let alone somewhere you can keep a pet." Emma pauses, one hand on her hip. "Of course, you would have if you'd only make up your mind to stay on at Otter House. I don't understand what the problem is. If you'd offered me a partnership, I'd have jumped at it."

"I know." I look at Ginge, who's pressed himself into the corner of the cage. I'd love to say yes, but I can't. And it isn't about the money or feeling like an outsider. My throat chokes up with emotion. I'll have to find a solution, because the more I think about it now, the more I want to stay.

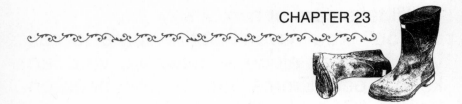

CHAPTER 23

Animal Magic

I SIT WITH GINGE FOR MUCH OF THE NIGHT, thinking it over. When I fiddle with his drip, he bites me—in the nicest possible way, I hasten to add. It's a mock bite, without teeth. By the small hours, he's sitting on my lap, a purring skeleton with bald patches where I've had to trim the worst of the knots away. I find it difficult to put him back in the cage, because as soon as he's confined in there he starts grumbling again. I smile to myself. He's going to get better—he's got enough fight left in him.

I've gained Ginge's trust, but I'm no nearer finding a way of regaining Izzy's. I'll have to talk to her. After all, I've got nothing to lose.

It's too busy first thing. Frances is at Reception, making appointments that seem to be coming thick and fast now Emma's back. Emma's in the office with a box of doughnuts to stave off morning sickness, going through the accounts with Nigel, and Izzy's whizzing around with rows of stainless-steel feeding bowls on her arm, like a silver service waitress. Raffles, some of the cats, and the small furries are still with us, waiting for homes. Ugli-dog has gone to one of Talyton Animal Rescue's long-term fosterers.

Suddenly, the buzzer goes off and there's a lot of shouting and banging of doors. Frances throws the door into Kennels open, letting in Chris, who's carrying a dog wrapped in a bloodstained towel in his arms.

"Emergency!" she calls. "Is there a vet in the house?"

"Oh, God." Izzy's face turns pale, and she drops her last bowl onto the floor before springing toward the bench where Chris is unwrapping his bundle. Her voice rises to a scream. "It's Freddie!"

"Someone's tipped some rubbish into one of our fields," Chris gasps. "He's cut himself. It's this leg," he adds helpfully, although there's no need to tell me. It's obvious which leg the blood's coming from. I unwrap Chris's temporary tourniquet, made from a well-used handkerchief, grab the top of Freddie's front leg, and squeeze it to stem the bleeding, which slows to a steady ooze.

Chris turns to Izzy, as upset as she is.

"I'm sorry, love. I didn't realize the dogs had got out. When I found them, Freddie and Meg were rounding up the sheep, would you believe it? Anyway, I whistled, they came bounding across the field, and Freddie caught himself on a piece of glass."

"It isn't your fault," Izzy says gently, seeming to have recovered from the shock of Freddie's arrival. She hands me a swab. I dab at the area, checking for glass. Freddie fidgets—a good sign, I think, because I have no idea how much blood he's lost—but the bleeding starts up again, spurting arcs of bright, arterial red, which spatter my scrub top, face, and hair.

"We'd better get him knocked out ASAP," I say, applying another tourniquet to Freddie's leg, which stops the bleeding, giving me time to anesthetize him. Izzy holds Freddie's head while Chris and Frances look on. Once Freddie's safely asleep, Izzy releases the tourniquet. I clamp off the severed artery and swab away the blood so I can assess the rest of the damage.

"How bad is it, Maz?" Chris asks.

"He's cut through a couple of tendons," I say. Freddie's bigger than when I last saw him, but he isn't fully grown yet. "I'm not sure how easy it'll be to reattach them."

"I hope they can be fixed," Chris says. "Just as he's proved he has the drive to be a working sheepdog, this happens. He'll be no good to me if he can only run on three legs."

"You will keep him though?" Izzy says quickly.

Chris smiles wryly. "A dog is like a wife—it should be for life." He turns back to me. "I take it you're doing the surgery, Maz."

I don't answer, aware that Izzy's staring at me as if assessing my competence and Freddie's chances if I should end up wielding the scalpel.

I clear my throat. "Frances, will you buzz Emma, please? I'd like her to do the surgery." I turn back to Izzy. "Is that all right with you?"

"Yes, that's fine," she says. "I'll set up in theater."

"Emma can't do it," Frances announces. "She keeps dashing off to the bathroom." She smiles. "I knew it. I knew she was in the family way."

"You mean she's pregnant?" says Izzy.

"Why else would she be craving doughnuts and feeling sick?" Frances says triumphantly. "You'll have to carry on without her, Maz."

"Izzy?" I say.

Izzy's brow creases with concern for Freddie.

"I'll be really careful, I promise."

"Go on then," she says, and a few minutes later, Freddie is in the operating theater. Izzy tells Chris to watch the bag on the anesthetic circuit to make sure Freddie keeps breathing, while she fusses around, making sure I have the right kit.

To be honest, Izzy's presence makes me nervous. Get a grip, I tell myself as my needle holders slip from my grasp and clatter to the floor.

"The spare set's stuck in the autoclave," Izzy observes. "You'll have to improvise."

Chris alters the angle of the light as I hunt for the ends of Freddie's tendons, which have pinged apart and disappeared under the skin higher up his leg. Izzy holds his leg in a position that brings the ends of the tendons back into view and gives me the best chance of reattaching them. It takes me a while, and the whole time I'm aware of Izzy watching over me. I can't afford to make the tiniest slip.

I can feel sweat pooling in my armpits, and dripping from my forehead, and soaking into my surgical mask. I glance up at Izzy's face, her eyes filled with worry.

"He is going to be all right?" she says.

I show her the repairs I've made. They're good enough for me, but will they be good enough for Izzy?

"I know I've made mistakes, that I'll never match up to Emma in your eyes," I begin when she doesn't say anything, "but—"

"No, Maz," Izzy interrupts.

No. With that one word, Izzy dashes my hopes of ever winning her round. I can't possibly stay on at Otter House now. My heart plummets, and my eyes mist with tears. I turn away, pretending to look for something on the instrument tray.

"Maz, I'm not saying you've done a bad job," Izzy says quietly. "I think you've done a fantastic job on Freddie's leg. No, what I'm saying is that it's true I've had my doubts about you—call it my suspicious mind, if you like—but I've seen how much you care about the animals, and the clients." She clears her throat. "Look at how kind you've been to Tripod, giving him a home as the practice cat. And Ginge. Most other vets I know would have put him down."

I turn back to her as she goes on. "I think you're a lovely person, Maz. And a great vet."

"Hear, hear," Chris says.

"You're making me blush," I say, "but thank you."

Smiling, Izzy looks past me as Emma enters and I start to try to work out how I'm going to find enough skin to close Freddie's wound.

"How's it going?" Emma asks anxiously as I begin to suture.

"Maz has saved Freddie's leg," Chris says.

"I hear you have some news for us," Izzy says, her eyes shining above her surgical mask.

"Ah," says Emma. "It's early days, so I was trying to keep it low-key, but yes, I'm expecting at long last."

"Oh, that's wonderful. I'd give you a hug, but for . . ." Izzy holds up her bloodstained hands.

"Save it for later," Emma says.

"RIGHT, THERE'S A LOT of tension across the repair," I say as I tie off the last knot a short time later. "We'll keep him in for a couple of days, and splint this leg for a while to give the tendons time to heal."

"I'll do the dressing," Izzy volunteers. "Chris, you hold Freddie's leg for me."

"I'll take over the anesthetic while Maz writes up her notes," Emma offers, bringing in a stool to perch on at Freddie's head.

A couple of minutes later, she looks up and stares across the table at Izzy. "What's that?"

Izzy stops partway through unwinding a bandage. She smiles coyly as she lifts the diamond ring dangling from a delicate gold chain around her neck.

"I never thought it would happen," she says softly, gazing toward Chris, who's turned red as beetroot under his tan. "I didn't think I'd meet a man I'd fall in love with, and he'd love me back. Chris and I are getting married next spring, after lambing."

"I'm not sure I can take much more good news," Emma says with a chuckle, and we both congratulate them at the same time, talking over and across each other.

"Freddie's going to be page boy," Izzy says once we've calmed down. "Maz, you will come back for the wedding, won't you? We want you to be there."

I glance at Emma, who's removing Freddie's ET tube. She takes a piece of cotton wool and wipes the drool from his face as he lifts his head up, his expression bemused, as if to say, "What am I doing here?"

I've always respected Emma for knowing exactly where she's going, and now I'm in a position to follow her example. I know exactly where I'm going. Nowhere.

"I'm sorry, Izzy," I begin, trying to keep a straight face. "I can't come back for your wedding."

"Why on earth not?" she says.

"Because . . ." I'm aware Emma's looking at me, her lips curving into a smile. "Because I'm staying on as Emma's partner."

Emma screeches with joy, Freddie tries to roll onto his front, and Izzy's jaw drops.

"I can feel a party coming on," Emma decides, and later in the day, Ben drops off a couple of bottles of champagne, which she puts in the freezer—yes, that one.

At the end of a busy evening surgery, she fetches wineglasses from the flat and calls Frances and Izzy through to the staff room to join us in a toast. Even Nigel is there to be part of the celebrations.

"Frances, you must have some champagne," Emma says.

"Not for me, thank you," she says. "A little bit of what I fancy always seems to do me in. I'll have lemonade, like you."

"First of all, please raise your glasses to Maz, my new partner," Emma says. "When I set up the practice, I always hoped that one day Maz would come and work with me." She turns to Nigel, who's wearing a short-sleeved shirt and spotty bow tie. "Here's to you, Nigel, for doing your best to keep Otter House Vets afloat."

"I reckon I have the toughest job around here, keeping you vets in order," he says smugly. Emma winks at me, and Izzy rolls her eyes.

"And to you, Frances," Emma says, "for coming back and sticking with us."

"Well, as I might have said before, I do love a good crisis." Frances's cheeks glow like the poppies on her tunic.

"If it hadn't been for you—and Fifi and her volunteers, of course—I don't think we'd have managed to rehome so many of Gloria's animals," Emma goes on. "Even the little cockatiel's gone."

"He'll be back," says Izzy wryly. "He'll drive his new owners mad with his constant chattering."

"Here's to the team then," Emma says.

"You've missed something, Emma," I point out.

"Oh yes. Congratulations to Izzy and Chris on their engagement."

"And one more." Emma frowns as I go on. "A toast to you and Ben, and the baby, of course." I take a sip of champagne, but it won't go past the lump in my throat.

"Thank you, everyone," Emma says with a sob. "I'm so happy . . ."

So am I, I think. It's been a difficult journey, but I've made real friends along the way. There's only one more thing that would make my happiness complete.

"Please don't cry, otherwise we'll all start," Izzy says, but it's too late and Frances has to dash out for her tissue box, which turns out to be empty.

"It's that Ally Jackson," Frances says. "Every time she's here, she empties it with her blubbering. Last time she broke down over each and every one of the rescues' stories. I'm surprised she could read her notes."

I think it's Emma who recovers her composure first. She offers me more champagne.

"I can't," I say. "I'm going out tonight."

"With Alex?" Izzy cuts in.

"I can think of a million men I'd rather see you going out with," Emma begins.

"It's a pity you haven't introduced any of them to me before," I say lightly. "Anyway, I'm not going out with him. I'm going to see him. There is a difference."

"I wasn't sure whether to believe the rumors that have been flying round. Do you really like him, Maz?" Emma asks.

I nod. I can't describe how I feel about Alex Fox-Gifford. Words aren't enough.

"In that case I'd better get over it, hadn't I?" Emma smiles. "I hope you have a lovely evening. I mean it."

I'm not sure how he's going to react, but I can't wait to see his face when I tell him that I'll be staying now. I check up on Ginge on my way out. He's out of the woods, so to speak, but he isn't all that grateful. Gloria was right—he hates being confined.

"I'll let you out with Tripod as soon as you're fit enough to look after yourself," I tell him. "You'll have to have butter on your paws though." It's an old wives' tale, but I'll try anything to make sure he doesn't run away again. I hope that, like me, he'll come to realize where he's better off.

WHEN I ARRIVE at the manor, the Fox-Giffords' pack of dogs come flying toward the car. One of them, an old black Lab, bares its teeth at the window.

"Good dogs." I open the door. "What good dogs you are." But the softly-softly I'm-your-friend approach doesn't work. The Lab raises his hackles and growls.

"Oh, push off!" I growl back, and the dog ambles round to the rear of my car and cocks his leg up the wheel while the rest of the pack trot back to the house, showing me the way to the tradesmen's entrance.

I head toward the barn though, wondering, when I find no one at home, whether I should have phoned first. A busy man like Alex is hardly likely to be sitting around waiting for me to turn up, is he? Old Fox-Gifford's Range Rover and Alex's four-by-four are here, and Liberty is back, looking over the door of the stable closest to the house. I walk up to the back door of the manor—it's open and the dogs are still milling around.

Hoping that I'm not going to run into Old Fox-Gifford and Sophia, I follow the muddy paw prints across a tiled floor, stepping over the wellies, dog beds, and water bowls strewn across my way. There's a strong scent of wet canine, sweaty horse, and boiled cabbage.

"Alex?" I call out, walking through another doorway and into a huge kitchen with an Aga, two butler's sinks, and a fireplace big enough to roast a whole cow but that instead houses a fridge and freezer that don't match. On the table in the center there's a preserving pan, a box of cornflakes, a bowl of what smells like tripe, and a pot of some horse supplement. I turn the pot so the label faces me—STROPPY MARE. "Alex?"

"I'm here, Maz."

"Er, hi. H-h-how are you?" I stammer, taken by surprise when he appears in the doorway on the other side of the room. If he's surprised to see me, he doesn't let on.

"Not bad," he says, "although I'm almost ready to turn vegetarian. The WI—bless 'em—keep turning up with chicken soup, cauldrons of the bloody stuff." He steps aside. "Come on through."

I follow him along a wide corridor and into another room.

I gaze around the room, trying to think of something to say. Alex's presence seems to have rendered me speechless. I notice the double doors that look out onto the lawn with views across the valley beyond, the oil paintings of various Fox-Giffords from the past, and the dogs slumped in a heap on the carpet. I don't think it's any old carpet—it could be an Axminster like the one Gloria had in her sitting room, but this one is several acres bigger and slightly better kept. I also notice the dead flowers in the grate, the rather shabby sofa and chairs, and the swirls of dog hairs in the corner nearest me. If the Fox-Giffords have a cleaning woman, there's not much evidence of her efforts.

There's something else, something behind the sofa, something breathing. I catch sight of a pair of pricked ears and flared nostrils.

"Alex, there's a pony in the house . . ."

He turns toward it. A tubby little Shetland, a black one, straight out of a Thelwell cartoon, nudges at a biscuit tin on a side table, rattling an oil lamp and an antique vase.

"Mind the majolica," Alex says. "That's Skye—Mother bought him for the children, but he bucked them off. He's more of a house pet now."

"I didn't think the Fox-Giffords approved of keeping animals as pets."

"Then you've been misled." Alex grins, and my heart flutters. "If you open the tin for him, you can give him a mint. That's what he's after." He picks up his phone and a set of keys from the elaborate marble fireplace. "How about dinner?"

Before I can argue with him, he's arranging a table at the Barnscote. He's a man who gets things done, I think. I like that. It's one of the many things I like about Alex.

"Right, I'll just let my mother know we're going out—I expect she's in the feed room up to her elbows in linseed and bran mash." He smiles at me, and it's like the sun has come out. "Did I tell you, you look lovely?" he says quietly.

"Thank you."

He hands me his keys. "Wait in the car. I'll be with you in a tick."

Less than two minutes after we've set out in Alex's car, his mobile rings. He glances toward me, his expression unreadable as Sophia's voice rings out loud and clear on the speakerphone.

"Hi, Mother, what's up?"

I sit, my hands balled together, my heart small and mean as Sophia says, "I wouldn't have called you unless I had to, Alexander, but Stewart's rung with a calving—he wants one of you over there straightaway."

"What about Father?" Alex says, his tone one of annoyance mixed with resignation. "He's on call tonight."

"You know he's in bed. His sciatica was playing him up, so I sent him upstairs with some painkillers and a hot toddy. He isn't in a fit state to calve a cow. In fact, he really shouldn't be doing the heavy work anymore. We need to look for an assistant."

"You know Father's view on that. Anyway, we'll talk about it another time," Alex says impatiently. "Tell Stewart I'm on my way."

"What's your ETA?"

"Ten minutes." The phone cuts out. "I'm sorry, Maz," Alex says. "The last time my father attended a calving, he couldn't work for a week."

"It doesn't matter. It's one of those things." In a way it's a relief, because I couldn't eat a thing, though I can't help but wonder whether this is Sophia's way of expressing her disapproval at Alex taking me out tonight. "I'll wait in the car."

"There's no need for that. I'm sure Lynsey can find you a cup of tea and a biscuit."

"I'd feel uncomfortable."

"This is about the dog, isn't it?" Alex says.

"I really couldn't face the Pitts again, not after some of the things Stewart said." My palms grow damp as I recall the expression on Stewart's face when I told him Cadbury was dead.

"He'll have forgotten about that by now," Alex says. "Anyway, I could do with some help getting all my kit up to the cowshed." He turns in to the farmyard and kills the engine. "You'd like to give me a hand, wouldn't you?"

"My shoes. I haven't got the right shoes on for wading about on a farm."

"I'm bound to have a spare pair of wellies, and a gown." Alex jumps out and opens the trunk. He hands me a pair of green wellies and a coverall that's several sizes too big and rich with the scent of cow.

"What's that for?" I point to the red toy stethoscope on top of the crates of equipment in the back of the car.

"My mother bought that for Sebastian when he was about three months old— hoping to keep the practice in the family for the next generation."

I can hear the pride in Alex's voice when he mentions his son, and I have to admit I admire the emphasis the Fox-Giffords place on family. Alex's parents obviously spend a lot of time with their grandchildren in spite of the fact that they live away with their mother; and Alex is very protective of his children, which I guess is another good reason for him not wanting to embark on a relationship with no future in it.

"I saw your parents with your children at the hospital. It was Sebastian who almost gave me away. I was hiding in the wash-down room."

Alex chuckles. "I won't ask why." He holds out his arm for me to grab on to so I can transfer my feet from my shoes to the wellies without putting them on the ground.

"Thanks." I stand up straight. "What happened about Australia? I've been meaning to ask."

"There's been a holdup, thank goodness. Astra and her new man have decided to stay in London—the firm he's with in the City extended his contract by another year, which gives me more time to work with my solicitor on what happens to Lucie and Sebastian." Alex hands me a set of calving ropes and a visit case, and he picks up a cesarean kit. "Come on, Maz. Hurry up."

It takes my eyes a while to adjust to the light inside the cowshed compared with the brightness of the summer evening outside. The single bulb that glimmers from a cable inside the ramshackle arrangement of cob, brick, hurdles, and corrugated iron doesn't help much, and the window, which has no glazing, is obscured by a bank of nettles growing outside.

An elderly man in a brown jacket restrains a black-and-white Friesian with a rope halter. Alex introduces him as Ewan, the Pitts' cowman. The cow bellows, filling the air with the sweet scent of her breath. One of the Pitt boys—Sam, I think—emerges from the shadows in pajama bottoms, a sweater that's far too big for him, and wellies. Stewart, stripped down to an undershirt with the arms of his coverall tied around his waist, enters the cowshed behind me and Alex.

My heart skips a beat at the flash of recognition as he catches sight of me.

"Maz?"

I force myself to hold his gaze.

"What the hell are you doing here?" he says, his tone one of curiosity, not anger.

"Meet my new assistant." Alex checks that his shirtsleeves are tucked behind the cuffs of his calving gown. "We were just off to dinner at the Barnscote when Mother rang."

"You and Maz? Well, I never." A broad smile spreads across Stewart's face. "You really know how to show a girl a good time." He slaps Alex on the back, then turns to the cow without giving either of us a chance to deny any involvement with each other, so far at least. "This is young Pepperpot—it's her first calving."

I smile to myself, thanking my lucky stars that I haven't had the opportunity to put my foot in it. The beast isn't a cow. She's a heifer.

Alex slips on a long plastic glove and starts to examine her. She groans with the onset of a contraction. The cowman scratches behind her ear.

"Cush, cush, my lover," Stewart murmurs.

Alex looks across the back of the heifer. "He says that to all the girls."

"You have to know how to handle them," Stewart says. "This one's mother is a devil at milking time."

Alex stands back slightly as the cow lifts her tail and drops a spattering of dung into the straw. The boy collects an armful of clean bedding from the corner of the shed and sprinkles it over the top.

"She's a good-looking heifer, don't you think?" Stewart comments.

"She is," Alex says, and I'm not sure whether they're referring to me or the patient. "I'm afraid I'm going to have to go in."

"A cesar?"

Alex nods.

"The calf's alive?"

"For the moment—I felt it sucking on my fingers."

"Two vets—I hope it isn't going to cost me double." Stewart's joking, but there's an edge to his voice. Stewart could easily end up with a big bill for a dead cow and calf. He nods toward his son. "Sam, go and tell your mum to put the kettle on. We need hot water, and tea. Milk and sugar all round?"

"No sugar for me," I say quickly. "Thanks."

"Sweet enough already, eh?" Stewart teases. "I should've guessed you two were an item. Alex hasn't stopped going on about you since you turned up."

"We aren't an item," I say coolly.

"Pity," Alex cuts in. "Still, it's your loss," he banters. "I'd make quite a good catch, wouldn't I, Stew?"

I'm still blushing some minutes later

when Sam returns, struggling with a steam-ing bucket and accompanied by Lynsey, who carries her baby daughter in a sling across her front, and a tray. Sam puts the bucket down, the water sloshing out over the edge, and Alex washes his hands in preparation for injecting the local anesthetic to numb the cow's flank for surgery.

"Alex is here with the vet who murdered Cadbury," Sam says, and immediately the last few weeks go into rewind, and I'm back in the operating theater with my hands in-side a dead dog. I want to run away and never come back. Sam's staring at me, and I can hardly look him in the eye, but I have to say something. I want him to know how much I regret what happened. I take a deep breath.

"I'm very sorry, Sam," I begin.

"No, I'm sorry, Maz," Lynsey cuts in. "She didn't kill him, Sam. It was bad luck." She rests the tray on a bale of straw. "You know what Alex said, that it could just as easily have happened if he'd done the op-eration."

Sam gives me the smallest smile, and I feel a rush of gratitude toward Alex for de-fending me.

Lynsey clears her throat as a sign to her husband to say something, but he's standing beside the cow, stubbornly staring at his mucky boots.

"Go on, my lover," she says. "It'll clear the air."

"All right, all right," he grumbles as he turns to me. "I'm sorry too, Maz. I said things I shouldn't have. I was tied up with the farm, and the new baby." And the fact his wife was threatening to leave him, I'd guess. "By the time I realized that Cadbury was really sick, he was too far gone. I must share the blame."

"Thank you," I say, wondering if he knows how much his apology means to me. It's like having a great weight lifted from my shoulders.

"We buried his ashes in the garden," Sam says. "I writ his name on a stone and put it on top of the grave: CADS RIP."

"We're looking for another dog," says Lynsey. "We were going to ask you if you knew of anything suitable, one of the rescues perhaps."

"There is one, actually. He's called Raffles. He's a funny-looking dog, but he's very bright. I'm sure you could teach him to do some party tricks. Would you like to come and see him?"

"Please, Mum," Sam cuts in. "Please, please, please."

"We'll pop in to the practice tomorrow," Lynsey says. She takes me aside as Alex continues with his preparations to make the operation as sterile as it can be. The cowshed with its dusty cobweb hangings and squishy carpet of mucky straw is a far cry from the operating theater at Otter House.

I notice how Lynsey pats and strokes the baby's back. Every now and then, the baby thrusts her arms and legs out straight and draws them back again, like a pond skater. "We've called her Frances, for obvious reasons. She's amazing, so much easier than the boys were. Stewart loves her to bits. We all do." Lynsey smiles fondly in her husband's direction and lowers her voice. "I don't expect you to understand, Maz, but I've forgiven him. I knew when I married him that he had a wandering eye."

It's more than his eye that wanders, I think, but never mind. It's Lynsey's choice.

"Scrub up, will you, Maz," Alex calls. From where he's checking the sensation in the heifer's flank with a needle, he gestures to the bucket. "We're almost ready to go. It's a big calf and it's breech. Let's make this quick."

But I don't do cows, I think, half panicking as I prepare to assist.

Minutes later, Alex is fishing about inside the cow's womb, tugging at the calf's fetlocks to pull it out.

"Hang on to those for me," he says. "I'll have to extend the incision a bit more."

We work together, and with a rush of fluid the calf emerges. We lower it onto the straw, where it lies very still. Alex starts closing the long incision down the cow's flank while I clear the fluid and membranes from its muzzle and watch the calf's chest.

"It isn't breathing," I say urgently.

Stewart steps forward and hauls the calf up by the hind legs to drain any fluid from its lungs before putting back it down.

"Anything?" he says, squatting down beside me.

I shake my head, and Stewart swears. Lynsey and Sam look on, tense and silent. Alex keeps on with his suturing, knowing the sooner he finishes, the sooner he can help us. He was right when he said it was a big calf. It would be pretty distressing to lose it now.

I rub the calf's body with handfuls of straw, trying to stimulate it to take its first breath. I pause and lean my face close to its muzzle to see if I can detect the movement of air through its nostrils. Nothing.

I'm just considering the practicalities of giving a calf mouth-to-mouth when Sam dives down onto his knees beside me and grabs a piece of straw. He sticks it up the calf's nose, at which it sneezes and shakes its head. "That's done it," he says, eyes gleaming in triumph.

"Well done, Sam," I say, watching the calf struggle onto its brisket.

"Boy or girl?" Stewart asks, the relief evident in his voice.

Sam pulls the calf's hind leg back.

"It's a heifer, Dad. That means she can stay on the farm and join the herd." He turns to Alex. "One day, Dad's going to let me do the milking all by myself."

"If we're still in farming," Stewart mutters, but I don't think Sam or Alex hear him.

"That's great, Sam." Alex ties off and snips the last knot. "I'm all done here.

Sam, your next job is to make sure the calf suckles."

"Like our baby sister." The boy man-handles the calf toward its mother, then helps it to stand. It wobbles like a drunk, then nudges against the cow's udder, latches on to one of her teats, which is already drip-ping with the first milk, and sucks noisily.

"Perfect." Alex washes his hands in the bucket and dries them on a towel. I follow suit, then help him pack everything away.

"So, how much longer are you staying in Talyton, Maz?" Stewart asks as he fol-lows us back to Alex's car.

"She came to see me to say good-bye," Alex says, his voice taut. "She'll be off soon, back to the bright lights of the city. I'm going to miss her."

If I'd had any doubts left about the wis-dom of staying on in Talyton, they've gone, banished by the warmth of Lynsey and Stewart's welcome.

"Actually, I'm not going anywhere," I say, smiling at the look of surprise on Alex's face. "Emma's asked me to be her partner at Otter House. I came to tell you I'm stay-ing on."

"Why didn't you say so before?" Alex

asks. His tone is scolding, but there's a smile on his lips.

"I tried to tell you when I arrived at the manor, but you took over and rang the Barnscote, and I decided I'd wait and tell you at dinner."

Stewart glances at his watch. "It's a bit late for dinner at the Barnscote now. They keep country hours—I think they close at ten. You could eat with us. Lynsey has a pot of stew keeping hot on the Aga."

Alex looks at me. His eyes flicker with mutual understanding. Going out for dinner was never going to be about eating . . .

"Thanks, but we have to get back," he says. "I've got the kit to clean."

It's dark by the time we're back on the road.

"What made you change your mind then, Maz?" Alex asks, his voice gently caressing.

"Lots of things. Gloria's funeral mainly. I realized how much I'd miss everyone, how much I'd miss Emma—and you."

At the bend at the old bridge, Alex changes down a gear, his hand brushing my thigh. The car shudders. My heart begins to pound with anticipation.

When we arrive at the manor, the dogs bark, then fall silent. A horse whinnies from the stables.

"That's Liberty." Alex opens the driver's door and jumps out. "Are you going to stay there all night?" he adds impatiently, and I slide out the other side and join him in the yard as Liberty whinnies again.

"Hi, my beauty," Alex calls back.

"How is she now?" I ask, following him across to Liberty's stable, where a light flicks on, illuminating the front of the stable block.

"Really well." He gives her a mint from his pocket and caresses her neck. "I'm going to turn her out this winter to recuperate and bring her back into work in the spring." He looks at me. "My parents tell me you don't ride."

I giggle at the memory of Alex's parents at the show. "They were horrified."

"I'll teach you sometime, if you like."

I'm not sure about getting up close and personal with a horse as large as Liberty, but the idea of Alex in those jodhpurs of his . . . Well, I wouldn't say no. I don't say no. I don't say anything as Alex takes me by the hand and leads me away from the stable, away from the car, and into the shadows cast by the barn.

"What about the cesar kit?"

"That can wait. I don't want to waste any more time"—he lowers his voice to a whisper, sending tiny quivers of anticipation down my spine—"time I could be spending with you."

"Oh, Alex," I breathe.

"Since the fire . . ." He falters, and I realize we haven't really talked about what happened on the night Buttercross Cottage went up in flames. "Since the fire," he starts once more, "I've tried to live every second to the full. I remember the beams coming down and thinking, I'm not going to make it out of here."

I open my mouth. He touches one finger to my lips.

"Shh," he whispers. "You were thinking of Gloria. I didn't have to go in after you." He lets his fingertip trail down my chin, down my throat, stopping just short of the shadowy cleft between my breasts. "Maz . . . Can we start again?"

"You bet." I lift my hand and draw him

closer until our lips touch, and my spirit soars as I realize that I've found what I've been looking for, and it's here in the country, in a sleepy market town, in Alex Fox-Gifford's arms.

Acknowledgments

I SHOULD LIKE TO THANK my family; my UK agent, Laura Longrigg, at MBA; my U.S. agent, Barbara Zitwer; Christine Pride, senior editor; and the rest of the team at Hyperion for their wonderful enthusiasm and support.

CATHY WOODMAN began her working life as a small-animal vet before turning to writing fiction. Cathy lives with her two children, three ponies, three exuberant Border terriers, and one very fluffy cat in a village in Hampshire, England.